THE LETTER
KILLETH

ALSO BY RALPH MCINERNY

MYSTERIES SET AT THE
UNIVERSITY OF NOTRE DAME
Irish Gilt
On This Rockne
Lack of the Irish
Irish Tenure
Book of Kills
Emerald Aisle
Celt and Pepper
Irish Coffee
Green Thumb

ANDREW BROOM
MYSTERY SERIES
Cause and Effect
Body and Soul
Savings and Loam
Mom and Dead
Law and Ardor
Heirs and Parents

FATHER DOWLING MYSTERY SERIES
Her Death of Cold
The Seventh Station
Bishop as Pawn
Lying Three
Second Vespers
Thicker Than Water
A Loss of Patients
The Grass Widow
Getting a Way with Murder
Rest in Pieces
The Basket Case
Abracadaver
Four on the Floor
Judas Priest
Desert Sinner
Seed of Doubt
A Cardinal Offense
The Tears of Things
Grave Undertakings
Triple Pursuit
Prodigal Father
Last Things
Requiem for a Realtor
Blood Ties
The Prudence of the Flesh

THE LETTER KILLETH

RALPH McINERNY

 St. Martin's Minotaur ⚞ New York

THE LETTER KILLETH. Copyright © 2006 by Ralph McInerny. All rights reserved.
Printed in the United States of America. No part of this book may be used or
reproduced in any manner whatsoever without written permission except in the
case of brief quotations embodied in critical articles or reviews. For information, address St. Martin's Press, 175 Fifth Avenue, New York, N.Y. 10010.

www.minotaurbooks.com

Library of Congress Cataloging-in-Publication Data

McInerny, Ralph M.
    The letter killeth / Ralph McInerny.—1st St. Martin's Minotaur ed.
        p.   cm.
    ISBN-13: 978-0-312-35143-4
    ISBN-10: 0-312-35143-7
    1. Knight, Roger (Fictitious character)—Fiction.   2. Knight, Philip
(Fictitious character)—Fiction.   3. Private investigators—Indiana—South
Bend—Fiction.   4. Mail bombings—Fiction.   5. University of Notre
Dame—Fiction.   6. College teachers—Fiction.   7. College stories.
I. Title.

PS3563.A31166L48   2006
813'.54—dc22

2006012808

First Edition: December 2006

10   9   8   7   6   5   4   3   2   1

For Bill Miscamble, C.S.C.

PART ONE

1   WINTER LINGERS IN NORTHERN Indiana, and snow continues to fall well into March, courtesy of Lake Michigan. Sometimes, of course, snow comes fluttering down with all the sweetness of a Christmas card, the weather almost balmy, puffs of breath before the face a delightful joke. More often than not, however, the temperature hovers around zero, and snow comes in on a blast of frigid wind that sends students scurrying across the campus from room to library to class to dining hall, all bundled up like Nanook of the North. Fortunately the campus walks are quickly cleared or it would have been impossible for Roger Knight to get around in his golf cart. For his brother, Phil, the Notre Dame winters were the only blemish in their current life. Not even following the fortunes of the hockey team could keep Florida from his mind as the days grew short and overcast and the snow deeper.

"You should go, Phil," Roger urged.

"But you can't get away now."

"What does that have to do with it? Phil, you know I don't golf or play tennis." Roger paused. "Of course, you smile. The thought is ridiculous. Check with the travel bureau."

"Maybe I will."

Later, Roger got on the Web and went to a travel site and looked into plane tickets and resorts in the Sarasota area. Of course, he could not make the arrangements final without Phil's go-ahead.

"You're trying to get rid of me."

"Of course, if you insist, I could resign from the faculty and go off with you."

"Ha. Actually, I'm beginning to like this kind of winter."

"Snow eventually melts, Phil."

Yes, and the sun also rises, but it would have been difficult to prove that in the gray and overcast days that lay ahead. How much gloomier it would have been without the snow.

Phil's decision to stay was not the result of anything Roger said. It was the letters.

Father Carmody called and told Phil, "You'll think I'm crazy."

"The weather getting to you, Father?"

"What's wrong with the weather?"

"Have you been out lately?"

"I am just this minute leaving the Main Building. I think I've taken on a fool's errand, and I want company. Can I come over there?"

"I could come to Holy Cross House."

"It'll be easier for me to come there."

Father Carmody was a reluctant resident of Holy Cross House, not because he did not like the accommodations of the retirement home for priests, but because of its associations. All the other residents save one or two were sliding slowly from this life, often having already left their minds behind. Father Carmody had his meals in his room so as to avoid the refectory where old men were spoon-fed by nurses, their chins wiped, all the while being talked to as if they were babies. Many of the most pathetic cases were men years younger than Father Carmody.

Father Wangle had given him excellent advice when he moved in. "Avoid all gatherings, refuse to take part in physical therapy, get your hair cut on campus."

The reason for the last remark became clear to Father Carmody when he saw the wheelchairs lined up, their occupants, many once prominent and powerful in the congregation or in the university, awaiting their turn to get a haircut that would have done a marine recruit proud.

"Stay active," Wangle said, summing it up.

Father Carmody had stayed active, perhaps too active for some. There were times when he felt like the Ghost of Christmas Past when he dropped in on the president or provost to give them the advantage of his thoughts on this or that. Once he had been a powerful presence in the university administration, not out front, but influencing the course of things from discreet obscurity. Officers came and went, golden boys rose and fell, but Father Carmody had always survived, ready to guide neophytes along the paths of effective administration.

Nowadays he did not speak softly, but he carried no big stick. In the provost's outer office, he took a chair and fell into conversation with a young priest he did not know. How pink and blond he looked. And nervous. Ah well, coming to see the provost was like a visit to Oz. Father Carmody sought to cheer him up, asked his name, found that he had studied in Rome.

"Ah, Rome."

"Have you been there, Father?"

Carmody looked sharply at the young priest, but neither humor nor insolence seemed to explain the preposterous question. No point in explaining that he had been in Rome as assistant general of the Congregation of Holy Cross during what he liked to think were the boom years. Obviously Father Conway did not recognize him. Well, for that matter, ten minutes had passed before he realized that Conway was an assistant provost.

"I'm thinking of visiting," Father Carmody murmured.

"We have a house there, you know."

This is what it will be like after I am dead, Father Carmody thought. Like grass of the field, swept away to be burnt, and no memory of it left. He had become a stranger in the institution to which he had devoted the long years of his life. Well, what did he want, a life-sized statue like those of Ned and Ted in front of the library? His name on a building or two? Better try to wring spiritual benefit from it. We have here no lasting city. Heaven's my destination.

The young priest was Tim Conway, and he had only recently been appointed assistant to the provost.

"And what are your tasks?"

"Troubleshooting. Mostly student affairs so far."

"Isn't there a prefect of student affairs?"

"You must mean Iglesias."

Father Carmody frowned. "The singer?"

Tim looked blank. "No, Ben Iglesias. Student affairs."

"He's the prefect?"

"He's a vice president."

"Of course."

What Father Carmody thought of the bureaucratization of the university and the resulting multiplication of administrative officers was a subject best brought up during a visit to the community cemetery, where he could walk the rows of identical crosses, communing with the dead and letting them know what Charles Carmody thought of what was going on around here.

Just then the provost emerged from his office and cried out, "Father Carmody! I thought I heard your voice."

Much shaking of hands, smiles all around, and did Father Conway realize who he had been talking to? In short, a great fuss was made over the unexpected visit of the old priest who had advised presidents since the early days of the Hesburgh regime. Carmody was beginning to think that being forgotten was preferable to this kind of attention.

"I was just going to tell Father Carmody about those letters," Father Conway said with a touch of obsequiousness.

The provost's eyebrows shot up and his eyes rounded, though his smile did not falter. "Let's go into my office, shall we?"

There, in a comfortable island of furniture in a corner of the vast inner room, they sat. Father Carmody refused coffee. The provost composed himself and began.

It was, he was sure, a tempest in a teapot. With a little

laugh, he took an envelope from his inner pocket and handed it to the old priest. The message was in block letters, some capitals, some not. BeWarE! yOUr ofFice WilL bE bomBEd. GOD is nOt moCked. The letters had been Scotch-taped to a sheet of paper.

Father Carmody read it a second time. "How did you get this?"

"My secretary found it slipped under the door when she arrived yesterday morning."

"Some student's idea of a joke."

"Of course." But the provost sounded dubious. "Others have received similar letters."

The dean of Arts and Letters. The football coach.

"The football coach?"

It was difficult to think that any student could be otherwise than elated by the abrupt reversal in the fortunes of the Fighting Irish wrought by Charlie Weis. That certain members of the administration or of the faculty might have their lives brightened by a bomb in their office seemed a pardonable student fantasy. To threaten to blow up the Guglielmino Center was something very much else.

"This is the sort of thing you always handled," the provost said.

"I'll take this." Father Carmody folded the sheet and stuffed it into a pocket.

"What will you do?"

"I'll ask Phil Knight for help."

The provost had to think. "The brother of Professor Knight."

"He is a licensed private detective. For that matter, so is Roger."

"Roger Knight is a detective?"

"Was. Before we brought him here as the Huneker Professor of Catholic Studies. His brother came with him. He is more or less inactive now, but he has been of help to the university on a number of occasions."

"We don't want any publicity."

"If we did, we would call in the South Bend police."

"Not even Notre Dame security knows of these letters."

"I should hope not."

The provost came with Father Carmody into the reception area, where a man rose from his seat, a look of expectation on his face. The provost blanched.

"Mr. Quirk."

Quirk hurried to Father Carmody and put out his hand. "Quirk, Ned. Class of '65. I'll bet you don't remember me."

Carmody smiled. "You lived in Dillon. You're from Kansas City and majored in electrical engineering."

"Civil."

"You changed your major?"

The provost threw up his hands in delight. "Father Carmody, you are remarkable!"

"The place was smaller then." He couldn't resist adding, "Once we didn't even have a provost. Only an academic vice president."

Quirk, smallish and rotund, bald as an egg, beamed. "I don't recognize the campus anymore."

Then, as it sometimes will to any administrator, an idea came to the provost. "Ned, why don't you discuss your suggestion with Father Carmody? I would be seeking his advice in any case."

This was a diplomatic bum's rush, of course, but Father Carmody fell in with the plan. He took Quirk's arm, and they went into the hall.

"What did they do to this building, Father?" Quirk looked around him with dismay.

"For the most part, simply restored it to its original condition. Not these grand offices, of course. Come."

In the elevator, he asked Quirk what he had wanted to talk to the provost about.

"Does the name F. Marion Crawford mean anything to you?"

"Is the pope German? Come on. We're going to visit the Knight brothers."

2 BEAUTY LIES, NOT IN THE EYE OF
the beholder nor in the mere thereness
of the beheld, but in some complicated relation between the
two. In fact, the beloved thing itself, or the person herself, is
seldom seen at all, if seeing lies in mere perception. What
wife ever sees her husband as does some neutral observer, if
such there be? What husband who might say of the wife of his
bosom that she walks in beauty like the night imagines that he
is describing her for all to see? Third parties are notoriously
mystified by what draws this man to this woman. They may
have eyes to see but are unable to see what for the smitten is
all in all.

Such thoughts and their expression characterized the discussion of the University Club of Notre Dame as the members
sought to deal with the news that the dear squat building, the
dining room with its vaulted roof, and the poky backroom bar,
where the discussions went on, were all doomed to destruc-
tion. An edict had gone out from the Main Building announcing that the club would be razed to make way for an extension
of Engineering, and the outraged members of the club were
thrust into the position of one whose spouse is spoken of by a
stranger.

In the dining room, at the facetiously named Algonquin table, in a corner where the self-described Old Bastards met for lunch, and at other tables where more random diners congregated, the sense that a Sword of Damocles hung over this familiar setting provided the common subject of the day. There is a music of anger, largely percussive and profane, and the club had swelled with it ever since the judgment had been circulated to the members.

The administrator with the hyphenated name was subjected to imaginative abuse.

"Who is he?" demanded Potts, professor emeritus of philosophy, surveying the other OBs with a rheumy eye.

"What do you mean, who is he?" Wheeler barked, as if his anger could be directed at Potts.

"I mean I never heard of him. How long has he been here?"

Potts had celebrated the golden anniversary of his joining the faculty, and anyone with less than a quarter of a century on campus had for him the status of an unregistered alien. Someone guessed, and Potts snorted.

"I knew Montana," Armitage Shanks said.

"The quarterback?"

"The architect. Frank Montana. He designed this building."

"Is he to blame for the acoustics?"

How sweetly sad it was to think that once complaints about the acoustics in the dining room might have provided topic enough to get them through a meal.

"Speak well of the dead," Shanks advised. "There's nothing wrong with the acoustics. It's your hearing that is defective."

"What?"

"Can he be stopped?"

"Who?"

"The man you don't know. The man who has no sense of the tradition of this place. He thinks it is just a building that can be torn down and replaced with another."

"It can be and it will be." Bingham, late of the law school, spoke with the mordant satisfaction of a magistrate invoking the death penalty. "We have been put in the position of those poor widows who learn that a new highway will be run through their living room. Eminent domain. Protests are useless."

A special meeting of the membership had been called, a committee formed, and an elaborate report prepared and sent to the Main Building. Its only result had been a statement that a new place might possibly be found for the club. Perhaps a donor could be found . . .

"A donor gave the money for this building!" Potts cried.

The Gore family had financed the building of the club with the understanding that a massive collection of beer steins would be housed there. And so they were, enshrined in a number of glass cases in the wall that separated the sunken dining room from a series of all-purpose rooms on a higher level.

"Have they been told?" Bingham asked.

"The original donor is dead."

"His family, then?"

"They are not pleased."

"They should be furious. Is there a statute of limitations on the recognition of benefactions?"

All looked to Bingham. He shrugged. "If they want to tear this place down, nothing can stop them."

"It'll be the Grotto next. Or Sacred Heart Basilica."

"The Main Building could simply be burned. That's a tradition."

The predecessor of the Main Building had gone up in flames in 1879 and within a year been replaced by the present edifice. Father Sorin, the founder of the university, had been away from campus when the terrible news came to him, and he returned immediately, vowing to rebuild within a year, and so he had.

"Where is Sorin now?" Potts asked piously.

"The question is theological."

"In the community cemetery."

Plaisance sighed. "It is enough to make one half in love with easeful death."

"Nothing lasts."

"The place has fallen into the hands of barbarians."

On and on went the discussion, engaged in with the peculiar satisfaction that morose delectation provides. Plaisance had come as near as any of them to the admission that this latest outrage promised to provide the subject of discussion for many future meals at the Old Bastards' table.

"We should march on the Main Building in protest."

"We could let our hair grow, and our beards. Only the unruly get a hearing."

"Not even God could grow your hair, Potts."

"What?"

They were interrupted by Debbie, the hostess, offering more

coffee. The thought of consuming more liquid caused unease, as she knew it would. They looked around and noticed as if with surprise that they were the last occupants of the dining room.

"We're going, we're going."

"Watch your language."

3 BILL FENSTER'S GRANDFATHER HAD made a fortune during World War II as a defense contractor, although to his dying day he described the conflict as Mr. Roosevelt's war. With the coming of peace, he had sold off everything and invested so wisely and widely that he had provided for his progeny into the second and third generation, and doubtless far beyond. In the postwar period, Grandpa Fenster had lent his support to the John Birch Society and to the campaign to get the United States out of the UN and the UN out of the United States. Bill's father, perhaps in reaction, had drifted leftward and worked for the doomed Gene McCarthy campaign. McCarthy's defeat and the later debacle of George McGovern had cured Bill's father of politics and provided his grandfather with satisfaction at this proof of his son's naïveté. The son, Manfred, called Fred, had then turned to religion and spent much of the year traveling to reported new apparitions of the Blessed Virgin. When Bill was accepted at Notre Dame, his father had attributed this to the intercession of the Blessed Virgin, whereas his grandfather was certain that in his generosity to the university lay the explanation. Thank God he hadn't put the family name on any buildings.

"Don't make my mistake," his father advised Bill.

"How so?"

"I never had to earn my living. Neither will you. I have come to think that money is a curse."

"You could disinherit me."

"Not even your grandfather could have done that. I'm afraid you're doomed to affluence. I have found that the best way is to live as if one were poor."

Bill's mother had died when he was four, worn out after a series of miscarriages when she was trying desperately to provide a brother or sister for him.

"Actually, she had dreamed of a huge family. Eight, nine, even more."

His father had never remarried. It was surprising he hadn't entered a monastery. He spent a week every year with the Trappists in Gethsemani, Kentucky. Bill had joined him there for a few days, once.

"It's not what it was," his father said afterward.

Bill said nothing. He had found it unnerving to be off in the woods like that, life on the farm, sort of, except for the services in church when the high-pitched keening voices rose to where he and his father knelt in the visitors' loft in the middle of the night. They could have used a second bass or two. It turned out that his father thought the life was not austere enough.

"It was like marine boot camp when I first went there. Their heads were shaved, total silence, no Muzak in the guests' refectory."

His father mimicked the life of a poor man and was half a priest himself, saying the office in Latin every day. It was from one of the readings in Advent that his father had typed out a text from Isaiah for Bill to translate when he had been in prep school: "Et aures tuae audient verbum post tergum monentis: 'Haec est via, ambulate in ea, et non declinetis neque ad dexteram neque ad sinistram.'" It had become Bill's motto and hung framed over his desk at Notre Dame.

"What's it mean?" Hogan, his roommate, asked.

"I thought you took Latin."

"In high school."

"It says, 'Your ears will hear a voice behind you warning: This is the way, walk in it, and do not turn either to right or left.'"

It wasn't political advice, of course, but Bill took it that way, too, determined to avoid the opposite extremes his grandfather and father had embraced. But he had accepted his father's advice about keeping secret that he already had the wealth most of his classmates dreamed of acquiring. He himself had financed the alternative campus paper he and Mary Alice and Hogan and some others had started. The *Via Media*.

"The donor prefers to remain anonymous," he said, which was true enough.

They put the quote from Isaiah on the masthead, in Latin. Recent issues had been concerned with the fate of the University Club, suggesting that the decision to tear it down and replace it was not only autocratic but indicative of a worrisome trend toward running Notre Dame as if it were a business. "The Bottom Line" was a regular feature in the irregularly appearing newspaper, chronicling the salaries of administrators and coaches, the swollen endowment that was never used to bring down the cost of a Notre Dame education to students. Nothing strident, just the chiding voice of reason. Bill had become a bit of an amateur in the history of the university. Sometimes he reminded himself of his father lamenting what had happened to the Trappists.

His father's visits to the campus were always unannounced. He would call from the Morris Inn and ask Bill to have lunch with him there. Today Bill found his father seated in the lobby. He rose and shuffled toward his son. Worn corduroy pants, baggy cable-knit sweater, tousled hair almost all gray now, he really looked like the poor man that he had wanted to let out of the very rich man he was.

"It was spur of the moment," he said unnecessarily, when they had been shown to their table near a window that looked out on the snowy world. "I forgot how cold it is here in February."

"There's not much going on."

"I want to look into the Catholic Worker House in town. Have you ever been there?"

"What is it?"

"Dorothy Day. Surely you've heard of her."

"Notre Dame gave her the Laetare Medal."

"That's hardly her claim to fame. Not that fame is what she wanted."

So Bill got an account of Dorothy Day and Peter Maurin and the Catholic Worker movement that still went on years after the deaths of its saintly founders.

"I ran into a classmate of mine," his father said, changing the subject. "It's the risk you run."

His father never returned for alumni reunions; he never came for football games. Yet he was a proud if critical alumnus. Bill had not told his father of founding *Via Media*. He hadn't told him of Mary Alice either.

"A fellow named Quirk. Why he remembered me, I don't know. It's even more surprising that I remembered him."

4   MARY ALICE FRANGIPANI WAS THE
eldest of six Frangipanis, a native of
Morristown, New Jersey, where her father was senior partner
in the law firm that bore his name. He had graduated from
Seton Hall, but his unfulfilled dream had been to go to Notre
Dame, and sometimes Mary Alice felt she was living out his
dream. He called every other day, avid for a blow-by-blow account of her life on the campus that was for him the earthly
paradise. He attended every Notre Dame football game, at
home and away, but Mary Alice did not find his passion
for athletics contagious. Her father was wild about Charlie
Weis.

"Do you know what they're paying him?"

"He's worth every nickel of it whatever it is."

"It started at two million dollars. Who knows what it is now?"

The whole family had attended the Fiesta Bowl on January
2, flying out in her father's Learjet. Her father had been in
ecstasy. He attributed the outcome to bigoted officials. You
would have thought they were all obtaining a plenary indul-
gence for cheering on the Fighting Irish.

Her major had been English until, in disgust, she had
switched to the Program of Liberal Studies. Her father had

thought English was a quixotic major, but the switch baffled him even more.

"What can you do with it?"

"Nothing."

"You better marry a rich man."

She thought vaguely of graduate school, maybe philosophy. If that thought was vague, anything beyond was vaguer still. Did she want to be a professor? The one professor she unequivocally admired was Roger Knight, and he was anything but typical. It was in one of Knight's classes that she had met Bill Fenster. They were taking another this semester, devoted to F. Marion Crawford. Neither of them had admitted that they didn't have the faintest idea who F. Marion Crawford was. Roger Knight could make a class on Edgar Rice Burroughs exciting. She had told him as much.

"Of course you couldn't connect him to Notre Dame."

"You're wrong, you know. When he was a student at what was called Michigan College he managed to schedule a game with Notre Dame."

"How do you know these things?"

"Constant attention to trivia. You know the name for the first three of the seven liberal arts?"

Why did such tangential things seem the very reason one wanted a higher education? When he first heard Bill's name, he had said, "Ah, window."

"Just don't defenestrate me."

"I'll spare you the pane."

Mary Alice hadn't followed that, but Bill explained it to her later. "I'm surprised he didn't comment on your name."

They both loved Roger Knight and seemed to be his favorites. After the first class of his they had attended, they came outside with him to his golf cart to find that the battery was dead. Bill plugged it in, and while it recharged he amused them by asking why the Battery in New York was called that. And why are the pitcher and catcher called a battery? How quickly the battery recharged, but they walked beside him as he drove to the apartment he shared with his brother, Philip.

"What does he do?"

"He's a private detective."

"Come on."

"It's true. And so am I. Or was. My being offered a chair here changed our lives."

He asked them in, but they were shy, thinking he was just being polite. Eventually, though, they did come to know him in his now native habitat. The whole apartment seemed a study, books everywhere, but also a giant television before which Phil was often sprawled in a beanbag chair watching some game or another. Mary Alice's father would have liked Phil. She didn't want to think what he would make of Roger Knight.

"Crawford was born in Rome, son of the sculptor who made the figure of Liberty atop the Capitol in Washington. His aunt was Julia Ward Howe. Although he was raised in Rome, he didn't become a Catholic until he went to India as a journalist. His first novel was based on his experience there. He lectured at Notre Dame in 1897."

That is how the class on F. Marion Crawford began. Roger

Knight's courses always related, one way or another, to the past of Notre Dame, and this was no exception, although there had only been that one visit to the campus by the author who in his day had known a popularity that was the envy of Henry James. Roger began with a discussion of *With the Immortals*.

"An unusual novel, not really a novel at all, but a sort of philosophical dialogue. I have always thought that the figure of Samuel Johnson is the most successful. We will be considering Crawford's theory of fiction later."

Mary Alice had written a profile of Roger Knight for *Via Media*. It gave her a chance to quiz him about his past. It turned out to be even more exotic than she had imagined. He and his older brother had been orphaned, but Phil had been old enough to keep them together and raise Roger. Had Roger always been so fat?

"I was briefly thin in the navy."

"The navy!"

"I enlisted after I got my doctorate at Princeton."

"In what?"

"They called it philosophy."

He had still been a teenager when he got his Ph.D. His age and his avoirdupois had made getting a teaching position difficult, and rather than subsist on postdoctoral fellowships, he had slimmed down enough to join the navy. Meanwhile, Phil had become a very successful private investigator. After Roger's discharge from the navy they settled in Rye, New York. Roger, too, got a private investigator's license, and they had accepted only cases of unusual interest. Their undemanding life had enabled Roger to pursue the life of the mind, and via the Internet he was in contact with kindred spirits around the globe. It was his monograph on Baron Corvo and its surprising popularity that had brought him to the attention of Father Carmody, who nominated Roger for the Huneker Chair in Catholic Studies, the funding for which Carmody had secured from a Philadelphia alumnus.

"Who is Baron Corvo?" Mary Alice asked.

"Was. His real name was Frederick Rolfe." And he told her a thing or two about the disenchanted convert to Catholicism.

"You should give a course on him."

"I have."

"I suppose you've given one on Huneker, too."

"Not yet."

Several agnostic courses in graduate school had been the prelude to Roger's own conversion to Catholicism. "Philosophy has been called the formulation of bad arguments for what you already believe. That is certainly true of disbelief."

"My father is here," Bill told Mary Alice after Roger's class today.

"In this weather? What's going on?"

"He came on impulse. He usually does."

She waited. Would he want her to meet his father? He seemed to be asking himself the same question.

"You could have dinner with us tonight. At the Morris Inn."

"Should I dress up?"

He laughed. "Wait until you meet my father."

5   WHEN FATHER CARMODY ARRIVED
with Quirk in tow, he displayed the let-
ter the provost had received. Phil levered himself out of his
beanbag chair and took the letter from Roger.

"A joke?"

"Who knows? Several other administrators and one faculty
member received similar notes, apparently. I haven't seen them.
Another went to Charlie Weis."

"Weis!"

Quirk seemed indifferent to Father Carmody's mission. He
stood, smiling at Roger and shaking his head.

"Is it true?"

"That depends on what you mean by 'it.'"

"You're interested in F. Marion Crawford?"

"I am giving a course on him this semester."

"You are! That's wonderful. I never even heard his name
when I was a student here."

Father Carmody rolled his eyes and took Phil into the study.

"Have you ever been to the Villa Crawford in Sorrento?"
Quirk asked Roger.

"You have."

"Several times. I have a great idea. Father Carmody tells

me you are just the one to propose it to the administration."

"I think he's pulling your leg."

Quirk ignored this. When he had entered, he had thrown back the hood of his parka, a commodious jacket with NOTRE DAME SWIMMING emblazoned on it. Roger commented on this.

"I was on the swimming team. Of course, there was only the pool in Rockne then."

"What is your great idea?"

Quirk rubbed his head as if to verify that it was hairless. He had not stopped smiling since he came in. Now he grew serious. Roger was aware of the many countries in which Notre Dame students could spend a year abroad. St. Mary's has a Rome program, and so does Architecture. What was needed was a place with associations with Notre Dame.

"Notre Dame as it was. Notre Dame as it should be."

"Is the villa for sale?"

"Everything is for sale."

"Isn't it a convent?"

Quirk tapped the tip of his nose. "I have reason to think that Notre Dame could buy the place."

"Villa Quirk?"

"What do you mean?"

"Most donors like their name given to the buildings they provide the university."

"Oh no no no. Good Lord, I don't have that kind of money."

"What kind of money would be involved?"

"Euros." His eyes widened and he laughed. "You mean, how much? Like everything, that is negotiable."

Roger was beginning to realize that Father Carmody had

palmed this enthusiast off on him. Despite Quirk's easy confidence that the villa Crawford had built in Sorrento on the princely proceeds of his fiction could be bought, Roger did not get the impression that Quirk was a practical man. The way he spoke of the purchasability of whatever one might covet and his vagueness as to what sum would be needed if his improbable scheme were adopted did not suggest a man at home in the rough-and-tumble world of buying and selling.

By this time, he had got Quirk into a chair and was trying not to glance enviously to where Phil and Father Carmody were huddled in conversation. Roger's curiosity had been aroused by the letter the old priest had brought, and he was almost as struck as Phil had been to hear that such a threat had been made to the football coach as well. Charlie Weis had taken Notre Dame football from the nadir to the peaks in a single year. Already, he was spoken of in the same breath as Knute Rockne, a comparison he of course dismissed. But he was indisputably a national figure, and the news that threats had been made on him, particularly after the Fiesta Bowl debacle, would be broadcast from coast to coast. Quirk, on the other hand, was completely absorbed in his quixotic project. Had he even understood the import of these threatening letters? Given the potential for bad publicity for the university, it was probably just as well Quirk seemed unaware of this.

"So you're an alumnus."

"Do you know that Father Carmody actually remembered me? Incredible. I was not, I can tell you, a campus luminary during my time here."

"And what have you done since graduating?"

"Wondering how I could have been so little interested in Notre Dame during the years I was here. A student's four years on campus are over almost as soon as they begin. You would be surprised how small a part of a student's interest is engaged in the classes he takes, in learning. Before you know it, you graduate and get swept up in life. Gradually it dawns on you that you all but wasted the opportunity of a lifetime. I have resolved to make up for that."

"Hence your interest in F. Marion Crawford?"

"Yes." He paused. "I collect Notre Dame memorabilia. Books about the place. I have someone who keeps on the lookout for me. She came upon a mention of Notre Dame in a biography of Crawford. You know he lectured here?"

"So did Henry James and William Butler Yeats."

"But they weren't Catholics! Have you read the chapter on Crawford in Louis Auchincloss's *The Man Behind the Book*? I wonder how much of Crawford he actually read. And he doesn't even mention his conversion to Catholicism." Quirk might have pronounced that scandalous sentence in italics.

"You yourself have read Crawford?"

"I have everything but a title or two. There were two complete editions, and he was very popular, so most of the books are easily found. But there are some that are very rare."

"I got my set for a song."

Quirk was on his feet. "Could I see it?"

Roger wished he had brought his chair from his study, the one he could wheel around in without getting to his feet. He rose slowly and with an effort.

"How much do you weigh?" Quirk asked wondrously.

"That depends."

"On what?"

"Whether I can get my brother to read the scale." He patted his rotund circumference. "I can't see it."

Roger waddled into his study, got into the specially built chair that made him mobile, and turned to find that Quirk had stopped in the doorway. His mouth was open as he looked around.

"What a room!"

"That wall is fiction. You will find Crawford there."

Quirk found them, ran his finger along their spines. "The Collier edition."

"The library has a good selection. I couldn't teach the course otherwise."

"He should be reprinted."

"Another costly project. I wonder how many would be interested in his style of fiction now."

"How can we know if he isn't available?"

"That doesn't sound like a premise any publisher would be willing to proceed on."

"Notre Dame Press should do it."

"Perhaps, with a subsidy . . ." Roger was beginning to feel the beginnings of impatience. He could have tolerated Quirk's enthusiasm if he would not far rather have been talking with Phil and Father Carmody of the threatening letter the priest had brought. Obviously, he wanted Phil to look into the matter.

"You're right, of course. But first things first. I mean the Villa Crawford. As it happens, I do have an idea where the money to buy it could be gotten."

"That wouldn't settle the matter, of course."

"This morning at the Morris Inn—I'm staying there—I ran into a classmate I had not seen in years. He lives a very simple life by the looks of him, and while he was here few people had any inkling of his background. He is rich as Croesus. Inherited money. I had an uncle who worked for his father, that's how I got the story. Manfred swore me to secrecy when I mentioned it to him."

"Manfred?"

"Manfred Fenster."

6 IN A DULL TIME, EVEN A SMALL task is welcome. Phil Knight felt that he and Father Carmody were colluding in making a mountain out of a molehill by pretending that the threatening letter the provost had received was anything more than a prank. What made it hard to dismiss was the fact that a similar threat had been made against the football coach.

"You really think there's anything to it, Father?"

"Even as a hoax it could make bad publicity for the university."

"Maybe that's the idea. Just a little rumble in the media."

"That's where you come in, Phil. Those letters have to be collected and their recipients warned against making them known." Father Carmody paused. "How many people already know of them? Someone is sure to say something that will be picked up by the press."

There seemed to be four letters in all:

to the provost
to the dean of Arts & Letters
to the football coach
to Professor Oscar Wack

"Who's he, Roger?"

Roger smiled. "He teaches theory."

"Theory of what?"

"He's in the English department. I think he has joint appointments in theology and law. He is a tireless writer to campus publications. That is odd since he is, as they say, widely published in his field. Cabalistic pieces on various works of literature. I am told he despises me."

"Do you know him?"

"He snubs me. When he sees me coming in my golf cart, he cuts off across the lawn to avoid me. He accuses me of corrupting the young."

"What?"

"I am sure I was his target. It was in a four part series he wrote for the *Observer*. He spoke of unearned and inflated reputations." Roger patted his tummy. "He inveighed against the resurrecting of authors who were enjoying a deep and deserved obscurity. I am told he is less oblique in class, where I am mentioned by name. The dark Knight of the soul, that sort of thing."

"Maybe you pasted together these threats."

"Oh, I did worse. I referred to him in my class as Wack, O. It was taken up by the students."

Phil went first to the Guglielmino Center to find that Weis was on the road recruiting. Father Carmody had prepared the way with a phone call, and an assistant took Phil into his office and handed him the letter.

"I thought the provost ought to know."

"He got one, too."

The man's face brightened. "He did?"

"There were others as well."

"Why do I find that reassuring?"

The letter to Weis had a different message. BewaRe! gOlden boWls brEaK. BoMbs awAy.

"Coach said ignore it. I didn't think so. What do you think?"

"Some nut."

"Some nuts are dangerous." The man looked around. "If anything happened to this place . . ."

"How many people know about this?"

"Here? Only me. And Coach, of course."

The office of the dean of Arts and Letters was a warren of rooms reached from a posh reception area. Phil was led as through a maze to the inner sanctum where the dean, in shirt sleeves and gaudy suspenders, rose, smiling a crooked smile.

"Phil Knight."

"I know. The provost called. I think he's making too much of this. I get threats all the time." The smile went away, and then came back. "Usually anonymous e-mails."

"Threatening to bomb your office?"

"That is a new touch."

"Could I see the letter?

A ladder leaned against a bookshelf, providing access to higher shelves. The dean went up a rung or two and felt along the top of the books. He brought down the folded page. He looked at Phil. "I told the provost about this, but no one else."

"As in no one?"

"It's not the sort of message one circulates."

Phil unfolded the paper. It had been put together in the same way as the ones to the provost and the football coach, but the message was different. AcHtung! A coNtraCt has bEEn taKen oUt on yOu.

"Any ideas?"

"I would say a faculty member. Because of the mention of contract. Maybe someone who didn't get renewed."

Phil asked him to explain and got more lore than he wanted about the various adjunct and auxiliary appointments to the faculty, men and women taken on for piecework, without tenure, and consequently vulnerable to being let go when the need for them lessened.

"How many people are we talking about? That didn't get renewed?"

"I made a list." He had it in a drawer of his desk, handwritten.

"You are worried, aren't you?"

"Not about violence. This is the kind of thing that can hurt the college, and the university. It would be pretty bad publicity that we have a nut running loose on campus. The fact that he or she is harmless would only add to the fun of it. From a journalistic point of view."

Oscar Wack proved more elusive. He was not in his office in Decio; there was no off-campus phone for him listed; the English department was reluctant to help.

"You've come from the provost?"

"That's right."

"And you want information about a faculty member?"

"I want to talk to him."

"Who exactly are you?"

"Why don't you call the provost's office."

But the fellow seemed to be signaling to someone behind Phil. He turned to face a spidery man of middle size with a great helmet of gray hair. His glasses were circular, the lenses thick. He looked from Phil to the secretary and back.

"Professor Wack?"

"Who is this?" He addressed the secretary.

"I'm Philip Knight. The provost asked me—"

"Knight!" He stepped back.

"Could we go somewhere to talk? It will just take a minute."

"We can talk right here."

The secretary nodded in vigorous approval.

"I don't think that would be very smart."

"What is this about?"

Oh, the hell with it. "You received a threatening letter."

"What!"

"Did you?"

"How would you have heard of that . . ." The grayish eyes had narrowed behind the circular glasses. He stepped back. "Knight. You're his brother, aren't you?"

"I have a brother, yes."

"So that's it.

"Look—"

36

"Is this part of the threat? You don't intimidate me, sir." But he backed away from Phil.

"Thanks for your time."

Wacko indeed. Phil headed for the bar of the University Club.

THE MAIN DINING ROOM OF THE
Morris Inn is called Sorin's, after the
founder of the university. It is a pleasant place for lunch, though
crowded, but even more pleasant for dinner. Bill had introduced Mary Alice to his father in the lobby. Mr. Fenster
reached out a hand, then hesitated, turned, and loped toward
the dining room. He was dressed as before, but then when
he traveled he carried only a duffel bag. They were shown to a
table and then, as if to make up for the gaucherie in the lobby,
Mr. Fenster said to Mary Alice, "I'm happy to know you."

What could she say but that she was happy to know him.
Suddenly, it threatened to be a long dinner.

"I went out to the Catholic Worker House."

"Did you rent a car?"

"I took a cab."

"How was it?"

"You really ought to volunteer there, Bill."

"Catholic Worker?" Mary Alice said.

This got for her the little lecture Bill had received at lunch.
What would Mary Alice make of all this?

"It would make a good article, Bill." She turned to his
father. "Of course you know about *Via Media.*"

"Cardinal Newman?"

"No, no. Our alternative newspaper."

"Tell me about it."

"I can't believe that Bill hasn't told you. Wait, I have an issue in my coat." She got up and hurried from the restaurant. Mr. Fenster stirred the ice cubes in his water glass, making a chiming noise.

"Is she a good friend?"

"Yes."

"She seems nice."

"She is nice."

Mary Alice was back, got seated, and opened the issue of *Via Media* for Mr. Fenster to see. "Bill found a donor to enable us to get started. Very hush-hush."

"He wants to be anonymous." He avoided his father's eyes.

"Not many donors do. What's this about the University Club?"

"They want to tear it down."

"I didn't know there was one. Is it for students?"

"Oh, no. For faculty, alumni, townies."

Mr. Fenster skimmed the story. "Will the same donor fund the proposed new building?"

"I gather the family isn't happy about the club's being torn down. A collection of beer steins was donated along with the cost of the building. They are enshrined in cases throughout the place."

"It must have been here when I was a student. I never knew about it."

A pudgy little man had entered the restaurant and was

listening to the hostess as he looked around. Suddenly his face lit up, and he hurried to their table.

"Fenster! What luck." He beamed at Mary Alice and Bill. "Have you ordered yet? I hate to eat alone."

The table could accommodate four. There seemed no way to refuse.

"My name is Quirk," the man said, as he got settled. The waitress appeared, and he ordered a scotch and water. "I hope I'm not drinking alone." Bill ordered a beer and Mary Alice a Diet Coke. Mr. Fenster said he would settle for his water. "Your father and I were classmates," Quirk said. "Well, I had a very interesting day. Do you two happen to know Professor Roger Knight?"

"We're taking his class," Mary Alice cried, delighted. "You wouldn't believe what it's about."

"F. Marion Crawford," Quirk said triumphantly. "And thereby hangs a tale."

"Who is F. Marion Crawford?" Mr. Fenster said, his voice heavy with disinterest.

"Now, Manfred, this concerns you. At least I hope it will. I know you're absolutely loaded, and this idea calls for a benefactor."

"What idea?" Mary Alice seemed unaware of the uneasiness Quirk's arrival had caused Bill's father.

Their drinks came. Quirk drank avidly, put down his glass, and hunched forward. "Listen, my children, and you shall hear."

Mary Alice would have been audience enough for the enthused alumnus, but Bill found himself caught up in this idea of using the Villa Crawford as the site of a junior year abroad.

40

"The place became a convent after Crawford's death, and one of his daughters joined the community. It is a magnificent structure, designed by the author himself, placed dramatically atop a cliff with the sea below."

"You've been there?"

"Several times."

"On business?" Mr. Fenster asked. He seemed to have decided to humor his old classmate.

"I'm retired, my dear fellow. On a pittance, to be sure, but enough to provide leisure to pursue my interests. I am trying to make up for the four years I wasted here. You'll know what I mean, Manfred."

Bill could not remember when he had heard his father referred to by his Christian name, one his grandmother had found in Dante, liking the sound of it, and unaware of the character it named.

"Of course Roger Knight immediately saw the brilliance of the idea."

"What will you do with the nuns?" Mr. Fenster asked.

"There are only a handful. The upkeep is funded by the Crawford estate, but it is still too expensive a proposition for a relatively small community. They should welcome the chance to move to more economical quarters. Now, Manfred, what do you think?"

"About what?"

"This would be a mere bagatelle for a man with your assets."

"You want me to pay for the purchase of this convent?"

"It is the Villa Crawford, man. It is steeped in history and

41

tradition. Crawford lectured here in the late nineteenth century. Do you know Russell Kirk?"

"The conservative?"

"It turns out that he was a great fan of Crawford. There is even a Crawford Society. My fear is that they will have this idea and purchase the villa."

"That would make sense."

"Notre Dame must buy that villa. What do you think?"

"About what?"

"Funding the purchase."

"I never discuss money at table." Or anywhere else, in Bill's experience.

Quirk lifted both hands, as if there were something promissory in the remark. "Okay. Okay. Later. Just let the idea simmer. Talk to these two about it." He looked pleadingly at Mary Alice, and she nodded. "Good, good. What's that paper?"

Mary Alice said, "It's an alternative campus paper that Bill and I and some others put out."

"Really? I have a story for you."

He looked over both shoulders and then again hunched forward.

"There have been bomb threats. To the provost, to the dean of Arts and Letters, a faculty member, and . . ." He paused for effect. "Charlie Weis."

"No." Now Mary Alice was hunched forward.

"You remember Father Carmody, Manfred?"

Mr. Fenster looked as if he would like to deny it, but he nodded.

"He brought the news to the Knight brothers when I was

there. I had heard of it where I ran into Father Carmody. He came along with me to the Knights. The brother Philip has agreed to look into it."

"Who else knows?" Mary Alice asked.

Quirk shrugged. "I don't know."

"Bill, this could be a real scoop. We have to ask Roger Knight about it."

8 EVEN GRANTING HE WAS PARA-
noid, a possibility that Oscar Wack did
not dismiss—he prided himself on keeping an open mind—
even paranoids have real enemies, as someone must have
said. He should remember who that someone was, but he
didn't. It was a troubling realization that much of what he
thought and said merely echoed what he had read and heard.
But no matter, who can own an idea, or a phrase? Last week,
in a lecture, he had told the story of the actress in the confessional asking the priest if it was a sin to think herself beautiful when she looked in the mirror. "No, my dear, only a
mistake." Even his students had found it funny. Where had he
read that? How unnerving then when the sinister Raul
Izquierdo, colleague, foe, occupant of the next office, breezed
into Wack's office without knocking, a Styrofoam cup of coffee
held before him as if he were about to propose a toast, crying,
"Congratulations."

Wack waited. There was irony and sarcasm in the very air
of the faculty office building.

"You're been reading the journals of the Abbé Mugnier.
And quoting him in class."

"I'm surprised you recognized it."

"When I myself quoted it in a recent paper?" Wack felt that he had been pounced on. As soon as Izquierdo said it, he remembered the one memorable sentence in the loathsome offprint his colleague had sailed onto his desk not long ago.

"It's hard to footnote remarks in class."

That was a counterthrust. The referees of a journal to which Izquierdo had sent one of his innumerable and unreadable articles had raised the question of plagiarism. Izquierdo had been unfazed.

"What would they say of *Ulysses,* or *Finnegans Wake*?" he had asked the departmental committee Wack had suggested look into the matter on the basis that such a charge touched on the integrity of them all. How sly to pronounce it *Finnegans Wack.*

"That they're works of genius," Wack said, his damnable voice contralto.

"Are you quoting?"

Once he had the committee laughing, Izquierdo was home free, and he knew it. It would be too much to say that Wack had made an enemy by demanding that the matter be looked into; he and Izquierdo had entered the meeting as enemies. They left the room together, Izquierdo's arm thrown over Wack's shoulders in a bogus gesture of bonhomie. "Nice try," he whispered. "I'll get you for this." The threat was made with a smile of Mexican silver.

"Why don't you take a few laps in the Rio Grande?"

"My family were landed gentry in California when yours were still swinging from trees in the Black Forest."

Now had come that absurd letter threatening to firebomb

Wack's office. Its provenance seemed obvious. The disturbing visit of Philip Knight to the departmental office shook his certainty, but not for long. He bided his time, left the door of his office open, waited for the sound of Izquierdo skipping off to the men's room. He looked out. Izquierdo had left his office door open as usual. In a trice, Wack was inside. He had to try several times to get the match to light, then he dropped it into the overflowing cornucopia of Izquierdo's wastebasket. He fled the building, but as soon as he was outside his teeth began to chatter with the cold. How could he have forgotten that the temperature was only seven above? But this was no time to be fainthearted. He circled the building and entered by another door, went up to the third floor, and huddled out of sight. He could see smoke curling from Izquierdo's office. And then came the awful realization. He had left his own door open!

He pulled open the inner door and ran down the hallway toward his office. Before he got there, Izquierdo was coming toward him from the opposite direction. Who knows what might have happened if Lucy Goessen hadn't emerged from her office and begun to scream. "Fire! Fire!"

Izquierdo came to a stop at his office door and looked with horror within. Surprising himself with his presence of mind, Wack pushed past him into the office, maneuvered the flaming wastebasket into the hall with his right foot, and turned to Lucy. "Water, please. Lots of it."

All she had was a mug of coffee. Wack took it and dashed it at the flames. Meanwhile, others converged on the scene. Again Wack called for water, and this time water was brought. Soon the wastebasket was a soggy charred mess emitting an odious smell.

"This is a smoke-free building," Wack said to Izquierdo. Tentative laughter all around, and then the full-throated laughter of relief. He distinctly heard someone refer to him as a wit. He was elated. "Better dump that somewhere."

Izquierdo glared at him with pure hatred. "You did that!"

"Put out the fire? Of course I did. Is that a sin?"

He had the onlookers with him. He felt a surge of self-confidence, the kind he sometimes felt when rehearsing his lectures before a mirror and finding them marvelous.

"No, my dear, only a mistake."

But no one heard Izquierdo. The offensive wastebasket was taken away; everyone retired to his or her respective office. Before disappearing into his, Izquierdo looked at Wack, who was seeking for some crushing final word.

"Maybe I should report this to the provost."

The unnerving memory of Philip Knight came. "What do you mean?"

"You can't fight fire with fire."

And he was gone. Izquierdo had gotten the last word. But what in the world did he mean?

9 ⟶ FRED FENSTER HAD SPENT MOST of his adult life feeling like the rich young man who had asked Jesus what he must do to be saved. "Keep the commandments." The young man already did, and so, too, did Fred. "If you would be perfect, sell all you have, give it to the poor, and come follow me." Like the rich young man, Fred had always turned sadly away from that counsel. He excused himself in part by saying that the legal complications of divesting himself of the enormous wealth his father had left him made it all but impossible. Besides, what right did he have to deprive his son of that patrimony? Bill had an independent legacy, of course, but compared with what he might inherit it seemed, in a Fenster perspective, modest. So Fred had settled for imitation poverty. He lived as simply as anyone whose sole income was Social Security. But of course it was a pretense, and he knew it, and was ashamed.

In his political phase, he had been a generous contributor to the causes he espoused, Gene McCarthy, Senator McGovern, Greenpeace; voices crying in the wilderness they had seemed, but what if they had been successful? The time came when Fred thought politics was simply a matter of misplaced emphasis. The only change that mattered was one the individual could effect in himself. He got religion, in the dismissive phrase of his sister, Vivian.

Vivian had been born to wealth and found it the most natural and agreeable condition imaginable. Her concern was the predatory forces bent on wresting her wealth and privilege from her. Her politics were somewhat to the right of what their father's had been. For her, the Republican Party had become a subservient wing of the Democrats. Her great heroine was Phyllis Schlafly, who had all but single-handedly stopped the Equal Rights Amendment. A pyrrhic victory. What the amendment sought had been gained by legislation. Pictures of women in combat gear could send Vivian into hysterics.

"Think of Joan of Arc," Fred suggested.

"Joan of Arc had a divine mission to drive the English out of France. Is Iraq a divine mission?"

He let it go. There was little to choose between winning or losing such arguments. All such things he had set aside as the things of a child. He visited Lourdes and LaSallette; he went several times to Fatima. He brooded over the messages of these apparitions, and they endorsed his conviction that personal holiness was the answer, not collective movements. He had been surprised when Quirk mentioned Garabandal.

"Have you been there?"

"Once. It's a devilish place to find."

Fred Fenster knew. "What did you think?"

Quirk studied him. They were in the bar of the Morris Inn, Quirk drinking Bushmills, Fred with a glass of mineral water. "That place scared the hell out of me."

"That's the idea."

"Look, I made a study of several apparitions. Fatima particularly. You would think that the end of the world is at hand."

Fred said nothing, sipped his water, wondered what he was doing sitting in a bar like this. Memories of the Catholic Worker House he had visited assailed him.

"I mean, what is She saying? The world is going to hell in a handbasket. War is a punishment, and if we don't shape up, it will get worse. Well, are we shaping up?" Quirk finished his drink and waved for another.

"Nothing's stopping us."

Quirk's third drink came, and he cupped it in both hands and leaned toward Fred.

"What do you think of Our Lady's university? I'm surprised you let your son go here."

"Really."

"Look, if you think this is the place we attended, forget it. Have you heard of this filthy play they've allowed to be put on here? What was the excuse? It wasn't the administration that sponsored it but certain academic departments! What a crock."

"What got you interested in Marian apparitions?"

"Remember Bastable?"

Bastable! Of course. Their classmate who had become the scourge of the Notre Dame administration. Shrewd investments had earned him the leisure to spend much of his time castigating what he regarded as the slide of Notre Dame into the status of an ex-Catholic university. Bastable had moved to South Bend, the better to be near the object of his wrath, and lived in a town house overlooking the St. Joseph River, managing his investments and firing off e-mails to one administrator or another at Notre Dame. One of the great dangers of coming to South Bend was that he might run into Bastable. Running into Quirk was almost as bad.

"Yes."

"We should get together with him."

"I can't. Not this time."

"When are you leaving?"

Fred looked at his watch. "Right now, I'm going to bed."

"Have another."

"One's my limit."

"Mineral water?"

"Did you ever taste it?"

Fred left the bar, crossed the lobby, and went up to his room, where he donned an overcoat and put on his beret. He took the elevator down, then went through the tunnel under Notre Dame Avenue and emerged in the McKenna Center. The outer doors were locked, of course, but only to prevent entry to the building. Fred let himself out and walked across the campus. The golden dome glowed in the lights trained on it; the clock in the tower of Sacred Heart looked moonlike in the darkness. He rounded the basilica and took the steps down to the Grotto, aflame with votive lights. It was a replica of the grotto at Lourdes, token of Father Sorin's devotion to the Mother of God. Fred knelt and shivered through several prayers. He had intended to say a rosary, but it was simply too cold. His prayer became an apology for his weakness.

Returning to the Morris Inn, ungloved hands thrust deep into the pockets of his overcoat, he felt himself to be a ridiculous figure. Fifty-eight years old and in many ways he still felt like an adolescent. His life seemed make-believe. Every day he read the *Liturgia Horarum*, he was a daily communicant, he longed to bring his life into line with the most austere ideal of the Christian life, but there remained the impediment of his vast inherited wealth.

Bastable. Several times, Bastable had waylaid him when he came to visit Bill. The man was a crusader. Almost literally. He was amazed that Fred wasn't a Knight of Malta.

"I'll put you up for it."

"I can't afford it."

Bastable laughed. "It turned me around, Fred. We take sick people to Lourdes, you know. That's when I first became aware of it, really."

Bastable had turned his interest in the shrine in a political direction. The messages of Mary at Fatima were a weapon he used against those who were betraying the Church. His public and private criticisms of Notre Dame were always put forward under the aegis of what the Blessed Virgin wanted. How could anyone resist such arguments?

A year ago, Fred had accepted Bastable's invitation to stop by his town house by the river. Mrs. Bastable was a comfortable overweight woman who seemed to spend the day reading jumbo paperback novels with glistening covers. But her passion was bridge. She played four days a week, leaving Bastable to grapple with the modern world. Fred wondered what he would be like now if Margie hadn't died.

"Don't ask," Bastable growled when Fred inquired about his children.

There was a photograph of a beautiful little Chinese girl on his desk.

"My grandchild. Adopted," he added, and looked out at the river.

Bastable's reforming zeal was apparently directed only at others. He dismissed the suggestion that proximity to the campus must make daily Mass an easy matter.

"At 11:30?" he said. "Come on."

Bastable reminded Fred of himself in his political phase. When Bastable wasn't buying and selling, he was dreaming up campaigns to get the Notre Dame administration to admit their perfidy and shape up. He had known many defeats, not least with their classmates.

"They think everything is hunky-dory. Look at all the new buildings, look at what they've done to the grounds, look at Warren Golf Course."

To keep up the level of his rage, Bastable pored over the *Observer,* the student newspaper, which he called the *New York Times Lite.* "The thing might just as well be coming out of Podunk Tech. Every stupid liberal cause is championed. And the faculty . . ."

Not a happy get-together. The worst of it was that Fred came away feeling smug. There but for the grace of God go I. What was the point of all this rage at others if one made no demands upon oneself? Not so comforting a thought when he reflected that any demands he made on himself were voluntary and, however secret, theatrical. *I should have been a*

pair of ragged claws scuttling across the floors of silent seas.
He smiled, then frowned. Why hadn't a verse from the psalms
occurred to him?

Roger was made uneasy when Mary Alice Frangipani and Bill
Fenster came to him and wanted to talk about the threatening
letters that had recently come to various administrators. "And
the football coach," Mary Alice added.

"Where did you hear that?"

"Mr. Quirk suggested it would make a great story for *Via
Media.*"

"I wish you wouldn't. It's not just that the provost would
like to avoid the publicity. My brother would be compromised.
He has been asked to look into those threats."

"How can they be kept secret?"

"Look, if you hear about them from some other source, one
that doesn't involve me or Phil, go ahead. Otherwise, I really
hope you won't write such a story."

They agreed—he had never doubted they would—but after
they were gone, he wheeled up to his desk and made the comparison that had started dark thoughts. It seemed pretty clear
that the letters pasted to the sheets of paper had been cut from
an issue of *Via Media.* The font was the same, and each of the
capital letters could be traced to a headline.

Roger sat and mused. After all, television networks had
staged battles in order to have a scoop when they covered them.
There had been too many instances of events contrived with an
eye to news coverage. Of course the Fourth Estate professed

shock when these were revealed, but a lesson had been taught, and Roger wondered if these young campus journalists had learned it. How better to advance the influence of their paper than to print an article about those threatening messages?

He looked again at the letters pasted to the sheet of paper. Of course anyone could have snipped those letters from the paper and concocted those messages. Those messages. It was silly to take a prank like that seriously, something he needn't tell Phil.

Phil had made the rounds of the recipients of the threatening letters.

"Are they all from the same source?" Roger asked him.

"See for yourself."

There was little doubt that the message on each sheet of paper had been formed from letters clipped from *Via Media.* The notion that the threats were an exercise in creative news would not go away.

Phil's account of his meeting with Oscar Wack seemed proof of the wild goose chase he was on.

"Is he nuts or what?"

"He teaches English."

"He seems to know you."

"I represent all that he dislikes. The amateur. I discuss books because they have given pleasure and the discussion promises greater pleasure in rereading."

"What's wrong with that?"

"Anybody can do it. Not equally well, of course, but there is no secret handshake or mystic doctrine separating the good from the best. My idea of a critic is Chesterton in his books on Dickens and Browning."

"What's the other way like?"

"You'll have to ask Professor Wack."

"I don't ever want to talk to him again."

"Don't underestimate him, Phil. He's famous in his own circles. His *Foucault, Flatulence, and Fatuity* won a prize."

"Have you read it?"

"You don't read a book like that. You decode it."

10 ⟶ TWO DAYS LATER THE SPECIAL
edition of *Via Media* appeared, featuring
a story on the conflagration in the faculty office building. The
tone was arch, the story could have been a spoof, but there
were pictures of the charred wastebasket, a long quotation
from Lucille Goessen, and a suggestion from Izquierdo that
students read Ray Bradbury's *Fahrenheit 451*. Oscar Wack
preferred to make a written statement.

> *The intellectual is ever under attack and nowhere more vigor-*
> *ously than in the university, the alleged redoubt for his ilk. A uni-*
> *versity is not a seminary or convent. Students may be unmarried*
> *but they are not celibates. The crushing suppressions of the past*
> *must be lifted. How can the mind be free when the body is not?*
> *All of us stand in solidarity with our colleague Izquierdo. We will*
> *not be intimidated.*
> *Wack, O.*

That is not the way the professor had signed his statement,
and he was furious when the issue came into his hand. He telephoned Bill Fenster.

"Is this the office of the *Via Media*?"

"Who's calling?"

"You answer first."

"Yes."

"Professor Wack. Why are you mocking me? For whom are you working? Who pays for this miserable rag of a paper?" His voice mounted as he spoke, and the last question ended in registers audible only to dogs.

"All that is made clear in the paper."

"That you are paid to harass the faculty?"

"Professor, we didn't light the fire in Professor Izquierdo's wastebasket."

"Someone should light a fire to you!"

He hung up.

"Maybe he'll send us a threatening message," Bill said to Mary Alice.

"It sounds as if he already has."

It was becoming ever clearer to Bill Fenster that even a twelve- or sixteen-page paper that appears irregularly is a stern taskmaster, demanding much of one's time. That would have been harder to take if Mary Alice weren't every bit as conscientious as he was. The others, well, it was a volunteer job and people came and went, but there were always enough around at crucial times. Newcomers had to be warned that they weren't interested in news.

"I thought it was a newspaper."

"No, it's a student publication. Let the others go scampering after news. We want to publish positive accounts of permanent aspects of the university. What do we know of the people who run the place, for instance?"

He was echoing his father here, of course. He could remember when his dad told him how liberating it had been when he just stopped reading papers and magazines and watching television news. The constant reader or viewer had his curiosity or indignation or anyway much of his attention engaged by some event, for the moment the most important event in the world, only to find that item replaced by another, and that by another, on and on.

"And none of them has any importance for me. More likely than not it's a distortion for sensational effect, or something I couldn't do anything about if I wanted to. How many remote weather disasters and crimes does one have to know about?"

"But how can you vote?"

"Only one or two issues are truly important, and it is easy to discover where a candidate stands on those."

His father had taken a look at *Via Media.* "It reminds me of the *Scholastic.*"

"The *Scholastic!*"

"Of long ago, when it was the sole campus publication. I like these long accounts of lectures given."

In their rivals, lectures, when they were reported at all, were reduced in the search for some controversial remark, with little sense at all being given of what had actually been said.

"You'll find no misspellings either. Thanks to Mary Alice."

Writing up the wastebasket fire in Decio had been meant as a spoof, so that was a lesson of sorts. Don't count on a sense of humor being widespread.

11 WHEN CRENSHAW OF CAMPUS
security showed up at the English department, he was not a welcome visitor. Hector, the secretary, eyed him warily when he asked about the fire in the building.

"It was in a wastebasket," he said.

"Your people know they can't smoke in this building, don't they?"

"No one in this department smokes!" His tone was shocked.

"I want to see the office where it happened."

"For heaven's sake. It was over before it began."

"Then why is it such a big story in this paper?" He produced the issue of *Via Media* as magicians produce rabbits.

"That rag!"

Crenshaw was getting nowhere, and he wasn't sure he regretted it. Members of the faculty sometimes treated campus security as if it represented the threat of fascism. Of course the main bone of contention was parking. With the expansion of the campus, faculty parking spots were ever more distant from their offices. No wonder that some sought to leave their cars in front of residence halls as if they were visitors. The bicycle patrol handed out tickets randomly, as traffic and parking tickets are always distributed, but Crenshaw wanted them to lean on the repeat offenders. Young Larry Douglas was a conscientious member of the bike patrol. It was too bad the fines didn't go to campus security.

A man entered, saw Crenshaw, turned, and went out.

"Who was that?"

"Professor Izquierdo."

Crenshaw went after him. "Professor, Professor, could I talk to you?"

The man turned, frowning, and looked up and down the uniformed Crenshaw. "Parking tickets are not a criminal offense."

"I'm here about the fire."

"I thought you were campus police."

"I am. Where can we talk?"

"Come in, come in." But Izquierdo entered his office first. Crenshaw looked at the wastebasket. It bore the marks of fire.

"Tell me about the fire."

"It's been written up."

"That's why I'm here."

Not quite true. Larry Douglas had come into Crenshaw's office two days before, so excited he had forgotten to remove the ridiculous helmet he wore while cycling around looking for cars parked in the wrong place so he could ticket them. Larry said he had overheard an old priest talking about bomb threats on the campus. Crenshaw had shagged the kid out of his office. The trouble with Douglas, he was so glad to have the campus job that he was overzealous. But then Crenshaw's secretary reported that there was murmuring among the staff in the Main

Building about strange messages received, threatening bombs and fire. It was the story in the alternative campus paper that decided Crenshaw to look into it.

Izquierdo tipped back in his chair. "How long have you been in your job?"

"Since I retired from the police department."

"South Bend?"

"Elkhart."

"I suppose they pay you peanuts."

"Well, I have my pension, too."

"Ah, pension. It's what drives us all on. We work in order to retire. And, in your case, to work again."

Izquierdo was a funny duck. If he had seen him on campus, Crenshaw would have thought he was in maintenance. He wore faded jeans, lumberjack shoes, and a T-shirt bearing a legend that said sexual perversity was okay with him. An old corduroy jacket hung limply from a coat stand, along with a baggy winter coat and a very long and gaudy scarf. A deerstalker hat crowned the coat stand. It might have been a scarecrow.

"About the fire in my wastebasket. It was set by my colleague Wack while I was in the john."

"Why would he do that?"

"What do you know about *The Vagina Monologues*?"

"What's that?"

Izquierdo seemed surprised. "You really don't know?"

"What's it got to do with the fire in your wastebasket?"

"Intimidation."

"You said a colleague started it."

"Oscar Wack. An unbalanced fellow. He is insanely jealous

of me. With reason, of course. I kept him off the committee sponsoring the *Monologues*."

"So he set fire to your wastebasket?"

"You probably find this ridiculous. It is. Life is ridiculous, when you come to think of it."

"Why didn't you call the fire department?"

"Because Wack staged the whole thing so he could look like a hero putting it out."

"Maybe I should talk with him."

"It would be wiser just to keep an eye on him."

"That isn't my job."

"I thought you wanted to know why I had a fire here."

The conversation went on like that. Crenshaw was glad to get out of there. The departmental secretary glared at him when he went by his door.

Outside, he sat behind the wheel of his car and thought of Sarasota. During his long years on the Elkhart police force he had dreamed of heading for Florida as soon as he hit retirement age. But then he heard of the opening at Notre Dame security. Crenshaw's father had served as an usher in the stadium during home football games—a visored hat, free entrance to all the games, minimal responsibilities. Notre Dame had long represented auxiliary income in the surrounding communities. The opening in security had seemed somehow a continuation of his father's connection with Notre Dame. Not for the first time, Crenshaw thought he had made a mistake in not heading for Sarasota three years ago. He knew that security was regarded as a version of the Keystone Kops. They had the equipment, a fleet of cars, the bicycle patrol, an expanding staff, the latest in technical wizardry, but they were still figures of fun. Never had he been more aware of the lack of dignity in his job than in talking with Professor Izquierdo. The man had to be stringing him along. What a great joke it would have been if Crenshaw had taken the bait and gone to quesion the colleague, Wack.

Bah. He started the engine and drove slowly away. A cop should always observe the speed limits he enforced. Except in an emergency, of course.

FATHER TIM CONWAY, NEW TO
the provost's office, had been assigned
the task of keeping tabs on Quirk. The alumnus seemed to
represent a recurring problem, as Tim gathered from talking
with others in the numerous offices that housed associate, assistant, and other adjuncts to the provost. He himself was tem-
porarily housed in an office with Roscoe Pound, a holdover
from the previous regime. They had gone off on the afternoon of
the day on which Tim had met Father Carmody to Legends,
where they sat over beer while Pound gave Tim the benefit of
his long experience.

"Quirk is a type. Check his record here as a student and
you will probably find nothing. People like him drift through
four years here. For most, football is their umbilical cord to
campus after they graduate, but many get religion. They are
the troublemakers."

"He wants us to buy a villa in Sorrento."

Pound chuckled. "I know, I know. But the idea behind it
is remedial, corrective. It is a criticism of the university as it
is now. He wants to bring it back to some fancied golden time.
I'll bet he mentioned the *Monologues*."

"That is a pretty raunchy thing to have put on here."

"Of course it is. No decent place would allow it."

"So?"

"We're no longer a decent place. Quirk is right, but it's important not to let him know that. Look, there are three Notre Dames, the one whose history you can trace, the one such alumni as Quirk imagine, and the one we are slowly becoming."

"And what is that?"

"Read Burtchaell, read Marsden."

Tim didn't ask him to explain. "I'd rather hear what you think."

"You are."

They had another beer. The place was noisy and crowded, just the setting to receive Pound's mordant view of things.

"You were in Rome?" Pound asked.

"For four years."

"And now you've come home."

"There's a chance I'll be sent on for a doctorate."

"Take it. One of our problems is that there are few priests of the Congregation on the faculty. The CSCs have become dorm mothers, campus ministers, supernumeraries."

"Who is Father Carmody?"

"Ah, Carmody. He is part of the history of the place. A second violinist. He goes back to Hesburgh."

"I had never heard of him."

"That is his genius. He was always in the background, whispering memento mori in the ears of administrators."

It seemed odd to Tim that he should be receiving such

information about the congregation he had joined immediately after graduation from a layman like Pound. It emerged that Pound was not Catholic.

"You're surprised. I was hired by a Calvinist."

The fact that Quirk had gone off with Father Carmody gave Tim an excuse to drop in on the old priest at Holy Cross House. Here in the last stage of their religious life were the ancient members of the Congregation. Preparing for death? Most looked just bewildered and frail. They watched the young man warily as he came onto the upper floor and said he had come to see Father Carmody.

"Oh, he wants you to meet him downstairs."

The nurse offered to show him where, but Tim told her he could find it. It was while he was going downstairs again that it occurred to him that he himself might end up here someday, but the thought was as remote as old age itself.

Father Carmody looked the picture of health after the specters Tim had just seen. The old priest sat in a room where visitors could be entertained. He closed his book on his finger, then flourished it at Tim.

"Dick Sullivan's book on the university. Have you read it?"

Tim asked to see it and leafed through it, not knowing what to say.

"It is a love letter to Notre Dame. Dick signed over all royalties from it to the university. No one found that odd in those days."

"You knew him?"

"In his last years. A wonderful, gentle man. He taught English and writing. He wrote fiction himself."

"I'll have to look him up."

Father Carmody proceeded to give Tim suggestions for other reading he might do on the history of Notre Dame.

"What do they tell you people in the novitiate nowadays?"

No need to go into that. Tim turned the conversation to Quirk.

"I wish those threatening letters hadn't been mentioned in his presence," Father Carmody said.

"They're just a prank, aren't they?"

"Let's hope so. Phil Knight seems to think so. I asked him to look into it. Do you know the Knight brothers?"

"I've heard of the one who teaches."

"Roger. A whale of a man, in every sense. As learned as Zahm, and yet he wears it lightly. He only teaches undergraduates. You should get to know him."

"Tell me about Quirk."

"He's an alum, of course. Engineering. He made a modest pile and decided to retire while he could put his mind to other things. Not that he has much of a mind. Of course he is disenchanted with what the university has become."

"In what way?"

The old priest considered for a moment. "There are two schools of thought on that. One holds that we are fashioning a new way to be a Catholic university. The other holds that we are ceasing to be one."

"Which school do you belong to?"

"Both."

"How is that possible?"

"Because things are never as simple as any theory demands. The idea of buying that villa in Sorrento isn't a bad one. We're throwing money at everything else. And Quirk thinks that his classmate Fenster might come up with the purchase money. Of course there would be maintenance. Always remember maintenance when a new building is proposed. You can pay off the building, but maintenance is forever."

"The provost hasn't rejected the idea."

"If he is smart, and he is, he will wait to see if the money is there."

"Who is Fenster?"

"He's staying in the Morris Inn at the moment if you want to meet him. He's not at all like Quirk. He has mountains of money and lives like a monk. His son is the editor of *Via Media.*"

Tim frowned. "Did you see the story on the fire in the English professor's office?"

Carmody nodded. "That wasn't the fellow who got the threatening letter, was it?"

"If he were, those threats could be taken as a prank. That was Wack. The fire was in the wastebasket of a professor named Izquierdo. He says Wack set the fire."

"No."

"Campus security checked it out."

"Campus security! Who told them?"

"I don't think those letters are a secret anymore."

"Ye gods."

13 HIS MOTHER WORKED ON THE campus cleaning crew, each morning tidying up the rooms of male students—the women looked after themselves—part of the contingent of serfs who were all but invisible elements of the infrastructure of Notre Dame. When she had gone to work there, Mrs. Grabowski might have done better just about anywhere else, but the idea was that her employment would smooth the way for Henry's admission as a student. And he had worked his tail off at St. Joe High, just as he worked his tail off all summer earning his tuition for the year. In high school, he had gone out for freshman football and been all but laughed off the field, but no matter, his sights were ever on the SATs, which together with his mother's employment at Notre Dame would get him admitted to the student body. Mr. Masterson, his advisor, encouraged him and, when the time came, wrote a recommendation.

"Don't put all your eggs in one basket, Henry. Apply at Purdue. Apply at IU. Of course, there is always IUSB." The South Bend campus of the state university. Henry had smiled away the suggestion. It was Notre Dame or nothing. And nothing is what he got.

He had applied for early admission so he didn't have to wait for the crushing disappointment. He read the bland letter so often it was etched into his memory like the legend over Dante's Inferno. He was devastated. His advisor suggested Holy Cross College, just up the road from St. Joe High, it, too, run by the Brothers of Holy Cross.

"Lots of kids are admitted from there as sophomores, even juniors."

Henry said he would think about it. But he was filled with a terrible proletarian wrath. He threw out his video of *Rudy*. His whole imagined future was ruined. He was filled with hatred for the university that had rejected him and all his youthful dreams. His mother was philosophical about it.

"You can get a job on campus." She added, "For now."

Maintenance, maybe even campus security. She had talked to a young man on traffic patrol, a South Bend native, Larry Douglas. She actually brought him home to tell Henry of the great opportunities to be had in Notre Dame security. So Henry applied but without hope, sure it would go the way of his application to be a student. He had been accepted, to his mother's delight. When he filled out the final forms, Henry felt he was becoming a permanent member of the underclass.

He and Larry became friends, more or less. What could you think of a guy who thought riding around campus on a bicycle dispensing parking tickets made him an integral part of the Notre Dame community?

"Think of the benefits, Henry." Larry meant hospitalization and retirement. Maybe also wearing the stupid uniform.

Henry's SATs meant that he had been more than qualified

for admission. He just hadn't been admitted. As he wheeled around the campus, wearing a helmet and dark glasses, he told himself that he was as at least as smart as any of the carefree students he passed. Those years of study at St. Joe, the reading he had done on his own, now seemed a joke, but he couldn't rid his mind of what he had learned, and he couldn't drop the habits he acquired. He began to collect syllabi of the courses he might have taken, and read the books assigned. He got to know Izquierdo when the professor came up while Henry was writing a ticket for his misparked Corvette.

"I'm about to leave," Izquierdo said, getting behind the wheel.

"I can't just tear this up."

"Give it to me." He took the long slip and tore it into pieces, grinning at Henry. "Now you don't have to."

"You're a professor." This was clear from the sticker on his windshield.

"Is that an offense?"

"What do you teach?"

"English."

"Yeah, but what exactly?"

"A survey of British literature."

"Do you do *The Vicar of Wakefield*?"

Izquierdo looked at him. "Have you read it?"

"Twice."

"What are you doing handing out traffic tickets?"

"It's a long story."

"My office is in Decio. Come see me. But not in that uniform."

That is how it began. The first time, they talked about Goldsmith's novel, then went on to other things. Henry asked if he could have Izquierdo's syllabus. He had read half the books on the list.

"Where did you go to school?"

"St. Joe High."

"I meant college."

"I was turned down."

"Where?"

"Here."

"Geez."

On Henry's second visit, Izquierdo developed the theory that Henry was better off as he was. "Your problem is you really want to use your mind. That disqualifies you. Students are engaged in job preparation. The degree is a ticket, that's all. So-called higher education has become a fraud. Maybe it always was."

"So why are you here?"

"To dig I am not able, to beg I am ashamed. Plus, the pay is great."

For all that, Izquierdo's negative attitude toward Notre Dame rivaled Henry's own.

"I suppose you're Catholic?" he asked Henry.

"I was baptized."

"Who wasn't? This is supposed to be the premier Catholic university in the land. Give me a break."

Izquierdo had put aside the faith of his fathers.

"You're an agnostic?"

"Ha. No halfway measures for Raul. None of that can stand up to what we now know."

"What's that?"

Izquierdo looked sly. "You think I think that what I just said is true."

"Don't you?"

He shook his head. "The thing is, it isn't false either. Look, there's no there there. No objective world to underwrite our sentences and make them true or false. The world is part of what we fabricate, not independent of it. Are you following me?"

This was exciting stuff, until Henry thought of the sentence "I was turned down by Notre Dame." But talking with Izquierdo fed his conviction that he was as smart as any student. Smarter. This wobbled a bit when he found out that Larry Douglas had a secret passion for poetry, but of the obvious sort.

"Why didn't you go to college, Larry?"

"Why didn't you?"

"All it is is job preparation. I've got a job."

Larry liked that. Why didn't they double-date some weekend?

"I broke up with my girl." There had never been a girl. All that study in high school had given Henry the reputation of being a nerd.

"My girl will fix you up."

Why not?

Larry's girl was named Kimberley, a real doll, but Henry got pudgy Laura, who worked in the office of campus security.

She kept telling him she hadn't wanted to come, she was only there to give Larry a bad time.

"What for?"

"Her. I was his girl for months, then she came along."

"Maybe we should trade."

Larry was driving, and he squirmed at the suggestion, but Kimberley turned and gave Henry a nice smile.

"Larry says you're quite a reader."

"Oh, a little poetry."

"Really?" Larry had given him the story about Kimberley's susceptibilities.

"Lasciate ogni speranza voi ch'entrate," he murmured.

"What's that?"

"Dante. No translation really captures the poem."

Henry knew two or three other phrases from the *Comedy,* but the one did the trick. When they got to the sports bar, Kimberley was as much with Henry as was Laura, who snuggled up to Larry.

"What other poets do you like?"

"I was just going to ask you who your favorites were."

Larry was following this exchange with a desolate expression. Laura had him pretty well pinned in a corner of the booth, and if Kimberley was just across from him, she had turned to face Henry.

"I suppose you think Emily Dickinson is too feminine."

"No woman can be too feminine for me."

"Hey," Larry said, "how about that fire in the professor's wastebasket?"

"Let's not talk business," Henry said, but Laura was all for the suggested topic.

"And he didn't even get one of those threatening letters," she said.

"What threatening letters?" Henry wanted to know.

"That's confidential," Larry said to Laura.

"Oh pooh. It's all they talk about in the office."

"Tell me," Henry urged Laura, and Kimberley turned pouting away.

So he got the official story. The provost, the dean of Arts and Letters, Professor Wack in English, and Charlie Weis, the football coach. Henry listened as if this were all news to him. He would have to tell Izquierdo of the reaction to those messages, if he didn't already know. Izquierdo talked as if he wouldn't mind firebombing Wack's office himself.

"Look," Larry said, assuming a tone of authority. "They're just a prank."

"So why the secrecy?"

"It would still be bad publicity. Who wants such a story about Notre Dame to get around?"

Who indeed? Henry pushed closer to Kimberley. " 'I'm nobody, who are you?' "

" 'I'm nobody, too.' " And she squeezed his arm. "I love that poem."

(14) THE STORY IN *VIA MEDIA* ABOUT
the fire in the wastebasket of Professor
Izquierdo set the Old Bastards' table aroar with excitement.
Armitage Shanks felt vindicated. When he had passed on the
rumor that threatening letters were circulating on the campus,
he had been scorned.

"I told you so," he said with all the satisfaction the phrase
conveyed.

"He probably dropped a cigarette in the wastebasket."

"You can't smoke in Decio."

"You mean you're forbidden to," Goucher corrected. "Pro-
hibitions don't confer incapacity." Goucher had taught philosophy for forty-two years, without great success.

"He blames a colleague. Some idiot named Wack."

A wide smile replaced the vague expression on Potts's face.
"Remember when we locked the dean in his private john?"

The faculty had resented the fact that the dean had a private washroom, and locking him into it had seemed condign
punishment. Chuckles went round the table. Debbie, the hostess, took an empty chair, singing softly, "I Don't Want to Set
the World on Fire."

"Is this a confession?"

"Are you a priest?"

"What do you hear about the conflagration in the waste-basket?"

"Just what I read in the papers."

"Maybe that's how they'll get rid of this place, burn it down."

Debbie put her hands over her ears. "I don't want to hear about it."

Armitage Shanks developed his theory that they had entered a period analogous to the phony war that had been prelude to World War II. War had been declared, but nothing much happened for months. He began to develop the parallel—the threat to the club, the countering protest, now long silence—but no one listened.

"Who was dean at the time?"

"At what time?"

"When he got locked in the john."

"Sheedy?"

"No, it was after him. Sheedy was all right. He was always hiding in the back room of the museum where he could read."

"He had one assistant dean."

"Devere Plunkett."

"Have you seen the present setup? I think the dean-to-student ratio is smaller than faculty-to-student. And they're all living like Oriental satraps. I'm surprised no one has fire-bombed the place."

"He was one of those threatened."

"How do you know these things?"

"I make them up."

"Guess who I ran into yesterday," Plaisance said.

"In your car?"

"An old student. He recognized me, I didn't recognize him. Quirk. He asked me why no one had told him about F. Marion Crawford while he was here."

There was a long silence. Finally Shanks said, "Crawford?"

"A novelist," Bingham said, emerging from wherever he went when he tuned out. "Late nineteenth century. I haven't heard him mentioned for years."

"You haven't heard anything for years."

"What?"

Plaisance reclaimed the chair. "He wanted to know what I thought of present-day Notre Dame."

"Who?"

"Quirk."

"Is that a real name?" Armitage Shanks wanted to know.

15 BECAUSE OF THE WEATHER, GREG
Walsh, assistant archivist, offered to
meet Roger halfway, so they were settled at a table in the pan-
demonium of the Huddle. A huge grainy television screen
overlooked the dining area but was ignored; perhaps it was
the watcher rather than the watched. Greg managed to say
this, despite his impediment, but then Roger Knight was one
of the few people with whom he could speak fluently.

"Big Brother." Roger laughed. "My brother Phil, that is.
Can you keep a secret?"

"Could I tell one, is the question."

Roger's many references to his enormous size made it easy
to refer to one's own disability.

"Several administrators, the football coach, and an English
professor have received threatening notes."

Greg nodded. "I heard."

"You did?" Roger sat back. "Well, so much for its being a
secret. Where did you hear?"

"There is an alumnus named Quirk on campus who drops
by the archives almost every day."

"Quirk. Of course."

"You know him."

"I've met him. He professes to have an interest in F. Marion Crawford, but all he talks about is his villa in Sorrento."

"He wanted to see any contemporary accounts of Crawford's visit here. He seemed to think all our visitors were Catholics and that the idea was to promote loyalty to our side. Sort of like football, I guess."

"He must have been reading George Shuster's little book."

"He didn't know it."

"But you told him of it."

"I'm not so sure he reads a lot, Roger."

"Early retirement is a mixed blessing."

"I'd like to try it."

"No you wouldn't."

Roger put a hand on his friend's arm. Greg had come by a circuitous route to his position in the Notre Dame archives. He had a doctorate in English and a law degree, but his speech impediment had impeded either a teaching or a legal career, so he had turned to library science and ended as perhaps the most versatile and learned archivist in the land. For the most part this light was hidden under the bushel of his stammer, but with Roger he was able to release wit and wisdom that had long been inaudible. He knew the Notre Dame archives like, in the phrase, the back of his hand.

"Did he ever explain why he is interested in F. Marion Crawford, Roger?"

"Rather than any number of other writers? No. It seems to have been a random choice. One of the novels found in a secondhand bookstore, I guess. But I really didn't press him on it. It is the villa that most excites him."

"What do the archives have on Crawford?"

Greg put a printout on the table. "Not much really interesting. But after all, a single visit."

"Everything he published is in the library."

"Well, as you know, he was the most popular author of his day."

"And the first who became wealthy by writing."

Roger himself approached F. Marion Crawford as a publishing phenomenon, perhaps the first in the country's history, although it was difficult to think of Crawford as an American novelist. He had spent very few years of his life in the United States, having been born in Rome and gone to India before he visited his uncle Sam Howe and his aunt Julia Ward Howe; two more quintessential Americans, or at least Yankees, it would be difficult to find. Most of Crawford's novels had foreign settings, Italy as often as not, but Roger had found *An American Politician* interesting if only because it recalled the time when senators had been elected by state legislators. It did not bear comparison to Trollope's *The American Senator,* but his history of Rome showed an easy erudition, as did his study of Pope Leo XIII. It was Roger's suggestion that the more typical novels—the Saracinesca trilogy—be read as deliberate alternatives to the theories of fiction of Henry James and William Dean Howells. Crawford was a professed romantic, for whom fiction commented on the human situation, not by seeking the most realistic contemporary setting, but rather by employing the exotic. It wasn't necessary to choose between the two schools, as if one were right and the other wrong. Best to take each novel by itself and analyze the

82

enjoyment it gave. The fact that the two literary adversaries, and friends, James and Crawford had both lectured at Notre Dame fascinated, and it was disappointing that there were such scant records of the two occasions.

As with a number of his other enthusiasms, Roger's interest in Crawford had been triggered by coming upon shelves of his books in the Hesburgh Library. How wonderful to discover a hitherto unheard-of author with a shelf, sometimes several shelves, full of his books. And he could always count on Greg Walsh either to have anticipated the enthusiasm or to joyfully take it up at Roger's behest.

Roger indicated the things on the list Greg had brought that he would like to see.

"I'm not as mobile as usual with all this snow."

"I'll bring photocopies around to your place."

So they left the Huddle by the east door. Roger's golf cart was parked just outside, and a uniformed young man, his bicycle propped on its stand, was looking it over. He turned when Roger and Greg came up.

"Is this your vehicle?"

"Yes, it is."

"You can't park here."

Roger hunted for and found his permit. "I don't like to just leave it hanging on the cart."

The young man now studied the permit. The task might have been easier if he took off his dark glasses. Roger said, "I thought you were Larry Douglas."

He took off the dark glasses. "Henry Grabowski." He handed Roger his permit. "This seems all right."

He wheeled away, and Roger and Greg sat in the cart, continuing their conversation. Ten minutes later, there was a tremendous booming sound, and Greg ran to the walk to look toward the sound.

When they came around the library, it was to see an automobile burning brightly in a No Parking zone.

PART TWO

"WAS IT INSURED?"

Even before the odious Wack, feigning sympathy, had asked this question, Izquierdo had put two and two together. That his colleague was nuts was a given, but who would have thought he was a pyromaniac? First the stupid stunt with the wastebasket and now this. Izquierdo, his unbuttoned coat pulled tightly about him, stamping his unrubbered feet in the snow, stared at the flaming carcass of the car on which he still owed two more years of payments.

"Against being set on fire?"

"Maybe the wiring." Wack's glasses were steamed over, and he wore an idiotic smile. Maybe he was just freezing to death.

The explosion had emptied Decio and Malloy, bringing professors through the snow to the blazing car. Izquierdo had known at once that it was his, the conviction encouraged by the way Wack loped along beside him. How do you set a car on fire? How would a zombie like Wack know?

"It's a car like yours, Raul," said Lucy Goessen, joining them.

"It is mine."

"Oh my God." She moved closer. "I'll take you home."

Her place? His place? He had to be careful with Lucy. She

had struck up a big friendship with Pauline, Raul's wife, and now Izquierdo got secondhand reports of what went on in Decio all day. He hadn't told Pauline about the fire in his wastebasket, it made him look foolish, but she had got a dramatic account from Lucy.

"You never tell me anything!"

"It's hard to get a word in."

Not wholly false. Pauline had a government job, downtown, dealing with drooling oldsters confused about Medicare and Medicaid. She filled his ear with pathetic tales over the dinner table, real appetizers, but as long as she was talking he didn't have to listen. He could imagine life as a long trek toward the office where Pauline worked, signing up for Medicare, on the dole at last, just when your days were numbered. Lucy's offer brought home to him what the immediate future would be like. They were down to one car, the Hummer Pauline had bought on eBay for a song.

"Hum a few bars."

"Oh ha. You're just jealous."

The reason Raul's car made such a nice fire was that it was an old, very old Corvette, all plastic. The fireman poured some kind of foam on the fire; campus security urged the onlookers to back up. Lucy wanted to know if Raul was going to tell the firemen or the security men or someone that it was his car. He shook his head. A delayed reaction came over him, a wave of melancholy memories of what that car had meant to him, the playboy professor, devil-may-care corruptor of youth. But the fun of being the unintelligible representative of continental theories had diminished because of the rivalry of Wack. At least Izquierdo knew it was a game; Wack preached nonsense with the conviction of Cotton Mather.

They began to walk back to Decio, Izquierdo bracketed by Lucy and Wack, his good and bad angels. Wack looked blue with cold and his teeth chattered. Weren't pyromaniacs supposed to get some kind of perverse thrill from observing their handiwork? Oscar looked immersed, psychologically let us say, in the icy bottom of the Inferno. The burning of the car took on Dantesque overtones, fire and ice both. Lucy held the door for him and he went into the warmth of Decio. The gallant Wack insisted Lucy precede him. She shoved him inside and followed.

"I have coffee made."

"Good," Wack said. Lucy just looked at him.

The coffee Lucy gave them in Styrofoam cups must have been made that morning, but it was too hot to taste anyway. She went on about her coffeemaker. It didn't turn itself off automatically and sometimes she forgot to do it and in the morning, oh the smell, and the cakey gunk at the bottom of the pot.

"I normally don't drink coffee," Wack told her.

"Just abnormally?"

Wack looked at him malevolently. "On special occasions."

"Whenever a colleague's car is set on fire?"

"Do you think someone did it?" Lucy was astounded.

"I doubt that it was spontaneous combustion."

"But who would do such a thing?"

"Who would light a fire in my wastebasket?"

"But you said that was an accident."

"To protect the culprit. How could I know what he would do next?"

Izquierdo was looking at a photograph on Lucy's bookshelf. "Who's that?"

"You wouldn't know him."

"He looks like the cabbie I rode with last week."

"It's my husband."

So the story she had told Pauline was true. Lucy turned the picture toward the wall.

Wack was thawing out, but it wasn't much of an improvement. Still, Izquierdo was glad the maniac had misinterpreted Lucy's invitation to coffee. He realized that he himself was in a state of mild shock, vulnerable to sympathy. He would be mere putty in Lucy's predatory hands. Before Pauline had got to know Lucy, Raul had been able to regale his wife with stories of Lucy's pathetic importuning. All imaginary, of course, as Pauline learned. The cabbie had proved a better audience, vicarious Leporello of Raul's amorous adventures.

"She is profoundly in love with a married man."

"What have I been telling you?"

"Her husband."

"She's married?"

"They're separated. He got mad because graduate school was taking her so long. Of course she doesn't believe in divorce. She intends to win him back."

This had been a revelation. How unobservant he had been. It turned out that Lucy attended the noon Mass in the chapel of Malloy, contiguous to Decio. Izquierdo had followed her there to be sure and lingered outside the door listening to the more or less familiar liturgy. He had half a mind to go in himself. Of course he didn't. He had lost his faith; he had destroyed Pauline's; he had no compunction about sowing doubt in the minds of his students. The funny thing was that he went on praying, addressing God as if nothing had changed between them.

"I better go." Wack had tipped forward and looked at the puddle of melted snow at his feet.

"It looks like you already have."

After Wack was gone, Raul said, "He did it, you know."

"Raul! It's melted snow."

"I mean my car. He lit that fire in my wastebasket, you know that."

"Do I? I thought it was an accident."

"He did it. Now my car."

"But that's . . ."

"I know, unbelievable. He's insanely jealous of me."

"He is."

"Over you, for one thing. You know he worships you."

"Oh stop it. Can't you be serious for five minutes?"

"Starting now?" He looked at his watch.

He accepted her offer of a ride home, just give him half an hour or so. "I won't have to call a cab."

She glared at him.

In his office he sought vainly for consolation in his unbelief. Someone was after him, there was no doubt of that, and he, too, found it difficult to think that it was Oscar Wack. He thought of all the students whose religious beliefs he had mocked. It could be anyone. He shivered. He had half a mind to start a fire in his wastebasket. The five minutes must be up. He found that he was addressing the God of his childhood.

"Don't let them get me."

"THERE'S GOT TO BE A CONNEC-tion," Crenshaw said.

"There could be."

"That car was set on fire deliberately. There have been threats of firebombing all over the campus. Not that I wasn't the last to know."

Phil Knight didn't blame Crenshaw for being uneasy. Nor for not liking it one damned bit to be told that the administration had brought in a private investigator to look into the matter they chose to keep secret from campus security.

"Whose car was it?"

Crenshaw displayed a twisted and charred license plate. "A faculty member. He shouldn't have been parked there."

"Give him a ticket."

But he punched Crenshaw on the arm when he said it.

The head of campus security had come to the apartment to see Phil as soon as someone in the provost's office told Crenshaw that a private detective was looking into the threatening notes that Crenshaw had learned of the hard way. Crenshaw thought there must be a connection between those notes and the torching of the car in front of the library. In the kitchen, Roger, swathed in a huge apron and sporting a Notre Dame baseball cap, was moving around in a cloud of steam making spaghetti. Meatballs simmered on the stove. This was the hour when Phil watched ESPN and argued with the experts on a sports panel, arguments he always won, of course. Crenshaw's visit, however understandable, was not welcome. And Roger had asked the head of security to stay for dinner!

Crenshaw had treated the invitation as an effort to compromise him. "I'll eat at home."

"As you wish."

Crenshaw couldn't figure Roger out. Well, few people could. Roger had already given Phil an eyewitness account of the burning before Crenshaw arrived.

"An exploding car?"

"Cars are designed to explode. Internally, that is."

Phil had been waiting for a call from Father Carmody, certain the old priest would make the connection that Crenshaw had.

Phil asked Crenshaw if he had spoken to the owner of the car.

"He wasn't in his office. I hate to bother him at home."

"How would he have gotten there?"

"Look, you're investigating this, not me. I'll leave it all to you."

That presumed that Crenshaw's presumption of a connection between the burning car and the threatening notes Phil had been asked to look into was correct. Well, maybe there was a connection.

"What's his name?"

"Izquierdo. Raul Izquierdo."

Father Carmody called after Crenshaw had gone, and Phil was able to tell him whose car had burned in front of the library.

"That's not the front," the old priest corrected. "That's the east side."

Phil told him the name of the professor whose car it was.

"I never heard of him."

"He didn't get a threatening note. As far as we know."

"Keep me posted. My dinner just arrived."

The phone went dead.

"*Mangiamo!*" Roger cried, and they tucked into the spaghetti and meatballs. Phil had a glass of Chianti, and Roger, who never drank alcohol, ice water.

"*Al dente,*" Roger murmured, approving the result of his labors.

"Do you know a Professor Izquierdo, Roger?"

"I've heard of him. One of the subversives."

"What do you mean?"

"A professor who subtly mocks in class the beliefs on which Notre Dame is built."

"You're kidding."

"I wish I was."

"Why would someone like that want to teach here?"

"Perhaps he isn't in demand elsewhere. Here he is an oddity. And our pay scale is AAAA."

"An irate student?"

Roger made the connection, thought about it, shrugged.

Roger had shown Phil the origin of the letters that had gone into those threatening messages.

"I know the kids who put out this paper. You do, too. They've been here. Bill Fenster and Mary Alice Frangipani."

"Are you saying they sent those messages?"

"No. Just that their newspaper provided the letters."

Jimmy Stewart, an old friend and detective on the South Bend police, called after supper.

"I hear you had a car set on fire."

"You busy?"

"Me? I'm a cop."

Phil had decided that he would pay a call on Izquierdo that night. Roger had approved. Strike while the car was still hot. The car had been taken downtown so that the cause of the fire could be ascertained, which is how Jimmy had heard of it. Phil had offered to pick up Jimmy, but he suggested they use public transportation, meaning his prowler. This was not the kind of errand Roger went on, curious though he was about Izquierdo. Jimmy was a grass widower and kept crazy hours; maybe that's why his wife had left him. He never talked about her, which was all right with Phil, a lifetime bachelor.

There was a Hummer in the driveway, and when Jimmy pulled in behind it, the lights in the house went out.

"Maybe we should have used your car, Phil."

They considered the situation. The fact that the Bulls were playing that night made the decision easier.

"We can talk to him on campus."

3 ⟶ LARRY   DOUGLAS   TOLD   LAURA
that Crenshaw was crazy for washing his
hands of the investigation into the torched car. Laura seemed
to think that they were reconciled, after the way Henry had
moved in on Kimberley during that ill-advised double date.
Double cross was more like it. He took some consolation in the
attention Laura paid to what he said. Crenshaw had shagged
him from his office when he offered to investigate.

"As a parking violation?"

Crenshaw resented the fact that Philip Knight had been
brought in by the administration to look into those threatening
notes. Who could blame them? There were too many retired
cops like Crenshaw in campus security. For them, the job was
just a lark, supplementing their pension, no real police work
involved. A rash of thefts in the residence hall had led to little
more than a list of missing items, and a warning to look out for
strangers in the dorms. Female joggers threatened on the lake
paths were advised to run in pairs. This was police work?
Larry, since being hired, had been reading up on criminology,
police investigations, the arts and skills of the profession.

"You should have joined the real police," Laura said.

"Maybe I will yet."

Had she lost weight? That was what had made him vulnerable to Kimberley, all that flab on Laura. It hadn't mattered when they were parked and whooping it up. In the night all cows are black. Remembering her affectionate nature, to put it obliquely, he was doubly pleased with her sympathy with his criticism of Crenshaw. He almost told her that, to hell with Crenshaw, he was going to do a little freelance investigating. Finally he did tell her, since he needed her help in filching a master key for Decio.

"I'll come along."

"Better not," he said in a husky voice.

"You don't want to ride your bike, or walk. I'll get a golf cart."

"Good girl."

He bought her supper at the Huddle, and when definitive dark had settled in, they set off in the commandeered cart. They were both wearing uniforms, but who would know because of their overcoats. It was kind of snug on the seat of the cart, bun to bun, so to speak, but through so many layers of clothes it would take an inflamed imagination to find it titillating. Laura drove. The frigid wind had died down; the snow under the lamps along the walkways sparkled. Who would believe it was nearly zero?

When they got to Decio, Larry hopped out, and Laura said she would make circuits of the walkways that stretched from the library to the stadium rather than just sit immobile. As it turned out, he did not need the master key for the front door of Decio, as several professors were emerging when he got there. One held the door for him, not really looking at him. And Larry was inside.

There was a glass case to his left that listed all the occupants of the building and their office numbers. Alphabetically. He found Izquierdo, Raul. Third floor. He took the elevator up and a minute later was standing at Izquierdo's door. He had taken the precaution of telephoning the office from the Huddle. The phone rang and rang, unanswered. Still, the fact that people had been leaving the building when he came in, and the many lights in offices that had been visible when Laura drove up to the entrance, suggested caution. He knocked. Very lightly. Nothing. He was about to knock again and then thought to hell with it. He slipped the key into the lock and turned. He went in without switching on the light, shutting the door first. When he flicked on the light he turned.

"Jesus Christ!"

Henry Grabowski sat behind the desk. His look of terror when the light went on melted into mere surprise, and then he was laughing.

"You scared the crap out of me."

Larry's own heart had stopped when he turned to see the figure behind the desk. A second or two went by before he realized it wasn't the professor, for crying out loud, it was Henry. He was dressed all in black, black turtleneck, a navy peacoat, a black woolen hat pulled down to his eyebrows.

"You look like a second-story man." Larry sank into a chair, almost giddy with relief.

"Actually this is the third floor."

"What are you doing here?"

"I might ask you the same question."

"Why were you sitting in the dark?"

"I turned off the light when you knocked on the door."

"Were you here when I telephoned?"

"So that was you."

Larry's breathing was more regular now. He looked around the office. He gave a kick at the wastebasket. "It was his car that was torched. But you already know that."

Henry said nothing.

"So what did you expect to find?"

"I'm not sure."

There was a loud knocking on the door, and Larry leapt to his feet. Henry sat calmly in his chair. "Better take off the coat so they'll see your uniform."

Good idea. Of course, they were here investigating a car torching. He opened the door. An owl-eyed little man skipped backward. The uniform had its effect; the man's eyes swept over it and his indignation drained away.

"Is Raul here?" He was trying to look around Larry, but Larry blocked the door.

"Who are you, sir?"

"I am Professor Oscar Wack. I was about to complain of the noise. These walls are thin as paper." Again he tried to look inside.

"Of course you know what happened to Professor Izquierdo's car."

A sly expression came over his face. "Well, I have a theory."

"Where is your office?"

"Next door."

"Could we talk there and let my colleague get on with his work?"

"Of course, of course."

Wack scampered to his open door and inside. He looked out to make sure Larry was following.

"Better close the door," he said when Larry was inside. "Please be seated."

"You said you have a theory."

Wack nodded. "You will find this incredible."

"I'm listening." Larry settled into the chair. This was more like it, the investigating officer taking depositions.

"Izquierdo is crazy. I mean that quite seriously. He set fire to his wastebasket some days ago and blamed it on me. I am certain he set fire to his own car."

4   "IT'S NOT ALL THAT EASY TO BURN
a car," Jimmy Stewart said. "It's not just
a matter of dropping a match or lit cigarette."

"*Planes, Trains, and Automobiles.*" Phil laughed, but Jimmy
did not understand the allusion.

"Of course, the technique was spread all over the world in
the coverage of those Arab riots in Paris."

The conversation turned to the once infamous front-page
article in the *New York Review of Books* instructing on how to
make a Molotov cocktail, complete with illustrations. Jimmy's
point seemed to be that while it is not an easy thing to blow up
a car—unless you want simply to drop a lit match into the gas
tank and add self-immolation to the crime—the knowledge is
easily available.

"The one safe guess is that the professor has enemies."

The two men walked to Decio from the Knights' apartment,
a mistake; Phil's face seemed frozen when they reached
the building. Jimmy wore a ski mask and monotonously sang
"Jingle Bells" as they hurried through the arctic weather.
There was an eatery on the main floor, and they stopped for
coffee, if only to have something with which to warm the
hands. They checked out Izquierdo's office number and got

into an elevator. As the doors were closing, a hand reached in, stopping them. A little man with a helmet of gray hair reminiscent of one of the Three Stooges followed the hand, ignoring those whose ascent he had delayed. The elevator stopped on the second floor and an angular woman got out, having to push the little man aside to do so. At three the door opened and, surprisingly, the little man let them exit first.

"Can I be of help?" He was studying Phil in a confused way. He obviously only half-remembered their encounter in the departmental office.

"What's your name?"

The question altered his manner. He backed away. "Wack. Oscar Wack. Who are you?"

Jimmy showed Wack his ID, lest the professor have a stroke. He peeked at it from a safe distance.

"Others were here last night."

"Is that right?"

"A young investigator and his assistant."

"Where could we talk about this?"

"Talk about it? Haven't they reported?"

"We always double-check, Professor."

"Ah." He nodded. "Come."

He hurried down the center of the hallway but at a given point veered to one side, his shoulder brushing the wall, then into the center again.

"Here I am."

Phil sat and sipped his coffee while Jimmy got Professor Wack to talk on about his night visitors.

"I went over there because I was vexed by the noise. I mean, one works late precisely in order to have peace and quiet. You can imagine what Sturm und Drang characterize the daylight hours. Anyway, I went over there to shut Izquierdo up. God only knew what I might be interrupting."

"Oh?"

Wack made a little moist sound, then gave himself permission to go on. "Given the things that have been happening, who knows what's relevant?"

"You mean the car burning?"

"Mainly that, of course. If I were his insurance company, I would look into that matter very carefully."

"The car is being examined downtown."

"Good. I won't bore you with the story of the burning wastebasket."

"We want to hear everything, Professor, just the way you told it to our colleagues last night."

Wack's story was told with malice aforethought—he obviously hated Izquierdo—but the story had a different meaning for Phil, and he was sure for Jimmy Stewart, too. Whatever it was Wack had interrupted in Izquierdo's office, it wasn't a police investigation. Phil had stepped into the hall and called Crenshaw to ask.

"I thought we agreed, that's your problem," Crenshaw said.

"I just wanted to make sure we weren't likely to interfere with each other."

Phil went back inside Wack's office. The professor was certain the investigator he had spoken with was in uniform.

"He showed his identification." He looked significantly at Phil. His memory had kicked in. "Something you failed to do when I encountered you in the departmental office."

Suddenly Wack put a hand over his opened mouth and looked from Jimmy to Phil through his little round spectacles. He lifted his hand and slapped his forehead. "You don't think he was genuine, do you?"

"You say there were two?"

"Only the one came here to my office. At my invitation! This was to permit his partner to continue investigating Izquierdo's office."

"Was he wearing a uniform, too?"

"The second one? I never got a real good look at him."

"But you did see him?"

"I heard them before I beat on the door. There were two, no doubt about it. Besides, I saw the three of them drive away from that very window. After the interview, when he went back to Izquierdo's office, I sat on. Of course, any hope of getting anything done was destroyed. I turned off the lights. This room is quite well lit from outside, you know. Not light to read by, but it isn't dark. Very restful, actually. I was drawn to the window, the snow under the lamplight, the moon above . . ." He stopped himself. "Dear God, I sound like Immanuel Kant. Anyway, I was at the window when the cart came by to pick them up. Oh, there were two of them, all right."

"And the driver."

"She makes three, yes."

"She?"

Wack seemed to have surprised himself. "How did I know that? Yet I'm sure."

"Intuition," Phil said, and Wack looked sharply at him.

"Is Professor Izquierdo in now?" Jimmy asked.

Wack cocked his head, listening. "I don't hear anything."

"Could you telephone him?"

He pulled the phone toward him and punched out numbers without delay. Phil listened for ringing in the next office but heard nothing. Then Wack straightened and hung up the phone.

"He's there."

5

HE HAD HEARD THE RUMBLE OF voices next door but thought nothing of it. Lucy Goessen called to say that Wack was entertaining two middle-aged gentlemen. She had had a spy hole drilled in her door, at her own expense.

"He's insatiable. But maybe they're from the IRS."

"You know, they could be."

Or from my insurance company, Izquierdo did not say. Pauline had brought him to campus in the Hummer that morning, truly a vehicle for this season. Pauline looked like a woman on an old Soviet poster behind the wheel of the massive vehicle. Woman liberated to do manual labor. They had spent hours the night before discussing the burning of his Corvette, the topic going to bed with them and keeping Raul awake after Pauline had slipped into sated slumber.

Suspecting Wack was to flatter the idiot. Oh, no doubt he had lit the wastebasket, but that on any scale of nuttiness was a three or four. Setting a Corvette aflame was something entirely else. Also, there was the undeniable fact that Wack had been in Decio when the explosion occurred and gone to the scene with Raul and Lucy.

The phone rang, and when he answered it went dead.

Izquierdo eased the instrument back into its cradle and stared at it. Who could blame him for being jumpy? Maybe Wack hadn't lit his wastebasket; maybe it was someone else, the someone who had torched his Corvette. There was a knock on his door.

"Come in!"

The knob rattled but that was all. He had locked his door. He never locked his door. He went around his desk and opened to two large men, the first of whom flashed his wallet and then returned it to his pocket.

"I didn't see it."

"Detective James Stewart." He let Raul study the ID.

"South Bend police."

"We are investigating your car."

These two must have been in the car that pulled into the driveway last night. Pauline had doused the lights.

"What's the point of that?" he had asked her.

She snuggled against him. At the moment, he felt as amorous as an anchorite.

Now he said, "What do you do with a burnt-out car?"

"You had insurance, of course."

"Of course." Pauline had checked that last night. But he would never find another Corvette of that vintage for any price he could afford.

"Your neighbor says someone visited this office last night."

"Wack? He's nuts, you know. Completely bonkers."

"He's quite a fan of yours, too."

"What did he say?"

"You wouldn't want us to tell him what you tell us."

Phil said, "Did you notice anything when you arrived today? Anything missing?"

Izquierdo pushed back from his desk and studied it from afar. He reached forward and opened the drawer. "Someone was in this drawer, that's for sure."

"Something missing?"

"It's the mess he made of it."

"He?"

"Whoever."

"Your colleague says there was a girl as well as the two men."

Izquierdo made a face. Phil was certain that if Wack said that every whole is greater than its part, Izquierdo would deny it. He was looking around his office now. Then he remembered something Lucy had said and had an inspiration.

"My pogo stick!"

"Your what?"

"What I exercise with. I can do it right here. But it's gone."

That seemed to be the only thing missing. Jimmy wanted a full description of it, even a crude drawing. Phil didn't need that. There had been such a pogo stick propped in a corner of Wack's office.

"Those pretty popular here?"

"What do you mean?"

"Do your colleagues get their exercise this way?"

"Hey, this is my little secret. Can you imagine what they'd say if they saw me jumping up and down on that thing? But why would anyone take that?"

When they left Izquierdo's office, the door of Wack's office was cracked slightly. Phil gestured him out, and on the second invitation Wack emerged.

"I just want to confirm something, Professor." Phil took Izquierdo to the door of Wack's office and pointed to the corner. "Is that the sort of thing you're missing?"

With a cry, Izquierdo sprang into the office. When he came out he was flourishing a pogo stick.

"You thief!"

"What is that? I never saw it before!"

"So you steal unconsciously?"

Wack took hold of Jimmy Stewart's sleeve. "He must have left it there last night. The investigator."

"Want to show us how that works, Professor?" Phil asked.

This flustered Izquierdo. A door across the hall opened and a lovely young woman appeared. "What on earth is going on?" She smiled when she said it.

Introductions all around. But it was the pogo stick that fascinated her.

"I haven't used one of those in years. Can I try it?"

"Watch the ceiling."

When Phil and Jimmy left, Professor Goessen was hopping up and down, with others who had emerged from their offices applauding the performance.

In the elevator, Jimmy asked, "Is everybody nuts?"

"Compared to what?"

AT HIS SON BILL'S INSISTENCE, Fred Fenster had given Roger Knight a call and invited him to lunch at the Morris Inn. The description his son had given him did not prepare him for the apparition that needed both doors opened in order to come into the lobby. A fur cap was pulled down over his ears; he seemed to have several layers of clothing beneath the massive blue parka with NOTRE DAME emblazoned in yellow across the back. His trousers were stuffed into unbuckled galoshes, which made his passage that of a tinkling Santa. His glasses fogged up immediately, and he removed them and looked myopically around. Fred went to his guest and introduced himself.

"Fred? But isn't it Manfred?"

"I'm afraid it is. My mother had no sense of humor. Or maybe she did."

"Of course you wouldn't remember Mighty Manfred the Wonder Dog."

"Tom Terrific! Of course I do."

"So we must have similar misspent youths."

Fred helped remove several layers of clothing of his guest's and pass them over the Dutch door to the attendant. Roger's entry into the dining room commanded everyone's attention as he maneuvered carefully between the tables, attended by the hostess, several waitresses, and the amused gaze of the assembly. Roger's smile seemed meant indifferently for them all. At table Fred mentioned that his mother had mistaken Manfred for Buonconte in the *Purgatorio* when she named him.

"Saved by a single tear."

"It is my hope."

"That is the CSC motto, you know. *Spes Unica.* An anchor and cross. I think the motto has Marian overtones as well. That's clear enough in the university's motto. *Vita, Dulcedo, Spes.*"

"You'd be surprised how little I know about my university." He had known what Roger said, but it seemed humble to pretend he didn't.

"No I wouldn't. Lack of curiosity about the past of the place seems widespread. Maybe we look ahead too exclusively. What do you do, Fred?"

This was always the difficult question. He could say what he was doing at the time, as if it were a profession or a job, but he found he did not want to mislead Roger Knight. He was beginning to understand Bill's devotion to this improbable personage.

"I'm afraid I am one of the idle rich."

"Retired?"

"Well, you see, I never had to work, to earn my living. Long ago, the guilt that induces drove me into politics. I mean as a supporter. But that's long over."

"And now?"

"I am guided by my putative namesake, trying to save my soul."

Neither of them wanted a drink. When Fred ordered the Sorin Salad, Roger put down his menu. "Me, too."

"I wanted to tell you what a good influence you have been on my son."

"He is a good lad. And the newspaper he and his friends are putting out is a good thing."

Fred smiled. "The heresy of good works."

"Dom Chautard."

"You know him?"

Roger shrugged. In the lobby there were stacks of the current issue of the *Observer*, but none of the paper Bill and his friends put out. Circulation was a problem, since they relied on volunteers to distribute copies to various places around campus. At first, piles of the paper had mysteriously disappeared. In default of his son's paper, Fred had paged through the *Observer*.

"That's an amazing story about the professor whose car was firebombed."

"Izquierdo? I haven't seen it."

"I don't know when I last looked at a campus publication, but I was astounded at how matter-of-fact they were about the man's atheism. An atheist teaching at Notre Dame? He seems to be something of a missionary as well."

"Professors aren't above posturing, you know."

In reading the piece, Fred had been truly shocked. It seemed preposterous that parents would send a son or daughter to Notre Dame in order to have someone seek to undermine their faith. He could imagine what Bastable would think of this piece on Izquierdo. Of course it could be argued that one will meet with assaults on his faith throughout life and that there was little point in putting it off. An untested faith is impossible. It was quite another thing to subsidize the attack on one's beliefs.

But he had not asked Roger Knight to lunch in order to discuss campus politics. Everything Fred had heard of the portly Huneker Professor had made him wonder if he might not, as his father had, give some financial support to Notre Dame. Quirk's campaign was having its effect. He dreaded the thought of calling on the Notre Dame Foundation, where professionals in the art of separating people from their money would have to be dealt with. What he wondered was whether he could not more or less directly underwrite the wonderful work that Roger was doing.

"Fred, I am paid far more than I am worth as it is. I sit in an endowed chair. I have a discretionary fund. There is nothing I need."

It occurred to Fred that Roger might be drawing the wrong inference from the clothes he was wearing: the same baggy sweater and corduroys with their wales all but gone. "My family has always given generously to Notre Dame. I mean my father. I'm afraid I've let that sort of thing go."

Small amounts of money, given to quite specific purposes, seemed more effective. Large sums, very large sums, seemed to satisfy some need of the giver rather than the recipient. Fred was struck by the way new buildings at Notre Dame bore the names of their donors. The pharaoh principle, more or less.

Thank God his father had not been in the grip of that kind of vanity.

"In any case, I appreciate the thought. Money isn't what Notre Dame needs most just now."

"And what is?"

Roger was wedged into his chair; his napkin was tucked into his collar and lay like a pennant on his massive chest. He looked at Fred. "Let me tell you a story."

It was Roger's story, orphaned early, raised by his older brother, dubbed a prodigy, and finished with college and graduate school when most boys were finishing high school.

"Swift as my passage through college and university was, delighted as I was to be able to pursue a dozen interests at once, from the beginning I felt something was missing. You have to take a course in Dante from a professor, and a good professor, too, who shares none of Dante's religious beliefs, to know what I mean. A man can teach Shakespeare well and yet not inhabit in any way the world of the poet's real beliefs. So, too, with Chaucer, Milton, Browning. It is of course far worse in philosophy. Schopenhauer, Nietzsche, certifiably mad, read as guides to what? The tail end of modernity makes clear that it was rotting from the head down."

"So what happened?"

A radiant smile. "I read Chesterton. I read Belloc. I read Claudel. I read Maritain. Then I knew what was missing. I became a Catholic."

"And came to Notre Dame."

"Eventually. It was a bit of a shock to find almost the same assumptions and outlook that I was fleeing here. It would be too much to say that people were ashamed of the faith; the fact is, many of my colleagues haven't the least inkling of the tradition in which the university allegedly stands. They have been trained as I was and simply accepted it as the way things are. It is tragic. A whole patrimony is ignored or, when taken into account, treated in the way I found so dissatisfying."

"And you are offering an alternative."

"In a small way." He patted his middle. "Insofar as I can do anything in a small way."

Roger tried discreetly to learn just what it was Fred did with his life, how he spent his days. He dodged the questions, again characterized himself as one of the idle rich. Much as Roger impressed him, stirring as what he had said was, Fred was not prepared to speak of his religious enthusiasms.

In the lobby, dressing to face the elements, Roger wrapped an *Observer* into his clothing and then, attended once more, went outside to where his golf cart awaited him. Fred waved him off and went up to his room. A message. He checked it out and groaned. Bastable.

HUGH BASTABLE WAS IN A RAGE. He paced from his study through the dining room and into the living room of the town house over-looking the St. Joseph River to which he and his wife, Florence, had moved with the idiotic notion that they would end their lives pleasantly near the institutions that, with the passage of years, seemed to have been the scene of the best years of their lives. They had come fleeing what seemed the debacle of their family. Young Hugh—he was thirty-seven now—had come out of the closet, as he put it ("The water closet!") and was now tossed about by the zeitgeist. Myrtle, their daughter, had married, three times so far, and had one neglected child for each of her discarded spouses. Florence subsided into silent resignation, but Hugh disowned them both, sold out, and moved to South Bend with Florence.

What had he expected to find? Florence had returned from her one and only visit to St. Mary's in wordless shock. And Notre Dame! What in the name of God had happened to Hugh's alma mater? During his active years, he had paid little attention to what was happening to the Church in the wake of Vatican II. The truth was that he hadn't been much of a Catholic, too busy, too successful, too whatever. There were disquieting moments when he wondered how responsible he was for the directions his children's lives had taken. But self-knowledge was not prominent among his gifts. He needed an external enemy, and by God he had found it. Day after day, he fed his discontents, and reading the benighted *Observer* was a reliable negative stimulus. Today's issue had provided a sympathetic portrait of the professor whose car had burned near the library. Izquierdo! Was the poor fellow the victim of some bigoted student, the reporter asked? That the man was an atheist and was noted for heaping abuse on the faith in his classroom was conveyed without the least hint that there was something odd about this. Surely this was the last straw.

The difficulty was that the past three years had provided one last straw after another, and nothing seemed outrageous enough for the university to finally shape up. Bastable had scanned the story and then faxed it to a dozen kindred spirits around the country. He sent out a spam e-mail to his classmates. Florence had diligently put together an almost complete list, with e-mail addresses, that facilitated the sending of such missives. He awaited a call from Fred Fenster. But what was to be done? Bad publicity? What worse publicity could be imagined than that chuckleheaded tribute to the campus atheist? Hugh had long since canceled his pledge of support to the university. But how could you punish an institution that was the beneficiary of endless floods of generosity from the most diverse sources? To make things worse, football, after having been in the pits for years, had suddenly been turned around, and the Fighting Irish were once more at the top of the heap. Which meant more money. Was even God

117

against him? Without three hours a weekday of Rush Limbaugh he doubted that he could go on.

No one in the administration would take his calls any longer. His letters to the *Observer* were countered by half a dozen disdainful and mocking replies, most from the faculty. One insolent young woman had suggested that Hugh Bastable was an all too fair example of the alumni the university had once turned out.

To his surprise, Fred Fenster called in person. He came in out of the cold wearing a bum's overcoat and a shapeless beret. When Florence took his wraps, there he was in a flannel shirt, a baggy sweater, and old corduroys. The man could buy and sell half his classmates, singly or collectively, and he looked as if he needed a handout.

"You got my message?"

"My, it is cold out there."

Florence offered hot chocolate, and Fred lit up like a kid. Hugh took him off to his study, what he liked to think of as his command center. On the radio a taped Rush raved on.

"Who's that?"

"You're kidding." Hugh turned it off. "Well, what are we going to do?"

"I don't know about you, but I'm going to Florida."

"We sold our place."

"Oh, I rent."

"Where?"

"Siesta Key."

"What do you do, just sit in the sun while Rome burns?"

"I walk a lot. And read."

118

Bastable shook his head. "Well, I can't blame you for wanting to get away from here."

"I had a nice visit, actually. I had lunch today with Roger Knight."

"I should look him up. What's he like?"

"My son is taking another class from him. I can see why."

"He's not an atheist?"

Florence came in with a cup of hot chocolate for Fred. She put Hugh's Bloody Mary on the desk.

"I also went down to the Catholic Worker House."

"Is that still going on?"

"Oh yes."

"Bunch of Commies."

Fred laughed. "What will you say if Dorothy Day is canonized?"

Hugh sought consolation in his drink. St. Dorothy Day? But he could believe it. He could believe anything now.

"Sometimes I think I've lived too long already."

"You're that ready to go?"

"What do you mean?"

"I'm going to stop at Gethsemani on my way south."

The river was all but frozen over now, and swirls of snow were blowing across the surface. The trees outside the window seemed black hands groping in the wind. It took an act of faith to think they would ever leaf again.

"You ought to join. You live like a monk."

"You could come along."

"Ha!"

"What do you know about Holy Cross Village?"

This was a retirement community run by the Brothers of Holy Cross, houses, apartments, terminal medical care.

"It's right up there on top of the cliff." Bastable pointed.

"I checked it out. Maybe that will be my monastery."

Bastable was excited. "You mean settle here permanently? Great. Why, together we could—"

Fred took one hand away from his mug and held it up, shaking his head. "You know the most effective thing you could do?"

"What?"

"Say a novena."

Bastable just stared at his classmate, but for all he could tell Fred was serious. Say a novena? Did he really think . . .

Bastable stopped the thought. Of course he believed in the efficacy of prayer. The trouble was you couldn't count on it. You had to do things. But suddenly he felt helpless. Do what? Get into a rage daily and harangue Florence about what was wrong with the world? He had a fleeting image of what he had become, but he dismissed it.

"Okay. I'll say a novena. What will you do?"

"I told you. I'm going to make a retreat with the Trappists."

Bastable gave up. "You can say a few prayers to Dorothy Day."

"Good idea."

8

⟶

"WHAT ARE YOU TALKING ABOUT?" Crenshaw demanded, when Jimmy Stewart asked if campus security had found anything interesting when they checked out Izquierdo's office.

"The inspection of the car turned up nothing. The professor himself was of no help. But you found nothing?"

"That is all in Phil Knight's hands."

Jimmy thought about it, then let it go. If Crenshaw wasn't interested, then he and Phil could find out who Oscar Wack had found examining Izquierdo's office. That it wasn't imaginary seemed proved by the presence of the pogo stick in the wrong office. Why had he thought of that young guy in the space-cadet helmet when Wack had described the supposed investigation going on in Izquierdo's office?

More snow was falling. What a winter this was. Phil had asked him out to watch a game, but the weather made that less attractive. Of course he would go. The thought of watching the game alone suddenly brought home to him what a lonely life he led. Not that he was given to self-pity. It hadn't been a shot in the arm to his self-esteem when Hazel told him she was going. He found himself unable to think of any good reason for her to stay. Her complaint was that he was too wrapped up in his work, but of course it was because they had no kids that her life was boring. He had suggested adoption, but she just made a face and wouldn't talk about it.

When he put down the phone after talking to Crenshaw, he wondered if that was his destiny. Get his pension and then apply for a job at Notre Dame security. Any real problems were foisted off on South Bend anyway, or lately on Phil Knight. He looked around his office and thought of Oscar Wack. Is that the way he looked to other people, a quirky bachelor? Geez. He got up, put on a storm coat, and headed for the elevator. He would waste the time before going to Phil's in a bar on Grape Road.

Downstairs he ran into Piazza, stamping snow from his shoes and looking around as if trying to keep time to the Muzak. He was in uniform; he preferred being in uniform, saying it saved on clothes. Piazza was always being kidded about using the prowler he took home as the family car. But he couldn't have got half his family in the thing, there being seven little Piazzas. They kept him on patrol duty because it was safer and because that was what his wife wanted. Sitting at a desk would have kept him out of harm's way, but Piazza would have none of it.

"Look, I was a clerk in the army. I had my fill of that."

He looked as if he had had his fill of lots of things, a real roly-poly. But then his wife was a terrific cook.

"Come watch the game tonight, Phil."

"I wish I could, Lou." And he did. It was hectic at the Piazzas', with all those kids, but the place was what a home should be.

122

"Big date?"

"I'll never tell."

"Ho ho."

Outside and through the snow to his car. Had Lou been kidding? Did others think he led an interesting life, now that Hazel had gone to California? There were times when he really missed her, even the nagging. He should give her a call. Of course she was still single. They had been married at St. Hedwig's, a big Polish wedding with a huge supper and dancing until all hours. How could you ever feel unmarried after a shindig like that? And of course they were Catholics. At first he had thought that Hazel would miss him the way he missed her and they would get together again. That was still possible, but the more years you added to a separation the more likely it was it would go on. Separation. That was all her pastor, old Senski, would permit her, and he had been against that. It had been something to watch the expression on the priest's face while Hazel tried to explain how awful her life was.

"You think I never get bored? What if I decided to just toss in my cards and go?"

"Well, at least you get to Florida in the winter."

"Take her to Florida," Senski had advised Jimmy.

"I don't want to go to Florida. I want a life of my own."

"Why no kids?"

"It's not my fault." She broke down then, crying like a kid. It broke Jimmy's heart to see a grown woman do that. From that point on, Senski's sympathy was with Jimmy, but that meant he was going to let Hazel call it a separation and head for her sister's in Santa Monica.

It took him fifteen minutes to scrape the ice off the windows. That was probably the most exercise he'd had all week. Maybe he would get a pogo stick and bounce around the house.

He had a couple of lonely beers before heading for the Knights', where Roger had made enough goulash for John Madden. Phil had laid in a supply of Guinness for the game, and during the hyped-up intro, with the set muted, Jimmy asked Phil if he remembered that kid on campus security that had been a help when they were on the Kittock murder. But it was Roger who remembered.

"Larry. Larry Douglas."

9

Roger's class on F. Marion Crawford, and
Roger had countered with the suggestion that Quirk give a guest
lecture.

"I never taught a day in my life."

"It's just a matter of discussing with other people some
topic you know better than they do."

"I'm not making any headway with the provost."

Father Carmody felt that he was getting a secondhand run-
around himself insofar as Quirk had been turned over to him.
Now, as a result of the dilly-dallying, they had lost the chance to
put the proposal to Fred Fenster. Of course Mendax in develop-
ment had checked out Fenster and came back whistling and
rolling his eyes. Neither Quirk nor Father Carmody had needed
such confirmation. Father Carmody had of course remembered
Fenster. He had been very active in campus politics on the liberal side and kept it up after graduation. He could afford it.
Carmody knew Manfred's father, a gentleman of the old school,
as only his friends would have put it. All the confidence of the
self-made man. But he had been generous to Notre Dame so
long as you listened first to his extended exposition of what was
wrong with civilization. Unlike others, he had never included

Notre Dame in his negative estimate of the modern world. Father Carmody could still remember old Fenster's eye damp with sentiment when he returned for home football games and was included in the select group entertained in the presidential aerie on the fourteenth floor of the library.

"Roger," Father Carmody said, bringing the Knights up to speed, "the problem is that Quirk wants to be generous with someone else's money. I suggested that he pledge something himself, to get the ball rolling. He thinks he's being stalled."

"Maybe he can't afford it."

"Ha. He's no Fenster, but he's got plenty."

"I'm surprised he hasn't just gone ahead and bought the villa in Sorrento."

"He tried to."

"He did?"

Carmody nodded. "Given the use to which it had been put in recent years, they want to turn it over to a religious order. So he asked, how about the greatest Catholic university in the world? They liked that."

"But he could have bought it himself?"

"I know what you're thinking, Roger. Why not just fork over the purchase money to Notre Dame and leave Fenster out of it? Sometimes I thinks he wants the project to fail."

"Has he been generous to the university?"

"Not lately."

Notre Dame alumni all looked alike at first, and then they fell into types and subspecies and ultimately into fierce singularity, no two really alike. Roger had classified Quirk among the nostalgics, and there was something to be said for that. His voice could get husky when he spoke of his time on campus. But he had a lot in common with what Roger thought of as alumni-penitents, men and women who bewailed the fact that they had wasted their undergraduate years. Some of these, like Quirk apparently, resolved to do belatedly what they had not done in their youth. But F. Marion Crawford, fascinating as Roger himself found the author, was an odd handle to take hold of initially. Then Roger began to suspect that Quirk's knowledge of the author was fairly superficial. He hadn't actually read much by Crawford. He had found *Ave Roma Immortalis* tough going, and of the novels he had read he preferred *The Ralstons*!

"Fred only reads saints and mystics," Quirk had answered when Roger asked him what headway he was making with Fenster. That had made Roger curious and he had gladly accepted Fred Fenster's invitation to lunch. And now the mysterious alumnus was gone.

"That's the way it always is," Bill said. "He shows up without warning, and then one day he calls to say so long."

"How often does he come?"

"A couple of times a year. His life is pretty much his own, you know."

Mary Alice said, "I think he really liked *Via Media*. Except for the symposium on aborutaries."

The question was, can force be used to protect innocent life, and one or two participants had been all for marching on the clinics and forcibly shutting them down. Even burning them down. The consensus had been against that, thank God. But to the zealous young it seemed a counsel of accommodation to recommend the slow path of legislative reform. The trouble was that the flood of abortions had not been begun by the passage of any law. Roger could share the anguish, who could not?

"What did your father say?"

"He said that in his experience any attempt to change others usually led to something worse."

"He suggested prayer and penance," Mary Alice said. "No one could stop us from doing that."

Quirk, on the other hand, applauded the more fiery contributions to the symposium. Not that he wanted to defend the position.

"It's just a gut feeling," he told Roger.

"Civil disobedience. Like Dorothy Day?"

That was sly, of course. Roger had gotten some sense of where Quirk stood on the Catholic Worker movement when Quirk mentioned that Fred Fenster had paid the local group a visit.

When eventually Quirk did show up for Roger's class on Crawford, he sat in a corner and said nothing, following the discussion but not taking part. He stayed around afterward, and it seemed that he had come to the class largely to talk with Roger.

"Did you know there's an atheist on the faculty?"

"You've been reading the paper."

"I can't believe it. It's not just what he might or might not believe himself. He preaches it in class."

Roger disliked feeling this kind of indignation. Quirk was puffed up with rectitude, a defender of the faith. Well, no need to doubt his sincerity. But Roger could understand why Fred Fenster had withdrawn into quietism.

10   OSCAR WACK GNASHED HIS TEETH in indignation. The story in the campus paper featuring Izquierdo should have been the kiss of death. Instead he was being hailed as a hero of academic freedom. The intrepid atheist. And he had stolen Wack's thunder! That hurt. That and the realization that he himself would not have had the guts to bare his soul to a student reporter. Now, of course, the burning of Izquierdo's car was seen as an attack on a man who had the courage of his convictions.

How accommodating could the university be? Did they imagine that a Holocaust denier would be feted at Brandeis? You could understand all the waffling about *The Vagina Monologues* and other activities of campus gay groups. To oppose those would invite being pilloried by the national media. That would have been a real clash of creeds. And Notre Dame blinked. But for God's sake, how could you sit still for a professor who used his classroom to argue atheism and mock Catholicism? If that wasn't rock bottom, Wack didn't understand the faith of his fathers. Yet Izquierdo was a hero.

Huddled at the desk in his office, muttering to himself, Wack asked half aloud when that blimp of a Roger Knight and his obsequious minions would take on Izquierdo. After

Izquierdo, Roger Knight was Wack's greatest complaint. So he had earned a Princeton doctorate when he was still using a teething ring; he had never held a teaching position, and his reputation reposed on a single monograph, the incredibly successful little book on Baron Corvo. That was the unkindest cut of all. Wack had long nursed a secret passion for the writings of Corvo. Not the sort of thing you could admit in the department, of course. Wack had every biography ever written on the tragic author, beginning with Symonds's *Quest for Corvo*. The man had fascinated many, but they were all outside the walls of academe. No matter. When his disbelief wobbled, Wack could curl up with *Hadrian VII* and feed his disdain for the church that regarded what was delicately called his sexual orientation as sinful. It had been the thought of subjecting himself to the humiliation of the confessional that had opened Wack's mind to the flaws in any proof for the existence of God and liberated him from the faith.

Of course his personal life was concealed behind the armor of indirection. Never anything overt! Stolen holidays, trying to live out his convictions in the Caribbean sunlight but always hampered by the repressive beliefs of his youth, that was as much as he dared. On campus Wack was as chaste as a Trappist and kept all crusaders at arm's length. Izquierdo, of course, was flamboyantly heterosexual, and Wack was not misled by the man's lip service to sexual liberation in the fullest sense. Izquierdo had guessed his secret, he was sure of it, though the taunting was always ambiguous enough. Item, his teasing of Wack about Lucy Goessen.

"Of course I know the impediment," Izquierdo had said,

his eyebrows dancing. Wack was furious. Was this a reference to his lisp?

"She's married."

"I didn't know that."

"Isn't that what holds you back?"

Oh, the homophobic beast. But it had drawn him closer to Lucy. How buoyant she had been when she displayed her agility on the pogo stick that had somehow ended up in Wack's office. That memory led on to the memory of that late-night investigation of Izquierdo's office. He sat back, and some of his anguish left him.

Were they on to Izquierdo, after all? Were they looking for something that would provide an oblique way of bringing the man down? Of course. Why take him on frontally and turn him into a martyr of academic freedom? Everyone is vulnerable in a dozen ways. Wack shivered at the thought of anyone rummaging through his office. It was sneaky, of course, entering an office when the building was empty for the night, or so they thought. What if someone else had come upon them, someone other than Oscar Wack? The enemy of my enemy is my friend. What did Lucy make of all this?

He went downstairs for a sandwich and saw Lucy huddled with a man at a table in the lobby. Oscar studied them as he moved slowly through the line. The man wasn't faculty, and he was too old to be a student. The conversation seemed anything but casual. Oscar made a beeline for the table when he had his sandwich and milk.

"Lucy!"

She looked up at him, startled. Oscar pulled out a chair,

smiling at her companion, and got a cold look in return. "I'm Oscar Wack. Lucy's colleague."

"This is Alan," Lucy said.

The man nodded and pushed away from the table. "I've got to get back to work." And he was gone.

Oscar was dying with curiosity but decided on indirection. "Have you seen Giordano Bruno today?" he asked Lucy.

"I know I should understand that."

"His statue is in the Campo dei Fiori. Burned at the stake for heresy."

"You mean Raul?"

Good Lord. But she did have a mind of sorts. Several solid articles on Kate Chopin.

"I didn't know he had a daughter," Izquierdo had said.

"Oh you."

"You think he's kidding?" Wack had intervened.

But there was no point in trying to score on Izquierdo, not when there were witnesses.

"I wish the weather would break," Oscar said.

"I've gotten used to it."

"If it gets too cold you can always touch a match to your car."

She leaned toward him. Honey-colored hair, green eyes. Had he ever seen green eyes before? "Do you think there is a connection?"

It had been a mistake to make Izquierdo the topic of conversation, but he had no gift for small talk. "Who's Alan?"

She seemed to be considering several answers. "A friend."

"Is it true that you're married?"

132

She sat back and stared at him with wide eyes. "Who told you?"

"Told me? It's not a sin."

Tears were leaking from her green eyes. And suddenly she was telling him all about herself; his gaucherie had proved the open sesame. Her husband initially backed her graduate studies, then came to resent them, finally saw that he would look like an appendage, and left.

"What does he do?"

"Do?"

"I mean workwise."

She lowered her voice. "He has a chauffeur's license." Her chin lifted. "He drives a cab."

"Tell me about it."

It was another world, but talking about it removed a barrier between them. He could imagine their becoming friends, even good friends. Brother and sister. Maybe he could be instrumental in bringing her and Alan together. The idea had the attraction of seeming aimed against Izquierdo. But all that would have to wait. She was off to class then, and Wack went up to his office.

His phone rang, and Hector, the departmental secretary, asked if he had seen Izquierdo.

"Did you try telephoning his office?" he said huffily.

"No answer. His wife is looking for him."

Hector hung up before Wack could slam the phone down. What insolence. After a minute, he stood and put his ear to the wall between his office and Izquierdo's. He could hear

133

nothing, but then he wasn't answering his phone. If he was in there.

Wack opened his door and looked out at an empty corridor. He slipped next door and wrapped his hand around the knob of Izquierdo's door. He turned it and the door began to open. That was a surprise. One didn't go away and leave the door of one's office unlocked. Not that investigators couldn't invade if they wanted to. He pushed the door open, flicking the light on as he did.

Izquierdo sat behind his desk, staring at Wack. Or staring at anything that looked at him. He didn't move. He said nothing. Wack had moved one foot back, preparing to flee.

"Your wife's looking for you."

The expression did not change. A horrible thought occurred. Wack moved closer to the desk. The eyes never blinked. He reached out tentatively, prepared to scoot if Izquierdo was putting on an act. Then his fingers came in contact with Izquierdo's forehead. It was ice cold.

With a shriek, Wack bounded into the corridor and began to spread the alarm.

PART THREE

1   WHEN THE SOUTH BEND PARA-
medics arrived on the scene, the Notre
Dame fire department was already there, and campus security was trying to cordon off the area on the third floor of Decio
where the dead body of Raul Izquierdo had been found, seated behind his desk, staring blankly into eternity. Professors
objected to this invasion of their space, of course, and diplomatic skills were called into play. Those having failed, everyone was chased from the floor and a burly sergeant was put on
sentry duty.

Flashes of light from the open door of Izquierdo's office
indicated that photographs were being taken. When Phil
Knight arrived, the sergeant waved him through to a murmur
of disapproval from onlookers. Phil found Jimmy Stewart in
the office, watching the technical recording of the crime
scene.

"How'd he go?" Phil asked.

"He looks as if he was scared to death."

"Why don't they shut his eyes?"

"Later."

Photographs having been taken, the desk and most of the
office dusted for prints, the coroner pronounced Izquierdo

officially dead. When he headed for the door, Jimmy stopped him.

"Well?"

"I'd say strangled."

"With what?"

"There's nothing here."

When Crenshaw arrived he had trouble getting past the sergeant and was in a mood when he confronted Jimmy. "No one called me," he complained. "The sight of all that equipment was my first realization anything had happened." They turned as a gurney with the zipped-up body bag rolled past. Crenshaw stepped back.

"Is that a body?"

"Professor Izquierdo."

"Good God." He thought. "I cede jurisdiction to you."

Jimmy let it go. There were lots of invisible curtains between town and gown, but dead bodies were not a university affair. Crenshaw looked around, then headed for a water fountain. It was almost a relief when he dipped to drink. He might have intended to symbolically wash his hands of the whole business. He came back.

"Izquierdo is the guy whose car was burned."

Jimmy nodded.

"You going to represent the university?" Crenshaw asked Phil.

"I guess."

"You guess?"

"I haven't talked to Father Carmody yet."

Crenshaw unclipped a cell phone and handed it to Phil.

Well, why not? Phil punched out the number of Holy Cross House and asked for Father Carmody.

"He's taking his nap."

"Lucky him. This is important."

A pause. He was asked to wait. While he did, Phil took Crenshaw's cell phone down the hall a bit. The sergeant was still keeping the faculty at bay. There had been a lull when they realized what was on the gurney that rolled by them, but now the grumbling resumed. Jimmy went to tell the sergeant it was okay now. Father Carmody came on, his voice cranky.

"Phil Knight. We have a body in Decio."

"Decio is full of bodies."

"This one is dead."

Silence. "Who?"

"Raul Izquierdo."

"The atheist?" A beat. "Well, he isn't any longer. Tell me about it."

"Things are still fluid. Crenshaw asked if I represented the university in this."

"Of course you do. It's a continuation of those damned notes, isn't it?"

No point in telling Carmody that Izquierdo hadn't received a note. At least he had never said so.

"I'll come by later with what we learn."

When Phil got back to Jimmy and Crenshaw, Jimmy had just asked the head of security if Larry Douglas was around.

"Douglas? What for?"

"Where can I reach him?"

Crenshaw took the cell phone, called his office, and said,

"Laura, where is Larry Douglas?" He listened, frowning. He folded up the phone.

"He called in sick."

"Is he a local boy?"

"You got a dead man here and you wonder about some kid who dishes out parking tickets?" But Crenshaw seemed to remember how Douglas had outshone him in the Kittock killing. "I'll let him know you want to see him."

"No need to do that. I was just curious."

"Sure you were."

Crenshaw wheeled and went down the corridor at a great rate. There are cops and cops, and Crenshaw was the other kind. Jimmy put the sergeant on sentry at Izquierdo's door and was about to go in when he hesitated, then went and knocked on the door of the adjacent office. He had to knock three times before there was the sound of a lock turning, the door opened slightly, and a terrified face looked out. "Professor Wack?"

"Yes, yes. What is it?"

"You found him, right?"

"Is he . . ."

"Yes. The body's been taken away."

The look of terror increased, then subsided as Wack slumped to the floor.

They pushed in, picked him up, and got him into his desk chair. He was white as a sheet and still out. Jimmy picked up a container half full of cool coffee and dashed it into Wack's face. He came spluttering to consciousness. He looked wildly at Jimmy and then began to dab at his shirt with a handkerchief.

"Tell us about it," Jimmy said.

The narrative gift is unequally distributed, and even those who normally have it can lose it in a pressure situation. Wack babbled more or less incoherently. Jimmy sat, and Phil did, too.

"Look," Jimmy said. "Did you ever make a general confession?"

"What?"

"The confessor runs down the list and you say yes and no. I'm going to do that, okay?"

Wack nodded.

"You discovered the body?"

"Yes."

"You went next door, walked in, and there he was behind the desk?"

Wack nodded, then closed his eyes. He opened them right away.

"Why did you go over there?"

He couldn't answer yes or no to that, but now he was less agitated. "The departmental secretary said his wife was looking for him."

"What's her name?"

"Him. Hector. A pardonable mistake."

Phil said, "Has she been told?"

"Professor," Jimmy said, "why don't you call Hector and have him call Mrs. Izquierdo. Just tell her something has happened."

Wack picked up his phone. Izquierdo's death apparently came as a surprise to Hector, so Wack told him what had happened.

"Yes, dead. At his desk. This place has been simply crawling with firemen, policemen, detectives, what-all. Just call her, all right?" Pause. "I understand. Just tell her that something has happened, that's all you have to say. And she should come at once."

Wack's eyes widened, and he looked at Jimmy. "Where should she come?"

"Campus security." Jimmy avoided Phil's eyes.

Wack repeated it, then hung up.

"So, Izquierdo's wife calls Hector and says she can't reach her husband?"

"Words to that effect."

"We'll speak to her later. So what did you do then? Go right next door?"

"Not immediately. No. But soon."

"You knocked?"

"The door wasn't locked."

"You tried it?"

"Yes."

"Having knocked?"

"I don't remember."

"And there he was, seated at his desk?"

"Staring." He shuddered. "I noticed his eyes didn't blink. I touched his forehead . . ."

And then he spread the alarm. Wack had no idea when Izquierdo had arrived in his office; he had been unaware of his even being there throughout the morning.

"Keep these memories fresh," Jimmy advised him. "We'll talk again."

142

Phil and Jimmy then went to Izquierdo's office, where Jimmy took the desk chair and began slowly to rotate it. Phil was looking at the spines of the books all neatly stored in their shelves. He said, "He should have put up a struggle if he was strangled."

Jimmy bent over and looked at the well of the desk, then studied the floor. "I think maybe he did. Unless he just enjoyed kicking the hell out of his desk. And you can see that the desk is not sitting in the indentations it made in the carpet. Whoever killed him must have tidied up before he left."

The plastic bag containing snippings from *Via Media*, a pair of scissors, and glue was in a bottom drawer of the desk. Jimmy removed it carefully and laid it on the desk, its contents visible through the clear plastic. He looked at Phil.

"No wonder he didn't get a threatening letter himself."

"Return to sender?"

They left the office in the care of the sergeant and took the elevator downstairs. Jimmy's car was parked on the sidewalk in front of Decio; when he came, he had just hung a left from the stadium.

When they were buckled in, Phil asked, "Why did you ask Crenshaw about that kid Larry Douglas?"

"Let's go see."

2

THE LOFT LARRY HAD RENTED after being hired by Notre Dame security was not much—his mother had wept when he showed it to her—but it was exactly what he wanted, a big room and no one to tell him to clean it up. The bed was emperor size at least, and he lay on his back in the middle of it staring at the ceiling. There was an overhead fixture with a fan that sounded like an airplane in trouble when he turned it on, something he didn't do in this kind of weather. He had two windows right under the eaves from which icicles hung now, glittering in the weak sunlight. The television was a reject of his parents', but he only used it for sports, and then he preferred a sports bar with Laura.

Laura. The interlude with Kimberley had been too good to last; she had deserted him for Henry, who had a line like Don Juan. Some contest. Don Juan and Don Quixote. So he was stuck with Laura again. She loved this loft, not that he let her up here very often. Any grappling had to go on elsewhere, usually in his car. He might be on his own, but his mother's presence hung over the loft like a persistent conscience.

The sad thing was that, once he had exchanged Laura for Kimberley, he had repented of those prolonged sessions in the car, and one day he went to Sacred Heart at eleven in the morning, his uniform concealed by a bulky jacket, and got in line at the confessional. He was still trying to figure out how to tell the priest when his turn came. As soon as the grille slid open, he blurted out that he had committed adultery.

On the other side of the grille, the priest stirred. "You're married?"

"No, Father."

"The woman is married."

"No."

A pause. "You had relations with her?"

Larry relaxed. The priest had been startled by the way he began, but this was his job. He said yes, he'd had relations with her.

Just the once?

"Many times."

"Three, four."

"Dozens of times."

Another pause. "Is she a student, too?"

"I'm not a student, Father."

"I see." He sounded relieved.

Kneeling during the long pep talk that followed, Larry began to think of the others waiting in line. How long had he been in here? He assured the priest that he had stopped seeing the girl, he meant never to see her again.

"Good. Good."

For his penance he was to say Psalm 32; he would find it in the red book in the pews. Would he do that?

"Yes, Father."

And then he was given absolution. He practically floated out of the confessional, drifting past those in line, avoiding their eyes. He went halfway down a side aisle and slid into a pew. How easy it had been. He sat, staring at the altar, at the statue of Mary in the niche high above on the back wall. He had recited the Act of Contrition before receiving absolution and promising to amend his life; that meant that from now on it was Kimberley, because Kimberley wouldn't allow him the liberties Laura had. He took out the red book and found the psalm.

That had been a month ago, and now, thanks to Henry, he was back in the danger area. Laura had reclaimed him with familiar warmth; he had let her tell him what a shallow person Kimberley was, just the sort of person someone like Henry would find attractive.

"You had a narrow escape, Larry."

Escape was what he thought of as they huddled in the front seat of his car. Laura did a lot of sighing that sounded phony to Larry. He was the phony, though. It wasn't just with Kimberley that Henry had asserted his superiority. He had come to treat Larry like an apprentice, even though they had been hired within weeks of one another.

On Sunday he had gone to Mass with his mother, and she didn't exactly quiz him about not receiving communion, but he could hear the wheels turning in her head. After dinner, she wondered if she shouldn't give that loft of his a good cleaning. It brought back memories of how she had prowled around his room when he lived at home. He didn't have to wonder what she would think of Laura. All that meat and no potatoes. He had come back here to his loft, alone, and told himself he had to go to confession again. He would know enough to call it fornication this time. But what was the point? He couldn't shake Laura, so he couldn't promise to amend his life. He felt miserable. That morning he called in sick.

"Oh, that's a shame," Laura said.

"I'll be all right." But he said it with a croaking voice.

"I'll stop over after work."

"No, no. That's okay." He added, "I don't want you to catch it."

"What is it?"

"Flu." Short for influenza. Influence. Bad influence. Lady, beware.

The thing about faking illness, you began to feel sick. So he had lain in bed, the covers pulled up to his chin, and stared at the blades of that stupid fan above.

When Laura called again he had actually fallen asleep.

"They found Professor Izquierdo's body in his office." Laura said it in a whisper as if she didn't want to be overheard.

Larry sat up like Lazarus. "What do you mean?"

"He's dead." She was still whispering.

He listened to her garbled account, sitting on the edge of the bed. Of all the days not to be at work! The South Bend police had been called, of course, and Larry would bet that meant Stewart. Stewart had liked him, had treated him with respect, and Crenshaw hadn't liked it, but to hell with him.

"I'm coming out," he said.

"With the flu? You stay right there."

How could he tell her he was faking? Then she was whispering again.

"I just hope they don't find out you know what."

"What?"

Of course he knew what. Laura had filched the master key for Decio and gone over there with him. Henry! My God, whenever he thought of opening that door and seeing Henry, dressed all in black, sitting at the desk, the hair on his head would almost lift.

"Yeah. Look, Laura, keep me posted, will you?"

"Of course. But get some rest."

Are all women mothers? Well, Laura was one big mama, that's for sure.

He showered and shaved, his ear cocked for the phone; he dressed and had a bowl of cereal as if it were morning rather than early afternoon. When the phone rang he flew to it.

"Yes."

"Larry Douglas?"

"Who's this?"

"Detective Stewart. I understand you're feeling under the weather."

"It's nothing. I feel much better." Did Stewart want his help?

"Could we talk?"

"Absolutely. Where?"

"What's wrong with there?"

"Not a thing. Come on over."

He hung up, looked around the loft, and began to straighten things up. He threw armfuls of clothing into the closet and closed it. He made the bed, more or less. He looked at all the

148

dishes in the sink but decided against doing them now. He spent the time before Stewart arrived pacing the loft. Maybe it was just as well he had called in sick. Crenshaw would have done anything to prevent Stewart from consulting with Larry. He realized he was smiling. He hadn't felt this good since he had come out of that confessional cleansed of his sins.

"Quite a place," Stewart said, when Larry let him in. Philip Knight was with him, and Larry was certain they were going to ask his help.

"You've heard about Izquierdo?"

He nodded, looking serious. "They called to tell me."

"How you feeling?"

"Much better. It must have been one of those quick bouts."

"You're sure?"

They went down to the car, and Stewart put Larry up front with him, while Phil Knight sat in back. The streets were a mess, icy snow, and the day was gloomy again, but Larry felt great. What were the chances of becoming a real cop? Maybe Notre Dame security would be a farm team from which he would rise to the majors. From the backseat, Phil Knight talked about the crime scene. That was where they were headed. Larry was glad he had put on his uniform.

Larry was a little startled when Jimmy just swung onto the sidewalk and glided along to the front of Decio.

"I won't give you a ticket," he said when Stewart had parked.

A big laugh all around. Larry felt terrific, a member of the team. They had come for him to ask his help! Wait until Henry heard of this.

Up the elevator and down the hall, three detectives on duty. The sergeant stepped aside, but Stewart went past Izquierdo's office and knocked at the next door. He had to knock again before Professor Wack opened. He looked annoyed, he looked frightened, and then he looked at Larry. His eyes narrowed.

"You put that pogo stick in my office!"

Stewart said, "You recognize this officer?"

"Of course I recognize him."

Larry felt as if someone had kicked him in the stomach. The memory of that crazy night when he had let himself into Izquierdo's office, when Wack had interrupted him and he had got the excitable professor back to his office, roared through his mind. But it was the expression on Stewart's face that plunged him into the depths.

He had been set up.

3   "GOD IS NOT MOCKED," ARMITAGE

Shanks observed the day after the body of Izquierdo had been found in his office. He turned the little flask of his executive martini in its bed of ice, as if he were dialing in the deity.

"Now, now," Potts said.

"How did he die?"

"Alone. The way we all will." Not a favorite topic at the Old Bastards' table in the University Club. It was one thing to derive pleasure from the general collapse of higher education and of the culture at large since their own active years, but the destiny awaiting them all was best left implicit.

"He was strangled."

"I thought he was poisoned."

Potts glared at Wheeler. "Where did you hear that?"

"The same place you heard he was strangled."

Their understanding of what had happened to Izquierdo was pieced together from hearsay, the story in the local paper, and what they had heard from Debbie, the hostess. The club was abuzz with recent events, and Debbie picked up bits and pieces from the various tables and relayed it all to them.

"I think the provost hired a hit man," Potts said with a wicked grin.

"I never met the man," murmured Tasker, an emeritus professor of English and an infrequent presence at the table. Tasker could have passed unrecognized through the current ranks of his old department. Not to know is one thing, not to be known another. The waters of Lethe had closed over them all and, in lucid moments, they knew it.

"When was the last time a professor was found dead in his office?"

Here was a tangent they could all pursue, dredging up from memory the several incidents of those who had died with their boots on, something they had all once resolved to do, but in the end all had been more than content to enter the ranks of the retired, where at least they were known.

"They took someone from campus security in for questioning," Debbie told them, taking a chair and resting from her labors. These consisted in leading diners to their tables, giving them menus, and then returning to her desk just inside the door of the dining room to doodle. Once she had been a waitress, something only those at this table were likely to remember, and she kept her hand in, bringing their initial drinks, pouring coffee and water for them, from time to time sitting in on the wake they were holding for the past.

"What do you mean, took him in for questioning?"

"I'm only telling you what I heard."

"He must have been the hit man," Potts said.

"Maybe now they'll decide to tear down Decio," Shanks suggested.

152

"The donor's still alive."

So they were back to the doubtful future of the club. It was the consensus that the place would not be pulled down in their lifetime.

"The whole thing is a false alarm."

Debbie laughed. "Don't count on it."

"Well, you're pretty cheerful about the prospect."

"That's what you think."

"That's why I said."

"How did Izquierdo die?"

Debbie frowned. "Good Lord, you're ghoulish. They say he was strangled."

"By someone in campus security?"

"Who knows?"

"*¿Quién sabe?*" echoed Plaisance. Once his department had been called Romance languages; now it was modern languages. What might it not be tomorrow?

"*Panta rei.*"

"Who's he?"

"It's Greek, my dear fellow," Shanks said. "All things flow."

The translation had an adverse effect on a table full of old bladders. Most of the other diners had risen and gone. It was time for their own exodus from the dining room, the slow procession up the ramp for the handicapped and on to the men's room beyond. Armitage Shanks brought up the rear in every sense of the phrase and looked with melancholy at the procession of his fellow emeriti.

"I had not thought death had undone so many," he murmured.

4 ⟶ LAURA WAS ON DUTY WHEN A hysterical Pauline Izquierdo burst into the office of campus security, demanding to know what had happened to her husband.

"Oh my God! Haven't you heard?"

"Heard what? Tell me. No one will tell me anything."

She paced frantically from one side of the reception area to another. Laura picked up the phone and buzzed Crenshaw. She couldn't handle this any more than this woman could handle the news about her husband, whatever it was. Crenshaw did not answer. She knew he was in there. Others came into the reception area and immediately did a 180 and got out of there.

"That stupid Hector won't tell me. No one will tell me. They said to come here. Where is my husband?"

Not many women can retain their beauty while screaming hysterically, but Mrs. Izquierdo was an exception. Ringlets of hair pushed out of the black woolen cap she wore. Her ankle-length belted storm coat was of kelly green. Her eyes flashed; her voice ran up and down the scale of anguish. Laura was so fascinated that she almost stopped being angry at Crenshaw for hiding in his office.

"Come on," she said. She came around her desk, took the woman's hand, and pulled her down the hallway to Crenshaw's office. Of course the door was shut. Laura opened it and led the hysterical woman in. Crenshaw had been on his feet. He retreated to the window and looked with terror at the two women.

"Mrs. Izquierdo," Laura said. "No one has told her her husband has been murdered."

Laura pulled the door shut after her, then stood listening to the aria of anguish in Crenshaw's office. She hurried back to her desk to call Larry. What a day to call in sick.

Larry didn't answer the phone. Dark thoughts went through her mind. If he wasn't in his loft, where had he called from? Her phone rang and she snatched it up.

"Larry?"

"Get Detective Stewart out here," Crenshaw said in a strangled voice. Mrs. Izquierdo's wailing was twice audible, from down the hallway and, more piercingly, over the phone. "And you come in here. Now!"

Throughout the next half hour, Laura was registering everything in order to tell Larry. She managed to calm down Mrs. Izquierdo, more or less, but Crenshaw was determined to get the banshee out of there. No one downtown knew where Jimmy Stewart was.

"Laura will take you down there," Crenshaw said. "You shouldn't be alone."

Mrs. Izquierdo was in phase two of her confused grief. Laura got into her coat; Crenshaw actually helped her.

"Take my car," he urged, pressing the keys into her hands. Laura took them.

With relief in sight, Crenshaw in shirtsleeves helped her get the woman out to his car. There was a Hummer parked in the middle of the street, its motor still running.

"Who the hell put that there?" Crenshaw roared.

"That's mine."

"No problem. I'll take care of it."

When she was in the passenger seat, Crenshaw slammed the door and then stood there hugging himself with the stupidest expression on his stupid face. Laura started the car and, even before she left campus, turned on the siren. It was either that or face the woman's questions.

"You said he was murdered." She looked at Laura as if she had confessed to the crime.

"The police will explain everything."

"The police. You're the police."

Laura turned up the volume of the siren and with lights flashing sped downtown, ignoring the icy streets, liking it as cars pulled off to the side to let her through. There was a near miss as she tore through a red light when a car braked and then began to slide sideways through the intersection. Laura went into a slide herself but regained control. This had the effect of subduing her passenger.

When she pulled into the parking lot downtown, she had trouble bringing the car to a stop on the icy surface. It slid slowly into a snowbank and came to a halt, killing the motor. The siren kept going and she had trouble stopping it. When they got out of the car, Mrs. Izquierdo was more or less under control. Laura led her like a zombie inside.

"Homicide," she announced to the cop on duty. How did a

fatso like that pass the physical? She pushed the thought away. "This is Mrs. Izquierdo, whose husband was found in his office on campus."

It was the new widow's cue to begin shrieking again. That was okay with Laura. She felt a bit like shrieking herself.

The next half hour or so was a confusing period. No one seemed to know of the murder on campus. Laura asked if they knew Detective Stewart. Of course they knew Detective Stewart. Well, this was his case, and this woman wanted someone in charge to tell her what had happened.

A tall man in a corduroy jacket with a Burberry coat over his arm, lining displayed, rose from a chair and became the voice of reason. He spoke soothingly to Mrs. Izquierdo; he stopped Laura when she headed for the door.

"Wait. I want to talk to you."

She waited. Finally the chief showed up. He knew less of what had happened than Mrs. Izquierdo, so Laura had to explain it to him, and to the man in the corduroy coat, while the horrified widow listened in.

"Where the hell is Stewart?" the chief demanded. "Get hold of Stewart."

Minions fled to carry out this order. The man in the corduroy jacket took Laura back to the reception area, got her seated, and brought her a cup of coffee. When he sat, he was holding a tablet. He licked the tip of his pencil.

"From the beginning."

All this was bearable because it was a story she was going to tell Larry. It was a strange interview, full of the oddest questions. Tell him all about Professor Izquierdo. Was he the campus atheist? Yes, yes, and the other day someone set his car afire. Her interviewer took this down eagerly.

The interview went on for twenty minutes, and Laura was more and more confused by the kind of questions she was being asked. Then the outside door opened and three men pushed through the revolving door. First, Jimmy Stewart, then Larry, and third, Philip Knight. Laura jumped to her feet.

"Larry!"

He stared at her and began to bawl like a baby. She took him in her arms. Stewart and Philip Knight shuffled and looked uncomfortable. Then Stewart asked what she was doing there.

"I brought Mrs. Izquierdo! No one had told her what happened."

"Ye gods."

"Laura," Larry said, burbling against her bosom. "They think I did it."

Stewart told Fatso to take Larry to a holding room so he could speak with Mrs. Izquierdo.

"Should I stay with him?"

"This officer will do that." He meant Laura.

When they were alone she coddled Larry as she often had, and he stopped whimpering. Honest to God, from a hysterical woman to a crying man. But this was Larry. He began to talk.

They had taken him to Decio. He thought they wanted his assistance. He looked at Laura and his mouth trembled. There, there. Then that creep in the office next to Izquierdo's recognized him from that night he had paid a visit to Izquierdo's office. Oscar Wack told them the whole story, which he seemed to think turned on planting a pogo stick in his office. He was sure Izquierdo had put them up to it, so he could be accused of God knows what.

"What did you tell them?"

"Nothing."

"You'll need a lawyer."

"Oh my God."

"Larry, what you did is not what they're after."

"They wanted to know why Wack spoke in the plural when he told the story. Of course he meant Henry."

"Did you tell them?"

"No! And don't you either."

"I think Henry should fess up."

"What good would that do?"

"Maybe you're right."

The door opened and the man in the corduroy coat came in and took a seat at the table. Larry stared at him. "Who are you?"

"Just tell it all in your own words. Have they charged you yet?"

They? "Who are you?"

The door opened again and Jimmy Stewart came in.

"What the hell are you doing here, Grafton?"

The corduroy jacket rose. "The public has a right to know, Stewart."

"Get out of here."

He got out of there. "Who is he?" Laura asked.

"Scoop Grafton. He calls himself a reporter. You can leave now. I want to talk to Larry."

"I'm part of it."

"What do you mean."

"I gave the master key for Decio to him."

Stewart slumped into a chair. "What did you tell Grafton?" He erased the question with an angry wave of his hand. "What the hell were you doing in Izquierdo's office?"

5   THE LOCAL PAPER WAS FULL OF
Scoop Grafton's story; there were lengthy
interviews with Laura and Larry, accompanied by what must
have been the photographs taken when they joined Notre
Dame security. Crenshaw said that both of them were on
indefinite leave, pending a decision on their future employment. The campus papers, both those subsidized by student
fees and the unsubsidized and independent, were full of the
story. The campus was being described as a war zone in which
cars were firebombed and dissidents murdered at their desks.
Grateful students of Professor Izquierdo gave testimonials to
his fearless attacks on Christianity. A girl who was writing her
senior thesis on Feuerbach under Izquierdo's direction said
that his course alone was reason enough for her having come to
Notre Dame. As a rule, faculty dodged reporters. Those inclined
to go on the record would doubtless submit op-ed essays.
Hector, the departmental secretary, basked in the attention
given him.

"He was one of the kindest men I ever knew." His eyes
flashed as he said this, lest the reporter dare to contradict hm.

"What did his colleagues think of him?"

"What do you mean?"

"He was a maverick, wasn't he?"

"We are all mavericks here."

He was shut up after that. Wack had lodged a protest that the departmental secretary should presume to act as spokesman for them all.

"Would you like to?" McCerb, the chair, asked.

"Ha ha."

"Of course, there would be a conflict of interest in your case."

What did that mean? What had that catty Hector said? He consulted Lucy Goessen about it.

"I suppose they mean you'll be called as a witness. I imagine I will be, too."

"But I don't know anything!"

"I wouldn't make it that sweeping." But she smiled and patted his arm when she said it. Oscar purred. He was again certain that he and Lucy could become good friends. Not colleagues, friends.

Larry Douglas's status was unclear. He was still being held for questioning, and his lawyer, a furtive fellow named Furlong, made a lengthy harangue about civil liberties, a phrase or two of which appeared in the newspaper accounts. On television, he was allowed to talk, but muted, while a voice-over explained what Furlong apparently wished to say. And then the scarf was found in Larry's loft.

It must have been five feet long, gaudy, striped. It was immediately recognized as Izquierdo's. It seemed twisted. It was rushed to the lab; results were collated with the coroner's report. It seemed that the murder weapon had been found.

"What did Larry say when you told him?" Roger asked. Jimmy Stewart and Phil were discussing this latest event in the Knight apartment. Father Carmody had been invited, but the continuing arctic weather had prevented it.

"The kid is almost catatonic."

Fauxhall, an assistant prosecutor, was trying to get Jimmy to sign on to a scenario. It is known that Larry was able to enter Izquierdo's office at will, thanks to the master key filched from campus security. Having established this, he bides his time. One night, while Izquierdo is still in his office, Larry enters. Imagine how surprised the professor must have been. But Larry would have been wearing his uniform. Some specious excuse must have been given. The scarf, with the professor's other wraps, is hung on a stand in the corner behind the desk. Did Larry marvel at the scarf of many colors, want to examine it more closely? Now he is behind the desk, he has the scarf, he loops it over the head of the still unsuspecting professor and begins to twist. There are signs of the struggle Izquierdo put up, kicking like crazy against the dying of the light. The desk itself is moved in the struggle. And then resistance ends. Larry removes the scarf, pushes the desk back approximately to where it had been, and leaves.

"Conveniently keeping the scarf in his loft so it could be found."

"I needn't tell you of the inconsistency of the criminal mind." Fauxhall might have already been addressing a jury. "Well, what do you think?"

"Even Furlong could make mincemeat out of that."

But it was Mrs. Izquierdo who did. She telephoned Jimmy.

"That is not Raul's scarf."

"Why do you say that?"

"Because it's here, hanging in the hall closet."

Jimmy went out to the house and looked at the scarf, identical to the one that had been found in Larry's loft.

"It's been here all along?"

"Of course it has."

"Where did he buy it?"

"I bought it for him."

From Whistler's, a men's store in the mall. The salesman took Jimmy to Whistler's office. When he learned the purpose of the visit, he wasn't sure he wanted his establishment mixed up in this.

"It already is."

"I am not responsible for what happens to items I sell."

"Of course you're not. Let's talk about this scarf." Jimmy had with him the scarf Pauline Izquierdo had given him. Whistler reached for it, then withdrew his hand.

"How many of these do you suppose you've sold?"

"I'm surprised I sold any."

"I see what you mean."

Whistler kept records, of course, and he found proof of Mrs. Izquierdo's purchase, but of no other. There had been three such scarves in his inventory. The scarf found in

Larry's loft had Whistler's tag in it. The explanation seemed to be that it had been on a discount table with dozens of other items that had not sold well. No record would have been kept of such a purchase, only a generic "special sale" designation.

"So who is trying to frame Larry Douglas?"

"When we know that, we will know who strangled Izquierdo."

Roger sat humming and shaking his head. "If I killed someone, I would want to get rid of the murder instrument rather than plant it somewhere."

"I needn't tell you of the inconsistency of the criminal mind." Jimmy crossed his fingers when he said it.

"And what of the plastic bag containing pages of *Via Media*, scissors, glue?"

Jimmy shrugged. No prints, but the pages had been compared with uncut pages of the paper, and it seemed pretty certain that the contents of the bag explained the threatening letters that had caused such interest some weeks before.

"None of those threats were actually carried out, were they?"

Phil suggested that, since they had been a spoof, they could have been sent by Izquierdo. Particularly since one of the addressees was the colleague he loathed.

"Oscar Wack." What interested Roger was Wack's assumption that Larry had not been alone the night he had surprised him in Izquierdo's office.

"That woman insists she was with him," Jimmy said.

"But waiting outside."

"So she says."

"Wack says he saw three people riding away in a golf cart."

"The third man."

Phil began to give an impression of the theme song of that old movie.

"I'd talk with Laura again if I were you," Roger said.

But first Jimmy talked to Larry. He had been released when Mrs. Izquierdo produced her husband's scarf. It had been assumed that the scarf found in Larry's loft had been the murder weapon, but the lab told the deflated Fauxhall that it could have been the other scarf. The marks made on the throat of Izquierdo pointed to such a scarf, but there was nothing on either scarf to enable them to decide which had been the murder weapon. And what else did they have?

"I'm still on leave," Larry complained. "Crenshaw let Laura come back to work, but I am still on indefinite leave."

Furlong, Larry's lawyer, had transferred his energies to combating the injustice with which campus security was treating his client. Furlong was a Democrat and thus despised the present occupant of the White House, but he argued passionately that providing security for a community often required unusual means. Larry was a zealous young man, his actions had been unusual, but his motives were clear. Furlong himself wasn't clear on what those motives were, but no matter. He had been given lengthy coverage in campus newspapers, editors being delighted to criticize the administration through a third party.

"Who was with you the night you entered Izquierdo's office?"

"Laura."

"Who was the third person?"

"What third person?"

"Professor Wack says he saw three people ride away in the golf cart."

"I don't know what he's talking about."

"He must be a great friend of yours."

"Who?"

"The third man who didn't come forward in your defense."

Larry just stared at him. Laura was no more help, but again Jimmy felt he was not getting the full story. So he began to keep tabs on the young couple. It turned out that Kimberley who worked in the coroner's office knew Larry. Feeley remembered that his assistant had gone out with the young man. So Jimmy talked with her.

"Oh yes," she said. "We went out a few times. We shared an interest in poetry."

"Ah."

"But that's all it was."

It turned out that she was now going with someone else in campus security, Henry Grabowski. Not that she volunteered this, but following her around for a few days brought this to the surface. Was Henry the third man?

Crenshaw began to shake his head as soon as Jimmy brought up the subject.

"You know I can't give out information like that."

"You don't have to, of course. It must be a pain in the neck having someone like Furlong on your case. I'd hate to get a court order and multiply your problems."

"A court order!"

"We've got a murder on your campus, Crenshaw. An unsolved case. I need to pursue what leads I get. Why are you covering up for Henry Grabowski?"

"Covering up? He works here. You know that, I know that, everybody knows that."

Finally Crenshaw let Jimmy see Henry's application. Among the letters of recommendation was one from a teacher at St. Joe High School, Masterson, who happened to be Jimmy's brother-in-law. They had more or less avoided one another since Hazel left him, but that was only because they were no longer comfortable together. Jimmy called him up and invited him for a beer at Leaky's near the courthouse.

"Bat, how are you? Take a pew."

Masterson smiled and slid into the booth across from Jimmy. "You're the only one who calls me that."

"What do your students call you?"

"Sir."

"Remember a kid named Henry Grabowski?"

"Of course I do. Why do you ask?"

"He's been taken on by Notre Dame security."

Bat's beer had come, and he made a face before drinking. "What a waste."

"How do you mean?"

Bat told him about Henry's record as a student, something Jimmy already knew, thanks to Crenshaw.

"He couldn't afford college?"

"He was a shoo-in for a fellowship, and there are loans. But it was Notre Dame or nothing. He wouldn't listen to me."

"Did he apply?"

"And was turned down. I told him thousands of applicants are turned down every year by Notre Dame. Tens of thousands. I suggested the route through Holy Cross College."

"Was he bitter or what?"

"All his life he had dreamt of going to Notre Dame."

"Well, he ended up there."

Bat shook his head and said again, "What a waste."

Professor Wack looked at the photograph Jimmy gave him. "Is he the man who was with Larry Douglas the night you surprised them in Izquierdo's office?"

"I didn't see him. I told you that. But I know this fellow. He and Izquierdo were thick as thieves."

"What do you mean?"

"He was up here a lot. I think Izquierdo was trying to tutor him. Raul wasn't all bad, you know."

Lucy Goessen also remembered seeing Henry when he came to see Izquierdo. "Raul said he was smarter than most of his students."

6   KIMBERLEY WAS RELUCTANT TO
show him around the morgue, but Henry
kept after her. What was a girl like that doing working in a
place like this? Feeley, the coroner, was another surprise.

"How did you end up here?" Henry asked.

"It's a long story."

"I'm listening."

It seemed almost noble that Feeley had abandoned all his
dreams in order to keep his father on the local political pay-
roll. It made them seem kindred spirits, in a way. "Did you
ever read 'Winter Dreams' by Fitzgerald?"

Feeley just looked at him. But Kimberley knew the story.

Stealing Kimberley away from Larry Douglas had not been
much of a triumph. Henry soon tired of her sentimental
response to what she read.

"You should read Nietzsche."

"Maybe I will."

She tried *Zarathustra* but didn't like it. So he told her what
Jeeves had said to Bertie Wooster. "You would not like Nietzsche, sir. He is fundamentally unsound." Kimberley began to
remind Henry of one of Bertie's girlfriends.

"I think Wodehouse is silly."

"Of course he is."

"So why read him?"

"For the silliness."

"Now you're being silly."

"That's because you think I think what I say is true."

But there was no point in trying out Izquierdo's nihilism on her. A limited mind. Pretty as a picture, of course, there was no doubt of that. Henry's trouble was that the future had ceased to interest him. Once his whole life had been aimed at becoming a student at Notre Dame. That would have put him on the one track he wanted. Meeting with Izquierdo was a poor substitute, but then it led nowhere, so that became its attraction. If he had been a real student, getting a high grade would have entered into it, but all he got from Izquierdo was the endorsement of his sense of superiority, and that only added to the bitterness of his disappointment. Putting the torch to Izquierdo's Corvette was an instance of what Izquierdo called an *acte gratuite*. Motiveless. Done in order to do it. And to get a rise out of Izquierdo. Raul's reaction was a disappointment. So one night he went to Decio and put the plastic bag with the cuttings and scissors and glue he had used in fashioning those threatening letters in a drawer in Izquierdo's desk.

When he heard someone outside the door, he quickly turned off the office light and sat as still as he could in Izquierdo's chair. A key in the lock. He prepared himself to greet Izquierdo, searching desperately for an explanation he might give of being here, and then he was looking into the terrified face of Larry Douglas.

171

For days now he had been mystified by Larry's silence about that night when they took him in for questioning. Henry had thought of going downtown and asking to see Larry, he had thought of quizzing Laura about it, but he didn't do the first, and Laura was suspended along with Larry.

Henry tried various explanations. Larry had told them that he had found Henry already in Izquierdo's office and they were keeping it quiet. Maybe he was under surveillance. The best response to that was to put Detective Stewart under surveillance. He called in sick, asking for Crenshaw.

"I've got the flu."

"Everybody's got the flu."

"I can't come to work."

"You better not. I don't want to catch it."

So Henry followed Stewart around. He watched him enter Whistler's and knew the reason. But who would remember buying a scarf from a table of discounted items? When Henry had seen the duplicate of Izquierdo's scarf—actually there were two on the table—he asked his mom to buy it for him. She did, but she thought it was ridiculous.

Nothing happened after Stewart's trip to the mall. Henry feared that his mother would be questioned about the scarf, but nothing happened. Henry breathed a little easier. When Stewart spent an evening at the Knights' apartment, Henry decided that the time had come for him to get a new faculty mentor. He found out where Roger Knight's class was held and asked if he could sit in. Knight just assumed he was a student.

"So what did you think?" Roger Knight asked him afterward.

He had been surrounded by students after the class, but Henry had waited for him by his golf cart.

"F. Marion Crawford?"

"Have you ever read him?"

"On my list, he comes right after Winston Churchill. The other one."

Roger's popularity was a mystery to Henry. He could understand that women students would feel motherly toward a man that helpless, shaped like a balloon, getting around a real effort. But his mind was too elusive for Henry, and allusive. He realized that Izquierdo had flattered him even while being condescending. Roger with his big blue-eyed baby stare could have talked rings around Izquierdo. What hadn't the guy read? But it was the simplicity of his religious faith that marked him. After Izquierdo, this was a real switch. Then Roger surprised him by saying he had heard Henry was a protégé of the campus atheist.

"Protégé?"

"I'm told you often visited his office."

"Only in daytime hours," Henry said, then wished he hadn't. For the matter of that, he wished he hadn't looked up Roger Knight. Of course Roger would know everything his brother knew and his brother everything that Stewart did. Henry felt a sudden impulse to talk to Roger, to ask his help, but he fought it.

Someone was playing him for a fool, and he just couldn't believe it was Larry Douglas. Why was he keeping quiet? The discovery of that scarf in Larry's loft should have turned him into a babbling cooperative witness, but even then, nothing.

It had to do with Kimberley, that must be it. He was too proud to point a finger at the guy who had walked off with his girl.

At home he went up to his room, telling his mom he would be right down for supper, but he had to check something first. He opened his dresser drawer, pushed aside the neat pile of Hanes shorts, and pulled out the many-colored scarf. It was still here. It had always been here. So who had tossed an identical scarf into Larry's loft? How many of them were there?

WHEN YOUNG FATHER CONWAY was asked to speak to the widow of Professor Izquierdo, he welcomed this opportunity for pastoral work. He hadn't endured all those years of study in order to occupy an office in the Main Building. Not that he thought this would be easy.

First, he made sure he had all the information about the late professor, and of course he was briefed by the university lawyer. That was when it dawned on Tim Conway that, for some, the main concern was that the widow would sue the university. So in some ways, he was engaged in making a pre-emptive strike. In his own mind, he was calling on her in his capacity as a priest. His lips moved in prayer as he drove. Please grant me the grace to say the right, the healing thing.

"Pauline," she said when he had addressed her twice as Mrs. Izquierdo.

"Tim."

"Oh, I couldn't call you Tim, Father."

"That's perfectly all right." There were laypeople like that, insistent on the dignity of the priesthood, sticklers for protocol and etiquette.

She said, "My father's name was Tim."

She was a woman of striking good looks, even a celibate could appreciate that. Dark hair with threads of gray, actually white, providing an intriguing contrast.

"Have arrangements been made?"

"Arrangements? Oh. The body is still at the morgue. There will be a cremation, that's what he would have wanted. You know he was an atheist."

"We will hold a memorial service in any case."

She surprised him by smiling. "If you think it will help."

"The university intends to give you all the help it can."

She nodded, waiting for him to go on. So he took a folder from his briefcase and outlined what the university felt, in these extraordinary circumstances, it could do to alleviate her sorrow.

"And there is of course the amount that accrued in his retirement fund."

"Maybe I'll stop working."

He felt like an insurance agent, not a priest, and she baffled him. From what he had heard of her reaction when she learned of her husband's death, Tim had steeled himself for hysterics, anger, accusations, whatever. Instead she sat on her couch with the flowing, florid housecoat dramatically draped around her and reaching to the floor, the picture of composure. He realized she was barefoot. Until they had sat, her feet were concealed by the garment she wore.

"I know it's difficult to speak of these things."

She shook her head. "I've had time to think, Father. Ours was what Raul called an open marriage." A little smile. "Meaning he could cheat on me."

"Did he?"

"He was a man."

"Well." He looked at the picture behind her. *The Temptation of St. Anthony.* "There are no children?"

"By me? No. We were too selfish for that."

"What about you? Your husband was an atheist . . ."

"Who every day recited the prayer to his guardian angel." She lifted her eyes and joined her hands. "'Angel of God, my guardian dear, to whom God's love entrusts me here, ever this day be at my side, to light and guard, to rule and guide.'"

"An atheist who prayed?"

"He was a bundle of contradictions. Maybe we all are."

"So he was raised Catholic?"

"We were married in the Church. The atheism came later."

"And you?"

"Have I lost my faith? I don't know. I don't think so."

"Well, we can talk of that later."

"Will they find the one who did it?"

He couldn't say. He supposed so. It was unthinkable that a professor could be killed in his office and the murderer go undiscovered. Did she have any suspicions?

"I'm glad I told the police about the scarf. I was certain that young man hadn't done it, and then I found Raul's scarf." She smiled. "Actually I thought the man they had arrested was someone else."

"Oh?"

"Someone Raul was tutoring. Also in campus security."

"You've had to discuss all this with the police?"

"They've been very nice. Very considerate."

"Good."

Her eyes drifted away. "Our parents were so happy when Raul was hired by Notre Dame. So were we." She looked at him and her eyes seemed moist. "Beware of answered prayers. Isn't that what they say?"

"I'll say a Mass for the repose of his soul."

"He wasn't sure he had one."

"Of course he did." It was all he had now.

Again she smiled. She made him feel younger than he was. He repeated for her what the university offered to do for her, and she listened carefully, and again he reminded her that her husband would have accrued a goodly sum in his retirement account.

"And there is insurance."

"Ah. Our substitute for providence. I'm quoting Raul."

He supposed it must be some consolation to know that she would be very comfortable, economically. There was also insurance on the car that had been burned.

"I noticed the Hummer in the driveway."

"That's mine."

"I've never ridden in one."

"It gives a sense of power."

A silence fell, and he didn't know how to break it. A sense of his own inadequacy swept over him. He began to gather together his papers and put them in his briefcase.

"I should have offered you coffee."

"I've had my cup for the day."

"Just one."

He nodded and rose. "Well, I'll keep in touch."

"Thanks for coming, Tim."

He thought of that farewell as he slipped and slid down the driveway to his car parked behind a drift beside the suburban street. He had four sisters, but that hadn't helped him figure out Pauline Izquierdo.

When he got back to campus, he stopped by Roger Knight's apartment and was glad to find the Huneker Professor of Catholic Studies in. He wanted to talk about his visit to Mrs. Izquierdo with Roger before returning to the provost's office.

8   YOUNG FATHER CONWAY COULD
not believe that Roger had never been to
Rome. The enormous professor spoke of the city as if he had
spent years there, and he could hold forth on the way Rome
was a palimpsest—Tim looked it up later—with the Etruscan
past under the republic and empire, over which the medieval
and Renaissance had been laid.

"How I envy you, Father, four years there."

But Roger knew that Tim Conway had not dropped by in
order to talk about his student years in the Eternal City, so he
stopped praising F. Marion Crawford's two-volume history of
Rome and busied himself making hot chocolate.

"I've just come from Mrs. Izquierdo."

"Can you tell me about it?" Roger had turned and looked
eagerly at the young priest.

"I don't see why not."

"Good, good."

And so they sat and Father Conway spoke of his chat with
the widow of Professor Izquierdo. An atheist who prayed.

"She said theirs was an open marriage."

"Open to adultery?"

"On his part anyway. She was very blasé about it. I had expected a hysterical woman, but not at all. Not that I know what the behavior of a wife whose husband has been murdered ought to be."

The account of the scarf got Roger's whole attention. It had been a lucky day for Larry Douglas when Mrs. Izquierdo informed the police that her husband's scarf was in the closet of their home.

"And now there are two."

"She said she was sure that young man hadn't killed her husband. Funny thing, though. She had mistaken him for someone else in campus security."

"She said that?"

"Well, in any case, there was the scarf."

Roger did not press the young priest. They sipped their cocoa, and then they were talking about the terrible weather, so the visit was coming to an end.

After Father Conway left, Roger went back to his study, settled himself in his special chair, and thought about the strange events of the past weeks.

Threatening notes had been received by the provost, the dean of Arts and Letters, the football coach, and Oscar Wack. The discovery of that plastic bag in Izquierdo's desk indicated that Izquierdo had fashioned those letters. Given his relations with Wack, it made sense that his loathsome colleague would receive one. Then there had been the strange episode of the burning wastebasket, allegedly the work of Wack, but who knew? Next had come the burning of Izquierdo's car and then the discovery of his dead body at his desk in his Decio office.

But before that, Larry Douglas had paid a clandestine visit to Izquierdo's office, only to be surprised by the ubiquitous Wack.

"What reason did he give for being there?"

"According to Jimmy, Douglas says he was investigating the burning of the car."

"What did he expect to find?"

Phil shrugged. "He didn't know. Maybe a threatening note."

But it was Wack's claim that Larry had not been alone in Izquierdo's office that night that interested Jimmy Stewart. It interested Roger, too, however slender a reed Wack was to lean on.

"He didn't see who it was?"

"Larry prevented that. They went into Wack's office to talk."

"And the pogo stick?"

"Larry says he doesn't know anything about that."

"Yet it belonged to Izquierdo and was found in Wack's office."

Wack's insistence that, from his window, he had seen three people drive away from Decio in the golf cart confirmed Jimmy's belief that there was a third man.

And neither Larry nor Laura would say who it was. Or admit that there was a third man.

"It had to be Henry Grabowski," Jimmy said.

"He sat in on my class," Roger said.

"Maybe you ought to pursue it," Jimmy said.

"He seems to be a brilliant young man."

"So what's he doing in campus security?"

"What are you doing on the police force?"

"I'm not a brilliant young man."

But Henry Grabowski didn't return to Roger's class.

9 LARRY'S LEAVE OF ABSENCE HAD been terminated, and he was back to work. Relieved as he was, it was as if he had been delivered over to Laura. Oh, she had stuck by him, she had been there when he needed someone, but that didn't mean he wanted to get back in the old rut. She thought he was nuts to keep Henry's name out of it.

"What would be the point of mentioning it?"

It was clear she didn't know. But Larry would never forget that Henry had already been in Izquierdo's office that night when he went to Decio with the master key. Larry had had time to think about that when he was under suspicion. He knew he hadn't killed Izquierdo, and he knew that whoever did had access to his office. An idea was born. Now that he was cleared, he was going to solve this case. He could never forget the elation he had felt when Detective Stewart had called and asked if he could be of help in the investigation. Only to find that what Jimmy wanted was to learn if Wack could place him as the nighttime visitor to Izquierdo's office. What a crushing letdown that had been. Even so, he was professional enough to appreciate what Jimmy Stewart had done.

So it had been important to convince Laura that mentioning

Henry's being there that night was simply irrelevant. Irrelevant, hell. How had he gotten into the office? And what was he doing there anyway? Larry's story was that he had been in search of clues to the burning of Izquierdo's car. Henry said the same. But the way Henry had been dressed, all in black, like someone out of *The Pink Panther*.

Had Henry killed Izquierdo? It was one thing to ask himself that when he was stewing downtown with that nut Furlong assuring him that they would beat this rap, but when he was with Henry again he found it hard to think that the guy could have done such a thing. It was the way that scarf had shown up in his loft that kept Larry on the trail. There was something screwy about Henry, smart as he no doubt was. And he was happy to talk about his sessions with Izquierdo.

"It was like a tutorial. I would read books and we would discuss them."

"Why?"

"All men by nature desire to know. Aristotle."

"Sure. But why would he give you all that free time?"

"He wanted to corrupt youth."

"How is Kimberley?"

Henry chuckled. "You can have her back, buddy. A great package, but it's empty."

Empty! What had drawn Larry to Kimberley was her love of poetry. She had been the first person he had been able to speak with about the poets he loved. Imagine discussing poetry with Laura. Well, maybe Angelou.

He didn't dignify Henry's magnanimous offer with a reply. Kimberley had liked him before she even heard of Henry

Grabowski. Larry was certain if they could just be alone and talk about, say, Richard Wilbur's poetry, or Dana Gioia's, all would be well. The difficulty was getting free of Laura. A difficulty doubled because he did not want her hanging around while he checked out Henry.

Where to begin? He remembered that ignominious scene in Decio when Wack had brought that stupid pogo stick out of his office, as if that was the point of bringing Larry up there. Not that the pogo stick wasn't a mystery. Then Larry had a distracting thought. What about Wack? The guy seemed to haunt the third floor of Decio; what had he been doing lurking in his office that night? And hadn't Izquierdo accused him of setting his wastebasket on fire? If a wastebasket, why not a Corvette? The more he thought about it, the more Henry faded from the picture and that creepy little Wack took center stage.

It was not an easy matter getting around campus on a bicycle in this kind of weather. He and Henry started off together, heading south from campus security, but Henry swung off to the right. Larry let him go, but then he doubled back and followed him. Henry locked his bike outside the Huddle and went inside. So that was his idea of being on duty. Disgusted, Larry set out for his original destination, Decio. As he pedaled, he remembered the woman professor, Goessen, illustrating the use of the pogo stick as Larry was led away by Stewart and Philip Knight.

When he came out of the elevator on the third floor, he thought of knocking on Professor Goessen's door, but he didn't know what he would say to her. So he continued on and knocked on Wack's door.

"Who is it?"

He knocked again, and again Wack spoke from behind the closed door, asking who it was. Larry waited.

The door opened and Wack stared at him. Larry had opened his coat so that his uniform was visible.

"What do you want?"

"Just a few questions."

Larry went in, with Wack moving backward, keeping the door between him and Larry. Larry took a chair and brought out a notebook.

"I have nothing to say to you."

"Let's start with that pogo stick. When did you remove it from Izquierdo's office?"

"Remove it? You put it here!"

It was hard to tell with a guy this excitable, but Wack appeared to be telling the truth. He decided to sit behind his desk.

"Okay. Then this is the mystery. You didn't take it from Izquierdo's office, and I sure as hell didn't put it here. So who did?"

"This is preposterous."

"If not you or me, someone else. Do you have any idea?"

Wack gave it some thought, grudgingly. "You're just trying to exonerate yourself."

"Oh come on. In itself, this is no big deal. A pogo stick. Even if it had been you or me, it's not a federal offense. Still, you and

I will want to know who did it." He paused. "It could be connected with something that is serious. Like Izquierdo's death."

Larry was enjoying this. Every time Wack spoke, he scribbled in his notebook.

"You must suspect someone. Has there been anyone, any stranger, lurking around this floor?"

"Oh, Izquierdo held open house. He didn't care how distracting it is to have students coming and going all the time. Or nonstudents, for that matter."

"Like?"

"You must know him. He works in campus security, too."

"Grabowski."

"I don't know his name, but he was up here several times a week."

No doubt while on duty.

"You never talked to him?"

"Well, I went over there several times and asked them to keep it low. I do most of my research right here."

"You're here a lot."

Wack just tossed his hair.

"When was the last time Grabowski was here?"

Wack couldn't remember. "I think Izquierdo gave him a key. Some professors let favorite students use their offices."

"He could have let himself in?"

"If he had a key."

This was going nowhere. Larry closed his notebook. "Well, I guess that's it for now."

"For now? This is harassment. If you come back, I will call your superior."

Larry pulled the door shut behind him. As he did, a door across the hall opened and Professor Goessen came out. Larry gave her a salute and she smiled.

"I thought they arrested you," she said.

"Mistaken identity."

"Who were they after, the other one?"

"What other one?"

"He wore a uniform, too."

"That's so we can't be told apart. You were pretty impressive on that pogo stick."

She laughed. "It's a knack you don't forget. Like riding a bicycle."

They went down in the elevator together. At the entrance, she bundled up. "Oh, this ungodly weather. And I had an offer from Florida State."

She pushed through the door, lowered her head, and started for the library. Larry's bicycle was not where he had left it. He looked all over for the darned thing. Henry. It had to be Henry. But why? He started off for campus security, not liking the prospect of reporting his bike had been stolen.

10

THE AFTER-CLASS DISCUSSION WAS
short—because of the weather, every-
one wanted to get back to his room—and Roger walked carefully out to his golf cart. Henry Grabowski was sitting behind
the wheel. He gave Roger a salute.

"Got the key?"

Roger slid onto the seat and handed Henry the key. He
turned it and depressed the pedal, and they moved off.

"I have to talk to you."

"You know where I live."

Henry shook his head. "Let's go to your office."

"You know where it is?"

Henry hesitated, then said, "Give me directions."

Brownson Hall is behind Sacred Heart Basilica, as old a
building as there is on campus, and one that had been put to
many uses since it ceased being the convent of the nuns who had
done the baking and cooking in the early days. The lower wing
now contained offices for various auxiliary and supernumerary
teachers, the lower rungs of the academic ladder. Roger's office
was there because he could park in the lot next to the building,
from which access to the building was easy for him. Roger

hadn't been in the office for a week or more, because of the weather.

Henry drove without talking, carefully guiding the electric cart along the shoveled walks, avoiding students who walked along in a frozen trance. He didn't need directions.

When he had parked in the lot next to Brownson, Henry waited for Roger to ease himself out, then took his arm and led him to the entrance.

"I feel that I'm in custody."

"So do I."

Roger had to unbutton his jacket to try several pockets, looking for his keys. They had been in a jacket pocket all along. He let them in, switching on the light as he squeezed himself through the narrow door.

Four walls of bookshelves, the overflow of his library, which continued to overflow as he made new purchases. Phil often asked him to weed out things he didn't need, but Roger would not have known where to begin. How do you know when you will need a book again? He hung up his great hooded outer garment, went around the desk, and sank with a sigh into his chair. He looked receptively at Henry, who sat opposite him, having dropped his jacket on the floor.

"They think I did it."

Roger smiled. "Who is 'they' and what is 'it'?"

"Stewart is investigating me. I know it. Your brother works with him, and I suppose he tells you everything."

"So we're talking about Raul Izquierdo?"

"I didn't kill him."

"Has anyone accused you?"

"Don't." His voice almost broke. "They will. Someone is trying to set me up."

The office was pleasantly warm, but Roger rubbed his hands, still a little numb from the cold. "Tell me about Izquierdo. I never knew him."

"I did. He gave me a lot of his time."

"In his office?"

Henry nodded. "We went through the books on his syllabus."

"What course was that?"

"It was called Criticism. There was a motto on the first page of the syllabus. 'Nothing is but what is not.'"

"Shakespeare."

"Is it? He hated Shakespeare."

"That's hard to believe."

"I think he hated literature."

"Tell me about your discussions."

"We pretty well settled down to Nietzsche. The works themselves. Some secondary stuff. There's a book, *Zarathustra's Secret*—"

"Kohler."

"You know it?"

"An odd book. But then Nietzsche was an odd man."

"So was Izquierdo."

"You were going to tell me about him."

After Henry began, Roger wanted to stop him, but he doubted that he could have. This was why Henry had waited for him and come to his office. His admiration for Izquierdo had turned to hatred.

"There was something diabolical about him. It wasn't just the delight he took in shaking the faith of students. He was a predator. Students, colleagues. He told me that he and his wife had an agreement. Maybe he just meant that she knew what he was up to. She certainly didn't approve."

Once when Henry was in Izquierdo's office talking with the professor, Mrs. Izquierdo burst in without warning. "She seemed disappointed to find me there."

So Henry had been introduced to Mrs. Izquierdo, and then she got in touch with him.

"She wanted to quiz me about her husband. She actually asked me to spy on him."

"And?"

Henry inhaled. "I fed her a lot of stories, made up, what she wanted to hear. I told myself it was the sort of thing Izquierdo would do. Anyhow, it wasn't much fun after that, talking about books."

"Why aren't you a student?"

"It's a long story."

Roger opened his hands. "I'd like to hear it."

It was the fact that Henry's mother worked on campus, a member of the crew that cleaned student rooms, that seemed most poignant to Roger. Her long employment might have lowered Henry's tuition, if he had been admitted. But he had been turned down.

"There are other universities."

Henry shook his head. He had defined his future so narrowly, alternatives were out of the question.

"What a disappointment that must have been."

"To put it mildly."

"Yet you took a job here."

"That was stupid. I wanted to be here and look at the students and tell myself I was as good as any of them, maybe better. So I became a freelance student. You let me sit in your class? Most of the time I did that without asking. I was flattered when Izquierdo took an interest in me."

"Not many professors would have been so generous with their time."

"Oh, it wasn't generosity. He wanted a disciple. I guess he got one in a sense."

After Mrs. Izquierdo burst in on them, the tutorials became sessions in which Henry became the unwilling confidante of Izquierdo's marital woes.

"He would quote Prince Andre to Pierre. Never marry."

Henry fell silent. He looked around the room, then over Roger's head.

"Now comes the worst part."

Izquierdo had urged Henry to seduce his wife.

Another long silence. Roger waited.

The office seemed to have become a confessional of the newer sort, penitent facing the confessor, trying not to make what he had done seem less awful than it was. Henry had fallen in with the scheme. His entree was to go to Mrs. Izquierdo and tell her, as if in shock, that her husband was carrying on an affair with Professor Goessen.

"She believed me. I believed myself. Maybe it was true. At first she was angry at me, kill the messenger, but then she started to cry, and . . ."

And he had taken the older woman in his arms, he had brushed away her tears, he had murmured a line of Swinburne.

"Then she laughed and pushed me away. Her laughing cleared the air. She made coffee and we sat and she told me what a bastard she had married. I already knew that."

She asked if her husband had sent him to her. He denied it but didn't think she believed him. The question put him in a light that alarmed him. What had he become?

"That's when I set fire to his car."

Henry waited for Roger to express shock, but Roger only nodded.

"The fire in his wastebasket suggested it to me. That and the threatening letters."

"Tell me about those."

"We composed them. I delivered them, the invisible messenger in his campus security uniform. He delivered the one to Wack himself, slipped it under his door. What a pair."

In the parking lot outside the window, car engines were starting up. It had grown dark, an early winter evening.

"Why did you and Larry Douglas go to his office that night?"

Henry smiled. "I was already there when Larry showed up. I don't know which of us was more scared when he came in and saw me."

"You were already there?"

"Izquierdo had given me a key. He told me I could use the office whenever he wasn't there. The idea was that in the evening it would be free."

"You went there often?"

"At first, when I was still impressed by him."

"You were just there working when Larry showed up."

Henry shook his head. "I was trying to figure out some way to really shake him. I thought his Corvette going up in flames would do it, but he was almost calm. He was sure his wife had done it."

"I can understand why you are worried."

He had a key to the office; he had come to loathe Izquierdo, feeling he had turned him into a monster like himself. Of course that would be considered motive enough to kill the man.

"I didn't do it."

But which "I" hadn't done it? It is all too easy for us to separate ourselves from our deeds. Augustine had developed that in the *Confessions*. The telephone rang and they both stared at it. Seven rings and then it stopped.

"That will be my brother, wondering where I am."

"Tell me what to do."

"Come home with me and have supper."

"I'll have to call my mom."

Roger pushed the phone toward him. He swung away while Henry talked to his mother. How his voice changed, softer, gentle. Then a long silence before he hung up.

"Stewart has been there. With a warrant."

As he got into his hooded outer garment, Roger said, "What I don't understand is the scarves."

"Neither do I."

Phil was waiting anxiously when Roger came in. "I've brought a guest."

"Jimmy's coming." Phil's tone told Roger that something was up.

In the kitchen, Roger donned his baseball cap and wrapped himself in a huge apron and put water on for pasta.

"There's beer in the icebox."

"I don't drink."

"Neither do I."

"That's more for me," Phil said, trying to sound cheerful.

Roger had already dished up when Jimmy Stewart came. He tried not to look surprised when he saw Henry Grabowski at the table. But he waited until they were finished, and the dishes taken away.

"I've been to your house," Jimmy said to Henry.

"My mom told me."

"With a warrant. You're in trouble, son."

Henry looked at Roger as if everything he had told him could help him now.

"I found this scarf in your drawer. Want to tell me about that?"

"My mom bought it for me."

"Now we have three of the damned things."

"Maybe I will have a beer."

Henry got up, started toward the kitchen, then dashed for the outer door, pulling it open and rushing outside. It took quite a struggle before Phil and Jimmy subdued him. Roger, still wearing his baseball cap and apron, brought Henry his jacket. The boy looked desolately at him when he was put in the backseat of Jimmy's prowler. Phil got in beside him. Roger stood in the snow watching the red taillights disappear into the night.

PART FOUR

1   THE   CASE   AGAINST   HENRY
Grabowski was, as had been that
against Larry Douglas, circumstantial—only there were
more circumstances. In Larry's case, it had been the fact
that he had surreptitiously gained entry to Izquierdo's office,
plus the scarf found in his room and thought to be the murder weapon. Mrs. Izquierdo's production of the identical
scarf from the hall closet in the Izquierdo home led to the
release of Larry, to the disappointment of Fauxhall, the
deputy prosecutor, and to the relief of Jimmy Stewart. Jimmy
had never been able to convince himself that Larry could
have done such a thing. He was having a similar problem
with Henry.

Listening to Jimmy and Phil discuss the arrest, Roger was
of two minds as to whether he ought to tell them things that he
knew only because Henry had confided in him. Of those
things, the most significant was Henry's claim that he had set
fire to Izquierdo's Corvette. At the moment, that seemed only
slightly more important than the fire that had been set in
Izquierdo's wastebasket, except of course that it suggested
something more than a mild dislike for Henry's quondam
mentor.

It was the testimony of Oscar Wack that Henry was a frequent visitor to Izquierdo's office, and Henry's own admission that he had a key to the office and had been told he might use it when the professor was not in, that weighed heavily against Henry.

"How often did you go there?"

"For a while, it was several times a week."

"During the day?"

"No. He would be there during the day." Henry made a face. "And of course I work."

"So it was only at night that you used the office."

"During the day, when I went, it was for tutoring. That's what we called it."

"You're a student?"

"I work in campus security." There was a bitter edge to his voice.

"It sounds to me that you were working more than any student."

"But less than a cop?"

Jimmy found him a smart-ass, but he liked him. Larry Douglas was the kind of eager beaver it was hard not to like, whereas Henry made it tough. But Jimmy had talked with Bat Masterson, and he knew the lifelong dream that had been smashed when Henry had not been admitted to Notre Dame. Sure, it was stupid for a kid with that much talent not to alter course and get an education, but Jimmy kind of liked the stubbornness of Henry's decision. It reminded him of himself in arguments with Hazel—and similarly disappointing consequences.

So Henry had opportunity; there were witnesses galore to that, along with Henry's own admission. He said he had never worn the scarf found in his room, the one identical to that found in Larry's loft and the other found in the Izquierdo hall closet. The lab couldn't verify that. All three scarves looked new. Motive?

Henry shrugged. "He was an arrogant SOB. At first I was flattered by the attention, but that didn't last."

Oscar Wack was sure that the pogo stick was the key to the whole thing. What more did anyone need? Admittedly, it had been planted in Wack's room by Henry's accomplice, the previous suspect, but there it was.

"Where is what?"

Wack narrowed his eyes. "They were both tools of Izquierdo. He had enlisted them in his war against . . ." Wack worked his lips. "Against his colleagues."

"Oscar, don't be ridiculous." Lucy Goessen sat at the table in the Decio eatery with Jimmy and Wack.

"I am not in the habit of being ridiculous."

"All it takes is practice."

"Did they or did they not put Izquierdo's pogo stick in my office?"

"Oscar, even if they did, he did, whoever did, there is nothing sinister about it."

"Has anyone ever left a pogo stick in your office?"

"I wish they would."

Oscar sniffed. "Perhaps Raul bequeathed you his."

"I'll ask Pauline."

Jimmy asked Mrs. Izquierdo about it and she just looked at him.

"A pogo stick!" He began to describe it, and she stopped him. "I know what it is. Belonging to Raul?"

"For exercising?"

"'Exercise is the simulated labor of the decadent.' I am quoting. One of his peeves was all the emphasis on healthiness. Wellness." She shuddered. "That I could sympathize with him on." She didn't have a spare pound on her, so she could afford to make light of exercise.

"Don't get me wrong. I run. It's all these machines, the factory look of the wellness center, that gets to me. Running is as ancient as cavemen."

"And cavewomen?"

Jimmy found himself responding to what he would have hesitated to call her flirtiness. Call it an irrepressible femininity. He hadn't felt this way since . . . Forget about it.

"So he didn't own a pogo stick?"

"Never."

Not to waste taxpayers' money, Jimmy mentioned it to Larry Douglas as something it would be nice to figure out. Larry got the message. Jimmy half expected him to lay a finger alongside his nose.

Jimmy himself sat in his office, staring at the wall. Someone had strangled Raul Izquierdo, and it looked as if Henry Grabowski would stand trial for it. By the time it got to court, the charge might have been whittled down to manslaughter; the jury would follow along, in their minds correcting procedures by reference to all the television dramas they had seen. The cops were the bums, the accused not only presumed innocent but all the more so because he had been accused. By the time it was over, Henry might be awarded a scholarship to Notre Dame.

Not funny.

Furlong had wangled a court appointment to defend Henry, who assured the lawyer he didn't have a dime.

"Justice isn't for sale."

"How much do they give you for representing me?"

Furlong ignored that. Jimmy left lawyer and client to their own devices. It was a dark thought that Fauxhall, the assistant prosecutor, had colluded in the appointment of Furlong. The little lawyer with the darting eyes could be the prosecution's secret weapon.

2 ──────▶ PHILIP KNIGHT STILL TALKED with Jimmy about the case, but he thought his work was done.

"At least it wasn't a student," Father Carmody said. He was getting his cigar ready for the match. Holy Cross House was smoke free, but when reminded of it Carmody always replied, "All right. Where are the free smokes?" The nurses weren't likely to insist on the rule with someone who had the gravitas of Father Carmody. Roger's phrase. The lawlessness of gravity? Phil shook his head. He had to get away. The next thing you knew, he would be auditing classes.

"More snow is predicted," he told Father Carmody.

Father Carmody smiled. He liked a snowbound campus. Notre Dame was the universe for the old priest, so he didn't feel deprived. His traveling days were over. Once he had spent a good portion of his time visiting various alumni around the country—around the world, for that matter—and bringing home the bacon for Notre Dame. He didn't miss it as much as he claimed. In any case, alumni came to him. Quirk. Reminded of Quirk, Father Carmody lit his cigar and disappeared in a cloud of smoke.

"I'm surprised he hasn't moved back here. Like Bastable."

"Bastable."

So Phil got the story on Bastable. Roger had called Phil's attention to the op-ed page in the *Observer* that had recently appeared. After a few swipes at the publication in which he was appearing, Bastable settled into the persona of an Old Testament prophet. His was an open letter to the president. Recent events on campus were the beginning of a divine judgment on the university. Warnings. There was still time to turn back. That a professed atheist had been on the faculty of Notre Dame indicated the extent of the decline from the days of yore. Who knew what other horrible revelations might be made? And please don't be deluded into thinking that the resurrection of the Fighting Irish was a sign of divine approval. Whom God would destroy, he first makes mad. Fanatic.

Bastable spelled it out. Fans. It was pretty bad. Right there he lost whatever wild sympathy he might have commanded. You don't talk that way about Notre Dame football. It didn't help that Bastable added that there are no atheists on the gridiron.

"You'd think he had been an English major," Father Carmody said.

What he was majoring in during his retirement years was divine discontent.

"Do you see much of him, Father?"

"I'm never in to cranks."

It was Roger's remark that he would like to meet Bastable that sent Phil to the town house overlooking the St. Joseph River. A large comfortable woman with her finger in a jumbo paperback, marking her place, answered the door. Phil told her who he was. She kept smiling. Then, stretching it a bit, Phil said Father Carmody had suggested he stop by.

"Carmody!"

She stepped aside, and the man who came forward was obviously Bastable.

"Philip Knight," the woman said, and slippered away.

Bastable's face lit up with delight. He had made the connection with Roger.

"Come in, come in." He took Phil's elbow and led him into what he called Command Central. He turned down the volume on Rush Limbaugh, then turned it off. "I'm taping it anyway. Why doesn't your brother ever return my calls?"

"This is quite a setup you've got here."

"State of the art. Where would we be without the Internet? At the mercy of the media, that's what. Take a pew, take a pew. Can I get you a drink?"

"No thanks."

"Diet Sprite. I drink six cans a day. It keeps the system running, if you know what I mean."

Phil was still standing, looking out at the river. "What a view."

Bastable stood beside him. "The awful thing is that I almost never notice it anymore."

When they finally sat, he told Phil of his plans for retirement. He and Florence would settle in South Bend, to be near the institutions that had formed them. "Florence is a St. Mary's girl." They had imagined taking part in campus events, attending lectures, plays, and of course sporting events.

"Who was it said you can't go home again? You can't go back to school again either. It's no longer there. But it isn't just that things are different. Tell me, what does your brother really think of Notre Dame?"

"We have an agreement. I don't speak for him, and he doesn't speak for me."

"Okay. What do you think?"

"I came for the sports."

"Sure. That's fine. But you must have some view on where Notre Dame is headed."

"Mr. Bastable, you have to understand, I'm not Catholic. Roger is, but I'm not."

Bastable stared at him. "Not a Catholic? I'm surprised they didn't offer you a professorship."

"I'm a private detective."

Bastable moved forward in his chair. "I had heard that." He seemed to be thinking. "How would you like a job?"

"Not particularly. I'm more or less retired."

"I would make it worth your while."

Phil shrugged. He found he wanted to hear what Bastable had in mind.

"Look, it can be as hush-hush as you want. You're inside, you have connections. I think that atheist who was strangled was only the tip of the iceberg."

He wanted Phil to dig up dirt on Notre Dame. What kind of alumnus was he? Bastable seemed to sense the question.

"You know what our trouble is as alumni? We refuse to believe anything bad about this place. You don't graduate from Notre Dame. At commencement you're turned into an alumnus. We trip over one another giving money to the place, and never ask what we are underwriting."

Phil heard him out. It was a shame that a man made himself as unhappy as Bastable clearly was. Maybe it was his way of being happy. Phil told him he wasn't interested.

"Think about it."

"I've met your classmate Quirk."

Bastable beamed. But then gloom returned. "He has some crazy scheme of getting Notre Dame to buy a villa in Sorrento. He actually wanted me to contribute." Bastable shook his head. "And he is pinning his hopes on Fred Fenster. Ha."

"You don't think Fenster will come through?"

"You know where he is right now? In a Trappist abbey in Kentucky. He thinks prayer is the answer."

"What's the question?"

"Maybe you're right," Bastable said enigmatically, and drank greedily from his can of Diet Sprite.

3

LARRY DOUGLAS FELT THAT HE was on His Majesty's Secret Service. He didn't tell Crenshaw that Jimmy Stewart had enlisted his help, and he didn't tell Laura either. She was as chummy as before, chummier, but Larry told her he wasn't sure he was completely over the flu.

"I need lots of rest."

"You shouldn't be working."

"Maybe not."

"I'll make soup and bring it over."

"I can't hold anything down," he lied.

Laura insisted that he go home immediately and get into bed. "I will explain to Crenshaw. Don't even answer the phone."

So Larry drooped and looked sick and got out of there. After hours on that damned bicycle it was good to get behind the wheel of his car. When he went through the campus entrance, he pulled in to Cedar Grove, got out his cell phone, and called the morgue.

"This is Larry," he said when Kimberley came on.

"I used to know someone by that name."

"I suppose you heard about Henry."

"Next they'll probably arrest your friend Laura."

"How would you like to do a little police work?"

"Like what?"

"I'll come by the morgue, okay?"

"We've got some free slabs."

It seemed a shame to be working for Jimmy Stewart and have no one know. He felt like a weasel, calling Kimberley with Henry under arrest, but after all Henry had grandly offered Kimberley to him on a platter. Have your old girl back. Henry was hard to like, no doubt about that, and Larry didn't know what he thought about the arrest. He remembered his own time downtown when he had been brought in by Jimmy and Phil Knight and there was Laura. He didn't like to remember how he had broken down and how Laura had comforted him. He stopped at his loft and changed and then went on to the morgue.

Feeley, the coroner, sat in his revolving chair, boxing the compass. He had been telling Kimberley for the hundredth time of his thwarted hopes for medical research, of the years at Mayo, of the bright future that had been dashed when he was told, run for coroner or your old man is on the street. If his father retired at sixty-five, Feeley still had years to go, and by then he'd be rusty, but he would try to get into Mayo's for a refresher. Why was he boring Kimberley with his sad story? Feeley was single and therefore, in theory at least, a rival, if Larry was in the running with Kimberley, that is.

"Business is dead," Feeley said sepulchrally when Larry asked if he could borrow Kimberley.

"Borrow me?"

" 'Neither a borrower nor a lender be.' "

Her eyes sparked; memories were enkindled. The way to her heart was through poetry.

"Let me use your phone book."

He turned to the yellow pages and looked up stores featuring athletic equipment, depressed to find so many. On the other hand, that meant a prolonged search.

"What are we after?"

"A pogo stick."

"Why not a unicycle?"

"We'll look at those, too."

The first half dozen stores said they didn't have pogo sticks in stock but they could order one for Larry. He told them maybe later, he would see if he could find a store that had one.

"I sold the only one I had two weeks ago."

"No kidding."

The clerk was adenoidal and had a bad case of acne. He couldn't keep his eyes off Kimberley.

"I sold it myself. To a real doll."

Larry had been about to get Kimberley out of there, but instinct told him to hold the phone. He asked the clerk to tell him about the customer and while he listened felt disappointment. He had been certain it would be Mrs. Izquierdo, but the woman the clerk was describing was more like Lucy Goessen.

"Did you get her name?"

"You want her name?"

"You don't have it?"

"I could look it up."

Larry flashed his Notre Dame security ID. The clerk looked

at it and then at Larry, but he had seen enough television dramas to know about undercover cops. "Come on."

The back office made Larry's loft look neat. Sales slips were tossed into a shoe box for later filing.

"Kimberley can help you."

"What are we looking for?"

"Goessen."

"Watch your language."

"Lucy Goessen."

"That's who it was," the clerk cried. Then he found the slip.

"I'll take that."

"Oh, I can't let you do that."

There was a photocopying machine in a corner of the office. Larry suggested they make a copy of the sales slip.

"Please," Kimberley added, and the clerk flicked on the copier.

When they went out to the car, Larry felt that he had hit pay dirt. His first impulse was to go out to Decio and confront Professor Goessen with what he had learned. But what had he learned? That she had bought a pogo stick. He decided it would be better to report to Jimmy Stewart.

"Want to come along?" he asked Kimberley, when he had explained his decision.

"Then what?"

"'Doubt that the stars are fire,'" he began, and she squeezed his arm.

4   IN ALL OUTWARD RESPECTS, Lucille Goessen was a daughter of her time. In departmental meetings, she voted with her sisters as a block, on every ballot for college council, academic council, whatever, she voted for females as her grandmother had once voted for all the candidates with Irish names. On the matter of the *Monologues,* she did not question the department's sponsorship of the event, nor did she snicker at the rape warnings pasted all over the door of Hilda Faineant's door. "Fair warning," Raul had commented, but Lucy only smiled, not a breach of sisterly solidarity. But the outer was not the inner.

Lucy taught eighteenth- and nineteenth-century fiction. English majors professed to be taken by *Nightmare Abbey and Crotchet Castle,* which always turned out to be a bit of a pose. *Rasselas?* Forget it. Sometimes Lucy felt that she was feeding the disgust for literature that seemed departmental policy. It was Jane Austen who divided the sheep from the goats. The goats signed on to the dismissive stance of Kingsley Amis; the sheep knew they were in touch with something real. For the latter, step one was to rinse their minds of all the cinematic distortions of the divine Jane and get them to wallow in the text. In her heart of hearts, Lucy wanted a world where women were women and men were men, where courtship was a prolonged ritual, where love was forever, the good were rewarded and the evil punished. Henry had turned out to be one of the goats.

When Raul told her of the campus cop who was brighter than any student, Lucy was ready to dismiss it as typical Izquierdian hyperbole. It might even have been a new version of his line. But the mention of Goldsmith's *The Vicar of Wakefield* caught her attention.

"He's read it?"

"Several times. Not my sort of thing. You should talk with him."

"Send him over."

Henry had read a lot, no doubt about that, but it seemed somehow ammunition in a battle he was in. Even so, it was obviously a waste that he was in campus security. Why wasn't he a student?

"I can't afford it."

She kept her door open during his visit, as male professors had once prudently done with female students. Hilda cruised by a few times during the session, her manner disapproving.

Henry failed the Jane Austen test, and that was a shame. If he could stop thinking of literature as a weapon, he could have been interesting. But he was already a disciple of Raul Izquierdo's, alas. Worse, Henry reminded her of Alan.

In graduate school it had dawned on her that she had joined something like the nunnery. Maybe a vow of chastity wasn't in prospect, but neither was anything like an ordinary marriage. Lucy was on track to becoming a female academic, and everything else in her life was presumed to be secondary to that. A few dates convinced her that the males were interested in arrangements and little more. Isn't that what feminism meant? And then on a fateful cab ride to campus she met Alan. He was driving the cab. When they got there, he got out, opened the door for her, carried her luggage to her door. He refused a tip and noted the address, and she went inside liking it that he had liked her.

He called. They arranged to meet. She didn't want her housemates to know. From the start, she felt like Lady Chatterley about it. He was smart but uneducated. They bowled; they went to sports bars; she watched more games on television than she ever had in her life. And they never talked about the fact that she was a graduate student in English. She loved it. He became her reality principle. Then, in a whoosh of romantic impetuosity, after she had passed her written exams and needed respite, they became lovers.

"So, when will it be?"

"It?"

"The wedding."

He meant it. My God. "But I'm going to be a teacher."

"I have an aunt who's a teacher."

They got married. A civil ceremony. She moved in with him, not letting her friends know he was her husband. She was leading a double life. What would it be like if she dropped out of school and . . . And what? When she was with Alan that seemed possible, but then she was awarded a Fulbright to England. He just looked at her when she told him. She tried to explain to him what a coup that was, nobody got Fulbrights to England. It was the first time they really talked about her academic life. She tried to convince him they could go to Cambridge together. He kept on staring at her. So she had to decide. In her carrel in the library, she tried to convince herself that being the wife of a cabdriver was preferable to having an academic career, but she lost the argument. Only he wouldn't have been a cabdriver anymore. It seemed to be his argument to keep her. He said he planned to drive a semi on the interstates of the country.

What would Jane Austen have done? They didn't get a divorce, they just separated. Lucy went on her Fulbright, published several articles on Peacock, and was hired by Notre Dame. Confused hopes for the future began when Alan moved to South Bend. He could drive a cab anywhere. Raul came on to her relentlessly, but she managed to keep it all on the level of laughter. Until Pauline showed up at her office, hair to her shoulders, wearing a fingertip-length coat and a colorful scarf that hung to her ankles. She came in, shut the door, and asked what the hell was going on. Lucy had no idea what she was talking about.

"Raul. Don't think I don't know."

"Sit down. What do you know?"

How do you convince a wife that you wouldn't take her husband if he came with the winning lottery ticket? In self-defense, she told Pauline about Alan. Like an idiot she wept while she told her story. Pauline sat looking at her with those beautiful big eyes that soon brimmed with tears. Then she told Lucy what it was like being married to Raul. Lucy felt a sisterly solidarity

Hilda Faineant would not have understood. When Pauline got up to go, they embraced.

"What a scarf," Lucy said.

"I bought Raul one, too."

Of course Lucy didn't tell her about Raul's shenanigans with women students. She must know about that. But why had he invented an affair with a colleague to tease Pauline with? What a relief it had been to confide in Pauline about Alan.

Then weird things began to happen. There was the fire in Raul's wastebasket; his Corvette was firebombed. Lucy wondered if this was Oscar Wack's revenge. Oscar was the only colleague she had told about Alan. It was Oscar who brought up pogo sticks, saying wistfully that he'd had one when he was a kid. So she bought one for him, bringing it to campus early one morning and getting the cleaning lady to put it in Oscar's office. Surprise, surprise. Only the surprise had been on her.

For days after Raul's body was found, Lucy avoided the third floor of Decio. The memorial service for Raul was in the chapel in Malloy, and Pauline was tragically beautiful wearing a fedora, a black coat with a fur collar, and that many-colored scarf hanging to her knees like a defiant badge of grief.

"May his soul and the souls of all the faithful departed through the mercy of God rest in peace."

At which words, Pauline whispered to Lucy, "He had no soul."

5 THE ONLY ENGLISH PROFESSOR
Mary Alice had ever liked was Lucy
Goessen, and she had kept in touch with her, more or less,
since switching majors. She had suggested doing a profile of
Professor Goessen for *Via Media* but been dissuaded. "I don't
have tenure."

Mary Alice understood. Any connection with the alternative paper could have been the kiss of death with Lucy's
colleagues. Mary Alice did cover the memorial service for
Professor Izquierdo and afterward talked with Lucy, waiting
until she was finished commiserating with the strikingly beautiful Mrs. Izquierdo.

"Come to my office," Lucy said.

So they crossed over to Decio and took the elevator to the
third floor. Before unlocking her door, Lucy stared at the
closed door across the hall and shuddered. When they were
settled with coffee, it was of Raul Izquierdo's death that they
spoke.

"There are so many things about it that don't make sense."

"Well, they've arrested the man who did it."

"Yes." She took a deep breath. "So tell me what you've
been doing."

Lucy seemed skeptical about her enthusiasm for Roger Knight, giving a little cry when she heard he was lecturing on F. Marion Crawford.

"Good grief."

"I know. But he can make anything interesting."

Lucy had never met Roger. Maybe that would have to wait until she had tenure, too. Mary Alice felt she was gushing when she explained what Roger's courses had meant for her. And she mentioned that Roger had been a private detective, with his brother Philip. Somewhat to her surprise, Lucy didn't express shock at this.

"I'd like to meet him."

"Oh, you should. I could set it up."

Lucy hesitated, then nodded. "Okay."

The following day, Mary Alice met Lucy in the library, and they walked through the parking lot east of the building to the village of graduate student houses where the Knights had an apartment.

Roger's size affected people in either of two ways, but Lucy's reaction was one Mary Alice understood. It made you want to mother the massive Huneker Professor. After the introductions, Roger sank into his special chair and then, realizing his guests were still standing, started to rise. They stopped him.

"If only I had behaved in a more gentleman-like manner," he said.

"Mr. Darcy!" Lucy cried, and from then on the visit was a dream.

Listening to the chatter about Jane Austen, Mary Alice was

aglow, having brought together two of her favorite professors to find that they were kindred spirits. Roger made popcorn and hot chocolate, falling snow was drifting by the windows, a Mozart piano concerto provided background music, it was wonderful. Inevitably, the conversation turned to the terrible events in Decio.

Roger said, "I know the detective in the case."

"Your brother?"

"Oh, Phil is just an auxiliary. I mean Jimmy Stewart."

Mary Alice described the memorial service and the beautiful Mrs. Izquierdo. "She was wearing the most colorful scarf. Long as a stole."

"I've met the young fellow who is accused of the murder," Roger said. "Did you know him?"

"He was a protégé of Raul's. What on earth he is doing working in campus security I just don't understand."

"That is curious, about Mrs. Izquierdo's scarf."

"Oh, they each had one," Lucy said. "A matching set."

Roger thought about it. "Well, that explains two of them."

Philip Knight came in then, and Roger introduced him to Lucy, but Philip was preoccupied. He had just come from downtown.

"Anything new?"

"Henry Grabowski has confessed to killing Izquierdo."

AFTER THE WOMEN LEFT, ROGER asked Phil to tell him all about it.

"He says he did it."

"What led him to say that?"

"The widow showed up and asked to see him. Furlong put up a fuss, but Jimmy let them talk."

"What was the point of the visit?"

"She said she wanted to see the man who had killed her husband."

Ten minutes after Mrs. Izquierdo left, Henry asked to see Fauxhall, the assistant prosecutor, and confessed.

"Of course, Furlong will plead him not guilty, but Grafton the reporter was lurking around and he heard of it, so it will be public knowledge that the accused confessed to the crime."

"What does Jimmy think?"

Henry's confession cleared up all kinds of loose ends. He had access to Izquierdo's office; that had been known for some time. The protégé had become progressively disenchanted with his mentor, particularly his boasting about all the conquests he made with women students.

"Is that true?"

"Oscar Wack says his colleague was an animal."

"I suppose it could be established one way or another."

"I doubt that Jimmy wants to get into that."

"Of course not."

In any case, fed up with Izquierdo, Henry had decided to act. The fire in the wastebasket in Izquierdo's office suggested firebombing the Corvette.

"He admitted doing that?"

"He told them to check out his car." There were an empty gas can and lengths of rags in the trunk as Henry said there would be. He thought that would be a nice touch because of the threatening notes that Izquierdo had pasted together. Henry had delivered them, in his guise as campus security, all except the one to Oscar Wack. Izquierdo wanted to do that himself. It was Izquierdo's stoic reaction to the loss of his car that elevated Henry's efforts to a tragic level. The murder had been committed in the early evening. Henry was using Izquierdo's office; the professor showed up, chuckling about the fact that his jealous wife had refused him entry to his own house. Henry ceded the desk chair; Izquierdo sat, that long many-colored scarf around his neck. Henry stepped behind him, grasped the scarf, and used it to strangle Izquierdo.

"But no scarf was found at the scene."

"He says he took it with him. For a lark, he tossed it into Larry Douglas's loft, with the result that we all know."

"Until Mrs. Izquierdo came to the rescue. So much for the mystery of the three scarves."

Phil opened a beer and checked the TV listings but didn't turn on the set. "So that's that, I guess. I'll have to let Father Carmody know."

"I said it the first time," the old priest said, when Phil telephoned him. "Thank God it wasn't a student."

Phil nibbled at the remains of the popcorn and finished his beer.

Roger said, "You don't seem very happy."

"It's all so neat."

"Oh, I don't know. What about the pogo stick?"

"Larry Douglas looked into that. It seems it was bought by Professor Goessen."

"The woman who just left?"

"I suppose Jimmy will talk to her. But what's the problem? The thing was hers, not Izquierdo's. At least she bought it. Pauline Izquierdo just laughed at the suggestion that her husband would have exercised with such a thing."

It was the following day that Roger called Professor Goessen to ask her about the pogo stick. Her explanation removed any need to explain how it had got into Oscar Wack's office. Roger wasn't surprised when she confided in him about her estranged husband.

"What does it profit a woman if she gets tenure and suffers the loss of her husband?"

"Why can't I have both?"

Phil and Jimmy Stewart had begun to wonder, first separately, then together, about Pauline Izquierdo. It was her visit to Henry that preceded his confession that each of them found intriguing. Was it some kind of absurd gallantry, or had the sight of the widow brought on remorse?

"Gallantry?" Roger asked.

"The kid's a romantic. He reads poetry."

"Ah."

But Roger was thinking of what Henry had confided in him about his unsuccessful seduction of Mrs. Izquierdo, prompted by her husband. When Phil and Jimmy went off to a Notre Dame hockey game, Roger called a cab. He had to have a talk with Henry.

Half an hour later, a cab pulled up in front of the building and Roger, all bundled up, moved slowly out to it. The driver hopped out and came to help him.

"Thank you, thank you. Do you think I'll fit?"

The cabbie laughed. "You should see the size of some of my passengers."

With an effort, and the help of the driver, Roger was wedged into the backseat, and they set off.

"The jail?"

Then Roger noticed the license displayed over the rearview mirror. Alan Goessen. His eyes met the driver's in the mirror.

"I'm going to visit a murderer."

"The kid who killed the professor?"

"That's his story."

"He performed a public service." They stopped for a red light. Alan said, "You know, I met the guy, the professor. What a jerk."

"How so?"

"I knew guys like him in the service. Real Don Juans, all they talked about was their conquests. Most of them fantasies."

"Where did you meet him?"

226

"He was sitting right where you are. I drove him home from the airport one night."

Roger remembered Lucy's story of how Pauline had come to her, accusing her of dallying with Raul. Hell hath no fury? But then came another thought.

"I know your wife, Alan. She's a brilliant woman."

The light changed, and the cab moved forward. Alan was avoiding the rearview mirror.

"Did Izquierdo talk about Lucy?"

The cab seemed to slow, then regained speed. "What do you mean?"

"She was one of his imaginary conquests."

"The guy was a jerk."

"There seems to be a consensus on that."

"His wife was no better."

"Oh."

"Driving a cab is like being a cop, you see the seamy side of everything. She was having an affair with that kid. I know, I drove him there."

"The night he killed the husband."

Alan hesitated. "You're right."

The rest of the drive was mostly in silence.

At the courthouse, Alan helped Roger out of the cab, then took his elbow and walked him to the entrance.

"Could you come back for me?"

"Sure."

"In an hour?"

Alan gave him a little salute, and Roger pushed through the revolving door.

"I'm Philip Knight's brother," Roger told the corpulent desk sergeant, who, looking at the massive speaker, seemed to grow thinner.

"So what?"

Roger sought and found his identification as a private investigator.

"I suppose it's all right."

"Think of him as a client."

"Is he?"

"You can ask him."

The sergeant thought about that, then decided against the effort it would take. He made arrangements for Henry to be brought to a visiting room and had an officer show Roger to it.

Roger was settled somewhat precariously on a chair when Henry was led in. He stared at Roger, then smiled. "What brings you here?"

" 'When I was in prison you visited me.' "

"Sure." Henry sat across from Roger.

"So you murdered Raul Izquierdo?"

Henry just looked at him.

"Someone confesses to a crime either because he did it or because he is trying to protect someone else."

"Does that exhaust the possibilities?"

"They are the only ones we need. So you think Pauline murdered her husband?"

"Look, I did it, and that's that."

Roger shook his head. "But you couldn't have."

Henry smiled. "Did implies could."

"An unassailable principle, whose counterpart is: could

not have, therefore did not. I refer to the second scarf, the one you say you put in Larry Douglas's loft."

Henry hunched forward. He was enjoying this as a puzzle. Roger could imagine the sessions Henry had had with Izquierdo.

"Why not?"

"Pauline put it there."

"Why would she do a thing like that?"

"The question is rather why you would have. You had no reason to throw suspicion on Larry Douglas. He was a friend of yours. The fact that you did not come forward when that scarf was found in Larry's place proves that you knew who did it."

"That's pretty flimsy."

"The truth is never flimsy. Of course, the scarf is relatively unimportant. More important is your alibi."

"What alibi?"

"I understand it is a delicate matter. You described your seduction of Pauline Izquierdo as unsuccessful. But it wasn't, was it? She is your alibi."

"That's crazy."

"And you are hers, aren't you? When did you leave her that night?"

Henry sat back. "You've been reading too many novels. That's a plot worthy of F. Marion Crawford."

"Indeed it is. You would confess, there would be a trial, and she would come to your rescue and say that you were with her at the time of the murder. That's the plan, isn't it?"

Henry smiled. "It's your story."

Roger put his hands flat on the table. "And Izquierdo was

already dead when you had your rendezvous with Pauline."

Clearly this had not occurred to Henry. Roger recalled for him the supposed time of the murder. "That was before you went to her, wasn't it?"

"Oh, come on." But there was a speculative look in Henry's eye.

"So you see, you can't be alibis for one another." Roger paused. "Something I am sure Pauline realizes."

Henry now had a realization of his own. He avoided Roger's eyes as if he were reviewing the events of the night Raul Izquierdo was strangled.

"She wouldn't do that to me!"

"Let's go back to your F. Marion Crawford plot. You think she killed her husband, she thinks you did. Which of you suggested your confessing? Of course, it could have been either of you who confessed, but noblesse oblige. You confess, the charade begins, she testifies, and the upshot is you are both exonerated. That was the idea, wasn't it? But why should she exonerate you if she did it?"

Henry pushed back from the table. "Save this kind of crap for your students."

"Do you trust her that much?"

Henry stood up, and the door of the room opened. An officer looked in. "Your cab is here."

"Would you have him come in here?"

"The driver?"

"Please."

"You through with him?" He meant Henry.

"Not yet."

Then Alan Goessen was standing in the doorway. He looked at Henry and Henry looked at him.

"Hi, kid."

Henry said, "Who is this?"

"Your real alibi, Henry. I regret to say that this is the man who murdered Raul Izquierdo."

POSTSCRIPT

There were some who expressed surprise at the way Alan Goessen had reacted to Roger's accusation, but Roger was not among them. It is for the Izquierdos of this world, and their apprentices such as poor Henry Grabowski, to so blind the eye of conscience that evil may parade as good. Alan's fundamental decency rendered him helpless before the truth of what he had done.

He did wheel and leave the room, and he might have left police headquarters if Phil and Jimmy Stewart had not arrived. An indication from Roger sufficed for them to prevent Alan's going, and then, feeling surrounded, almost with relief, he acknowledged the truth of what Roger had said.

Ahead lay the slow turning of the wheels of justice. Roger found that he felt sorrier for Lucy than he did for her husband. There must be some elemental sense of the rightness in killing a man who had wronged one's wife. The irony was that, whatever the truth of Raul Izquierdo's claim to be the playboy of the western world, South Bend division, there had been nothing between him and Lucy. When the truth of this was brought home to Alan, he looked at his estranged wife with an indescribable expression. She took him in his arms, and in a broken voice he asked her forgiveness. When a plea of innocence was entered for him, it seemed to have some plausibility.

"He'll probably walk," Jimmy Stewart said. He didn't sound regretful.

Larry Douglas had been accused, and he was free. Henry Grabowski had been accused, and he was free. The two young men were not true precedents for Alan Goessen, but who knew what might happen in the present state of the courts?

The liberated Henry had been reunited with Kimberley, whose mind now seemed adequate enough to match her beauty. Larry Douglas stopped by with a possessive Laura clinging to his arm, her unmittened hand displaying a diamond.

"Congratulations!" Roger said, but it was Laura who said thank you.

BETWEEN THE NOTES

Between
the
Notes

BY SHARON HUSS ROAT

HARPER TEEN
An Imprint of HarperCollinsPublishers

HarperTeen is an imprint of HarperCollins Publishers.

Between the Notes
Copyright © 2015 by Sharon Huss Roat
All rights reserved. Printed in the United States of America.
No part of this book may be used or reproduced in any manner whatsoever
without written permission except in the case of brief quotations embodied in
critical articles and reviews. For information address HarperCollins Children's
Books, a division of HarperCollins Publishers,
195 Broadway, New York, NY 10007.
www.epicreads.com

Library of Congress Control Number: 2015933430
ISBN 978-0-06-229172-1

Typography by Kate J. Engbring
15 16 17 18 19 CG/RRDH 10 9 8 7 6 5 4 3 2 1

First Edition

TO RICH, SEBASTIAN, AND ANNA

Between the Notes

ONE

I came home from school on a Thursday in early September to find my parents sitting on the couch in the front room, waiting for me. I knew immediately something wasn't right. We never sat on that couch. We never even walked into that room, with its white carpet and antique furniture. And what was Dad doing home from work, anyway?

My mother was wringing her hands, literally, like she was squeezing water out of her fingers, too preoccupied to ask me to take my shoes off in the foyer.

"What's wrong? Where's Brady?" I naturally put the two together before I realized it couldn't be him. They would not be sitting here so calmly if something had happened to my brother. There'd be a note on the kitchen counter, a frantic phone message from the hospital.

"He's at school. He's fine. Kaya's fine," said Mom. "Everything's fine."

Dad squeezed my mother's hand. "Have a seat, sweetie.

There's something your mother and I need to talk to you about."

Clearly, everything was not fine.

I dropped my book bag on the carpet with a thud that mimicked the feeling in my stomach, and lowered myself into one of my mother's favorite wingback chairs.

"What did I do?"

Mom laughed, about an octave higher than usual. *"Nothing! Nothing."*

Then Dad cleared his throat, and they broke the news like it was a hot potato, tossing it back and forth so neither of them actually had to complete an entire, terrible sentence.

"You know, my business . . ."

"Daddy's business . . ."

"It hasn't been good."

"This economy . . ."

"The whole printing industry, really . . . It's been . . . a difficult few years," said Dad, nodding and then shaking his head.

"And with Brady's therapy bills . . ." said Mom.

My spine went stiff. My parents never blamed anything on Brady's disability. It was an unspoken rule.

"We got behind on some payments," Dad was saying.

"And the bank . . ."

"The bank . . ."

They paused, neither one of them wanting to catch the next potato.

"What?" I whispered. "The bank what?"

Then Mom started to cry and Dad looked like the potato had slammed into his stomach. "The bank is foreclosing on our house," he said. "We have to move."

I suddenly felt small amid the lush upholstery, like the chair might swallow me whole.

"Huh?"

"We've lost the house," Dad said quietly. "We're moving."

I couldn't seem to process what he was saying, though it seemed plain enough. "This is *our* house," I said. They couldn't take *our* house. We couldn't move. Not away from my best friend, Reesa, who lived next door; and my lilac-colored room with its four-poster bed; and the window seat with its extra-fluffy pillows; and my closet where I could see everything; and . . . and my piano room, and . . .

"We can't move," I said.

They shook their heads. They said, "We're sorry," and "We hate this, too," and "There's nothing we can do," and "It's the only way . . . ," and "We're sorry. We're so, so sorry."

I threw a dozen what-if scenarios at them: "What if Mom gets a job?" "What if I get a job?" "What if we just stop buying stuff we don't really need?" "Get rid of my phone?" "Sell the silver?"

"Your mother *is* getting a job," Dad said. We wouldn't be buying anything but necessities, the silver had already been sold, and yes, they'd be canceling my cell phone service. Even with all that, we still couldn't afford the mortgage. In fact, we'd barely be making ends meet in the way-less-expensive apartment we'd be renting.

"What about Nana?" My grandma Emerson lived about two hours away in a farmhouse. She had chickens and made soap from the herbs in her garden. Lavender rosemary. Lemon basil. She always smelled like a cup of lemon zinger tea. "Can't she loan us money?"

Dad dropped his chin to his chest.

"Ivy," said Mom, "she lives off Social Security and the little bit she makes selling her soap at craft fairs. She can't help us."

"Aunt Betty? Uncle Dean?"

My parents shook their heads. "They have their own problems, their own bills, their own kids to send to college," Dad said.

The air went out of my lungs; my bones seemed to go out of my limbs. I couldn't even lift an arm to wipe my tears.

"I know this is hard, but it's necessary." She paused. "Please don't cry. The twins will be home soon. We don't want to upset Brady."

I took a shuddery breath, but the tears were refusing to stop. Mom looked nervously out the front window.

"The bus is coming," she said. "Here." She offered me a wad of Kleenex.

I nodded, took the tissues from her hand, and sniffled my way to the stairs. We didn't cry in front of Brady. We didn't raise our voices or have freak-outs of any kind if we could help it.

My little brother had a seizure disorder when he was a baby. His brain had been wracked by spasms for months, and while they had finally stopped, he now struggled to walk and talk and understand the world around him. If you got angry or emotional in front of him, he thought you were upset with him or, as the doctors said, he "internalized." Then it took hours to pry his hands away from his ears and calm him down.

I went upstairs to the music room and closed the door. It had taken a special crane to get the baby grand up here through French doors that opened onto the balcony. I sat at the piano bench and played a tumble of scales and chords until my hands turned to heavy bags of sand and I dragged them over the keys. The resulting noise was satisfying. It sounded exactly how I felt.

Out the window, I saw Brady and Kaya walking up our long driveway. They were six years old and I was sixteen. I remembered when my parents brought them home from the hospital. Brady was perfect then. The seizures didn't start until six months later. We were so worried Kaya would get them, too, but she never did.

She held his backpack for him. It always took a while for them to make their way to the porch, because Brady stopped every few steps to pick up a pebble or stray bit of asphalt and throw it into the grass. We had the cleanest driveway on the planet.

When they neared the house, Mom and Dad walked out to greet them with hugs and pasted-on smiles. I wasn't ready to pretend everything was okay, not even for Brady.

I just continued to play my piano.

When I saw where we were moving a week later, my throat closed up and I could barely breathe. Mom made it all sound like a fabulous adventure, like camping in a deluxe cabin.

"It's really very nice," she said. "Three bedrooms, two baths, walk-in closets. Even wifi."

"Golly, Mom. Do you think we'll have running water? And heat?" Sarcasm was one of the few ways I could say what I truly felt in front of Brady, as long as I paired it with a smile.

"Of course, sweetheart." Mom smiled sarcastically right back. "Refrigeration, too. And bunk beds!"

"Brady get bunk bed!" he exclaimed with a sweet smile.

It was amazing how easily six-year-olds could be won over by the promise of narrow sleeping surfaces stacked on top of each other. Mom and Dad were just relieved he wasn't traumatized by the whole thing, and made no attempt to redirect him to a new topic or coach him to speak in complete sentences like they usually did.

I ruffled his soft, blond hair, the hair I wished I could trade for my mop of brown, frizz-prone curls. "Bunk beds are cool." We'd been talking up the benefits of the bottom bunk in particular, so he wouldn't want the top. It was too dangerous for him.

He hugged my leg. "Ivy bunk bed!"

I kissed his head and quickly turned back to the dishes I was wrapping in newspaper. My bags and boxes were packed with what little I was allowed to take to our new home. Essentials and favorites only, Dad had said. The rest would go into storage or be sold, because the new place was "more economical." I was pretty sure that was code for "crappy little apartment," but I wouldn't know for sure until Dad got home and took us to check out the place.

The phone rang and I heard Mom answer in the next room, a den with a circular fireplace we always sat around on New Year's Eve to roast marshmallows.

"Oh, hi, Reesa. . . . Yes, she's here. Why don't you come over? Ivy's just—"

I lunged for the kitchen phone. "Mom! I've got it. You can hang up."

I waited for the click. "Hey. I'm here."

"I kind of noticed that when you screamed in my ear. You want me to come over?"

"No!" I closed my eyes and took a calming breath. "No, I'm . . . Mom has us all doing chores. She's, um . . . she's giving a bunch of old dishes away. For a charity thing."

I wasn't quite ready to tell her that *we* were the charity thing. I kept thinking if I didn't tell anyone, it wouldn't happen.

"Then you totally need me. I know how to pack china so it won't break," said Reesa. "Remember my job at the antiques store?"

"You worked there for one day. They made you dust."

Reesa laughed. "Okay, fine. But I did learn how to wrap flat-ware before I quit."

"That's okay," I said. "I'm almost done, and we have to go out when my dad gets home, anyway."

I managed to rush her off the phone before she could ask where we were going. When I hung up, Mom joined me across the table. She slid a dish onto newspaper and folded four corners to its center. "You haven't told her?"

I shook my head. "Not yet."

She wrapped another plate, and another, alternately stacking hers with mine. When I placed the last plate on the pile, she rested her hands on top and sighed. "We're moving this weekend, sweetie. You should tell your friends."

"I will. I'm just waiting . . ." I didn't know what I was waiting for. That sweepstakes guy to show up with a gigantic check for a million dollars and a bouquet of roses, maybe? "I want to see it first. That's all."

As if on cue, Dad walked into the kitchen and laid his brief-case heavily on the counter. He didn't say a word. He didn't have to. His look of nervous resignation was enough to announce it was time to go see our new place, ready or not.

We loaded into the Mercedes SUV, which now sported a hand-made FOR SALE sign in the rear window. Mom chattered on about how nice the new apartment was. Her voice sounded thinner than normal, like she couldn't get enough air. "It's smaller, of course. But plenty of room for the five of us. Three bedrooms..."

She kept saying "three bedrooms" like it was a huge deal. I should've known the sleeping accommodations were the least of my troubles. It was like worrying that your tray table is too small on an airplane that's about to crash.

I hid my face behind the FOR SALE sign, picking at the tape that held it in place, while Brady and Kaya bounced in their booster seats. My father steered the car down our long, curving driveway. The wrought-iron gate swung open as we approached, triggered by a motion sensor that was perfectly timed to release us without a moment's delay. My parents hadn't installed the gate or the fence around our property to keep people out, but rather to keep Brady in. He had a tendency to wander. Still, it kept visitors from stopping by unannounced, so none of my friends had discovered we were moving yet. I was hoping to keep it that way.

My nail polish, a glossy fuchsia, had started to chip. I scraped one thumbnail against the other as we passed Reesa's house. Their gate was sculpted of copper with an ornate letter M for Morgan in the middle. It was flashy and curvy and shiny like she was. But more important, it was right next door. The distance between her kitchen door and ours was precisely seventy-seven steps—or fifty-three cartwheels. Though we hadn't traveled via cartwheel in a few years, we had sworn to always live next to each other, even when we went off to college. Even when we got married. "Our kids will be best friends," we always said.

I lifted my head like a prairie dog. "Maybe the people who buy our place will rent it back to us."

Daddy darted a warning glance at me in the rearview mirror. Brady and Kaya didn't know the house was going to be sold. "Nobody's buying our place," he said.

My parents wanted to spare the twins the full details of our situation, so they wouldn't be overly traumatized. (Was there such a thing as moderate trauma?) We were telling them this was a temporary move while work was being done on the house.

A big fat lie, I'd said.

A little white lie, Mom insisted.

"Oh, yeah." I winked at Kaya, who squinted back. She was totally onto them, but also very well trained in the ways of the let's-not-upset-Brady bunch.

I twisted around to watch the rolling hills of Westside Falls disappear behind me as we headed toward the city of Belleview, then slouched back down in my seat. Maybe the new place wouldn't be so bad, after all. Small, but cozy. Like Brady's bunk bed. Maybe it would be located on one of those cute streets in the city where the houses were like Manhattan brownstones, and I'd be close enough to walk to my favorite shops.

We hadn't been driving long, maybe six or seven minutes, when my father turned left at an intersection we usually went

straight through. I sat up taller, the fine hairs on my arms standing at attention as we passed some industrial buildings and
warehouses, an abandoned gas station, and a vacant parking lot
with weeds sprouting through crumbled asphalt. "Wait, we're
not . . . where is this place, exactly?"

"It's in district." There was definitely something weird about my
mother's voice. "You won't have to change schools or anything."

I froze, swallowing hard. "But it's . . . it's not . . ." Another
warning glance from my father confirmed what my arm hairs
had been trying to tell me.

We were moving to Lakeside.

Like Westside Falls, Lakeside was a suburb of Belleview. But
that's where the similarities ended. Lakeside was a bad neighborhood that had been added to our otherwise posh school district
a few years ago when they redrew the boundaries. There wasn't
even a lake there, only a reservoir where they'd flooded a valley
years ago to provide water to the nearby city of Belleview. I'd
never actually been to Lakeside myself—we never drove this way
when we went downtown to shop or go to restaurants—but I'd
heard plenty. Somebody's cousin's best friend's mom got car-
jacked when she took a wrong turn and asked for directions. And
everyone said if you wanted to buy drugs, all you had to do was
look for a corner where a pair of high-top sneakers were dangling from the phone wires above.

The worst part was how all the Lakeside kids who attended
Vanderbilt High rode a single bus to school, and everyone joked

that it came from the state penitentiary, which was on the other side of the reservoir.

No way was I riding that state pen bus to school.

We slowed down as an exceptionally ugly apartment building loomed ahead, its sign promising GARDEN TERRACE ESTATES though there was neither a garden nor a terrace in sight. It did have balconies, though, which were strewn with deck chairs, grills, and . . . was that a giant, inflatable snowman drooping over the railing? I closed my eyes and didn't open them until the car bumped to a stop and Daddy said, "Here we are."

The twins scrambled out, squealing. I opened my left eye, and it immediately started twitching . . . as if trying to protect me from what it was about to see. I pressed my palm to the lid to make it stop and squinted through the other eye. Mom pulled my car door open and held her hand out to me. I finally lifted my arm and slipped my fingers into hers.

I was relieved, at first, that what stood in front of me didn't have balconies full of deflated Christmas decorations. It wasn't an apartment building at all, but a tall, skinny, brown house on its own little plot of land. It looked like a row home that had lost its neighbors and might teeter over sideways in a stiff wind.

"I thought you said we were moving into an apartment." I stayed close to the car, figuring they'd made some kind of mistake.

"We are." My father pulled some keys from his pocket and strode up the steps to the front porch. "Top two floors are ours, plus the attic. The owner lives downstairs."

He jiggled a key in the lock and held the door open as the twins scampered inside. Brady almost tumbled over backward craning his neck to view the steep flight of stairs in front of him before turning around to scoot up on his bottom. I wanted to turn around, too. And *run*. My feet shuffled backward until I was leaning against the car, staring at the exterior of our new home. The vinyl siding was the standard Crayola shade of brown (no chestnut or copper or raw umber for us). The fake shutters were painted a slightly lighter brown, like a chocolate mousse, and the front steps were the color of mud. The lawn was more weeds than grass, but at least it was green. Ish.

I walked toward the porch steps but couldn't bring myself to go any farther. It was my mother's face that stopped me. For the thinnest whisper of a moment, her brave smile had slipped, and I caught her reaction. The same panic and dread that clenched my stomach were reflected back to me in her eyes.

She was as scared as I was.

"Coming in?" Mom held the screen door open, her everything-will-be-just-fine mask back in place.

"Sure," I said. "In a sec."

I waited for her to disappear inside before attempting my escape but only made it as far as the edge of our yard, all of ten paces away. I stood there, looking around. The neighborhood didn't appear to be laid out in any sort of grid. Houses were scattered at random angles, as if they'd sauntered up the hill, spied an empty lot, and plopped down. A gravel road meandered between them. Our house was the only one taller than two stories, dwarfing the squat little houses and cabins around it. Bungalows? I wasn't sure what to call them.

Some kids on bicycles came tearing around the corner, skidding on the gravel road. They headed for the playground across from our house, bumping over the grass and dirt and hopping off their bikes to make a pass across the monkey bars. They noticed me standing there, and one of the little girls stared for a minute, then said something I couldn't hear to the others and they all leaped back on their bikes and rode away.

I vaguely registered the creak of door hinges behind me and expected to hear my parents calling me inside. But they didn't. Nobody was there when I turned. I looked toward the neighboring house, a small brick ranch surrounded by a tall hedge. Nobody there, either, but I noticed for the first time an older-model Jeep parked out front. It was bright red and immaculately clean, the only vehicle I'd seen so far that wasn't covered in a film of dust from the gravel road.

I was staring at the Jeep, thinking it didn't belong here any more than I did, when its engine revved. Jumping back, I fell against the rear bumper of our car. The Jeep lurched forward and rumbled my way. I regained my balance and stood there like I'd never seen an automobile before as it covered the short distance between us and rolled to a stop in front of me.

A tattooed arm, lean but muscled, stuck out the window. It

looked familiar, and when I lifted my gaze to the driver's face, I knew where I'd seen it before. Or, rather, where I'd *ignored it before*.

The tattoo—an intricate pattern of chains and gears—belonged to none other than Lennie Lazarski, a senior at Vanderbilt High School and its most notorious druggie.

His black hair, always tied in a short ponytail at school, hung wet and loose around his face like he'd just showered. He drummed his fingers on the outside of the Jeep's door, flexing his tattoo as he looked me up and down. Then the corner of his lips curled into a lopsided grin.

"Ivy. Emerson." He punctuated my name like that, slowly, in two parts.

I didn't think it necessary to acknowledge that I was, indeed, Ivy Emerson. Or that I knew who he was. Not that I could've spoken if I'd wanted to. My mouth was suddenly very dry, and my throat . . . my throat was doing its squeezed-tight thing. I stared at him, blinking. Hoping he'd disappear.

Lazarski's eyes darted from me to our car to the brown house and back to me. He let out a single, raspy snort of laughter, then gunned the Jeep's engine again and drove off, stirring up a cloud of dust that billowed at my feet.

TWO

" hou hast thine period?" Reesa said in a British accent. She was trying to guess the source of my agony as we sat in her bedroom after school on Friday.

Moan.

"Thy mother hath readeth thine diary?"

Reesa had been talking like this since we started studying Chaucer in AP English the week before. I shook my head, moaned some more. I didn't keep a diary, exactly. It was more of a journal, where I scribbled bits of poetry and song lyrics and occasional rants I couldn't rant about in front of Brady.

"They didn't have the dress thine wantedeth in a size zero?"

Already I felt the wedge, a little sliver of a thing at first, start to wiggle its way between us. In Reesa's world, the one I'd lived in until last week's big foreclosure reveal, the worst imaginable causes for distress were things like cramps. And a dearth of cute dresses.

"Not even close," I said.

She plopped down next to me. "I giveth up."

I took a deep breath. "You need to swear you won't tell anyone or laugh or stop being my friend. And you need to promise you will lie, if necessary, to protect me."

"Oh, my God, yes, yes, yes," she said. "Tell me. What is going on?"

I lifted a stuffed koala bear from her bed and pressed it to my face, peering over its fluffy head to gauge her reaction as I spoke the horrible words. "We're moving. To Lakeside."

Her eyes got big. "Uhhh . . . what?"

"We're moving."

"Yeah, I got that part, which is just . . . wrong. But I could swear you said you're moving to Lakeside. And that's insane."

"We're moving into an apartment over there. In a house. It's behind a long-term storage place off Jackson Boulevard, you know?"

Reesa did not know. Her blank stare got blanker.

"There's a Save-a-Buck store at the corner. Or Save-a-Cent. Whatever it's called. It's . . . it's over there." I waved feebly in the general direction of my new neighborhood.

"B-but, why?" She could not have looked more shocked and disgusted if I'd announced I was pursuing a career as a pole dancer.

"My parents are totally broke. The bank is foreclosing on our house. We're . . ." I lowered my voice. "We're *poor*."

"That's not possible. How is that possible?"

I tried to explain what my parents had told me, how my father had put our house up as collateral on a business loan right before the economy tanked. It hadn't seemed like much of a risk at the time because sales had tripled the year before. Then everything bottomed out, and Brady started having all kinds of therapy. My mom had to stop working to take care of Brady, and they couldn't keep up.

"It came down to paying our mortgage or paying for Brady's therapy," I said. "And they couldn't exactly stop teaching him how to talk and stuff."

Reesa squeezed her cheeks between her hands, nodding. She knew. Outside our immediate family, she was one of the few people who knew the challenges Brady faced, how hard everything was for him. She watched him take his first steps, applauding along with the rest of us. She helped me teach him how to clap. He still claps whenever he sees her.

"Couldn't they, like, declare bankruptcy or something? That's what my uncle did and he didn't have to give up his house or his boat or anything," said Reesa.

"I don't think it's an option." Or, at least, not one my father was willing to consider. I had overheard my parents arguing about it months ago, one of many signs of our impending doom that I'd ignored. When I walked in and asked what was wrong, they said everything was fine. *Nothing for you to worry about, sweetie.*

Maybe they'd thought they could fix it, that something would come up. But it hadn't. They'd put off the inevitable as long as they could. "Dad said we just have to live within our means. Make it work."

"Like *Project Runway*."

"I wish." I flopped back on the bed. "Try 'Project Poverty.'"

Reesa crinkled her nose as if she'd just taken a whiff of the girls' locker room at school. I had thought it would make me feel better to tell Reesa, to hear her say everything would be all right, that it wasn't so bad, that nobody would even notice or care. But she didn't say any of those things.

She said, "That sucketh."

I hadn't even described the house yet—its overwhelming brown-ness, my closet-sized bedroom. "It's not that bad," I lied, suddenly afraid of scaring her off entirely. "Kind of cozy, actually."

Reesa pouted. "I'll never see you. You'll be too busy smoking pot. And getting tattoos."

I rolled my eyes. "No, I won't." I had already decided not to mention Lennie Lazarski. Even a friend as loyal as Reesa might run screaming if I mentioned that he lived next door.

"Move over." She put her head next to mine on the pillow and we both stared at the ceiling. There were still a few of the glow-in-the-dark stars we'd stuck up there in the shape of constellations when we were twelve. "I can't believe you're leaving me."

"I'll see you at school every day, and I'll get Mom to drive me over here on weekends, and you can . . ." I almost suggested she visit me, but I didn't want to trigger that smelly-locker-room sneer again.

"I'll call you," she said. "All the time."

I pulled my phone out, dialed her number, and showed her the NO SERVICE message that popped up on the screen. "I'm officially a total loser. Just, please . . . don't tell anyone. Okay?"

"Someone might notice if you never answer your phone again."

"I'll make up some excuse. Nobody has to know I moved. *Nobody.*"

Reesa nodded, knowing exactly who I was talking about: Willow Goodwin and Wynn Davies, a.k.a. Wicked and Witch. We ate lunch with them every day, went shopping together, attended the same parties. They were among our closest friends.

And we couldn't stand them half the time.

Willow's mother was "old money" and her dad worked as an attorney, not that he had to work at all. *The only reason my dad works is so he doesn't have to hang out with my mom all day,* Willow told us. She insisted that she hated her mother, but she didn't mind the perks that came with being Frances Goodwin's daughter, like getting the role of Clara in *The Nutcracker* after her mother donated a million dollars to the Belleview Ballet.

Wynn was spoiled, too, but more so by the absence of her parents. They took their role as socialites seriously, and that meant Wynn was practically raised by a revolving door of nannies du jour. Her parents bought her whatever she wanted to keep her happy.

The two of them sat at the tippy top of the social ladder of Vanderbilt High School and made it their business to know *everything* about *everybody*.

"They'll find out," said Reesa. "They always do."

My throat tightened. I knew girls fed gossip to Willow and Wynn, simply to avoid being targeted themselves—a preemptive strike of sorts.

"Can't your parents borrow money from someone?" Reesa reached for the Tiffany-blue, polka-dotted piggy bank on her nightstand, as if its contents would make a difference.

I shook my head.

"My parents are packing up the last of our stuff right now, so we can move this weekend," I said. The bank wasn't officially foreclosing on the house for another month, but it would take a few weeks to sell all the furniture we weren't taking with us.

"This weekend?" Reesa sucked in a sharp breath. "As in tomorrow?"

I closed my eyes. "Yeah."

"This is bad."

Duh.

"But it's not, like, permanent, is it?" Reesa was going through the same five stages of Oh-Shit-This-Can't-Be-Happening that I had: denial, denial, denial, denial, and denial.

I could only shrug. My father had assured me the apartment

was a temporary fix. We'd find a regular house in Westside Falls once the debts were paid and some of our savings replenished. But he wouldn't say if "temporary" meant a few weeks or a few months. I didn't want to consider that it might be even longer.

THREE

Saturday morning I rode shotgun in the truck Daddy rented to haul our stuff. Mom was planning to follow in the car with the twins and Brady's little fish tank once she packed up the food from our fridge. I hadn't showered. My hair was knotted into the same messy bun I'd slept in, and my sweatshirt had toothpaste down the front. Not that it mattered. Nobody important would see me today.

"The red couch from the den will go in the living room," said Dad, seemingly oblivious to my unenthusiasm. "Your mother's little writing desk will fit in your room. That small dresser of Kaya's will be yours, too. . . ."

I zoned out on his detailed inventory of what we'd brought from our old house. My piano hadn't made the cut, of course. None of my bedroom furniture had, either. All of it was too big to fit in the tiny attic room that would be mine.

". . . and Carla asked one of the neighbor boys to put together a moving crew to help us unload, so it shouldn't take long."

"Who?" I said, panic rising in my throat.

"Carla Rodriguez. Our landlady. She's very nice. Your mother's already spoken to her about watching Brady and Kaya from time to time. I think you'll like her. She's—"

"No, what neighbor boy?"

"Hmm?" He bent over the steering wheel to see out my side-view mirror. "I think I just cut that guy off. Sorry!" He waggled his hand toward my window. "Give him a wave, so he doesn't think we're jerks."

I leaned out the window and offered what I hoped was a we're-not-jerks sort of wave. In the side mirror, I saw an arm shoot out of the passenger side, wave, then give me the finger.

"I'm pretty sure he still thinks we're jerks," I mumbled. I rolled up my window and ducked down in my seat.

The car continued to follow us into our new neighborhood, stopping in front of the Lazarskis' house as we pulled in front of ours.

"Uh, Dad? I think the guy we cut off is part of our moving crew . . . or he wants to kill us," I said. I slid down in my seat even more.

"Oh, great. I can apologize in person." Dad jumped out and strode over to their car. The whole embarrassing scene was visible in the driver's side-view mirror.

"Sorry 'bout that, boys," Dad said, sounding like one of those annoyingly reasonable and cheerful fathers on a 1960s sitcom. "It's harder to drive that thing than I thought." He gestured toward the truck and I ducked down farther—I was practically on the floor at this point—so they wouldn't spot me.

There was some muttering among them that I couldn't make out, and the squeak of a screen door. Someone shouted, "Lazo, my man!" A voice that I presumed was Lazo's said, "Gentlemen." And the decidedly-not-gentlemen laughed.

More muttering. Then Dad was back, opening the door to the truck. "Are you coming? Do you want to meet the boys?"

"No." I shook my head. "No way."

"Ivy, please."

I shook my head again and Daddy sighed, closed the truck door, and walked up to the front porch. I heard a woman's voice, and the door to the house closed.

Then laughing. Hooting. "'Sorry, boys,'" someone mimicked my dad's deep voice. More laughing. Then, "Shut it, dickwad," "I need a smoke," and "Are we gettin' paid to carry that asshole's furniture, or what?"

I pulled the hood of my sweatshirt up and pressed it to my ears. When Daddy came back to the truck, I would tell him to make them go away. I'd rather carry every single box up three flights of stairs myself than let any one of them step foot in our apartment.

Suddenly, the passenger door I was leaning against was yanked open, and I nearly rolled out backward.

"Shit, Emerson." Lennie Lazarski caught my shoulders from behind and shoved me back in. "What the fuck are you doing?"

A kid with a scar under his lip stood behind him laughing.

"Nice language," I said, scrambling onto the seat.

"Yeah, nice language, Leonard," said Scar Face. "Is that any way to talk to such a fine piece of Westside ass?"

Lazarski smirked. "She's not a Westsider anymore, is she?"

I wanted to shout that I was not a Lakesider and never would be, but I was *here*. In a moving truck. Waiting for my belongings to be unloaded. It was kind of hard to claim that I wasn't one of them. I reached for the door handle instead and slammed the door closed, punching the manual lock down with my fist.

"Go away," I said through the glass.

Lazarski crossed his arms over his chest and tilted his head back so he could look down his nose at me. "You gonna carry this stuff inside all by yourself?"

I took a deep, shuddery breath and cranked the window down a couple of inches, to make sure he could hear me. "Yes, we are. Your services are no longer required, so you and your friends can go home."

A slow smile spread across his lips. He uncrossed his arms and did a deep, exaggerated bow, swishing his hand in the air like he was bowing to the Queen of England. "As you wish, Your Royal Highness."

Sauntering away, he threw an arm over Scar Face's shoulder and called out to the guys, "Hear that, gentlemen? Our services are no longer required."

They all started talking over one another. "Great." "I got out of bed for this shit?" "What'd you say to her?" "This is bullshit, man." "Dude, I'm hungry." "Yeah. Let's eat." "Vinny's?" "Yeah, Vinny's."

I lay on the truck seat with my arms wrapped around my head until I finally heard four car doors slam shut and the sound of tires spinning out on gravel.

A few minutes later, the front door to our house swung open. I lifted my head to see Daddy step onto the porch, followed by a slender, dark-haired woman. Carla, I presumed. They looked toward the puff of gravel dust the car had left in its wake.

"Where'd everybody go?" said Dad.

Carla took a few steps toward Lazarski's house. "Leonard?"

I scrambled to the driver's-side door and pushed it open, jumping down to the road. Lazarski was nowhere to be seen.

Dad turned a befuddled face toward me. "What happened?"

"Nothing, they . . ." I lifted my chin, refusing to cry. "We don't need any help. We can do it ourselves."

I walked shakily to the back of the truck and pulled the lever to open the cargo doors. A box of pillows tipped over and spilled its contents onto the road. A single bark of laughter came from Lazarski's backyard. My sincere hope that he'd left with his friends was dashed. Slowly, I bent to collect the pillows and put them back in the box. I would *not* cry in front of that jerk-off. I would *not*.

Dad joined me at the truck. "Ivy," he said gently, "are—"

"Let's just get this done, Dad. Okay?"

He nodded, and we quietly started carrying things upstairs.

By the time Mom and the twins arrived, we had already made twenty trips each. As soon as I dropped a box in whichever room Mom had marked it for with her blue Sharpie, I turned around and went down for another. Carla helped us wedge the couch up the stairs and kept an eye on Brady while we hauled everything else up. We took a break a few hours later, ate sandwiches standing around the tiny counter of our new kitchen, then went back to hauling boxes.

I overheard Mom hissing at Dad when she didn't think I was listening, "We should've hired someone ourselves. Or asked some of the guys from the shop."

Dad gave her a funny look. He obviously didn't want his employees to see our new neighborhood any more than I wanted my friends to. "Too late now," he said, heaving another box from the truck. "Won't take much longer."

Six hours later, it was done.

Brady was happily introducing his fish to their new room. The tank was so close to his bed, they were practically sleeping with him. He was thrilled.

I made a final climb to my attic room, lay down on the bare mattress of my single bed, and stared at the boxes filled with the remains of my life. I didn't even have the energy to search for my earbuds and plug them into my not-a-phone-anymore to listen to music. As I closed my eyes, the noise of the neighborhood drifted in—car doors and dogs barking and the pounding bass of a passing car stereo. I took pride in being able to find music in

nearly every sound. The rustle of leaves, a squeaky swing swaying in the breeze, the slamming of lockers . . . laughter, footsteps,
sighs, even sneezes. Finding my own voice was sometimes hard,
but I could always hear the music around me.

But here, in Lakeside, I wasn't sure I'd ever hear it again.

FOUR

Someone had slipped off my shoes and unpacked a blanket to cover me. I'd slept in my clothes on that bare mattress straight through to Sunday morning and didn't wake until the sun hit my little dormer window at just the right angle to shine in my face.

I went down to use the bathroom, which was next to my parents' room on the third floor, and down again to find my family unpacking the kitchen. Mom fussed over me. Made me eat an egg. Brady wanted me to see his bunk bed. My legs ached. But I followed him up, huddled with him on the bottom bunk for a while.

I really needed to brush my teeth and shower, but the thought of climbing stairs again to get my stuff made me want to cry. The apartment was so vertical, I wondered if we wouldn't have more space if we laid the building on its side. Carla lived on the lower level, which had a kitchen addition out the back that made it a bit more spacious than the upper floors. A narrow stairway led from the front door to the second floor, which contained our living room and kitchen, and there was a little landing out the back with another set of stairs to the backyard.

Mom was not amused when I referred to the staircases as "two means of escape."

Next to the twins' bedroom was a little hallway where more stairs led up to my room, a.k.a. the attic, the fourth floor, the tippy top. Somehow, when I'd imagined living in a penthouse someday, this wasn't exactly what I'd had in mind. There wasn't even a proper door, just a rainbow-striped curtain I could pull across the opening at the top of the stairs.

The "walk-in closet" my mother had promised consisted of a bar mounted between the sloping walls of my attic room. It was more of a dive-in closet, since the single bed occupied the entire width of the room and I had to leap over it to get to my clothes. The tiny desk and dresser sat on either side of a dormer window that looked out the back.

The view out my window wasn't as bad as I'd expected. No snarling dogs pulling against chains. No yards littered with broken-down cars. There were some lawn ornaments you might not find in Westside Falls—like the small flock of plastic pink flamingoes a few houses down. But the yards were neat and tidy for the most part. People were out on their stoops or hanging their laundry or fixing their cars, talking or laughing or arguing.

Nobody I knew ever hung laundry outside or fixed their own cars.

On the road behind ours, sitting next to someone's trash, I

spied the answer to at least one of my problems: a bicycle with a FOR SALE sign taped to its spokes. My parents had sold mine in a last-ditch online auction frenzy, thinking I wouldn't care since I hardly ever rode it. But now that I faced total humiliation on the state penitentiary bus, I cared.

Our new neighborhood might have been light-years away from my old life, but it was only 3.5 miles to Vanderbilt High. So I pulled the last of my dwindling cash from my purse and walked over there.

"How much for the bike?" I asked the elderly man who answered the door.

He limped outside, leaning heavily on a cane, to size me up. I wished I'd thought to put on scruffier clothes. "Fifty," he said.

"For that old thing?" The bike was rusty. I didn't even know if the tires could hold air. "How about twenty?"

The man gasped and held a hand to his chest. "You insult me," he said. "That's a classic Schwinn. Vintage. People pay a lot of money for bikes like that."

I nodded slowly. "Well, thanks, anyway." I smiled and headed back toward the road. I had fifty dollars, but that was *all* I had. Considering the man had sat the bike so close to his trash, I had a feeling he'd take my twenty bucks. Nobody else had come up to make an offer in the hour I'd watched out my window. And from what I could tell, every other kid around here already had a mode of transportation.

The man cleared his throat a few times as I walked away.

"Now, wait up. Just a minute. I didn't say I wasn't willing to negotiate. You can have it for twenty-five."

I stopped and turned around. "If you throw in a tire pump, you have a deal."

He paused, then shuffled over to a little shed and dug around in it until he found a tire pump. I took it, gave the man his twenty-five dollars, and wheeled the bike away. It squeaked and rattled, but it rolled.

I searched for a place to hide it. The playground across from our house was surrounded by woods. I found a path that cut through the trees and tucked the bike behind a snarl of vines a few feet off the trail. Secrecy was my new best friend, apparently. It was a matter of survival, I told myself. My parents would never let me ride that thing to school. They'd have plenty of good reasons: too dark, too bumpy, no headlights, no helmet. And there were stretches where the road to school had no shoulder.

But the bus? So much scarier. I might survive the bus trip itself without being physically harmed (I heard an armed police officer rode along), but I'd be seen. And everyone would know. And that would be worse. Westsiders and Lakesiders did not mix at our school. We sat on separate sides of the cafeteria and in different sections of the bleachers at football games. It was bad enough Lennie and his friends knew I lived here, but I could be fairly certain they wouldn't be chatting with any of my friends about it. Stepping off the state pen bus in front of the building, though? I might as well announce it at a school-wide assembly.

33

Satisfied that the bike was sufficiently concealed, I turned for home—or, rather, that brown thing we were living in. I spotted Lennie walking from his backyard toward a pickup truck that was idling along the gravel road in front of our houses, so I lingered in the shadows of the tree line. He handed something through the driver's window, and the guy took a few bills from his wallet and flipped them into Lennie's hand. They chatted, laughed. I couldn't hear what they were saying, but had a pretty good idea what they were doing.

And it happened three more times that day. I saw out of our window a vehicle arriving, Lennie going out, an exchange, and the car driving off. Each transaction took less than five minutes.

"Shouldn't someone report that?" I asked when the fourth one had come and gone.

"What?" Dad continued ripping tape off empty boxes and flattening them under his foot in the backyard.

I told him what I saw.

"Don't jump to conclusions. You have no idea what's going on there."

Oh, I had ideas, all right. I just couldn't believe the guy was so bold about it.

By the afternoon, we were settled in. When your living space is roughly the size of a shoe box, it doesn't take a whole lot of time to unpack. Clothes were jammed onto that bar across my room and shoved under the bed in plastic bins. Still, I'd left at least half my wardrobe behind. "The half you've worn once and never looked at again," my mother pointed out. I could've added, *Because Willow or Wynn said it made me look fat, or wasn't the right color, or was frumpy or bunchy, or OMG their cleaning lady had the exact same blouse!* Mom was taking it all to a consignment shop, where other unsuspecting girls could relive my fashion faux pas at half the price.

The bunk beds and a marathon game of hide-and-seek had kept the twins entertained for most of the weekend. Kaya didn't even mind that Brady crawled under the exact same box whenever it was his turn to hide. She still searched and searched, calling out his name before finding him. I took them to the playground and helped him up the ladder and down the slide about eight hundred times, and he squealed with delight every single time. The monotony of it would drive most people crazy, but Brady's smile was probably the only thing keeping me from crying. So we kept on sliding.

Then came bedtime and we tried to go through our usual routine, but Kaya started noticing which of her toys were missing, like the sock monkey she hadn't played with for three years. Suddenly, it was her all-time favorite. Brady fixated on his train puzzle, one stupid train puzzle that hadn't made the cut when Mom packed their favorite things.

Kaya's shoulders quivered as she tried not to cry, but eventually, the tears came. She just couldn't hold it in anymore. I knew how she felt. Brady started rocking back and forth on the floor saying "train puzzle train puzzle" over and over again. I found a different puzzle, with dump trucks on it, but he merely clapped his hands to his ears and squeezed his eyes shut tight.

Dad appeared in the doorway to the twins' bedroom and pressed his forearms against its frame, as if he was holding the walls from crashing in on us. We all stared up at him. The crying and rocking stopped.

"Kids?" His tone was grave. "This isn't going to be easy, adjusting to our new home. It's a lot smaller. Everything we had before won't fit here. Okay? But we all need to try our best, and make do with what we have."

Kaya started whimpering again and Dad held up his hand like a stop sign, as if that would work. But, oddly, it did. She pressed her lips hard together and held her breath.

"We will make one more trip to the house. You may each pick one item to bring back. Just one. Then that's it. Got it?" His eyes locked on mine first, then Kaya's, then Brady's. We each nodded in turn.

"Get in the car," he said.

"Like this?" I gestured to the pajamas we were all wearing.

"Yep. Let's go."

Mom let out a huge sigh, and the air went back into the room. We all tumbled down the stairs and into the car. Nobody said anything the whole way there. Brady even stopped his puzzle chant. When we pulled up the driveway, our house looked so dark and empty, so lonely. So enormous.

I went to my room first, scanning the remains for that single left-behind item that would make my life in Lakeside bearable. The one thing I wanted wasn't in my room, though. It had a room of its own.

My mother had purchased my piano before I was born. It was one of the reasons they'd bought this house. She'd seen this room and known immediately it would make the perfect piano room. I started playing when I was three, but ever since the talent show debacle in fifth grade, my performances were reserved for the twins only.

Mom came up behind me then and laid her fingers next to mine on the keys. "We'll get you a keyboard for the apartment," she said. "I promise. Everything will work itself out. You'll see."

I nodded and closed the lid. We both knew it wouldn't be the same. Leaving my piano behind was like chopping off an arm. No . . . more like wearing a blindfold. Music helped me see things. Whenever I was confused or upset or frustrated, I went to the piano like it was my own private shrink. Reesa called it "Dr. Steinway."

"You're selling it," I said. It wasn't a question.

Mom nodded and stroked her hand along the curved body of the piano. "Not right away, though. The realtor for the bank said she'd find out if the people who buy the house want it."

"That's nice." I don't know why I said that, because it wasn't nice at all. But it gave me a little glimmer of hope. Maybe the house wouldn't sell. Maybe we'd get to come back and my piano would be here waiting for me.

Maybe I was still in denial.

"We have to do this for Brady," she said quietly. "We need the money. If he doesn't get the therapy now . . ."

"I know, Mom." I strode to my room before she could remind me how much the sacrifices we made now would mean for Brady's future. Even with twenty hours a week of therapy— speech and physical and occupational—his life would be a constant struggle. Without it, he didn't have a chance. Didn't I want the best for him? I would say, "Of course I do." Because I did. I only wished it didn't mean the worst for the rest of us.

I went to my wall of shelves to search for that special something to take with me and ran my fingers across the spines of my favorite books. I wanted them all, not just one. So I had decided to leave the lot of them behind. Good-bye, *Will Grayson*. Farewell, *Jane Eyre*. See ya, *Stargirl*.

I looked around. Resting on the top shelf was the ukulele my aunt Betty had given me. I hadn't played it much. It was too quiet. It could never make the entire room vibrate like the Steinway could. I reached for it and blew the dust off its frets, strummed a badly out-of-tune chord. Maybe I'd give the uke another chance. Maybe it was just the right instrument for our tiny apartment and the smallness of my voice when my throat felt tight. I tucked it under my arm and went down to the car. Dad smiled but said nothing.

Kaya got her sock monkey. After tearing through the entire house in his Superman pajamas, Brady had decided he didn't want his train puzzle after all. He chose a small, fuzzy accent pillow from the couch in the TV room. Dad raised an eyebrow, but he certainly wasn't about to argue. We'd made our choices, and that was that. Mom hadn't picked anything, though, so Dad disappeared into their room and came out with one of her slinky evening dresses.

"I don't think that'll fit you," she joked, but wrapped her arms around his neck. "Shouldn't you pick something more practical?"

He gave my mother a long kiss, long enough to make Kaya hide her eyes. "Just because we can't afford a beautiful house doesn't mean you can't have any beautiful things," he said. "It doesn't mean we'll never have an occasion to celebrate again."

Mom looked up at the house, swept her hand from one end to the other as if brushing it away. "We never needed all this," she said. "I don't know why we bought it in the first place."

The mother I knew, the one who took such pride in our home and fussed over every tiny detail of its décor—the fringe on every pillow, the angle of every chair, the potting of every plant—seemed to disappear before my eyes.

I knew our furniture would be disappearing soon, too. At least we wouldn't be there when it was carted off by the auction house. Mom said they'd get better prices than she could, but I had a feeling she just didn't want to witness our life being sold to the highest bidder, piece by piece.

Back at the apartment, my father tucked the twins into their bunk beds and read to them. Their room was directly below mine, and I could hear their soft voices filtering up the attic stairs. When Dad snapped the book shut and kissed their cheeks, I heard that, too. He flipped off the light. Click.

"Ivy sing," said Brady.

"Yeah," said Kaya. "We didn't get our song."

I'd been singing to them at bedtime since they were babies, when they'd finally put on enough weight to come home from the hospital. At our old house, the piano room was in between their two bedrooms. I would sit there and play and sing until they drifted off to sleep. It was our thing. I didn't perform anywhere else, or for anybody else. *Ever.* Not since my spectacular display of stage fright during the district-wide talent show when I was eleven. I had frozen onstage like some shocked victim of Medusa. After that, the mere thought of performing made my throat close up, like someone was strangling me.

But it was different at home—at our old home. I could play and sing there, safe behind walls of stone and layers of insulation and acres of yard and trees and space. Not these paper-thin walls.

Dad took a few steps up and poked his head in the opening to my room. I pretended to be sleeping. It was a decision my body made before my mind could convince it otherwise. I loved singing to the twins, and I hated to disappoint them. But I felt so exposed here. It was a warm night and the windows were open. People might hear me. People like . . .

"You awake?" Dad whispered.

I didn't answer. Because I'm a coward. And a liar, apparently.

Dad went back down and told the twins I had fallen asleep, that he would sing to them instead. Kaya said, "Blackbird," and Dad obliged with his soft, breathy version of the Beatles song.

When he finished, I heard the rustling below as he tucked and kissed and closed the door. Then, through the thin walls, a tiny, off-key voice:

"La-la-la-la-la." Brady was trying to sing his own la-la lullaby. That's what we called the bedtime songs I made up for him that used only the sound "la" so that he could easily sing along.

He sang his la-las over and over again, eventually lulling himself to sleep.

FIVE

There was a split second when I first woke up the next morning that I didn't feel like I was going to vomit. But then I remembered where I was, and what I faced. I hadn't heard from Reesa all weekend. No calls, and no email since we hadn't had a chance to set it up yet. No cell phone meant no texts, either. Reesa and I always used to text each other in the morning—what we were wearing, how horribly our hair was behaving. Reesa saw things in her breakfast cereal and would send me pictures: DO THESE CORNFLAKES LOOK LIKE STONEHENGE OR IS IT JUST ME?

But she'd been silent, and it felt like I'd moved to another planet.

The morning was a jumble as my family got in each other's way dodging and reaching for cereal, milk, toothbrushes, shoes, coats, backpacks. I had calculated that our new home was about the same total square footage as my parents' bedroom, bathroom, and closet in our old house. We now lived in about one-tenth the space we had before. The strangeness of it confused Brady.

It must've reminded him of a vacation house we once rented in Sea Isle—which had an outside shower but only one bathroom inside—because he kept asking, "Which way the beach?"

"Which way *to* the beach," I said, tying his shoes.

My parents hadn't corrected his speech in days—which was bad because of the way he locked onto things. It was hard for him to unlearn something once he'd gotten it wrong.

"Which way to the beach?" He smiled, proud of his good sentence.

"No beach here, buddy. But I'll take you to the playground after school. Okay?"

He gave me one of his signature kisses—a press of wet lips to my cheek, followed by a smacking sound. He hadn't quite coordinated the two yet. I kissed him back, extra hard.

My plan was to slip out by six twenty, retrieve the bicycle, and get to school before the buses. I figured Mom and Dad would be too distracted to realize I was leaving a half hour early. But I hadn't counted on Kaya watching my every move.

"Where are you going?" She stood blocking the top of the stairs that led down to the front door, arms crossed and hip jutting out.

"School," I said.

"It only takes three minutes to get to the bus stop. I timed it." She tapped her pink glitter watch.

"I like to be early. Just in case." I avoided her lie-detector gaze.

"Since when?"

"What?" This conversation was wasting precious time. I pulled my backpack onto my shoulders.

"Since when do you like to be early?"

I sighed heavily. "Since none of your business. Can I get through here, please?"

She stepped aside and waited until I reached the bottom step to cup her hands and call down to me, "Have a nice ride!"

"How did . . ." I spun around but snapped my mouth shut. Maybe she was referring to the bus ride, not bicycle. I was being paranoid. "Thanks," I managed. "You too. Let the bus driver know if anybody messes with you or Brady, okay?"

She nodded and disappeared into the living room, and I flew out the door like a claustrophobe escaping an elevator. It was much darker at six thirty than I'd expected. I stumbled around the woods searching for the Schwinn, which I'd hidden so well, nobody would ever find it. *Including me.* Using my not-a-phone-anymore as a flashlight, I swept its beam across the trees until I spotted my trusty getaway vehicle. The handlebars were cold against my bare hands. I flung a leg over the seat and steadied myself, then kicked off and pedaled across the playground toward the road.

The bike groaned beneath my weight, rattling over the gravel. My legs seemed to be groaning, too, after all the stair climbing I'd done over the weekend. But I picked up speed once I hit the paved road, the wind whipping my hair into my eyes. I hadn't thought to tie it back. At the first stop sign, I yanked my hood up and cinched it tight around my face, tucking every last stray brown curl inside.

God, I hoped nobody saw me.

The transportation office at school had given Mom a map of our new bus routes, which I'd used to figure out the most direct route by bicycle. It seemed easy enough, only one right turn and one left . . . but it all looked so different on the ground in the dim light of dawn than it had on the map. Every car that passed sent a shiver through me. Nobody knew I was out here. Someone could knock me off the road or kidnap me, take me to a soundproof cell in their basement and imprison me there. I'd never see my family again.

Maybe I was exaggerating the dangers of bicycling through Lakeside. Or maybe I should've just sucked it up and taken the bus.

I pedaled faster, swerving to miss potholes I swear were big enough to swallow small children.

My thighs were burning as I made my final turn and saw Vanderbilt High looming ahead, the lights of the parking lot casting an eerie glow through the morning mist. No buses in sight, though. Still, I didn't want to ride up to the front of the school on this thing, so I headed to the loading dock out back by the faculty parking lot. There was a hedge along the side that looked like the perfect hiding spot. I swerved toward it, bumping onto the grass and squealing to a stop. The gap between the hedge and the wall was only about ten inches wide, but if I turned the handlebar sideways a bit, the bike slipped right in. I shoved it far enough back that nobody could see it, then scanned the parking lot to make sure I wasn't being watched.

A sleek black sedan pulled in, so I crouched low and waited, wondering which of our teachers drove such a nice car. But it wasn't a teacher who stepped out, at least not one I'd ever seen before. It was a guy. Tall-ish, blond-ish, cute-ish. If he was a new student, Willow would probably be dating him by lunch. He pulled a messenger bag from the trunk and threw it over his shoulder, then walked in my direction. I ducked farther behind the wall. Why was he parking there? Maybe nobody had told him this lot was for teachers and staff only. Or was he worried his fancy car would get scratched in the student lot? I heard his footsteps approaching and, realizing I was about to be discovered squatting behind shrubbery, leaped to my feet as he rounded the corner. He jumped sideways, his startled eyes flashing to mine.

"Sorry," I squeaked. My face felt so hot, I was afraid there might be steam rising from it. "I . . . uh . . . was just . . . um."

He took in the scene of me and my bicycle hiding in the bushes, and one of his eyebrows shot up.

I went catatonic. He was standing so close and he had beautiful, pale-blue eyes. They rested on mine for a second, then drifted up to my hair, which was crammed into my hoodie.

"Oh, God." I fumbled with the drawstrings under my chin and shoved the hood back. My hair sprang out like a can of rubber snakes. I tried to flatten it down.

He took a step back and looked at his feet, like maybe he was trying to give me a moment to collect myself. But I was pretty much uncollectible at this point, so I just stood there staring at him, all sweaty and panting like a dog.

When he looked up, he tipped his chin toward the bicycle crammed into the hedges behind me. "You, uh . . . do this every day?" A sweep of sandy-blond hair fell across his eyes, and he pushed it back.

My face went redder than it already was. I didn't need a mirror. I could feel it. "I, no . . . I just . . . my bike . . ."

He teetered back on his heels a bit, hands shoved in his back pockets.

"This is the first time," I said, finally managing to form a complete sentence.

"Oh. Cool." He looked anxiously toward the front of the school. Probably eager to get away from the crazy girl in the bushes. "Well, I better go."

I nodded. "Right. Okay."

But he didn't go right away. He hesitated, like he was going to say something more, then just smiled. "Bye, then."

"Bye."

As he walked away, I felt a trickle of sweat drip down the small of my back. He must have thought I was a complete idiot. At least he was new and didn't know anybody he could blab to about my unfortunate appearance and bizarre behavior.

I knelt beside the hedge to deal with my perspiration situation, unzipping my sweatshirt to let the cool air dry my damp skin. I found a tissue in my backpack and dabbed it across my face. When I pulled it away, I saw a brown smudge. With legs.

I whimpered, shoving the dead-bug tissue into my pocket and hoisting my backpack to my shoulder. School buses were arriving. I moseyed out of my hiding place like it was perfectly normal to enter the campus through a hedge, and merged onto the sidewalk.

I was almost home free, zombie-shuffling toward the building like everyone else, when someone fell into step directly behind me. I scooted to the side to let the kid pass. But whoever it was stepped sideways right along with me. Assuming it was Reesa goofing with me, I stopped abruptly.

And then Lennie Lazarski sidled up beside me and murmured in my ear. "Hi, neighbor."

I stopped, sucked in my breath, inhaling the dead-giveaway, burnt-leaf scent of a pot smoker.

"You really should wear a helmet, you know."

"I have no idea what you're talking about," I said, picking up my pace.

He laughed. "Okay. But I still saw you."

I stopped and glared at him. "Saw me what?"

"Hiding your bicycle."

"I wasn't hiding it. I, uh . . . don't have a lock, so I parked it back there so nobody would—"

"Steal it? You think someone's going to steal that thing?" He barked out that annoying laugh of his, a single, loud "Ha!" Every-one walking within a five-mile radius turned and gawked.

My face burned for the second time that day, and it was barely seven o'clock. "It happens to be a classic Schwinn. People pay a lot of money for vintage bicycles like that, you know."

He chuckled. "Looks more like something you found, oh, I don't know . . . lying in the trash by the side of the road?"

"It wasn't in the trash, it was . . ." I snapped my mouth shut. "Why am I even talking to you?"

"Just being neighborly?"

I ran up the stairs, hoping to distance myself from him before we reached the entrance. But he took the steps two at a time and lunged to open one of the double glass doors for me.

"Thank you," I muttered.

"You're very welcome." There were two sets of doors, and he leaped ahead of me to get the second one as well. I told myself he'd go away then. He'd go his way and I'd go mine, and . . .

"So, how's life in Turd Tower so far?"

"In WHAT?" I immediately regretted the volume of my reply as another dozen people registered me talking to Lazarski. I imag-ined tiny little cameras snap, snap, snapping away, like paparazzi. "What are you talking about?" I asked, trying to speak without moving my lips.

"Your house," he said. "Don't tell me you haven't noticed it kinda looks like a giant turd. A very tall one."

My mouth dropped open, but I was too stunned to cough up a

clever retort. He was absolutely right. My new brown-on-brown-on-brown home looked like shit. And I was living in it.

Having it rubbed in my face by Lennie Lazarski was more than I could bear. My eyes started to burn with hot tears. I spun around to escape him and marched down the hall toward my locker.

Where Willow and Wynn were waiting for me.

SIX

" -vy!" Willow waved to make sure I'd seen her, in case I missed her shouting my name with her megaphone voice. Wynn greeted me with a more delicate wiggle of her fingers, lashes fluttering. I knew better than to be fooled by their sweetness.

"Hey." I continued walking, hoping they'd go back to their usual favorite pastime of admiring themselves. But the clomp of their heels followed in my wake. When I reached my locker, they pulled up on either side of me, like tennis players preparing to volley.

"New boyfriend?" Willow nodded toward the entrance.

"Huh?" My eyelid twitched.

"We saw you talking to Loser Lazarski," said Wynn.

I pressed the knuckles of my right hand to my twitching eye. "He's not . . . I wasn't talking to him. He opened the door for me and I said thank you. It's called being polite. You should try it sometime."

"To him?" Willow gave a fake shudder. "No thanks."

Wynn reached over and plucked something out of my hair. A leaf. "Nice. Were you rolling around in the grass with him or something?"

I grabbed the leaf from her hand and let it fall in crumbled bits to the floor. "No! I barely spoke to him."

"We're kidding," Willow said in a monotone. "God, lighten up."

I wasn't sure that was possible, what with the quicksand of my life swallowing me whole.

"Where were you this weekend?" Willow twisted a stray hair around the dancer bun she always wore. "You didn't return our texts."

Wynn made puppy-dog eyes. "Are you mad at us or something?"

"No, I . . . uh . . . lost my phone."

"That sucks," said Willow. "When are you getting a new one?"

I shrugged. "I'm thinking maybe I don't really need a phone—"

"Right." She laughed, then realized I might actually be serious. "Tell me you're kidding."

For a few seconds, an alternate conversation went through my head in which I confessed the truth of my situation, that my family was broke and living in Lakeside, next door to a drug dealer. But the look of disgust on Willow's face at the mention of no cell phone was so horrible, I just wanted to make it go away. I broke into a smile. "Of course, I'm kidding. My dad's ordering a new one through his work. It might take a few days."

Willow sighed. "Don't joke like that."

Wynn yanked me into a hug, then quickly pulled away. "Ew. You're all sweaty."

"I, uh . . . had to run for the bus."

They glanced sideways at each other. Willow put her fingertips on my sleeve. "Text us as soon as you get your phone, 'kay?"

"Sure."

Wynn air-kissed my cheeks, both sides as she had been doing ever since her family went to Europe last summer. Then they were gone.

An irrational sense of relief flooded over me, like I'd successfully tiptoed through a minefield. My hand smoothed nervously over my unruly curls, which seemed to have picked up even more altitude than usual. I quickly opened my locker, got the books I needed for first period, and hurried to the bathroom. Windswept was not exactly a good look for me. Wetting my hands, I combed through my hair, then dried my damp arms with a paper towel.

My exterior appeared almost the same as usual, but it didn't feel that way on the inside. In homeroom, I stood for the pledge and pretended to listen to announcements, certain everyone was staring at me. Was it on my face in some way?

I caught up with Reesa on the way to first-period AP English. "Do I look different to you?"

"What do you mean?" She dabbed some gloss on her lips.

"I don't know." I dropped to a whisper. "Poor?"

Her gaze swept from my head to my toes and back up again. "Nope. Same as always, you skinny bitch."

I smiled. "Thanks, Rees." Reesa was always complaining about her curves, and I was always complaining about my lack thereof. The only thing I had that wasn't straight was my hair, and Reesa was the opposite.

We walked into AP English and took our seats as the bell rang. Mr. Eli wrote *The Canterbury Tales* on the board and underlined it three times. There were a few sputters of nervous laughter. Our assignment had been to memorize the opening part of the prelude, as it was originally written in Middle English, and recite it in front of the entire class.

I sat as still as possible and kept my eyes on the floor. Mr. Eli strolled the aisles between our desks until everyone was settled and quiet. "Now, don't strain yourselves volunteering all at once," he said.

The door opened and I said a silent thanks for the disruption, then looked up. It was the guy from the hedge this morning. He had this adorable way of tipping his chin down and looking out the top of his eyes, through his hair. He was doing it to Mr. Eli right now.

"Can I help you?" Our teacher took a step toward him.

Sitting next to me, Reesa sucked a breath through her teeth. "Be stillith myith heart."

The boy handed Mr. Eli a paper. "I'm new," he said. "Is this AP English?"

Mr. Eli nodded. "Yes, uh . . ." He looked at the paper. "James Wickerton?"

James nodded. Mr. Eli said, "Welcome, James." Then he turned to the class and said, "This is James. Find him a seat."

There was an empty desk on the other side of Reesa's. She nearly dislocated her shoulder trying to alert James to its availability. He smiled at her and started walking toward the desk, his eyes sweeping the room. I dropped my forehead to my hand and looked down at my notebook in a classic don't-call-on-me-I-have-a-terrible-headache stance.

Mr. Eli picked up where he'd left off. "*The Canterbury Tales*. The first eighteen lines. Who's ready? Who hath learned thy Middle English?"

I peeked out over my hand to observe that I was not alone in dreading this assignment. While my stage fright only reached paralytic proportions when I was standing on an actual stage or otherwise attempting to sing for an audience, I still got very nervous for anything remotely performance related. In classes, going to the board definitely made my palms sweat. I was usually fine answering questions, as long as I could remain seated safely at my desk. It was best if I didn't have to sit there anticipating my turn and getting worked up over it. But that didn't mean I wanted to go first, either.

Mr. Eli lifted a book from his desk and walked over to James. He flipped to the correct page and laid it down. "We've been studying *The Canterbury Tales*," he said in a low voice. "I won't make you memorize since you're just starting with us, but maybe you'd like to start us off today by reading from the book?"

James's face went slightly green. "Uh . . ." He licked his lips and squirmed under Mr. Eli's gaze. I knew that squirm, that heart-racing discomfort.

"I'll go." I jumped to my feet, knocking the desk with my hip so it scraped loudly across the floor. Everyone who had been watching James turned to gape at me.

"Miss Emerson?" Mr. Eli looked at me with surprise. Reesa looked at me with surprise. The part of me that hadn't gone totally insane looked at me with surprise. "Thank you for volunteering," said Mr. Eli.

I swallowed and began before my brain could fully process what I'd done, what I was about to do.

"'Whan that Aprill with his shoures soote, the droghte of March hath perced to the roote . . .'" My voice quavered, but the strange words spilled out in the proper order. I had put the poem to music in my head, a trick I always used to memorize things. Separating it now from that melody was like reading backward, but it kept my mind off the fact that everyone was watching me. Closing my eyes helped, too.

When I finished, there was a polite smattering of applause and I took my seat. Or rather, I fell into my seat as my knees gave out. Reesa was still staring at me like an alien had possessed my body. "What was that about?" she whispered.

I shrugged as Mr. Eli called on her next. She hopped up and launched into the poem. I let my eyes flutter over to where James sat. He was staring back at me, a curious eyebrow raised. I looked back at the front of the classroom and didn't budge for the rest of the class.

"Glad that's over," Reesa said after the bell rang. She linked her arm with mine and looked back over her shoulder as we left class. I followed her line of sight and saw James standing in front of Mr. Eli's desk, teetering back on his heels, now with his thumbs hooked through his front belt loops instead of shoved into his back pockets. "He's hot," she said.

"Who?" I said.

"Sir James. Me thinketh he's divine."

My throat felt dry. "You think?"

"Oh, yeah," she said. "Tall, dreamy. And quiet. You know what they say about the quiet ones."

"Um, they don't talk a lot?"

"Actually, I have no idea what they say about the quiet ones. But it must be good." She laughed at herself. "They have a secret. They're hiding something, like—"

"Bodies? The quiet ones are serial killers?"

Reesa put a hand on her hip. "Don't talk about my future boyfriend like that. I was referring to a secret passion. Quiet on the outside, crazy and sexy on the inside. Something like that." She gave a meaningful wink. "I'll let you know when I find out."

She sauntered off with an exaggerated sway of her hips, putting her dibs on James Wickerton. I didn't like it. The guy surely thought I was an idiot, and I'd rather my best friend didn't date someone who thought I was an idiot. But, to be honest, what really bothered me was that she hadn't even mentioned his eyes. How could she not have noticed how they were icy blue and warm at the same time?

Because he hadn't looked at her.

SEVEN

I didn't see James for the rest of the day. But Lennie was suddenly everywhere. Grinning, leering, sneering, materializing out of nowhere—like my own personal Cheshire cat. Sometimes he was surrounded by his friends, the moving boys from Saturday morning. But fortunately, Lennie was the only one who seemed to remember me.

Reesa noticed one of his more blatant stares when we passed him in the hall on the way to chemistry. "Who's that?"

"Nobody," I said too quickly.

She turned to get a better look. "What's his name, Lizinsky? Lewinski? Isn't he, like, a drug lord or something?"

"No idea. Can I borrow your psych notes? I kind of zoned out during that ethics lecture."

"Sure." She dug a notebook out of her bag as we were walking. "But why is that guy . . ."

"Can we not talk about him, please? He stared at me. End of story." I walked ahead of her without taking the notebook.

She hurried to catch me. "What's wrong with you?"

"Seriously?" I wanted to bang my head repeatedly against the lockers.

She rolled her eyes and handed me the notebook. "Don't be so sensitive."

"Easy for you to say. You weren't the one ripped from your home and thrown to the wolves. You act like nothing's changed, like I'm just . . . I don't know, having a bad hair day or something."

She glanced up at my hair. "Well, you kind of are. And you *told* me to act like nothing had changed. Remember?"

"I told you not to *tell* anyone. There's a difference."

Reesa took a deep breath and exhaled it loudly. "Obviously, whatever I say is going to be the wrong thing, so I'm just going to shut up." Now she was the one walking away from me.

"You didn't even call me," I mumbled to her back.

She spun around. "You don't have a phone!"

"Shh! Do you have to announce it to everyone?"

Reesa closed her eyes and spoke low. "You're in a mood. I get that, and I get why. But you need to stop acting like a crazy person. Okay? We're going to be late."

I followed her down the stairs to our last class and tried my best to act like a noncrazy person, fully engaged in the wonders of science. But my mind kept straying to my next challenge: retrieving my bicycle from the hedges at the end of the day without attracting further attention.

And when the final bell rang fifty minutes later, I dodged my way to an upstairs bathroom to avoid my friends, who might notice if I didn't head out to catch a bus or a ride home. I waited for a turn at the mirror. Reesa wasn't kidding about bad hair day. I scrounged through my backpack for something to tie it back, but all I could find was one of those big black-and-silver metal binder clips. I grabbed a fistful of hair and clipped it back. It looked . . . well, pretty stupid. But it would keep my hair out of my face on the ride home. My standards were clearly falling already.

The hallway had grown quiet. Aside from a few kids sitting around some lockers at the far stairs, the coast was clear. I started walking toward them, but Mr. Cook, the assistant principal, appeared at the end of the hall and started interrogating them. I dived for the nearest door and ducked inside.

Mr. Cook was notorious for giving detention, and that was the last thing I needed. The room I'd entered was pitch-dark. I stood, not moving, just listening for footsteps and trying not to breathe too loud. Behind me, in whatever this room was, something was dripping. It started to freak me out, so I swept my hand along the wall until I found a switch. A long fluorescent light flickered on, illuminating a storage room with floor-to-ceiling shelves stacked with cardboard boxes and big multipacks of toilet paper. The drip was coming from a utility sink in the corner.

Beyond the supply shelves was a long, narrow hallway. It was too dark to see exactly where that led, but I noticed another small room off to the side. It was a tiny little sitting room, a break room for the janitor, maybe? It had a table and lamp, which I switched on, and an orange faux-leather chair like the ones in the library (only this one had a tear in it that was patched with duct tape). The wall was lined with shelves that were empty except for a few boxes of paper clips. The discovery gave me a little tingle, like I'd stumbled upon the secret tunnels of Vanderbilt High.

I closed the door and sat in the chair, which was surprisingly comfortable. The cement walls blocked out every sound from the outside world. It was the perfect place to hide after school. All I'd need was a few good books to pass the time. I pulled out the beaten-up copy of *The Great Gatsby* I had in my backpack from a summer reading project and set it on the shelf—a little start to my secret reading room. I switched off the lamp and closed the door as I left.

It had been ten minutes, and the hallway was eerily quiet and empty now. My pink Chucks squeaked along the waxed linoleum. When I reached the double doors, I hesitated. Someone was in the stairway. I peered through the little window and saw the one person I least wanted to see: *Lennie*. He was talking to some guy wearing a black slouch hat.

"It's top quality," Lennie said, handing him a small paper bag.

Slouch Hat looked into the bag, then rolled it up and shoved it in his front pocket. "How much?"

"Twenty."

The kid took a bill from his wallet and handed it over. "I'll call you if I need more. I know some guys who might want to check out your stuff, too."

"You know where to find me," said Lennie.

Oh, my God. I ducked down so they wouldn't see me through the window. Had I just witnessed what I thought I'd witnessed? *Unbelievable.*

The door pushed against me and I jumped back. "Ahhh!"

"Emerson," said Lennie. "Can I help you?"

I stepped away. "No."

He came through the door, letting it swing shut behind him. "Were you spying on me?"

"Of course not." I glanced behind me, now wishing Mr. Cook would appear. "I was just leaving."

I attempted to walk past him to the door, but he sidestepped into my path, glaring down at me. "What are you doing here?"

I remembered what someone once told me about vicious dogs. They could smell your fear. I straightened my shoulders and lifted my chin. "I might ask you the same thing!"

He nodded. "You might. And I *might* have a very good answer."

"Such as?"

"Such as I help out in the au-to-mo-tive shop after school." He articulated the word like he was trying to sound aristocratic. "Fully approved and sanctioned by the administrative powers that be. And you?"

"None of your business," I said, desperately wishing I'd had a better comeback, something that seemed to escape me whenever I was in Lennie's presence.

"Better be on your way, then." He glanced up at the big, round clock that hung over the doorway. "Mr. Cook is due to pass through here on his daily rounds in approximately two minutes."

My eyes widened. He had it all timed perfectly.

"Unless you want a ride," he added, grinning.

"No, uh . . . I don't think so." I brushed past him to get to the door. As I started to pull it open, he slid his heavy boot in the way. I stared down at it, fingers squeezing the door handle so tight my knuckles went white.

"It's just a ride," he said in a low voice. "I wasn't asking you out or anything."

I swiveled my head to look up at his face, which was now inches from mine. "That's not what I thought. I would never think that."

The grin that had been taunting me through most of our conversation fell from his face. He pulled his foot out of the way. "Of course you wouldn't."

My heart was now thumping visibly through my shirt, I was sure of it. I yanked the door open and nearly flew down the stairwell. I was almost to the bottom when I heard the door above swing open again.

Lennie called out, "Love what you've done with your hair, by the way!"

I put a hand to my head, felt the giant binder clip, and groaned inwardly as I pushed through the doors to the downstairs hallway.

EIGHT

I pedaled home. Fast. My legs screamed. All I kept thinking was that I had to beat Lennie home. I didn't want him there waiting to taunt me again. I'd also nearly forgotten about the twins' bus, and the disaster it would be if I didn't arrive in time to greet them. Mom was usually there, but she had an interview today for a job at a newspaper. I bumped onto our gravel road just as the bus squeaked to a stop and deposited Kaya and Brady at my wheel, along with a handful of other kids from the neighborhood. A few gave Brady funny looks, but Kaya funny-looked them right back and they ran off. Kaya was Brady's fiercest defender, and most of the time he didn't even know it was happening. He automatically assumed everyone was nice, like he was.

"Hey." I panted. "How was school?"

"Fantabulous," said Kaya. She nudged Brady's arm.

"Fan-tah-lah-bus," he tried. Kaya attempted to teach him a new word on the bus every day. She was responsible for additions to his vocabulary including "chili cheese dog," "holy bagumba," and "butt head," among others.

"Fan-tah-*byu*-lus," she tried again.

Brady didn't respond. He was staring at his feet, then looking toward our house in the distance, and back down to his feet. His little mouth fell open as he squatted down, patting the stones with both hands.

"Oh, no," said Kaya. "The rocks. He wants to clean up the rocks. Like at home. The driveway. Remember?"

He picked one up. Just one bit of gravel from an entire road made of gravel, and threw it toward the grass. It didn't quite make it, so he went to where it had fallen and tried to figure out which one it was. He finally picked up a stone and threw it again, then squatted down for another.

"Brady," I said, "the rocks *belong* here. In the road. It's not like home." That was the understatement of the year. Our driveway at home was beautifully paved with an ornate brick border. Here it was just gravel that crunched when you drove on it.

"Come on." Kaya gently took his hand. "Let's go."

He let her lead him to the side so they could walk along the edge of the grass. I followed, pushing the bike. Kaya glanced at it but said nothing, clearly too nervous about the precarious situation with Brady and the gravel. You never knew what might set him off.

When we got to the house, I quickly wheeled the Schwinn around back and tucked it under the stairs. Brady and Kaya were standing out front. I watched from the side of the house. Sometimes it was best to just let him process things. He was staring intently at that gravel road, no doubt trying to figure out what he was going to do about it. The poor kid had spent all of last year clearing our driveway of every stray bit of stone, like it was the most important job in the world. *His* job. It was a huge source of pride for him, and now it was gone.

God, I hated this place.

As the three of us stood there, Lennie's Jeep rumbled to a stop in front of his house. He climbed out and started walking toward his front door, glancing from Brady to the road. He took a step toward the twins, and I was about to run out to protect them if he got any closer, but he didn't.

"Whatcha doin'?" he called out.

Kaya kept looking out at the road and said, "My brother is trying to figure out what to do about all those rocks."

"Ah," said Lennie, nodding. "They get everywhere, don't they?" Then he reached down, picked up a piece of gravel from his front yard, and threw it into the road.

Brady swiveled his head to look at Lennie, who bent down to pick up two more pieces. He tossed them one at a time, underhand so they arched up high before dropping with a satisfying clatter.

Brady watched each rock as it soared into the street. A big smile came across his face. He studied the grass around his feet, squatted, and selected one of several bits of gravel. He stood and threw it with all his might. It landed about three feet away.

Lennie laughed. He threw another rock, then Brady threw one. Then Kaya joined in, and they all took turns. The threat of a major Brady meltdown had been avoided. I kept watching from the side of the house, not sure what to do.

Lennie looked up and saw me, then let the rock he was holding drop to the ground. He turned to Brady. "Gotta go, dude. Keep up the good work."

Brady smiled at him, and waved—a perfectly normal exchange, which was *not* normal for my brother. It usually took him weeks of behavior therapy to master an interaction like that.

I waited for Lennie to go into his house, then hurried to collect the twins and take them inside. Brady was loath to leave his work unfinished, but I assured him he could continue later. There had to be at least a year's worth of gravel in our little yard to clean up.

"How was school?" Mom asked an hour later. She kicked off her shoes and opened the refrigerator.

"Fine."

"The bus?"

"Fantabulous," I said. "How did your interview go?"

"Also fantabulous," she said, not even realizing it was Brady's word of the day. "I got the job."

"That's great! Doing what?"

"Copyediting. Writing obituaries, the police report, stuff like that. It's just two afternoons a week for now. I'll need you home to get the twins off the bus those days. Okay?"

"Yeah." I heard the distinctive rumble of Lennie's Jeep and watched out the front window as he drove off. My chest unclenched the slightest bit, knowing he was gone. "You probably won't have to go very far to get stuff for your police report."

Mom raised an eyebrow. "Why's that?"

"Am I the only one who's noticed that our neighbor is a drug dealer?"

"Mr. Lazarski?" Mom chuckled. "He's sixty-five years old and disabled. I hardly think he's dealing drugs. He can barely feed himself, apparently. Carla told us a car fell on him, if you can believe it. He used to be a mechanic."

I peered out the kitchen window toward their little house. There was one broken-down car parked in the grass along the far side, and one of those prefab sheds shaped like a miniature barn. I'd seen Lennie coming and going from it, but nobody else had stepped out of the house.

"I wasn't talking about Mr. Lazarski, Mom. I was talking about his son."

Mom pulled a box of pasta from the cabinet. "Trust me. We checked everyone out thoroughly before moving here. It's not a bad neighborhood, sweetie. No arrests, no incidents at all in the past year."

"That just means they haven't been caught yet," I mumbled.

Mom gave me The Look, as Kaya came bouncing down from the bunk bed room and described the gravel incident in painstaking detail. In her version of events, Lennie hadn't absently thrown a few rocks into the road. He had practically swooped in wearing a superhero cape to save the day.

Mom turned to me and said, "See? He's not so bad."

"He knows how to throw rocks," I said. "Doesn't exactly make him a model citizen."

"I'm sure he's a perfectly nice boy." She disappeared upstairs to check on Brady.

I took the phone to my room and dialed Reesa's number.

She answered on the first ring. "You got a phone?"

"Landline," I said flatly. "Same number as before. Didn't you recognize it?" We must've dialed each other's home phone numbers a million times when we were kids, before we got our own.

"Oh, yeah." She recited the numbers, superfast. "Sorry about not calling. I didn't think they'd let you have the same number over there."

I know she didn't mean it as an insult, but it felt that way. "What, like there's a special number for poor people?"

"No, I . . . never mind. That was stupid."

An awkward silence fell between us. This phone call was not taking my mind off my situation as I'd hoped. "So, what are you doing now?"

"Deciding what color to paint my nails."

"Choices?"

"Sassy Librarian's new colors are out. I couldn't decide so I got them all."

We had discovered this teen boutique and bookstore in Belleview last summer that made its own nail polish, with literary-inspired names. There was "Shatter Me Silver" and "Lovely, Dark, and Deep Purple," and "Every Day Red." We loved them more for the names and the fun of figuring out which book they referred to. And if you bought the polish *and* the book, you got a 20 percent discount.

"How many?" I asked.

"Six," she said. "And books, too. Mom said we'd call it a back-to-school present."

I started calculating in my head what six polishes and matching books would cost, but stopped myself before I reached an exact figure. One polish was out of my budget now. "That's great," I said weakly.

"Wait till you hear the names."

I sighed. "I should probably do homework."

"Oh, okay. Fine." She sighed. "I'll show them to you this weekend. We're still going to Little Invisibles concert, aren't we?"

"Oh, crap," I said. "I can't."

"Ivyyy," she whined. "You told me we'd go next time they played at the King."

"That was before I became a person with an allowance of zero," I said.

"It's only twenty dollars!"

"It might as well be a hundred," I mumbled.

She paused. "I guess New York's out, too?"

I'd forgotten all about the trip we'd been planning—to take the train into the city to shop, maybe see a show. Even if I didn't actually buy anything and we stood in the discount ticket line at Times Square and walked everywhere instead of taking a cab, it would still be a four-hundred-dollar day. "I don't think so, Rees."

"I'll loan you the money. You can pay me back when things clear up."

"Things aren't just going to clear up, Rees. And I'm not going to be your charity case," I said. "I'll get a job or something."

"A job?" She was wrinkling her nose, I could just tell. "Then you won't have time to do anything. You'll always be working."

"Yeah, well . . ."

"I have two words for you," she said. "Rich. Boyfriend."

I sighed. "Because destitution is so attractive. I'm sure they'll be lining up outside my crappy apartment."

There was a rustle and clunk on the other end, like Reesa had dropped the phone. "Hold on," she said, then I was on speaker. She always put me on speaker when she was painting her nails. "Maybe James has a friend."

"Uh, James . . . who?"

"My future boyfriend. James Westerton. Wickering. Whatever his name is. The new guy who sat next to me in English. He of the golden, wavy hair."

I wanted to tell her his last name was Wickerton, not Westerton or Wickering, and his hair, while definitely worthy of running one's fingers through, was not his finest feature. But I was too busy feeling slightly nauseated at the thought of James and Reesa becoming an item. I didn't begrudge her a hottie boyfriend, but the guy had seen me with bugs smashed to my face. The last thing I needed was to hang out with him and Reesa all the time.

"Wonder what kind of car he drives," she mused.

I should've said something then, that I'd seen him in the parking lot. That he drove a nice car, a black one. Mercedes, or maybe a BMW. But I kept it a secret. Maybe because secrets were all I had left. Or maybe it was inertia . . . an object in motion stays in motion? Once you start keeping secrets, it's kind of hard to stop.

NINE

Tuesday. Lakeside, day four. I contemplated carving hash marks on the wall of my room, but didn't want to make the place feel any more like a prison sentence than it already did. I left the apartment five minutes earlier so James wouldn't see me bug-faced and shrub-hiding again, so Lennie wouldn't walk in with me, so the Witches wouldn't pounce. So, so, so many reasons. My hair was tied back. No looking like a possessed sea anemone today.

I went into our backyard to get my bike but stopped short when I saw a white plastic bag in the basket. If my parents had noticed the bike, they hadn't said anything. Maybe they assumed it was Carla's. But somebody had found it.

I poked at the roundish shape, then lifted it far enough to see the blue-and-green Ike's Bikes logo. My dad had taken us to get our custom bicycles there. It was a nice shop. Expensive. I reached in and pulled out a bicycle helmet. Had my parents . . . ? No. They definitely would've said something.

A light went on over at Lazarski's house. I saw a shadow pass in front of the window. Then a light in another room. My eyes went back to the helmet in my hands. I started to get that nervous feeling like when you think someone's following you on a dark street.

You should really wear a helmet, you know, Lennie had said.

I dropped it into the basket as if it was scalding hot. Why would he buy me this? What did he want from me? I couldn't wear it. Absolutely not.

But the cars did whiz by really fast.

I picked the helmet up again and turned it over in my hands. It was gorgeous, and that is not a word that usually appears in the same sentence as "bike helmet." The surface was smooth and cream colored, with pale gray-and-white flowers screen-printed on the side.

I hated that he'd paid for this . . . *if* he'd paid for this. I'd be indebted to him. Maybe I could wear the helmet until I had a chance to buy one of my own. Then I'd give it back to him. I wouldn't owe him a thing. I flipped the helmet onto my head and snapped the buckle under my chin.

It fit perfectly.

When I got to my locker, relatively nonsweaty in the fresh shirt I had packed, Reesa was waiting. She waved a sheet of paper in my face. "This is the answer to your problem. Right here."

"Which problem?" I said, pushing it aside to get to my locker. "I have several, you know."

"Your cash flow problem."

I took the flyer. The country club her parents belonged to was looking for someone to play piano and sing in their hoity-toity bar and restaurant, and to perform "light background music" at dinners and receptions. I pushed the sheet back into Reesa's hands. "I don't think so."

"What? It pays fifty dollars an hour. Plus tips."

"A, everyone we know goes to that country club; and B, I can't sing." I turned back to my locker.

"Yeah, and Adele totally sucks, too." Reesa was the one person, outside my family, who had ever heard me sing. And only because she was sneaky and had a key to our house.

"I can sing at home. That's it." And I couldn't even manage to do that anymore.

Reesa slapped the flyer on top of the books I had pulled from my locker. "Come on. People will start noticing if you never have spending money. And this isn't like a *job* job. You could totally do this."

A graceful arm swept over her shoulder and snatched the flyer. "Do what?"

I tried to grab it back, but Willow held it out of my reach as she read. "You sing?"

"No," I said, but Reesa drowned me out with a loud, "Yes! She sings."

Willow looked at us like we were crazy, which we probably were. "Like, in the shower?"

"Yeah. Something like that." I grabbed the flyer and shoved it into my backpack while giving Reesa a don't-say-another-word-under-penalty-of-death stare.

"God, Ivy. It's been six years," Reesa muttered. "Get over it."

Air hissed out between my teeth. She might as well have stuck a knife in my chest. I knew how ridiculous it must seem that I hadn't gotten over my stage fright from that stupid talent show yet. It should've been ancient history by now, but the further away I got from that day, the darker and more frightening its shadow became.

"Thanks." I stared daggers at Reesa. "Thanks a lot."

Willow tilted her head to the side and tapped her dangly earring. "Wait," she said. "Are you talking about . . . Oh, my God. I forgot all about that!"

I groaned.

"What was that song you were supposed to sing? Something about summer from the perspective of a butterfly?" She giggled and nudged me like I was in on the joke, not the butt of it.

"Summerfly," I mumbled.

"Awww." She pushed out her bottom lip, then her face brightened. "I won that talent show, remember? I danced Clara's solo from *The Nutcracker*."

"Yes." I gave a weak smile. "I remember." She hadn't actually witnessed my humiliation, thankfully. She'd been off somewhere "getting into character" or stretching her foot behind her head.

"Didn't some kid have to drag you off the stage because you froze up?"

I nodded, though "drag" was a bit of an exaggeration. There was a boy who gently took my arm and led me off. At least, that's what my mother told me. All I noticed were the bright lights and the front few rows of faces staring at me.

Willow pulled me into an awkward hug, my books pressed between us. Then someone down the hall behind me caught her attention. "Ooh, gotta go." She waved and sashayed off.

"Well, that was fun," I said.

Reesa grimaced. "I'm sorry."

I shrugged.

"I'm really, really sorry. You know I just want the rest of the world to hear your amazing voice. And for you to have spending money so we can have fun." She pressed her palms together, fingertips to her lips as if in prayer. "Forgive me? Please?"

I rolled my eyes. "You're forgiven. Just promise you won't throw me under the Willow bus again, okay?"

"I promise," she said.

We started down the hall, walking shoulder to shoulder and swerving to miss people without breaking contact. It was something we'd started in middle school as our own secret good-luck charm. If we made it to class without separating, we'd get whatever we were wishing for that day. As we approached the stairway, Willow twirled away from her locker and pushed straight between us with a laugh. We stopped and glared at her back.

"I hate her," Reesa growled. "Remind me why we're friends with her?"

"Must've done something awful in a past life."

"We're such losers," said Reesa. "It's sad, really."

"Really sad."

"Lame."

"Pathetic."

We went on like that all the way down the hall, belittling our-selves, turning it all into a joke. But as I sat down in homeroom, I wondered why we let her rule over us the way we did. It was just as much our fault as hers, I suppose. We were all complicit in the state of inertia that governed our friendship. It was just easier to keep going along the way it was than to change direction.

When we got to AP English, James Wickerton had not yet arrived and Reesa took the opportunity to scoot her desk closer to his. She did it casually, like she was just trying to get her things situ-ated and comfy.

"Seriously?" I shook my head.

"What?" She smoothed all her hair to one side of her neck and adjusted the collar of her blouse so it displayed her décolletage.

I slouched a few inches lower in my chair and let my hair fall around my face like blinders. Reesa was an accomplished flirt, but I didn't like to watch. It made me feel like a third wheel.

The room got a little quieter when James walked in. Reesa waggled her fingers at him, and his face brightened with recognition as he walked toward the desk she'd saved for him.

"Good morning, James," she practically sang.

"Hey." He gave a quick smile and sat down.

"I'm Reesa."

James nodded, his eyes darting from her to me.

"Oh, and this is Ivy." Reesa leaned back so there was a clear line of sight between him and me.

"Yes," he said, "We've . . ."

"Nice to meet you," I said quickly, before he could reveal that we'd already met. He frowned, confused, but I ignored him and opened my notebook, paging through it like I was in search of some very important notes. I could still see them out the corner of my eye, though.

Reesa leaned over to rest her hand on James's arm. "If you need, like, help finding a classroom or the library or something, don't hesitate," she said. "You can ask me anything."

"Oh, uh. Thanks," he said.

We suffered through the remaining recitations of *The Canterbury Tales*, the words sounding like mush by the time we were done. Mr. Eli made one more attempt to get James to recite, but he politely declined.

And when class was over, I darted. I didn't want James to mention the bike, the bushes, or the bugs in front of Reesa. She wouldn't understand why I was keeping secrets from her. I didn't understand it myself, except it was all so embarrassing.

As soon as I reached my locker, I realized I'd forgotten my hoodie. I quickly swapped my English book for chemistry and hurried back, hoping Mr. Eli hadn't left for his free period yet.

I was relieved to find the door ajar. But someone was in there with him, so I hesitated before waltzing in.

". . . smale foweles maken melodye, that slepen al the nyght with open ye . . ."

It was a deep, rich voice that managed to put feeling into the words that had lost all meaning coming out of the rest of our mouths. I listened as if transported to fourteenth-century England, where my now-favorite poet was whispering the melodious verses into my ear.

". . . The hooly blisful martir for to seke, that hem hath holpen whan that they were seeke."

When the poem ended, a shiver shot down my spine, jarring me back to the present. I peeked through the narrow slit but could see only Mr. Eli, tilting back in his desk chair.

"Excellent," he said, looking more than a little astonished. "I wonder why you didn't want to do it for the class."

James?

"I don't know. Nervous, I guess. I'm not very good at public speaking."

"Our Shakespeare section should help with that. We'll be reading from various plays," said Mr. Eli. "If you want full credit, I'll expect you to participate."

"Yes, sir."

The warning bell for second period rang and I didn't want to be late. But I didn't want James to think I was stalking him, either. My hand was poised over the door handle when he pulled it inward. He caught me in an awkward, about-to-steal-a-cookie pose.

"Oh, hi," I squeaked, sounding like a helium addict. I withdrew my fingers from the handle and we did a little you-first, no-you-first dance in the doorway.

He laughed and stepped aside. "After you."

"I, uh, forgot my jacket." I pointed to where it was draped over the back of my chair.

He took three long strides back to my desk and snatched it up, and then held it out by the shoulders to help me put it on.

Mr. Eli cleared his throat. "Don't you have somewhere to be? I know I do."

The bell rang for second period. "Can I get a pass?" I asked Mr. Eli.

He nodded and I went to his desk. When I looked back at the door, James was gone. Mr. Eli scribbled out a pass for me and I hurried off. The hall was empty, except for a lone figure approaching the far end, messenger bag slung over his shoulder and a huge book under the other arm. I watched as he opened a door near the stairs and slipped inside.

Though chemistry was in the opposite direction, I followed

the path James had taken to see which class he was in. But when I arrived at the door I was certain he'd entered, it wasn't a classroom. It was the same unmarked door that led to my secret room. I put my hand on the knob and turned.

It was locked.

TEN

When I returned to the supply room at the end of the day to wait out the after-school rush, the door was unlocked. It hadn't occurred to me to lock it before, but James had done it, so I pressed the button to make sure nobody walked in on me. Then I quickly found my way to the secret room and switched on the lamp.

Everything was just as I'd left it, but my tattered copy of *The Great Gatsby* was no longer the only item on the shelf. It was now dwarfed by a three-inch-thick hardbound book. I pulled it down to read the cover: *The Complete Works of William Shakespeare.*

Not my first choice of reading material. But James was proving to be not-your-average cute boy. I sat and thumbed through the book. Almost every page had something highlighted, with notes scribbled in the margin. Words defined, explanations of what was really going on. I flipped to the front cover to see if James had signed his named, but found only the initials J.A.R.

I closed it tenderly and returned it to the shelf, gathering my stuff to go. But something called me back. I don't know if it was the secret feeling of the room or my new life of secrets, but I wanted to know more about the owner of that book. I took out a pencil and scrawled a note under the initials.

And what do you read for fun?

I smiled as I closed the book again and left. I avoided the stairwell where I'd seen Lennie yesterday, got my bike, and pedaled home as close to happy as I'd been all week.

Mom was sitting on the living room floor with papers spread out around her and all over the coffee table. She looked up as if she hadn't been expecting me and quickly scooped everything into a pile.

"What's all that?" I asked.

"Nothing." She shoved it all into one of those brown accordion folders. "Just paperwork."

"Bills?"

She smiled. "Nothing for you to worry about."

My stomach twisted. That was what she'd been saying for months. I knew better than to believe her now.

"Mom—"

"How was your day?" she asked brightly.

I told her what *she* wanted to hear. "It was great, Mom. Really great."

She sighed as if the weight of the world had lifted. "I'm so glad to hear that. Things have a way of working out, don't they?"

She disappeared into her bedroom with the papers, and I wondered what bad news they might contain. We'd already lost our house and most of our possessions. How much worse could it get?

The next morning I gazed longingly at some of my cute skirts and dresses and boots but again chose a more cycling-friendly outfit instead: a pair of skinny jeans, my Converse sneaks, a vintage T-shirt, and hoodie. My new uniform.

Mom and Dad were already in the kitchen when I went down, arguing in hushed tones. I stopped and stood on the middle stair.

"Please tell me we didn't lose everything for . . . for nothing," said Mom.

"If we get the university contract, we'll be fine," said Dad.

"And if we don't?"

"Something will turn up."

My mother was making coffee, noisily slamming the pot into place. "You've been saying that for weeks, Mark. And look what turned up."

The step I was standing on suddenly creaked, and their conversation came to a halt. When I arrived in the kitchen, it was all sunshine and roses again.

"Hey, princess." Dad smiled in his usual way, but I could see the sadness in it now. I wondered how long he'd been hiding it.

"Hey, Daddy," I said, snarfing down the jelly toast Mom offered. "Gotta go!" I left before the twins were up. Another sign my parents were distracted by their financial woes? They hadn't even noticed how obscenely early I was leaving for school.

It was my third day on the Schwinn, and everything was going okay until one mile into my ride, a car zoomed past so close I swore it brushed my arm. Someone thrust a hand out the window and gestured at me with an angry fist. *Jerks.* Like it would kill them to share the road with my elbow, which was the only part of me that might have crossed the white line. I gripped the handlebars tighter and veered to the side, leaving plenty of room between me and the car lane. But the loose, gravelly surface of the shoulder sent my wheels skittering and sliding. I swerved back onto the smooth road to get control of the bike.

Another car came up behind me, and I slowed to let it pass. Black BMW. What were the chances James took this road to school? Small, I told myself. Minuscule. He had to live in Westside Falls. Still, watching it go up the hill in front of me was enough to take my eyes off the road long enough that I didn't notice the rainwater drainage grate coming up in front of me. And when I did, it was too late.

My front tire dropped through the metal slats to a jarring halt, slamming me into the handlebars. I toppled forward and landed smack on the top of my head in a grassy ditch, then flipped onto my backpack like a turtle.

I lay there for a minute, the wind knocked out of me. My ears were ringing, and then rumbling.

No, that was a car.

I scrambled to right myself and discovered one of my shoes was missing.

"Looking for this?" Lennie sauntered up with my pink Converse dangling from his fingertips.

I nodded, and he tossed it to me. My fingers fumbled the laces as I tried to tie them. I was shaken up but uninjured—as far as I could tell—if you didn't count my pride. I stood and brushed myself off.

Lennie lifted my bike from the ditch. "Chain's off," he said, pointing to how it dangled loosely. Before I could think what to do about that, he had the whole thing flipped upside down, balanced on its seat and handles. I watched numbly as he returned the chain to its gears and slowly rotated the pedal until it was running on track.

"Should be okay now." He set the bike upright and rolled it over to me. "Are you?"

I nodded again and walked toward him, took the handlebars in my shaky fingers.

He didn't let go. "Could you say something so I know you're not brain damaged?"

"Something," I murmured.

Lennie pulled a cell phone out of his pocket. I was officially the only person in our entire school without my own functioning cell phone. He swiped his finger across the screen.

"Want me to call someone?"

I shook my head. "No, that's okay."

He studied me for a minute, his eyes slowly scanning my body from top to bottom, then settling on my face. He gestured back toward his Jeep. "Sure you don't want that ride? I could throw your bike in the back."

I shook my head again. "No, I'm fine."

"Of course." He snorted and backed away. "Wouldn't want anyone to see you with me, huh?"

It was true, I couldn't deny it. I stood there and watched him walk back to his Jeep. Before he got in, he turned back to me.

"Good thing you were wearing a helmet." He knocked on his head, then got in and peeled away, leaving me in the dust for a second time that week.

I arrived at school without further incident, hid my bike, and checked myself. No scratches, no blood. The bruises would show up later, no doubt. I'd given myself a complete pat down in search of rips or holes, and found none. Unfortunately, I wasn't contortionist enough to see my own rear end, so I didn't realize it was one gigantic grass stain.

Willow kindly alerted me to the situation at a decibel level roughly equivalent to the blast of a foghorn when I walked past her in the hall. "I-vy! What the hell is all over your ass?"

I instinctively went into defensive mode and leaned my back

against the wall. Wynn scurried over to spin me around. "Oh, my God!"

"What?" I said, twisting myself backward to see what everyone was looking at. For one terrifying moment I worried that I'd landed in dog shit. "What is it?"

Molly Palmer stopped to observe the commotion. Molly had been one of "us" until she and Willow had a huge falling-out freshman year. I secretly envied Molly for standing up to Willow. It had cost her nearly all her friends, but she didn't seem to care. She walked over now, looked at my butt, and shook her head. "It's just a grass stain," she said. "Haven't you nitwits ever seen a grass stain before?"

"Who asked you?" said Willow.

Molly snorted. "Like I need your permission to speak?" She pulled a sweater out of her backpack and handed it to me. "You can borrow this, if you want. To cover up."

"Thanks," I said, clutching it to my stomach.

Willow snatched it out of my hands and threw it at Molly. "She doesn't want your ugly sweater."

Molly shrugged and pushed the sweater back into her backpack. She glanced over at me before she walked away. "Don't be such a sheep," she said.

I watched her disappear into the crowd that continued to stare. *At me.* Reesa came pushing her way through. "Nothing to see here! Move along. Move along." She took one look at me and went into crisis mode.

"What happened?" she said.

My eyes started to water. It was too much to explain. "I fell."

Willow and Wynn were suddenly all "Poor Ivy, are you okay?" Neither one of them objected when Reesa handed me a sweater from her locker. "Here," she said. "Tie this around your waist."

I hoped she could read the gratitude in my eyes, because I was finding it difficult to speak. She helped me position the sweater to conceal the damage.

"Can't you call your mom and ask her to bring you something?" said Wynn.

I gave her a withering look. Her own mother was never home to bring a change of clothes. But she had the nanny. "I'm just going to use the bathroom," I said.

Reesa followed, as I knew she would. As soon as we were alone, she whispered, "What really happened?"

"I fell off my bike." I didn't mention that Lennie had helped pick me up.

"What bike?"

"The one I've been riding to school."

Her eyes widened. "I thought your mom was driving you."

I shook my head. "We only have one car now." And the complication of getting both of my parents to their jobs was difficult enough without adding me into the equation. Even if I had my license—I was still on the six-month learner's permit I got when I turned sixteen—we didn't have a second car I could drive, anyway.

Reesa's eyes went all "poor you" and she touched her fingers to my arm. "As soon as I get my license, I'll pick you up, okay? It's only three more months."

That was a lifetime. But I gave a quick nod and busied myself, pretending to fix my hair. Reesa fiddled with the sweater around my waist, trying to tuck in the sleeves, then giving up when she couldn't make it look like something it wasn't.

"You know, I read somewhere that downsizing is trending."

"What does that even mean?"

"I don't know. The headline was 'Hashtag Downsizing' or something. It was about people going off the grid, making do with less, shopping at thrift stores, using lemon juice instead of deodorant."

I crinkled my nose. "People do that?"

"I totally read that somewhere," she said. "Citrus has natural deodorizing properties. It's all very Bohemian."

My brain was starting to hurt. Considering how our own high school treated kids from Lakeside—even putting them on their own separate bus—I'd have to say being poor would never be trendy.

But I was too weary to attempt to set Reesa straight on that particular point. "Let's just go."

"I'll walk you to homeroom." She leaned her shoulder to mine as soon as we were out of the bathroom, but separated suddenly and squeezed my arm. "Oh, God. There he is. Should I talk to him? I should. I should talk to him."

"Who?" I swiveled my sore neck in time to see James striding toward us. His head was down, though. I did a quick spin-and-drop maneuver, crouching to tie my shoe. Then I dug through my backpack until he passed.

"Shit, shit, shit." Reesa stamped her foot on the last shit. "He didn't even look at me."

I stood and returned her "oh, well" shrug, hoping it hid the relief I was feeling. Maybe she'd lose interest in him.

"He drives a black BMW, you know," she said. "A really nice one. I saw him pull into the back parking lot. But I couldn't find any listings for a James Wickerton."

"Listings?"

"Google, Facebook, Twitter. It's like he doesn't exist. There's only one explanation I can think of."

"He's not into social networking?"

"He's a vampire," she said, breaking into a playful smile. "But still, probably loaded. Vampires always have money. Centuries of saving, stealing from their victims. It's all very lucrative."

"You should definitely stay away from him." I tried to make it sound like I was joking, but Reesa didn't take it that way.

"Why?"

I pretended to flip casually through my notebook in search of something. "He doesn't seem like your type."

Her bottom lip jutted out. "You don't like him?"

"No, it's just . . . I don't think he's right for you is all."

She gave me a long look, then patted my shoulder. "You

must've bumped your head in that fall. Because if tall, dreamy, and rich isn't right for me, then I don't know what is."

When I entered our first-period AP English class, Reesa was twirling her hair at James. "We go into the city a lot. You should come with us sometime."

"I'm not much of a city boy, actually."

"Not even to visit?" she said, looking slightly aghast.

He laughed. "Not if I can help it."

"Then what do you do for fun?"

He glanced over to me as I sat down. "I read a lot."

Reesa frowned. She loved to read, too, but I don't think that was exactly what she had in mind with James. What she wanted, I realized, was to ditch me and go to New York with someone who could afford it. So much for "hashtag downsizing."

Mr. Eli called us all to attention and launched into a soliloquy on Shakespeare that drew James's full and rapt attention, and put Reesa into a coma. About halfway through the class, she escaped with the bathroom pass and gave me an unobstructed view of James. I slid my eyes his way and found him looking at me, too.

He smiled a quick smile.

I quick-smiled back.

Mr. Eli gave the class an assignment to do at our desks. "Take five minutes," he said, "and write whatever comes to mind when you think of Shakespeare's plays. The characters, the language, the plots . . . What are your impressions? If you completed the eighth grade, you've already studied at least one of his plays. What are your perceptions of his work? How does Shakespeare make you feel?"

Kids started calling things out: "bored," "confused," "like slitting my wrists."

James frowned and bent over his notebook, writing furiously. I stared at my blank page for a moment, bent over it to write a single word, and held it up to show him.

Curious.

He smiled more widely and took out a fresh piece of paper, scribbled something quickly, and held it up to me.

Alive.

I put a finger to my lips and shifted my eyes around to look at our classmates.

He laughed, and that's when Reesa walked in. I dragged my gaze away from James to my own paper, but not soon enough. Reesa glared at me when she sat down. She scribbled out a note and tossed it on my desk.

Thought you didn't like him.

I mouthed, "Who?" and gave her the best confused-and-befuddled expression I could muster. A shadow fell over my desk and I looked up to see Mr. Eli hovering there. He plucked the note out of my fingers, tucked it into his shirt pocket, and kept strolling.

Reesa and I exchanged cringes. I stifled a moan. Mr. Eli told everyone to finish up their work and pass their papers up to him. "We'll revisit these at the end of our section on Shakespeare," he said, "and see if anything has changed."

Then he pulled Reesa's note from his pocket and glanced down at it before crinkling it into a tiny ball. "Everything is not as it seems!" he bellowed. "A common theme in Shakespeare's plays, you'll find. Right, Ivy?"

My head snapped up. "Um, right?"

Mr. Eli chuckled, dropping the note on my desk as he walked past. I scooped it up and kept my head down for the rest of the class. When the bell rang, I darted out, avoiding James but not quite fast enough to escape Reesa, who cornered me at the end of the hall.

"You like him."

"No." I shook my head. "I was just being friendly."

Her eyebrows pinched together in the middle. "Promise? Because he's the first guy I've liked in so long. I know this sounds crazy because I've hardly spoken to him but . . . I think I'm falling in love."

I laughed to myself—Reesa was always dramatic. But I took a deep breath and told her what she wanted to hear, because she was my best friend. I couldn't afford to lose her. And the lie was easier than the truth.

"I promise," I said. "He's all yours."

ELEVEN

'd been without my piano for four days now and I was beginning to feel the effects, my hands shaky with unplayed emotions. So, instead of heading to the cafeteria for lunch, I veered off toward the band room.

It was empty and quiet, except for a set of hi-hat cymbals tinkling against each other as if an invisible drummer had left his foot on the pedal. An upright piano sat facing the wall in the corner, next to the smartboard. I walked to it and let my fingers slide across the keys.

Pressing my thumb to the middle C, I let the sound mingle with the shimmer of the cymbals. I added my middle finger and pinkie, plunked a C chord. The piano was slightly out of tune, but I could feel the soothing vibration all the way up my arm. Playing always calmed me, as long as no one was listening. I slid onto the bench and lifted my left hand to the keys as well and slowly played the ascending chords, key by key, majors then minors. I was drawn to the minor keys today. They matched my mood.

I let my thoughts mingle with the scales, adding syncopation and rhythm to the notes I played. Why did Reesa assume James was wealthy? Just because he drove a nice car? Maybe he'd worked for it, earned it with his own money. Maybe he was the kind of guy who wouldn't care whether a girl lived in a mansion or a shoe.

The notes spilled from my hands, taking me back to the argument between my parents I'd overheard that morning. Low and soft and anxious. Then racing, like my heart had been. Pedaling fast, falling, knocked so numb and senseless, I'd actually been relieved to see Lennie, the fear returning when he sped away, riding shaky and slow—it all came out in a frenzy of sound. Then smiling, a quick and happy note to James and back. A laugh. Alive and curious, two playful melodies coming to an abrupt halt. Then taking it back. My happiness undone.

If anyone knew how to listen properly, they'd hear all my secrets in the song I played.

A calm came over me once I finished dumping my day onto the keyboard. I then played something familiar, comforting— one of the lullabies I'd written for the twins. I sang the melody as softly as I could, so nobody would hear me out in the hall.

"That's nice."

I spun around to see Molly Palmer sitting there, partly hidden by a bass drum, with a clarinet on her lap.

"Sorry," she said. "Didn't mean to scare you or spy on you or anything. I just sat down to practice when you walked in. I thought you saw me, but then you started playing and, well . . ."

"It's okay." I quickly closed the lid of the piano and hurried for the door. I had forgotten Molly even played the clarinet. Her dad was a musician, I remembered. They had a little recording studio in their basement.

"You're good, you know," she said. "I'd love to hear more."

I stopped and looked up at her. We used to tease her for the crazy flowered dresses she wore when we were friends in ninth grade, but there wasn't a flower to be seen on her anymore. She was still quirky, though. Beat-up army boots with tight, faded jeans and a cable sweater so big and baggy it nearly swallowed her knees. She looked like she might have escaped the 1980s.

"No, you wouldn't," I said. "I'm a sheep, remember?"

She smirked. "I said 'Don't *be* a sheep.' That's what happens if you stay friends with Willow Goodwin too long."

"I'm not really her friend. I just play one on TV."

She laughed, a bit too loud. "Well, you don't *sound* like a sheep. You have a beautiful voice. And whatever you were doing on the piano before? That was crazy good, too."

I shook my head. "Not really."

"Uh, yeah," she said. "Really. What *was* that?"

I laughed, a sudden gush of nerves. "I just made that up. It was nothing."

"That was *not* nothing. Seriously. It gave me the chills. I felt like I was somewhere else there for a minute. Or *someone* else."

As a musician, I could never hope to receive a more

meaningful compliment. To create music that was transformative, that changed how people felt *about themselves?*

"Thanks." I took a step toward her. "Nobody ever said that about my music."

"I've never heard anything like it. And I listen to a *lot* of live music."

"Where?" I asked.

"The King Theatre in Belleview. They do an open mic night once a month. I always go."

"To perform?" I was impressed.

"No," she said quickly. "Nobody wants to listen to a lone clarinet squawking away. But if I had a pianist to accompany me . . ." She left the suggestion hanging there.

My throat started to get tight just thinking about it. "I, uh . . . usually only play for myself. By myself, I mean. At home."

"Oh. Sure. I understand." She rolled her eyes and started pulling her clarinet apart to put it back in its case.

"No, really. I get stage fright," I explained. "Really bad. Like completely paralyzed bad."

"Have you tried therapy?"

I shook my head. "I couldn't do that."

"Why not?"

I thought of Brady, the therapy he needed just to deal with normal, everyday stuff like talking and using a pencil. Paying for it had cost us our home. Getting therapy for something as lame as stage fright felt a little self-indulgent.

"The piano is my therapy," I said. "You know when you feel like screaming or crying or laughing really hard? I just do that on the piano." I'd never really explained this to anybody before, and here I was telling Molly Palmer.

"That is awesomely weird," she said. "And I mean that in the best possible way."

I smiled as the bell rang. "Maybe I'll see you next time. We can practice together." The words came out before my brain had a chance to realize what I was saying. Practice together? I *never* did that.

"Sure," she said. "Just don't tell Willow. You'll be banished from the herd."

I nodded and left, feeling more like myself than I had in a while—though I wasn't exactly sure who "myself" was anymore. The thing was, I hadn't told a single lie to Molly. I hadn't worried what she would think or who she would tell. And there was nobody else I could do that with. Not even Reesa.

I started to fantasize about that secret room in the supply closet, about hiding in there all day with James's books. I could read all the notes in the margins of his Shakespeare and nobody would bother me. Maybe James would find me there and we'd sit and talk and ignore the rest of the world. I was thinking about that when Reesa caught me trying to disappear upstairs after last period, and my face went red. I could feel the heat shoot up my neck into my cheeks.

"You're mad at me," she said.

"No." I only wanted to get to my secret room to find out if James had answered my question, and the guilt of lying to Reesa about James was eating at me. "Why would I be mad at you?"

"Because I invited James to New York since you can't go and that is a totally sucky thing for a best friend to do and then I freaked out when you smiled at him or whatever because I'm paranoid and crazy?"

It took a minute to process. "Right. I'm totally mad at you," I said.

"You are?"

"Um . . . no."

Reesa slumped against my arm. "You are the best friend on the planet. Gotta go. I'll call you later."

She ran for the bus. I realized I hadn't asked her how it was without me. We used to sit together, put our backpacks on the seat over the wheel hump, and slouch down in the one behind it. We had an ongoing game of "Guess What's Happening to the People in that House." All it took was a single sighting of a human entering or leaving a house to get us started. The scenarios we imagined usually involved wild affairs with gardeners or mysterious packages being delivered to spies. A woman with luggage? *She's leaving him,* Reesa would say. *She's fed up with his affairs.* Then she'd get quiet and I would know she was thinking about her parents, who were always on the verge of divorce.

I reached the supply room and slipped inside, locking the door. It was easy now to find the switch and the little room. I noticed some paper towels missing, and the mop bucket was in a slightly different place. The secret room, however, was untouched— except for the addition of a book on the shelf.

It rested on top of the Shakespeare. *The Hitchhiker's Guide to the Galaxy*.

I picked it up and smiled. How could you not love a book whose characters had names like Zaphod Beeblebrox and Gag Halfrunt? I flipped open the first page and read the brief note penciled there, presumably for me:

Your turn.

I assumed he was lobbing the question of what he read for fun back to me. But I hadn't brought a book. I'd have to leave something in the morning, though my collection at home was a little sparse at the moment. Most of my books were back at our old house, waiting to be sold off along with everything else.

I flipped through *Hitchhiker's* for a while, then closed up the little room and checked to see if the hall was clear. There was one place I could grab a book. I took the back hallway to avoid Lennie's stairwell. All the English classes were taught there, and Miss Poppy's free book bin sat outside her door. I stopped to peruse. There were eight copies of Homer's *Odyssey*, five of Dante's *Inferno*, one *Wuthering Heights*, and a single cover-missing copy of

Jane Eyre. Maybe nobody else would classify *Jane Eyre* as "fun," but I'd read it three times, and not for any class.

I pulled the book from the bin and hugged it to my chest. There was something about Jane. She was refreshingly uncomplicated amid a complicated life. If only I could be that way.

I rushed back to the secret room with Jane and slipped her onto the shelf, wishing I could take up residence there, too. Jane was in good company. It was more than I could say for myself.

TWELVE

On Thursday morning, I met Reesa by our lockers. Our conversation was a game of dodgeball. It was "James this" and "James that" and all I could think about was whether or not he appreciated *Jane Eyre* and would he leave me another book today.

I managed to avoid smiling at him in AP English, but I worried he'd think I didn't like him as much as I worried that Reesa would think I *did*. He played along, or maybe he didn't care for my smiles after all.

Molly caught my eye in the cafeteria as I sat down at my usual table with Willow. She gave a quick and sympathetic grin but didn't say hi or wave or give any indication that we might be the slightest bit friendly. Her discretion only made me feel like a bigger fraud.

Reesa never mentioned James in front of Willow or Wynn, so I wasn't the only one telling lies of omission. She probably worried they'd swoop in and nab him for themselves. He was a senior, and even though he was taking my junior AP English class to make up some credits, he didn't eat lunch our period.

Willow wouldn't have allowed him at our table, anyway. She had a "no boys" policy, claiming that lunch was reserved for girl talk. I suspected it had more to do with her tendency to grow tired of boyfriends after about five weeks. She didn't want to have to give up *her* table to some guy.

"Mark your calendars, ladies," Willow announced. "Halloween is on a Friday this year, so we're having our party the Saturday *before*." The Goodwins threw a huge bash every year, and it was a terrible faux pas, her mother believed, to host a Halloween party in November.

"Theme?" Wynn asked.

"Mom's still deciding," said Wynn. "It's either the Roaring Twenties or Broadway."

"Flappers or Cats." Reesa held her hands up like claws.

"Ooh," said Wynn. "I want to be a flapper." She mimed holding a long cigarette.

The previous year, we'd all rented elaborate—and expensive—dresses for a medieval theme, with laced-up bodices and flowing sleeves. "I vote Broadway," I said, thinking I could dress as an orphan from *Annie*.

"Your preferences will be taken under advisement," said Willow with exaggerated snootiness. It wasn't that different from her regular voice. "But Mom has her heart set on this jazz band she saw at the Lincoln Center. Her assistant is finding out if they're available."

The party always featured a live band. The Goodwins put up

a circus-sized tent and erected a wood dance floor on their lawn. It was crazy. I couldn't help thinking what our family could do with that party budget. Probably pay our mortgage *and* Brady's therapy for a year.

"So, ladies," said Willow, "if there's anyone special you want on the guest list, speak now or forever hold your peace."

Wynn started rattling off the cutest members of the basketball team, lacrosse team, and soccer team. "Jeremy Dillon, Evan Stans, Andrew Hudson . . ."

Willow held up a hand to interrupt. "Suffice it to say that every cute guy in this school will be invited," she said.

"Even . . ." Reesa started, then snapped her lips shut.

"Even who?" said Willow.

Reesa darted a warning glance my way. She'd almost said James's name but must've remembered she was keeping him a secret from Willow. "Nobody . . . never mind."

"How about Molly Palmer?" I suggested. "We all used to be such good friends. She's—"

Willow nearly choked on her portobello sandwich. "Why the hell would I invite *her*? I heard she lives in Lakeside now. Some trailer park or something. I would *die*."

I glanced at Reesa, our eyes holding the growing number of secrets we kept between us. As for the ones I kept from her, I swallowed them with a gulp of my chocolate milk.

* * *

Following my new routine, I made my way to the tiny room in the supply closet at the end of the day. *Jane Eyre* sat untouched where I had left her on the shelf. I flipped through her pages, front and back. *Nothing.* Maybe he'd gotten bored of the little game we were playing. I left, disappointed, after my required twenty minutes of waiting.

When I pedaled into our neighborhood, Lennie was leaving in his red Jeep. I steeled myself for some kind of harassment, but he just drove by. Didn't even glance my way.

I tucked my bike under the back stairs and trudged up to our apartment, muscles still complaining from my accident the day before. I let myself into our miniature kitchen, rounded the half island with its three stools, and went for the fridge to get a drink. Mom had stuck a note there with a magnet advertising a local pizza joint. In our old house, she never let us stick papers on the Sub-Zero.

> *Ivy~Walk over to the store and get potatoes. See coupon on counter. Six bags, if you can manage it.~Thx, Mom*

I picked up the six dollars she'd left on the counter, and a two-for-one coupon on five-pound bags of Yukon Gold potatoes. How exactly did she think I was going to carry thirty pounds of potatoes? And what was she going to do with that many potatoes, anyway? The store she referred to was not Bensen's, the gourmet market we used to frequent, but the Save-a-Cent on the corner. I could walk it, lug four bags in my backpack and one in each hand, or I could take my bike with its trusty basket.

I left my backpack on the kitchen floor and headed back down the stairs. The Save-a-Cent had a bike rack out front, next to some metal boxes that dispensed newspapers. I rode right past them and parked behind some Dumpsters, then cut through the parking lot before heading to the main entrance.

Yanking a cart free, I spun it around and rolled into the store, ignoring the stacks of ginger snaps and clementines near the entrance. Not in the budget today. My mouth started to water thinking about them, though. They weren't even my favorites, but suddenly they were an extravagance. I headed for the produce department, where I spotted the BUY ONE, GET ONE FREE sign above the potatoes. I dug into the giant mound, counting out six bags. Someone stepped up to pick through the loose baking potatoes beside me. He chose one and dropped it into his handbasket alongside a T-bone steak and a small bunch of fresh green beans. I had this silly urge to start a conversation with "Hello, single-steak guy. I'm crazy potato girl." Then I glanced up and realized, with a gurgly choking sound, that it was him.

James.

He turned, no doubt alerted by the embarrassing noise I'd just made, and spied me standing there with a bag of potatoes clutched in each hand. One of his eyebrows cocked upward.

"Hello," he said.

"Um, hello."

"We've got to stop meeting like this."

"Right. Yeah." A nervous laugh erupted from my throat. I snapped my mouth shut and plopped the potatoes into my cart. "You, uh . . . shop here?"

He lifted his basket to indicate that yes, he did, indeed, shop here.

"Stupid question." I grimaced.

"The prices are good," he said. "I've been comparing."

A bargain shopper? Reesa would be devastated. "Research for a home ec project?" I said, "Or, uh . . . just a hobby?"

The corners of his lips tweaked up a tiny bit. "Trying to save money. That's all."

I glanced toward my haul. "My mother sent me. She's preparing for Armageddon, apparently."

"That's a lot of potatoes." He peered from my cart into his own basket. "My groceries are feeling a little intimidated."

My laugh came out normal this time, and I felt like an almost-regular person for a second. Until a tall, tattooed figure approached. I tried to blink him away but he kept coming.

"Are you following me?" said Lennie. He was wearing a green apron with the Save-a-Cent logo across his broad chest.

"No, I . . . uh, you work here?" Again, my grasp of the obvious was stunning.

"Nah, I just like wearing the uniform." Lennie hitched his thumbs under the straps of his apron, like a farmer tugging on his overalls. "Fetching, isn't it?"

He looked around me and spotted James, wiped his hand on his apron, and reached his tattooed arm out to shake.

"Hi. I'm Lennie."

"James," said James. He took Lennie's hand and pumped it twice.

My heart was thumping double time but my brain seemed to be working in slow motion. I should've noticed the evil grin that came across Lennie's face and hurried out of there. But I wasn't fast enough.

"You want some bananas?" Lennie leaned over my cart and spoke in one of those conspiratorial whispers loud enough to wake the dead. "I got some in the back I'm supposed to trash. They've only got a few brown spots, though."

I shook my head. "No. No thank you."

"You sure?" He was trying to embarrass me in front of James and doing a fine job. "I could set some aside for you. That was your bike I saw parked out behind the Dumpster, wasn't it?"

"I . . . I don't need bananas." I pleaded with my eyes. *Please don't do this to me.*

He glanced at James. "How 'bout you, Jimbo? Bananas?"

I bowed my head in a silent prayer that a trapdoor would appear in the dingy linoleum and swallow me whole. But James responded as if free, overripe produce was offered to him every day. He didn't even flinch at the nickname Lennie had given him.

"Thanks, man," he said. "Another time?"

"You bet," said Lennie. He made a clicking sound and pointed his finger at James like it was a gun, then holstered it in his apron pocket. He sauntered to the double doors at the back of the produce area and pushed them open saloon style.

I exhaled.

"Your friend is . . ." James paused.

"He's not my friend," I blurted. "I hardly know the guy. He's . . . I think he's a drug dealer."

"Oh. Well . . . he seemed cool."

Way to go, Ivy. He probably thought Lennie was a great guy now, and I was a total bitch. I maneuvered my cart to face the exit. "I've gotta go."

"Oh." His voice was soft, almost sad. "Good-bye, then, Ivy Emerson."

My eyes widened at his use of my full name, and the way he said it in that soft, low voice, at the realization that he knew my last name at all. "Bye!" I chirped.

I hurried to the checkout and loaded my potatoes on the conveyor belt. My fingers were shaking when I handed the coupon and six dollars to the cashier. She noticed and looked at me funny. I quickly grabbed my bags and ran out. Lennie was standing by my bike. He started wheeling it toward me.

I stormed over to him, piled the potatoes into the front basket, and snatched the handlebars away from him. All the maybe-he's-not-so-bad feelings I'd been having since he rescued me by the side of the road had completely evaporated. "Are you trying to ruin my life?"

"No, I . . ."

"Can you just leave me alone, please?"

I pedaled off and got about ten feet from where he was standing when one of the bags fell and broke open. Potatoes rolled across the asphalt. I jumped off to pick them up, but my bike didn't have a kickstand and I couldn't lay it down or the rest of the potatoes would spill.

Lennie watched it all without budging. When I whirled to see if he was going to help, he held his hands out by his sides, palms up. "You said to leave you alone."

I got back on my bike, tears stinging my eyes, and rode off—leaving the potatoes scattered across the parking lot.

THIRTEEN

"Where's Mom?" I leaned the bike against the side of the house and lugged the bags of potatoes toward the back stairs, where the twins squatted with their sticks. It was rare to see Brady unsupervised, because wandering off was a constant worry. He'd collected an impressive pile of gravel that had migrated all the way to the backyard.

"Upstairs," said Kaya. She pointed to the first-floor apartment. "Miss Carla is watching us. She went in there."

"Then she's not watching you, is she?" I shifted my lopsided load of potatoes, my shoulders aching under their weight.

Kaya silently mimicked my grumpy remark. I made like I was going to swing an armload of potatoes at her and she ducked.

I hadn't really spoken to Carla since we'd moved in. I knew what kind of underwear she wore, however, because she hung it to dry on a line out back. When she emerged from the house, I was struck by her style, which did *not* scream "Lakeside landlady." She was tall and fit and slender, with dark, spiky hair that shimmered with a hint of deep purple highlights. She wore silver hoops in her ears and a vibrant blue scarf over a simple white blouse, jeans, and black boots.

I looked down at my drab hoodie and jeans and felt under-dressed.

"Hello, Ivy." She spoke with the slightest tinge of a Spanish accent. "Did you have a nice day at school?"

I nodded. "Mm-hmm."

She held out a plate. "Cookie?"

"No, thank you." My arms were about to fall off. "I'm just going to put these away."

I climbed the stairs, let myself in our back door, and dropped the potatoes on the kitchen counter. Mom was in the shower, I could tell, thanks to the high-pitched whine that reverber-ated through the pipes. I peered between the kitchen blinds to make sure Carla wasn't ignoring the twins out there again. She had placed the cookies on a small plastic table and was pour-ing glasses of a bright-orange liquid from a pitcher. The twins gobbled and gulped, wet orange mustaches curling up around their lips. I had a feeling it wasn't the organic, all-natural juice my mother used to buy for us.

Plopping on the couch, I let my head fall back to stare at the ceiling. It was that kind of ceiling that looked like stucco. It hid cracks and flaws but was impossible to clean. You could see where someone had tried and rubbed off a section of the nubby surface.

My brother and sister were all giggles and chatter outside. The windows were closed, but I could hear every word through the thin walls.

I started thinking how nice it would be to stay on the couch for the rest of the day (the week, the year, my entire life . . .), just slip between the cushions and hide until the movers came and took us back to where we belonged.

Things got quiet outside, so I lifted my head to make sure the twins were still alive. They weren't at the plastic table anymore, and their mud hole was vacant. I heard the music then, and felt it. A dance beat pulsed from below, setting the glassware in the kitchen cabinets vibrating. Our landlady was partying with the twins? I threw open the door and ran down the stairs.

Kaya answered Carla's door when I knocked, a silky purple scarf wrapped around her head. She shimmied to the Latino pop song blaring on the stereo. "*Hola*, Ivy!"

Behind her, Brady danced around in a too-big cowboy hat, with castanets on his fingers.

His eyes sparkled. We'd all been so worried about how he'd adjust to the new place, but I swear he was handling it better than I was.

I looked around Carla's apartment, which was so much nicer than ours. Its hardwood floors were covered with richly colored rugs, not the wall-to-wall beige carpet we had. The couch was a creamy white. A large, rustic wood table took up most of the space, though. It was draped with fabrics, books, and magazines.

I didn't even see Carla sitting there until she jumped up and turned down the music. She was a chameleon blending into her surroundings.

"Come in, come in." She handed me the cookies again and this time I took one.

"So, you're at Vanderbilt High?"

"Yes," I said, biting into the cookie. It was still warm, and a bit gooey—delicious.

"Then you must know Molly Palmer. She lives around the corner. And Lennie, of course." She took a cookie and bit into it, watching Kaya dance in front of a floor-to-ceiling mirror.

So Willow was right about Molly living in Lakeside—though our neighborhood was hardly a trailer park. Maybe some of the houses were trailer-ish, but ours definitely was not. Unless someone had turned a trailer on one end and slapped a roof on the other.

"Has he offered you a ride yet?" Carla was still talking to me, I realized. "Lennie. He said he would. It's silly for you to be riding that bicycle. . . ."

"I'm fine," I said quickly.

She studied me for a moment. "I see. Well, I'm sure he'd be happy to take you if you change your mind. He's a good kid. Smart, too."

"Mm-hmm." I blinked a few times. He clearly had her fooled. And if Lennie was so smart, why wasn't he in any of my AP classes?

"You should get to know him," said Carla.

"Yeah, I don't, uh . . . We're not going to be living here very long, so . . ."

Carla's eyebrows raised upward a hair but she didn't say anything, just kept smiling. Which was infuriating.

"We better go." I scooted the twins out the door. "Thanks for watching them. And for the cookies."

"Oh, sure." She stared at me. "Anytime." She saw us out and leaned in her doorframe with arms crossed as we clambered up the stairs.

"What happened to the sixth bag of potatoes?" Mom barely waited for me to get through the door before she started in on me.

"I dropped it," I said. "It isn't exactly easy to carry thirty pounds of potatoes, you know. Want me to go pick them up off the side of the road?"

She huffed. "No need to be surly about it."

"Whatever," I mumbled, and retreated to my room. I tried to focus on my trig and chemistry homework, but my brain wouldn't cooperate. Half of it wanted to talk to Reesa, tell her about Lennie and the potatoes and James. The other half was considering a lobotomy. It felt like I was playing a board game with the wrong pieces or something. Nobody was matching up to who they were supposed to be or where they were supposed to go. Lennie Lazarski, "a good kid"?

Mom declared it breakfast-for-supper night, Brady's favorite. I came back downstairs, ate my pancakes and scrambled eggs in silence, then retreated back to my room to continue my homework. I heard Dad singing "Blackbird" again and looked at my clock; it was bedtime for the twins. As the melody rose up into the attic, my chest ached. I missed it so bad, singing to them. But I couldn't do it here. This wasn't the right place.

I dug my earbuds out from the depths of my backpack. It was silly to take them to school, since I couldn't exactly walk around listening to music on a phone that was supposed to be lost. Desperate to block everything out, including my own thoughts, I quickly scrolled past my usual homework-friendly choices of Vivaldi and Bach, and blasted Queen. If Freddie Mercury couldn't banish "Blackbird" and Lennie from my brain, I didn't know who could.

Around midnight I closed my books and fell asleep to "Crazy Little Thing Called Love." When I woke an hour later, the music had stopped and the wind was howling in a way I'd never heard before, like wolves in the distance. I scrambled to the head of my bed, reaching for the corner post, but it wasn't there. This wasn't my room . . . *this wasn't my bed*.

I fumbled for my lamp in the darkness but my knuckles knocked up against a wall. *Not my wall.*

Then it all came flooding back to me.

I found the lamp on the wrong side of my bed but didn't turn it on. No need to illuminate what I didn't really want to see. This wasn't the lavender-and-white room I'd grown up in, the room that held all my memories.

What would happen to those memories now?

I felt detached from them, from my old life. From myself. I sank under the covers and turned to the wall, running a finger along a peeling edge of flowered wallpaper. I tried to push it back into place but it kept springing out, farther each time.

I pulled my knees up to my chest and hugged them in the darkness. I just wanted to go back to the way things were.

FOURTEEN

The next morning passed without incident. But then lunch came. After packing for a few days, Mom calculated the expense and decided I should start buying what the cafeteria offered. "I tried for the free lunch program, but we didn't qualify. Still, it's much less expensive to buy something," she declared. "Just make sure you grab whatever fruits and vegetables you can."

When I arrived at the table with my tray, you'd have thought I'd slapped a dead chicken carcass on the table.

"Ew," said Wynn, looking at my chicken patty on hamburger bun with pickle and a side of corn. "That's nasty."

Willow opened her designer lunch bag. "How can you eat that?" She took out her usual portobello and sun-dried tomatoes on focaccia.

I closed my eyes and took a bite. "It's not that bad."

Reesa held her apple out to me. "Trade you for the pickle," she said, nodding at the limp sliver of green on my plate.

"Ew," said Wynn again. There were days when it was the only word in her vocabulary.

"You sure you want it?" I waggled the droopy pickle at Reesa. She nodded, so we made the swap. I snarfed down the apple because it was the only edible thing on my tray. Reesa never touched the pickle.

As I finished eating, Reesa kicked me under the table, her eyes flicking up to someone approaching from behind me. "Incoming," she whispered as Willow and Wynn sneered. I turned slowly, just in time to catch the object Lennie tossed to me.

A potato.

Every ounce of blood in my body raced to my face. I held the potato in my hands like I was cradling a baby chick.

"Good catch," he said. "You dropped that. I can bring the rest of the bag by your . . ."

"No! Uh, no." I was desperate to stop him from revealing my location. That he knew where I lived at all. "That's okay. I don't need them. Thanks."

Lennie's eyes flitted from my face to my friends behind me. I could only imagine the looks they were giving him. He put his hands up. "Whatever, dude. Have it your way. You know where to find me if you change your mind."

There was a moment of silence. Several long moments, really, until he was out of sight. I still had the potato cupped in my hand when I turned back around.

"What. The. Hell?" said Willow. "You know where to find

him? Who does he think he is?"

"He's nobody. He works at the grocery store. I dropped some potatoes. That's all." I tucked the potato into my bag and picked up my chicken sandwich. "He's nobody," I mumbled. No chance I'd be able to swallow anything, but I took a bite, anyway.

"What store? Not Bensen's," said Willow with dismay.

I shook my head. "Some crappy store my mom stopped at the other day. I don't even remember the name of it."

"But where . . ." Willow pressed.

"Who cares where he works?" said Reesa.

Wynn ducked low to the table. "He could be stalking you. Wasn't he bothering you the other day? And you were talking to him. You should never engage with a stalker. It encourages them."

I shook my head. "He's not a stalker."

"You talked to him?" said Reesa.

I wanted to yank my own head off and throw it across the room. "You mean when I thanked him for opening the door for me?"

"You shouldn't encourage him," said Wynn.

I took a few breaths and spoke slowly. "I am *not* encouraging him. Can we please just drop it?"

Reesa tossed the uneaten pickle back onto my tray. "Just stay away from him, Ivy."

I stared at the pickle, trying to figure out what Lennie was up to. If he was trying to be nice, he had a funny way of showing it. He knew the school hierarchy—why would he keep trying to talk to me, especially in front of my friends?

As soon as lunch was over, Reesa shuffled me down the hall and into a corner under the stairs. Her face was red. "Please tell me you are not hanging out with Lennie Lazarski."

"I'm not hanging out with him. He lives in my neighborhood. In the house beside ours."

"Lazarski lives next door to you?"

I shushed her and explained how he offered me a ride and gave me the bike helmet, and what happened at the Save-a-Cent with the potatoes. I left out the part about seeing James.

"And he stopped and helped me when I fell off my bike." It was like a confessional, and I had sinned.

"Great," said Reesa. "So what, you're, like, buddies now?"

"We're neighbors. That's all."

"Look," she said, "I'm trying to cover for you, but if you're going to start hanging out with the scariest guy in the entire school? There's not a whole lot I can do."

"I told you," I said, teeth clenched. "I am not hanging out with him."

"Well, he obviously didn't get the memo." Her nostrils were flaring. "Just tell him to stay away from our lunch table, okay? I don't want to be associated with him . . . and you shouldn't be, either. People will start to think we're dealing drugs."

I watched her storm off, absorbing her anger like a sucker punch. I gasped for breath. How could *she* be mad at *me*? And what exactly was she mad at?

I stumbled up the stairs, away from my locker and my next class. I needed to pull myself together, and the secret room beckoned.

When I got in and shut the door, a sense of quiet calm washed over me. I looked over at the shelf. There were only *Gatsby*, Shakespeare, *Hitchhiker's*, and *Jane Eyre*. But I found a note penciled on the inside flap of *Jane Eyre*.

> So serious? Love me some J.E., but what do you read for laughs?

I smiled. I knew just the book to offer in reply. I simply had to steal it back from my sister, who, unlike me, had been smart enough not to leave all her books at our old house.

FIFTEEN

On Monday, nobody said a thing about the potato incident and I was foolish enough to consider it forgotten. Then the cafeteria served mashed potatoes on Tuesday. Jeremy Dillon brought an ice-cream-scooped blob of it to me on a napkin. "I heard you really like potatoes," he said, laying it on my tray while the rest of the basketball team laughed.

Willow and Wynn wasted no time bailing on me and laughed right along with everyone. I turned to Reesa, who wasn't laughing but moved away from me, clearly mortified.

"Uh, no thanks." I handed the napkin of potatoes back to Jeremy.

"Oh, I get it," he shouted to his friends. "She only likes Lazarski's potatoes!"

The entire cafeteria erupted in hoots and the gossip started flying.

"Lazarski gave her a potato?"

"Sure it wasn't a dime bag?"

"Are they dating?"

Willow and Wynn inched away from me now as well, as if I had suddenly contracted a highly contagious disease. I tried not to make eye contact with anyone, until my gaze landed on a familiar face at a distant table. Molly was sitting there smiling at me, in a see-how-it-feels? sort of way.

Molly's banishment had been set off not by her move to Lakeside, but by her saying yes when Trevor Freebery asked her to the Jack Frost dance freshman year. Willow had been planning to go to the dance with Trevor (unbeknownst to Trevor, but that's beside the point). Rumors started circulating about Molly—that her dad was in jail, that she was pregnant with the baby of a guy who was in jail, that she was a cutter, that she was having an affair with a teacher . . . all kinds of crazy stuff. Trevor swore he'd never even invited her to the dance, that she'd made the whole thing up. Then she disappeared from school for a couple of months, and when she came back, she didn't talk to any of us anymore. She sat by herself or with the other outcasts.

Caught in Molly's gaze, all I could think was: *I barely made it a week.*

For the rest of lunch period I kept my eyes on the table in front of me, not even looking at Reesa, who seemed just as uncomfortable as I felt. I finally mumbled some excuse about using the bathroom and left early, shuffling toward my next class upstairs. As I passed the supply closet, I saw a light on under the door.

I had snuck in earlier—before school started—to leave the

book I'd snagged from Kaya's shelf . . . the one book that always made me laugh, no matter what: *The Essential Calvin and Hobbes*. I could skip class, sneak in there and see if James had found it and left a note. He'd barely acknowledged my presence in English, but I had a feeling that had more to do with avoiding Reesa, who kept asking him nosy questions.

"I asked him where he was from, and he said, 'around' all mysterious," she told me after class. "Around where? Why won't he tell me?"

"Maybe he's in a witness protection program," I offered.

"Then he'd have a whole story prepared," she said. "And I don't buy that 'country boy' stuff. He's wearing Diesel jeans. They don't sell those at Walmart."

"How do you know? You've never been to a Walmart."

She shot me a look. "He's too well dressed to be some hick."

It didn't occur to Reesa that maybe James wasn't interested in her, that maybe he was interested in someone else.

I stood outside the supply room door, looking at the slit of light beneath it, and listened for a sound. I knocked quietly, not really thinking what I'd do if someone other than James answered (or if James answered, for that matter). But no one came. So I knocked again, louder. Nothing. I was about to walk away when the light went off. My breath caught as I wrapped my fingers around the knob. I pulled the door open and peered into the darkness.

"Hello?" I waited for an answer, but all I heard was a rustling and a soft click. Somebody was in there. I fumbled for the light switch and slipped inside. The door closed behind me. Slowly, I stepped through the narrow space and into the corridor that went past the secret room. This time, there was a light coming from the other end, around a corner.

I walked toward it. The corridor bent in an L shape to the right and back to the left to another exit. With a sharp intake of breath I opened that door and found myself in a main hallway, the one that ran along the back wall of the school, parallel to where I'd started. There were a few students still straggling into classes, and small clusters gathered around their lockers. Looking past them, I spotted James—his sandy hair, his smooth gait. He turned down the stairwell and disappeared.

I hurried after him, not exactly sure what I'd do if I caught up. At the end of the landing at the top of the stairs were huge windows overlooking the faculty parking lot. I peered out. A lone figure emerged from the exit door located almost directly below where I stood.

James was leaving the building?

He opened his messenger bag and dug through it as he walked, and the trunk of his car popped open. I watched him put the bag inside and slam the lid shut. He moved to the driver's side and got in.

I sighed a heavy breath that steamed the window so I could barely see through it anymore. I was tempted to pound on the pane, call out to him. But it was too late. And I wasn't that brave. I didn't want to cause another scene. I lifted my finger to the glass and wrote in the steam: *W-A-I-T*, knowing he wouldn't see it. Knowing I shouldn't want the boy my best friend wanted, anyway.

I'd never cut school before, but I had an overwhelming urge to disappear. I couldn't face all the gossip about Lennie and that stupid potato. And my bicycle was waiting. I took the stairs leading to the same back entrance James had exited, and pushed open the door, expecting to see an empty space where his car had been.

But it was still there. And so was James.

He stood by the open car door, looking straight at me. He glanced up at the window above, then back down at me. Then crossed his arms over his chest and leaned against the side of the car, as if to say, *I'm waiting.*

The decision should've been harder. I should've hesitated for a second or two at least, to consider Reesa's feelings. I had promised. But I was fresh from the sting of her scorn, and my only thought in that moment was to put Lennie's damned potato and my lunch humiliation behind me. It was all I could do to keep myself from sprinting over to James, and I almost succeeded in walking across the lot like a normal person.

"Ivy Emerson." He did it again. Said my name like it was a work of art, and framed it with the most adorable, shy smile I had ever laid eyes on.

"James Wickerton." It was the first time I'd spoken his name aloud and I loved the sound of it.

"I, uh . . . got your message." He pointed to the window.

"Fortunately, I can read backward."

The letters I'd drawn in the condensation were still faintly visible. *T-I-A-W*. "I didn't . . . I thought you were gone."

"Still here." And still smiling.

"Shall we make our escape?"

"We're escaping?" he said. "What do you need to escape from?"

My presumption that he and I would leave school together now struck me as a bit, well, weird and presumptuous. "Oh, I, uh . . . what I . . . um, that's . . ."

James left me stammering and walked around to the front passenger door, swinging it open with a flourish. "Your chariot awaits. Would you care to ride shotgun?"

I smiled. "Yes. Yes, I would." I slid into the black leather interior, placing my backpack at my feet.

He snapped the door shut gently, ran around to the driver's side, and got in. Then he shifted into gear and pulled out of the lot.

"I wanted to thank you," he said, "for saving me the other day, in English."

He had hardly needed saving, the way he'd read those lines to Mr. Eli. "I wanted to get it over with," I said. "The longer I sit there getting nervous, the worse it is."

"I know the feeling. You did great, though."

"Thanks."

A million questions bounced around in my head: *Are those your books in the supply room? (Or was I flirting with the janitor by mistake?) Did you really read all of Shakespeare's plays? Where did you come from?*

Probably not the best conversation starters.

I looked out my window to stop myself from staring at him. That's when it hit me—I realized I had no idea where I was. I had driven off in the middle of the day with a guy I barely knew. It was exactly the kind of thing my parents had warned me against for years.

"So, where are we going?" The slightest hint of worry had crept into my voice.

He pulled up to an intersection and stopped, looking past me out the window to check for crossing traffic, then back the other way. "One of my favorite places," he said. "I hope you don't mind hanging out with dead people."

SIXTEEN

"Excuse me?" I squeaked.

"Okay, I hope this doesn't creep you out, but there's this cemetery I like to go to sometimes. It's a great place to think, to unwind. Whatever. It's quiet. Nobody bothers you. It has these massive old trees, and . . ."

He glanced over to gauge my reaction. "You . . . don't like trees?"

"Love trees. Trees are good. I'm not so sure how I feel about the graves, though."

"You'll like these graves." He nodded knowingly.

"We'll see," I said.

"You're a skeptic. Not a blind follower, then."

I remembered what Molly had said. "I don't want to be a sheep."

"I always thought sheep should have different names for singular and plural," he mused. "Like, one sheep and two sheepies. Or one shep and two sheep."

"Same with moose," I said. "One moose and two meese."

"Or one moo, two moose."

I laughed again. "I *really* don't want to be a shep or a moo."

"Or a deer," he said, pointing to one of those fake deer standing behind a low hedge in someone's yard. It had been decapitated. "Especially *that* deer."

I laughed. It felt so good to laugh.

We sort of giggled back and forth for the next mile or two. This neighborhood we were driving through was some sort of haven for weirdness. I spotted a tree-shaped sculpture made with sticks and empty wine bottles. Just as we passed that, we saw an all-white house with a single window on the second floor with a bright-yellow frame.

"What do you think?" I asked, nodding toward the house. "Paint job interrupted? Or unusual design choice?"

James stroked his chin as if he had a beard. "Maybe it's a portal to another world, a bright-yellow one. I've been trying to figure it out for a week now."

"You could knock on their front door and ask," I said. "Solve the mystery once and for all."

"Nah. What if it's some lame reason?"

I shrugged. "At least you'd know the truth."

"Truth is overrated," he said. "It's hardly ever as good as what you imagine."

I nodded, keeping my eye on the yellow window until it disappeared from sight. We drove in silence for a few minutes. My relationship with the truth was complicated at the moment, and if James wanted to stick to imagination, I was all in favor.

He pulled into a little strip mall and parked in front of a flower shop. "I'll be right back," he said, jumping out. He returned with a small bouquet of daisies, and for a split second I thought they were for me. But he put them in the backseat.

"I like to bring flowers," he explained.

"Oh! Is someone you know buried there?"

He hesitated, which seemed strange. Either he did or he didn't. But he said no, and explained, "I come here a lot, so they all feel like family, I guess. I just like to leave flowers."

"That's sweet."

He flashed me an embarrassed smile as we turned into the parking lot of a large brick building with a white steeple—the Northbridge Methodist Church. The cemetery was massive, with stone pillars on either side of a black arching gate. James grabbed the daisies and we walked toward it. He lifted the heavy latch and swung the gate open far enough for us to squeeze through. It clanged loudly when he pulled it shut, the noise echoing off the sea of tombstones sprawling out before us.

"This way." He started up a grassy hillside, cutting diagonally across a row of graves dating back to the early 1900s, and glanced over to make sure I was following.

I stepped gently, calculating where the coffins might be buried in relation to the headstones and trying to walk around their edges.

"You can't hurt them, you know. They're already dead. And they like visitors." He waved to some nearby graves as if they were old friends. "Hey, folks. This is Ivy. Ivy, that's, uh . . . Eunice and Gerald."

I pretended to curtsy. "Pleased to meet you."

James laughed. "See? They love you already."

"As long as they don't start talking back."

He leaned down to speak in a hushed voice, as if the tombstones might hear us. "That's why I like it here so much. Nobody talks, nobody tells you what to do, nobody judges. They only listen. That's all they can do."

I smiled. "I think I like this," I said.

"Told you." James beamed at me and stretched out his hand. "Come on."

He pulled me along the rows, zigzagging between stones. *Holding my hand.* This was so much better than sitting in the cafeteria with everyone staring at me.

A twinge of guilt fluttered in my stomach. If Reesa knew where I was and who I was with, she'd kill me. But James had barely spoken to Reesa, I reminded myself. How could she claim to like him so much?

James slowed our pace among the tombstones, swinging my hand in his left hand and the daisies in his right. We took turns reading the names of people who were long gone, imagining who they were and how they had died. There were entire families buried together. One man had a beloved wife on both sides. The first had died young, only twenty-eight. The other had outlived him. James pointed to one who shared his birthday. I couldn't find any with mine. We entered the oldest part of the cemetery, where some of the stones were barely legible. I started to read out the more interesting names: *Adaline, Selinda, Cletus, Bertram*. We saw plenty of men named James, but not a single Ivy.

"There's got to be an Ivy somewhere," I said. "Maybe if we went row by row . . ."

"I've done it," said James. "There aren't any."

"Oh!" I blinked a few times. *He searched the entire cemetery for . . . for a dead woman with my name?*

He noticed my expression and his eyes went wide. "I mean, I've walked all the rows. Lots of times. I would've noticed . . . if I saw . . . I'd remember an Ivy, is all." He swung the daisies nervously from hand to hand but kept strolling.

I walked a bit closer to him, so our arms brushed, and after a bit he took my hand again. This time it wasn't a sudden grab and pull but a gentle slip of his fingers between mine. It sent tingles up my arm. He pointed to the far end of the cemetery, where a giant oak tree stood. The rows of graves fell away from it like folds of a billowing skirt. "That's where we're going."

I had a sudden urge to run, to release all the tension and worry that had been coiled up inside me these past few weeks. And the coffin-width path of grass before me was so inviting.

"Race you."

"Serious?"

"On your mark, get set . . ." I dropped his hand and took off.

"What happened to 'go'?" he called, laughing. I could hear his feet pounding after me.

It was a straight shot for fifty yards or so; then I'd have to cross a few other rows of headstones and run up a hill. I pumped my arms and sprinted, then darted at an angle, weaving between the graves on the final stretch. James appeared in my peripheral vision, leaping over the stones like a gazelle. He surged past me but slowed just before reaching the tree, so we both touched the trunk together, panting.

"You're fast," he said, dropping the daisies to the grass so he could lean both of his hands on his knees.

I shook my head, still trying to catch my breath. I leaned my back against the tree. "You're like a track star."

"I never hurdled dead people before," he said. "Hope they don't mind."

From this vantage point, the tombstones looked like seats in an amphitheater. And we were at center stage. They sat quietly, patiently. Listening.

"I don't think they mind," I said softly.

He leaned his shoulder against the tree, next to me. His face was inches from mine, close enough that I could see the silvery bits that made his pale-blue eyes shine the way they did. As if sensing I wanted a better look at them, he pushed his hair back. It flopped right down again.

"Need a haircut," he murmured.

I shook my head. "No."

James bit his lip as an awkward silence passed between us. Was he going to kiss me, here in the cemetery? I couldn't decide if that would be romantic or creepy. My lips felt dry thinking about it, but if I licked them now, he'd know I was thinking about kissing.

He picked up the daisies instead. "Here."

"For me?"

He smiled. "Or you could pick who we leave them for."

My eyes widened. "Ooh, yes," I said, clasping the daisies to my chest.

He nodded toward the nearest row of tombstones, and I strolled along, reading the names and dates. I stopped in front of a heart-shaped stone that happened to memorialize a man named James and his wife, Clara.

"This one," I said. "James Aloysius Robertson and his wife, Clara Rose."

James had a funny look on his face, like he really *had* seen a ghost.

"Do you know them?" I said.

He shook his head. "No, I . . . uh . . ." He stepped back and sat on the bench in front of their grave. "I always sit here when I come. It's just funny you picked that one."

I squatted in front of the stone and traced my fingers over the dates etched there. They had both passed in September, five years before—Clara on the sixteenth, and James on the twenty-third.

"That's today," I said. "He died exactly five years ago today."

James nodded. "A week after his wife," he said quietly. "Couldn't live without her."

"It's sweet, isn't it? In a sad way," I said.

I laid the flowers in front of the stone and joined James on the bench. We sat quietly, the breeze rustling the leaves above us. A few fluttered to the ground with each gust of wind.

"You were right," I said. "It's nice here. The trees . . ."

"Trees are good," he said, smiling.

I was tempted to ask him if the books in the supply room were his, to be sure. But I liked the secretiveness of it. It got me through each day, anticipating a book or a note, a little treat just for me. If I revealed myself, it wouldn't be the same.

James stood up suddenly. "I have to show you something," he said.

I got to my feet and followed as he led me to the edge of the highest point of the hill overlooking the cemetery. We faced the rows and rows of headstones. Then he said the one word that frightened and excited me more than any other in the English language.

"Sing."

I snapped my head around to face him. How did he know? How could he . . . ?

"Or yell, or shout, or recite poetry, or tap-dance." He held his arms out wide. "Yodel, maybe."

"Yodel?"

He laughed. "Maybe not. Here. I'll show you."

James gently nudged me to the side, turning my shoulders to face him. "No laughing."

I shook my head.

Then he spoke, with a hint of a British accent. "'But, soft! . . . What light through yonder window breaks? It is the east, and Juliet is the sun.'"

He flashed me a quick smile.

I'd never seen or read the play version of *Romeo and Juliet*, but I'd watched a movie version with my mom, the one with a very young Leonardo DiCaprio and Claire Danes. I hadn't understood everything they were saying, but the way they looked at each other was explanation enough.

I lifted my hands to my face, squinting at James through my fingers.

"'See, how she leans her cheek upon her hand! O, that I were a glove upon that hand, that I might touch that cheek!'"

He stopped, backed up as if stepping off the stage, and was James again. "Good timing with the hands," he said. "Now your turn."

I kept my face covered and shook my head. "Uh-uh."

"Come on." He grasped my wrists and pulled them toward his chest, shaking me gently. "It's fun. Dead people make a great audience. You can do anything."

My wrists were still in his hands, and I made no move to take them back. His hands were warm and strong, and I needed all the strength I could get if I was going sing to these tombstones. Or scarier yet, to James.

But then I saw my watch peeking out between his fingers and the time . . . oh, no. "What day is it?"

"Uh, Tuesday?"

"Oh, my gosh. I'm supposed to be home for the twins' school bus. I promised I wouldn't forget." It was already four o'clock, and the bus would be dropping them off in ten minutes. "If I'm not there . . . if my brother . . . Can I use your cell?"

"I don't have one." He patted his empty pockets. "There's a phone back in the church, though."

I started walking. Fast. As we got closer to the gate, James said, "This way," and led me down a little path that emerged between some trees at the edge of the parking lot. Our feet pounded on the asphalt as we sped for the church. James yanked open the massive door and I dashed inside, blind for a moment until my eyes adjusted to the darkness. The scent of candle wax and old Bibles wafted over me.

"In there." James motioned to a vestibule off the entrance area. A black phone hung on the wall, with a sticky note posted above it. "Dial 9 for outside line." I picked up the receiver and punched 9 on the keypad, then stopped. If I called my mother, she'd be furious. I couldn't call Reesa, who was already mad at me for consorting with the enemy, and anyway, she might refuse to drive to Lakeside. For a single, crazy moment I considered

Lennie but quickly shook that awful idea from my head.

"You going to call somebody?" said James.

"Yes, I . . ." It had to be Carla. But I didn't know her number. "I need to look up a number."

James found a phone book on the cloakroom shelf. I flipped through it and found Carla's name and my own address. I dialed quickly and the phone rang three, four, five times. It was ten past four now and the kids would be stepping off the bus any second, locked out of their house and alone. I wasn't even sure the driver would let them off if there wasn't an adult to meet them.

On the sixth ring, Carla answered.

"Carla? This is Ivy. Ivy Emerson, from upstairs."

"Well, hello, Ivy from upstairs."

"I'm running late and the twins'll be home any minute, and Brady . . . I was wondering, if you . . . would you mind . . ." I hadn't been very nice to Carla the other day and I felt weird asking her for help.

"No problem," she said. "I see the bus pulling up right now."

I let out the breath I'd been holding. "Thank you. Thank you so much, Carla. I owe you one."

"I better go out and greet them."

"Yes. Okay. I'll be home soon," I said, staring into the receiver before placing it back in its cradle. I took a deep breath and turned to where James had been waiting, but he was gone.

"James?" I checked the sanctuary, and another room off to the side. I found a piano, but no James.

Then I heard the unmistakable purr of his car engine outside. I was in my seat and buckled in seconds, and he tore out of the parking lot.

SEVENTEEN

"'ll drive you home instead of back to school," said James as we passed the house with the yellow window. "Where do you live?"

I didn't want him to see. *The truth is never as good as what you imagine.* "Actually, it's okay. I need to grab my bike."

"You sure?"

"Yeah. It's fine. I'd never hear the end of it, anyway, if I showed up with a strange boy."

He tossed his hair to the side. "I am *not* a strange boy."

I laughed, for the umpteenth time that afternoon.

"I had a really good time," I said as he pulled into the faculty parking lot. "This was exactly what I needed."

He smiled and said, "Me too."

I headed in the direction of my old neighborhood first, so James wouldn't see me pedaling toward Lakeside. Then I cut down a side street and found my way back to Jackson Boulevard. I was soon rattling down the gravel road toward our house, where I saw four figures in the yard. The two small ones were the twins, and the woman with purplish hair was easy enough to identify. But it wasn't until I'd rolled up close that I recognized the other one.

Lennie.

He was leaning against the front steps, chatting with Carla like they were old pals. I wheeled past them to stow my bike under the back stairs, dropping my helmet to the ground.

I went straight for Carla. "Thanks so much. You saved me."

She waved my gratitude away like a pesky gnat. "That's what neighbors are for." She nodded toward Lazarski. "You know Lennie."

I turned my head slightly but didn't make eye contact with him. "Yes."

Carla crossed her arms and studied us for a moment. "What have you done to her, Leonard?"

"Nothing!" He lifted his hands in mock surrender. "I swear."

I grimaced as Brady ran over to Lennie and tugged on the front of his T-shirt. "Airplane?" My brother stuck out one foot and one arm, nearly toppling over.

"I don't know, Brady—" Instinctively, I reached over to stop them, to protect him. It might make him dizzy. He had a hard enough time with his balance as it was. But Lennie had already grasped him by the ankle and wrist and was lifting him off the ground. Brady let his other arm and leg fly out wide as Lennie spun him around. Just once. But to Brady it was like the ride of a lifetime. He lay on the ground laughing while Kaya took her turn.

Lennie swung her around and around. Carla must've told him about the twins, about Brady's disability. He seemed to know to take it easy on him. I was surprised.

"Again!" Brady said as soon as Lennie was done spinning Kaya.

Lennie wobbled over to Brady. "I need a break, dude."

I hurried over and grabbed the twins by whatever I could get my hands on—the shoulder of Brady's jacket and the strap of a Kaya's jumper—and led them to the back steps. "Anyway, we have to go in now," I said to Carla. "Thank you again for watching them."

"Anytime."

Brady pulled free of my grasp and ran back into the yard. "I play with Lennie." My grip on Kaya loosened and she darted off as well. The three of them stood there staring at me, awaiting my verdict.

"You play with Lennie, too," said Brady, looking up at Lennie. "Can she?"

"Sure," said Lennie, grinning. "Ivy can play with me anytime."

I gritted my teeth. "One more spin, each of you, then inside. And I mean it. Mom'll be home soon." I made my way up the stairs and peeked out the kitchen window to make sure they were okay.

The twins begged him for more but he stopped at one each, actually obeying my edict. They hollered, "Bye, Lennie!" about a million times and finally came in. It took a while to get them settled at either end of the coffee table with a drink and a snack and some coloring books. Fifteen minutes later, I glanced out the window to the backyard. Lennie was lying on the grass, staring skyward. Aside from blinking occasionally, he didn't budge.

I walked downstairs and poked my head out the door. "They're not coming out again. You can go now."

He kept gazing at the sky. I craned my neck to see what he was looking at, but there was nothing but clouds.

I checked the twins once more to make sure they were still okay coloring, then pulled the door closed behind me and stomped down the outside stairs. I circled around him to stand where I could keep an eye on our apartment, my arms crossed.

"What are you doing?"

He shrugged. "Nothing in particular."

"Then would you mind doing it in your own backyard?"

He crossed his legs and laced his fingers behind his head. "Something tells me you didn't appreciate the gift I brought you in the cafeteria on Friday."

"Are you serious? You call that a gift?"

"I did purchase a whole new bag of potatoes for you with my very own money so, yes, technically, that's a gift."

I glared down at him. "No, I did not appreciate it."

He nodded over to where my bike was leaning under the stairs. "That's a spiffy new bike helmet you got there."

I knew the helmet must've come from him, but didn't want *him* to know I knew. "I thought it was . . . someone else. I'll pay you back for it."

"Not necessary," he said. "But a thank-you would be nice."

I glanced up at our kitchen door. It wasn't good to leave Brady alone this long. "Thank you for the helmet," I said quickly. "And the roadside assistance. I didn't ask you to do that." I didn't know why he was being so nice to me, either.

He shrugged. "It was my pleasure."

The way he said *pleasure* made it sound like he'd done something way more stimulating than purchase some protective headgear and fix my bike chain. I should've gone inside then, ignored him, but I couldn't help noticing that his shirt had hiked up a bit to reveal his abs, and they were disturbingly six-packy.

"Stop undressing me with your eyes, Emerson," he said.

I gasped indignantly. "I was not!"

I jumped over him to head home, but he sat up at exactly the wrong moment and my foot accidentally kicked him in the side of the head. I fell to my hands and knees.

"Ow, shit!" Lennie's hand flew to his eye.

"Oh, my God." I crawled to his side. "Are you okay?"

Lennie rocked back and forth holding his left eye.

I reached out to touch him. "I'm so sorry, I didn't mean to—"

He shoved my hand away.

"I'll get you some ice." I started for our back stairs.

"Don't bother." He got to his feet and stalked away, still holding his eye.

"Lennie . . ." I got up and took a few steps toward him but he kept walking. "I'm sorry!" I called after him. "I really am!"

He didn't turn back, and I stood in the yard until I heard the door of his house slam.

"Shit," I said.

Kaya's face was pressed to our living room window above, watching the whole thing with saucer eyes. I knew Carla had probably seen it, too. Or heard it. And Brady . . . I ran upstairs to find him curled up on the floor, bawling.

"Now look what you've done," said Kaya.

I knelt beside him and spoke in the most soothing voice I could muster. "It's okay, Brady. Everything is okay."

He banged his fists to the sides of his head. "You hurt Lennie."

I groaned. "I'm sorry. It was an accident. I said I was sorry."

Kaya gave me a stern look and took over, gently rubbing Brady's back and cooing softly in his ear as I latched the back door so he couldn't escape. I moved next to Brady, who started crying loudly again.

"Just go away," Kaya said.

"Fine." I backed off. "When Mom gets home, tell her I'm in my room."

Feeling like crap, I climbed the two flights of stairs to my attic room, sank into my bed, and pulled the edge of the comforter around me.

EIGHTEEN

It was dark outside when I woke up—seven o'clock, and I had slept through dinner. Without my piano, sleep was my only escape. There was no fear of being found out or humiliated, of losing my best friend or falling for a boy who was too good for me. Or the wrong boy.

There was nothing.

When I went downstairs, everyone was sitting around the coffee table playing Chutes and Ladders, Brady's favorite.

They were all crowded together on our single couch, Kaya and Brady crawling across our parents' laps to take their turns. My father would nudge them to the side or pin them under his elbows when he reached to spin the wheel, and they'd squeal.

Back home, in our real house, we had so much space to spread out. You could get away, to think or read or breathe without the entire family witnessing your every move. Brady's therapists used to come and work with him at our house; now Mom had to take him to their offices.

I sighed. I missed my piano room.

I missed my window-seat bedroom.

I used to sit at my window, surrounded by soft pillows, talking to Reesa on my cell phone. She'd walk over to my house with her phone to her ear and I'd wave to her as she crossed the yard. We'd keep talking until she was in the house and up the stairs and sitting next to me and we'd say bye and hi without skipping a beat.

I missed that so much. Thinking about who had replaced her as my neighbor made my stomach ache.

I picked up the remote to the small television from our old kitchen that now sat in the corner of the living room. A black screen of static blasted me when I turned it on, so I quickly muted and flicked to another channel, and another. Only a few local stations came in, and they were fuzzy. "What's with the TV? We can't get cable here?"

My father slid his player down a chute. "Essentials only, Ives. The less we spend, the quicker we pay off our debts."

"And get the hell out of here?"

"Language." Mom said sternly, snatching the remote out of my hand and turning off the TV. "Come eat some supper."

"I don't want any supper. I want to get out of this stupid place. I want to go home."

"Ivy!" said Mom. "We are home. What's gotten into you?"

"She had a fight with her boyfriend," singsonged Kaya.

"He's not my boyfriend, Kaya." I stomped into the kitchen, which wasn't particularly satisfying as far as dramatic exits go, since it was only three steps away. I climbed onto one of the bar stools with my back toward the living room, and folded my arms on the counter so I could bury my head in them.

Mom heated up a plate of sausage risotto and slid it in front of me. It was my favorite. "You want to talk about it?" she asked.

"No." I picked up a fork and shoved a bite into my mouth.

Mom poured a glass of milk and set it down next to my plate. "Delicious, nutritious, and affordable. Reminds me of when your father and I were first married. We hardly had two nickels to rub together, but we—"

"Can you please stop trying to make it sound like some great adventure? Because it's not. You moved us to the worst possible neighborhood in the district. Brady's got the freaking drug dealer next door for his new best friend, and the entire school is laughing at me. This place sucks, and nothing you say is going to make it suck any less." I pushed my plate away so hard, it accidently fell off the counter and clattered to the floor.

Mom leaped back with a gasp. "You think I wanted this?" She bent down, scooped up a handful of risotto, and splatted it into the sink. "You think I didn't do everything within my power to stop it from happening?"

"How would I know?" I shouted. "You've spent the past year telling me everything was just fine. Nothing to worry about. Nothing at all!"

The expression on my mother's face then made me stop, and she wasn't even looking at me. She was looking at the rest of our family. I spun around to see. Dad had an arm around each twin, hugging them to his chest and covering their ears. Brady was pounding his own hand on top of Dad's, and his mouth was wide open in what appeared to be a silent scream. I'd never seen him do that before.

Mom rushed to them, took Brady's face in her hands. "It's okay, sweetheart. It's okay." She shushed quietly until he stopped pounding and the silent scream turned to hiccupy tears. Dad kept his arms around them all, a big hug of family that didn't include me.

I turned to the risotto mess I'd made and began wiping it up with paper towels. When I'd cleaned most of the goop off the floor, Dad appeared with a bucket and mop and handed them to me.

"Your mother is working very hard to make the best of a difficult situation," he said quietly. "Maybe you could put a little effort into making it easier on her. Not harder. Huh?"

I nodded, feeling like utter crap . . . again. "Okay."

He stepped closer and spoke even lower, so nobody else could hear. His jaw was tight. "I don't ever want to hear you talk to your mother like that again. Understood?"

I nodded again. "Yes, sir."

Daddy went back to Mom and the twins while I mopped the kitchen floor. He and Kaya resumed their game of Chutes and Ladders. Mom held Brady on her lap next to them, still shushing.

I felt my throat tightening. Tears hovered dangerously close to the surface.

Daddy caught my eye. "Join us?"

I shook my head. There wasn't any room for me, anyway. "I've got homework," I mumbled.

After the twins got so upset that first night about missing their favorite toys, Dad had started spending every evening doing something special with them, no matter how tired he was when he got home from work. They played games, or he pushed them on the swing in the park across the street, or they made up silly stories. They played "Would You Rather" and Daddy always asked if they'd rather have cake or ice cream, snowdrifts or sand dunes, kisses or hugs. My own personal version of the game was not so fun: Lakeside or Westside? Embarrassment or total humiliation? Losers or druggies?

I retreated to the attic and opened my laptop, which was the only computer my parents hadn't sold. They agreed I needed it for homework, and I just had to let Mom and the twins use it sometimes. No cable in this joint, but at least we had internet access. A little red circle popped up on my email icon, alerting me to sixteen new messages. I scanned through them, deleting the spam and ignoring Wynn's links to cat videos. That left three from Reesa. They had all had been sent after lunch, while I was racing through the cemetery with James. A pang of guilt rang through me when I saw the subject line of her first email: SORRY. I clicked the window open to find a short message.

> Sorry about the idiots at lunch. I dropped some mashed potatoes into Jeremy Dillon's sweatshirt hood after you left, if that makes you feel any better.

I smiled, hoping he'd discovered it by putting his hood on.

The next email was titled YOU MUST DO THIS! It was the ad for the job at her country club. She wrote:

> Auditions on Saturday!

I hit DELETE.

Her next email was a link to a Little Invisibles video, a song called "Breathless." I loved this band because the lead singer was a girl, and she played keyboards, right up front in the middle of the stage. She also sang with her eyes closed most of the time, like she was a little afraid to see the audience out there. And I totally got that.

I closed my own eyes and listened, mouthing the words she sang, pouring my frustrations and fear into the silent song.

When I looked up, my mother was standing in the doorway. "Were you singing?"

Was I? I snapped the laptop closed. "No."

"Thinking about it?" She sat on the corner of my bed.

"Just memorizing some lines. For AP English. *The Canterbury Tales.*"

"Hmm." She studied my face. "Reesa's on the phone."

I tensed. "Okay," I said. "I'll be right there."

Mom padded away and I made my way down to the kitchen to take the call. My parents had vacated the living room to put the twins to bed, so I curled up on the couch with the phone to my ear.

"Hey, Reesa."

"*Hey, Reesa?* That's all you have to say to me?"

"Um . . . how are you?"

There was a strangled, growling sound on the other end. "Where *were* you? You were supposed to meet me in the band room after school."

"I was?"

"You didn't get my note?"

Since I'd joined the land of the cell-phoneless, we'd been leaving notes inside each other's lockers. She knew my combination and I knew hers. But I hadn't gone back there when James and I returned from the cemetery.

"Sorry. I went home early. I . . . uh . . . didn't feel well."

Reesa snorted. "That's great. I waited for an hour. Molly Palmer was in there playing her clarinet."

"Did you talk to her?" I was nervous, yet oddly hopeful. If Reesa and Molly became friends again, maybe I could stop sneaking around about everything.

"No, I did not talk to her," Reesa snipped. "She looked at me like she was going to bite my head off if I got too close. I waited in the hall."

"Why were we supposed to meet there, anyway?"

"So you could practice! For the country club thingy. Auditions are next Saturday. I thought . . ."

"Wrong," I said quietly. "You thought wrong."

"But you'd be perfect, and the money . . ."

"It's not happening, Rees." Yes, I needed spending money. It would raise fewer questions if I didn't have to decline every single activity that cost more than five dollars, which was the amount Mom had decided we could spare for my monthly allowance. But . . . no. I couldn't sing for people like that. "Can we talk about something else?"

She huffed, gave me a few seconds of silent treatment, then said, simply, "James."

Not the subject I was hoping for.

"I've been doing some research," she said. "His car has New York tags."

"It does?" I hadn't even noticed that.

"So I focused my search on New York. And I found them. They're loaded."

"Who's loaded?"

"The Wickertons. Ever hear of Wickerton Investments?"

"Uh, no?"

"I hadn't, either. It's some hedge fund or something. The owner is this guy Joseph Wickerton. He's on the list of the richest people in America. Number twenty-nine. Worth like nine billion dollars. I found an article about him in the *New York Times*. He and his wife are big philanthropists. They give all kinds of money to charity."

"So what makes you think they're related to James?"

Reesa sighed. "His name is Wickerton. And he's from New York."

"That's all you got?"

"For your information, Wickerton is not a very common name. They were the only Wickertons I found. Anywhere. They have to be related. Plus, in the article, it said they had a teenage son and a daughter in college. But they didn't mention their names. I'll have to keep digging on that."

A dozen questions came to mind.

"It can't be him," I said. "Why would he live *here*?" Sure, he looked the part. And he was well dressed and charming. But he was my secret and that would all change if he was a bajillionaire. He'd be special and I'd be . . . not. *Please don't let it be him.*

There were muffled sounds on Reesa's end, which I recognized as her shouting to someone while holding her hand over the phone. When she came back, she said, "Mom needs me for some bullshit."

"Okay. See you tomorrow."

"Oh! I didn't even tell you what happened with Lazarski."

"What?" I forced myself not to scream into the phone.

"Coming!" she shouted, and then to me, "Sorry. Tell you

about it tomorrow. You're gonna die."

"Wait . . . what?"

The phone clicked and Reesa was gone. And I was left feeling as helpless as a game piece on the Chutes and Ladders board, never knowing when I'd be sent tumbling downward again.

NINETEEN

In the haze of half sleep and early dawn, I wondered why so many birds had chosen top of our house for their morning perch. And also, why were they tap-dancing? But the sound soon revealed itself as rain thrumming on our roof, a few inches from my head. I bolted upright.

Shit. Rain.

I'd be soaked if I tried to ride my bike to school. The day I'd been dreading was here. *Already.* I was going to have to take the bus. The state pen bus.

My bed thought I should stay, bury myself in its warm folds and forget school. Forget everything. I wanted to listen to it, but ditching school a second day in a row probably wasn't the best idea. Plus I needed to find out what Lennie could've done to earn a you're-gonna-die rating from Reesa.

I selected my favorite ankle boots, a pair of tights, my vintage paisley dress with the short flowy skirt, and a cropped jacket. Might as well go down looking fabulous.

"Can you drive me today?" I gave my mother a pathetic, pleading look as I spooned cereal into my mouth. It was worth a try. "Please? Don't make me take that bus."

"Sorry, Ivy. I've got to get myself ready, see the twins off on their bus, and drop your father at the office, then get to work myself. I'll barely make it on time as it is." The newspaper had offered Mom additional work hours two mornings a week, and this was one of them. "Did something happen on the bus yesterday?"

Sometimes it was hard to keep up with my lies. "Uh, no, nothing."

I zipped my backpack and found an umbrella hanging on the coatrack by the door. It had purple and pink cats and dogs all over it, but at this point, what difference did it make? I carried it down the front steps and pushed the umbrella out the door ahead of me as I opened it into the wind. Maybe the dress wasn't such a brilliant idea. I clutched it tight against my thigh with my left hand while wrangling the cats and dogs with my right. The rain was coming down hard, spraying my legs. The narrow walk that led to the road was mostly puddles. I jumped from the lower step to the first spot of high ground, and another and another until I reached the gravel drive and turned toward the main road where the bus picked up. It was about a thousand puddles away.

I leaped to the middle of the road, which appeared to offer the driest path, and walked slowly.

A car horn beeped and I spun toward the sound. Lennie's Jeep sat there, its low rumble masked by the pounding rain. I puddle-jumped over to the tinted driver's-side window, which he rolled down about an inch to keep from getting drenched. I could barely see him in there.

"Nice umbrella," he said.

"Thanks." Any other day I would've had something far less gracious to say, but I'd been humbled. And he could bring up assault charges against me for what I'd done yesterday.

"Sure you don't want a ride?"

I contemplated my options as water seeped through the seams of my boots. Standing in a puddle is always a nice place to discover your footwear isn't waterproof. A ride with Lennie wouldn't have been my first choice, but it was a clear winner over riding the Lakeside bus. I finally nodded, walked as gracefully as possible to the passenger side and climbed in, dropping my soggy umbrella to the floor. "Thanks," I said again.

His only reply was to push the gearshift roughly into place. The Jeep was warm; he had the heat cranked. I wondered how long he'd been waiting out there.

"I'm so sorry, Len, about kicking you yesterday. It really was an accident. I didn't—"

He held up his hand. "It's okay. I guess I had it coming."

"Still . . ."

Lennie kept his face pointed straight ahead as we drove past a couple of umbrellas with legs waiting for the bus, and rumbled out onto the road. The rain was coming down in torrents, and the

Jeep's wipers couldn't keep up with it. It was almost impossible to see where we were going. He leaned toward the windshield.

"Be careful," I said. "Can you see?"

"Yep."

It was raining so hard, I doubted anyone would look up from their mad dash into the building to notice who had chauffeured me to school, but still I was glad when Lennie parked in a small lot along the side of the building. Less chance of being spotted there. When he cut the engine, I unbuckled my seat belt and shifted to face him, but he kept staring straight ahead.

"Look, I'm sorry," I said. "It's been hard, moving from Westside to Lakeside . . ."

"Must be awful for you." He nodded.

"No offense, it's just . . . not what I'm used to."

"Yeah, we're kind of short on limousines and butlers."

"We didn't have those, either," I said. "I just don't want to make a big deal about it. Okay? The entire planet doesn't need to know that we moved to Lakeside. It's embarrassing."

"You mean I'm embarrassing."

The guy had an amazing bullshit-o-meter. "Okay, fine. You're embarrassing me. You threw a potato at me in front of everybody in the cafeteria. I was embarrassed."

"Come on. If one of your friends had done that, nobody would've blinked."

Was he really going to make me spell this out? "My friends don't have your reputation. Which isn't exactly stellar."

He gasped in feigned shock. "It's not?"

"Might have something to do with the fact that you come to school every morning smelling like a bong."

"I don't smoke pot."

"Okay." I laughed, rolling my eyes. "Sure you don't."

He started to say something, then stopped and continued to stare straight ahead.

We waited for the rain to stop or for somebody to say something else. I wasn't sure which. But we sat and waited and watched others go into the building. The five-minute warning bell rang.

"You go ahead," Lennie finally said. "I'll wait here, so I don't embarrass you or anything."

I sighed. "Whatever."

It was weird, the way he wouldn't look at me. I picked up my wet umbrella and climbed out. Instead of walking toward the school, I rounded the front of the Jeep and approached his window. It was still raining and I couldn't see more than a blur of him sitting there, but I knew he could see me.

I tapped.

He again rolled it down barely far enough to expose the top of his head.

"Roll it down, Lennie. All the way."

He chuckled, in an it's-not-really-that-funny sort of way. The window squeaked down. I knew it was coming but the sight of it made me cringe. The socket of Lennie's left eye was colored a hideous shade of bruise. Purple and yellowish brown. I'd given him a serious shiner. And his eye wasn't open the whole way.

"Here's lookin' at you, kid." He tried winking at me with the bad eye and winced.

"Oh, Len. I'm sorry."

"Stop saying that, would ya?"

I stood on tiptoes and leaned in the window to get a closer look at the damage I'd inflicted. As my head was tilted to the side inspecting his eye, he leaned down and kissed me on the cheek. Soft and gentle. Just like that.

I stepped back and lifted my fingers to my cheek. "I'm sorry," I said again.

He grinned and pulled his head back into the cab. "Don't worry. I'll survive."

TWENTY

y hand trembled as I dialed the combination on my locker. I made a fist, digging my nails into my palms, forcing them to be calm. *Lennie kissed me.* Why? And why had I said, "I'm sorry"? I was sorry I kicked him. I was sorry I'd given him a hideous bruise. *I was sorry I let him kiss me?*

My wet jacket dripped a puddle around my feet. I stripped it off and hung it on the hook in my locker and grabbed the books I'd need for my first two classes. Amid the scramble of students hurrying to beat the bell, I heard the hooflike clomp of four heels, approaching me in purposeful unison. Maybe if I stood perfectly still, they wouldn't . . .

"Ivy." Willow growled my name.

I turned around slowly. She and Wynn crowded up against me. They both had potatoes clutched in their fists and pushed them at me.

"What is with Lazarski and these effing potatoes?" said Wynn.

I stared down at the potatoes I was now hugging to my chest. "W-what?"

"He gave me that potato yesterday after seventh period. He yelled my name in the hall, and when I turned around, he tossed it to me! I'm lucky it didn't hit me in the face. The guy is seriously twisted," said Willow.

"He did the same thing to me," said Wynn. "After school, out in front of the building. What is his deal?"

I shrugged. My mind bounced through the possibilities of what Lennie had been up to. "No idea," I mumbled.

Reesa walked up to us, saw the potatoes in my arms. "He's giving them to all the prettiest girls in school," she said casually. "Bethany Bartell got one, too, and Shawna Evans. He even gave one to Chandra."

Chandra Mandretti was a senior, and the most gorgeous creature ever to walk the planet. Harps played when she passed by, I swear. She had a long, thick, wavy brown mane that belonged on a TV commercial for hair care products. And her body was like a work of art. Toned and curved and shazzam in all the right places. I would kill for that body.

"Chandra?" Willow and Wynn said in unison. They looked stunned, and then . . . I couldn't believe it . . . pleased.

"Yeah." Reesa laughed. "She asked Lazarski what the potato was for, and he told her it was a tradition where he's from to give potatoes to the most beautiful girls in town."

"What?" I screeched.

"That's what I heard. He said it was a rite of passage of sorts, like a bar mitzvah or something. Chandra thought it was really sweet and funny." Her lips curled into an exaggerated pout. "Now I'm kinda pissed I didn't get one."

Willow and Wynn gave Reesa the most ridiculously insincere "poor you" faces and assured her she was stunning. Lazarski simply hadn't gotten to her yet, of course! Then Willow snatched her potato back from me and Wynn did the same. They smiled smugly and clomped off. With Chandra's blessing, Lennie's potatoes were now a coveted symbol of beauty.

I shook my head as they flounced away. "You cannot be serious."

Reesa's face broke into a wide grin. "He did give potatoes to Shawna and Bethany, but I made the rest up."

"Chandra?"

"Total bullshit."

"The tradition of . . ."

"Utter fabrication," said Reesa, clearly pleased with herself. "Someone had to save your ass."

"Thanks." But part of me knew full well it wasn't only my ass she was saving. She didn't want to lose me as a best friend, but she also didn't want to be the best friend of a loser.

I slipped into my homeroom seat as the bell rang, still unnerved by my own bizarre behavior. And Lennie's. The potato thing was . . . weird. When I'd left school with James yesterday, everyone was chattering about Lennie and me and the potato. This morning, it was diffused. Four other girls had received potatoes, so the gossip was no longer focused on me.

Maybe it wasn't Reesa who had saved my ass. Maybe it was Lennie.

But, I reminded myself, Lennie was the one who got my ass in trouble in the first place.

As our homeroom teacher took attendance, the speaker came on with a fuzzy blast and one of the office receptionists said, "Excuse me, Mr. Dalton? Could you please send Ivy Emerson to the office?"

"Okay," said Mr. Dalton. "She's on her way." Everyone made the ooohh-you're-in-trouble sound. My face did its I-am-a-beet impersonation.

The speaker gave another fuzzy blast and then the morning announcements began as I left the room. The Pledge of Allegiance reverberated down the hallway, accompanied by the squeak of my wet boots. I waited outside the office door until the pledge was over, but I could see James sitting in there, studying the floor between his knees.

He didn't smile or nod or lift an eyebrow when I entered, merely held my gaze. Under the fluorescent lights, his eyes seemed dimmer than they had in the cemetery. No reflection of bright-blue sky today. No light from within. I gave him a faltering smile but his face didn't change. He looked like he might be sick.

The assistant principal, Mrs. Lanahan, stepped out of her office and asked us both to follow her. James stood and gestured for me to go first. We took seats facing her desk.

"Ivy. I'm surprised to see you here." Mrs. Lanahan was in charge of discipline and had been for years. She flipped through a manila folder with my name of it. I knew it was filled with honors and perfect attendance. "I'm told you missed your afternoon classes yesterday, but I have no record of an early dismissal. Explain."

"Oh, um, I wasn't feeling well and wanted to go home." I glanced at James. His presence here meant she knew we'd been together. "James offered me a ride."

"I see," she said. "You know you can't simply leave school because you feel like it. Even if you're ill, you must ask to be excused. Why didn't you go to the nurse?"

"I don't know, I needed some air, I guess. . . ." My voice trailed off.

She turned to James. "And you, Mr. Wickerton, are studying here under special circumstances, as a part-time student." She picked up a thinner, blue folder with his name on it. "You are free to leave the premises after your classes. But if I learn that you are transporting other students off the property before their dismissal time . . ."

"It won't happen again."

"I expect it won't," she said, and looked back at me. "Ivy, I'm letting you go with a warning, because of your perfect record.

Next time, you'll be enjoying a stay at camp detention. Got it?"

"Yes, ma'am."

She waved the back of her hand toward the door. "Get a late pass from Miss Bennett. James, stay a moment."

I collected my things and scooted out her door, pulling it closed behind me, then wishing I hadn't. What was she saying to him that she didn't want me to hear? I waited for my pass, straining to catch bits of their conversation. It was all too quiet and muffled until the door opened, and I heard the last bit.

". . . can't hide the truth forever," she said.

The hall was empty as we headed toward class. James walked about as far away from me as he could get and still looked slightly green. I felt like my own skin must've turned a lovely shade of creamed asparagus.

What did she mean, "can't hide the truth"? Surely, my parents had submitted a change of address, maybe even explained our circumstances. If that woman told James anything about it, I would report her for . . . for breach of privacy or confidentiality. Or something.

"Sorry to get you into trouble like that," said James, merging over to my side of the hallway.

"It was my idea. Remember?"

He smiled. "In that case, thanks a lot for getting me in trouble."

I shoved him gently with my elbow. He shoved back.

"So . . . ," I said. "You're part-time? I didn't even know that was allowed."

"Technically, I'm homeschooled." He made little air quotes around the term. "That's the only way they'd let me enroll for just two classes—AP English and art history. But that's all I needed." A guilty expression came over his face, like he couldn't believe he was getting away with it.

"To graduate?"

He nodded. "My last high school was pretty intense."

He didn't elaborate further and I didn't ask. The only schools I knew of like that were private and expensive. There was an all-boys boarding school people said was like the first two years of an Ivy League college. Kids came from as far away as California to go there. Maybe Reesa was right about James and the wealthy Wickertons.

As we started for the stairs, James took my wrist and pulled me into the same corner where Reesa had reamed me out over Lennie the day before.

"I have something for you." He reached into his messenger bag and handed me a piece of notebook paper that was folded into a small rectangle.

I started to unfold it.

"Not now," he said. "It's too embarrassing. Open it later, okay?"

The door at the top of the stairwell swung wide and one of the math teachers came plodding down. He gave us a dirty look. "Passes?"

We pulled ours out and showed them to him.

"Move along," he said.

James motioned for me to go ahead of him. When we reached Mr. Eli's room, he put one hand on the doorknob and the other on the small of my back. It was a simple gesture, but it melted me. He looked into my eyes, opened the door, and poured me into the room.

I quickly wiped the swoon off my face when I realized the entire class was staring at us, including Reesa. Mr. Eli took our passes and even he gave us a funny look. I sat and tried to focus on what he was saying. I gave up after about two minutes and pulled out the paper James had given me, discreetly smoothing it flat inside my notebook.

Then I looked down at it and ... *Oh, my God.*

It was the most incredible drawing, a crazy collage of our trip to the cemetery. The wine-bottle sculpture was there, and the headless deer, and the giant oak tree and tombstones. And he'd drawn us on the hill as Romeo and Juliet. It actually looked like us, except I wasn't wearing a hoodie for a change. He'd depicted me in a flowing dress with wings—like an angel. It was insanely beautiful. Around the edges of the paper he'd colored in a yellow frame—like the one on the house we'd driven past—our portal to another world.

At the center of it all was a little illustration of an open book, and on its pages a note in old-fashioned cursive handwriting:

Our sweet adventure ended far too soon,
Please meet me in the library at noon.

I had to stifle a laugh. It was like the last two lines of a sonnet! I snapped my notebook shut and looked straight ahead, my face nearly bursting with giddy surprise. I wanted to look at it again, but Reesa was shooting curious eyebrows my way and I *definitely* didn't want Mr. Eli to confiscate this note.

James dropped his pencil then and it rolled under Reesa's chair. He smiled at me over her head when she swooped down to retrieve it for him. I don't know if he did it on purpose, but it distracted her long enough so I could pull myself together.

I refolded the note into a rectangle and slipped it in my pocket.

TWENTY-ONE

My swelling heart dropped into my stomach when I saw Reesa's face after class. She was glowing. "He touched me, right there," she said dreamily, rubbing a knuckle on her right hand. "I'll never wash it."

"Aren't you being a little dramatic?" I mumbled.

She ignored me. "And he said 'thank you.'" She mimicked James's deep whisper. "And his eyes . . . oh, man. His eyes are like . . . like . . . I don't know, like pools of liquid heat. But icy. Icy heat, like . . ."

"Bengay?"

"No. Like a hot angel boy. Or something." Reesa giggled and nudged me down the hall. Any hopes I'd had that she'd lose interest in James were officially dashed. She'd seen into his eyes. Hello, mesmerized.

The illustrated note in my pocket suddenly weighed as much as a brick and was just as bulky.

"Cute hat," I said in a feeble attempt at diversion. "Where'd you get it?"

Reesa's hand went up to the pink ribbed-knit beret that tipped back on her head. "Bloomie's."

"Nice." I almost asked what it cost but knew the answer would only depress me.

"Are you jealous or something?" she said.

I reached into my bag for a roll of mints and slipped one into my mouth. "Of your hat?"

"No." She grabbed my mints and took one for herself. "Of James and me. Because you keep changing the subject whenever I mention him."

I almost choked. "Uhh . . . no. I'm . . . uh . . ."

"I mean, I'd understand," she said. "With him being a super gajillionaire and everything, and your financial situation being what it is. You won't be jealous, will you, if he asks me out?"

"N-no. Of course not." I fingered the paper in my pocket. "You think he, uh . . . likes you?"

She nodded and smiled knowingly. "The way he dropped his pencil right under my desk?"

Though I knew otherwise, her confidence gave me doubts. Reesa was gorgeous, after all. And if James was as wealthy as she said, he'd quite possibly want nothing to do with me when he found out where I lived.

I heard myself say, "I'm sure you'll be very happy together," and it was like tearing my own heart in half. I wanted James for myself but I wanted to keep my promise to Reesa, too. I stopped in the middle of the hallway and just stood there. For a few seconds I couldn't seem to move forward or backward. Literally.

"What's wrong?" said Reesa.

"Nothing, I . . . uh . . . I forgot something." I spun on my heel before she could question me further and went straight for the supply room. Maybe he'd be there. I'd seen him go in there after English that one time a few days ago. We could escape again to the cemetery or even just lock the door to that tiny room and shut out the world.

I was a horrible friend and Reesa would never forgive me but he'd drawn me as Juliet to his Romeo and I had *wings* and I wanted to fly away with him. I turned the knob and cracked open the door enough to slip inside and . . . it was completely, absolutely, totally dark. Nobody was there.

I don't know if it was pent-up anticipation or emotion or the lies on top of secrets, but I felt tears prick at my eyes. I stumbled through the dark to the tiny room. I switched on the lamp and quickly checked the bookshelf. Everyone was there: *Gatsby*. Shakespeare. Beeblebrox. *Eyre*. *Hobbes*. But they were now joined by none other than Ponyboy.

He'd left *The Outsiders*. I smiled and wiped the lone tear off my cheek. If only he knew exactly how appropriate that book was. I was a refugee from the world of the Socials—the Socs—now hiding smack-dab in the middle of greaser territory.

I flipped open the cover to see what he'd written. Like his other notes (though unlike his crazy beautiful drawing), it was brief:

Greaser or Soc?

I loved that I never knew what to expect from James. He was this amazing surprise. The cemetery, the snippet of sonnet, and these cryptic little secret notes. I loved it all.

So I sat in the orange, duct-taped library chair with *The Outsiders* and contemplated my own brief response. If this book was about our school, my friends and I would be the Socs. Lazarski's gang would be greasers. But everyone hated the Socs in that book. They were all bullies, except Cherry. She was the only one who crossed sides. I pulled a pencil out of my backpack and scribbled a single word. Not Soc. Not Greaser.

Cherry.

Reesa caught me leaving the supply closet after second period, when I should've been in chemistry. I had stayed in there until I heard the bell ring so I wouldn't have to walk into class halfway through.

"Is that where you disappeared to? What's in there?" she said, trying to peer around me through the door before I pushed it shut. "And why is your face so red?"

"It is?" I put a hand to my cheek and a guilty lie stammered out.

"I was, uh . . . just looking for a place to practice for that country club audition." It was the first stupid lie that came to mind, and the second those words spilled out of my mouth, I wanted to swallow them back down.

But Reesa's face split into a huge smile and she squeezed my arm. "This is going to be so great! I'll help you. We'll meet in the band room after school. There's a piano. It's no Dr. Steinway, but it's a piano! And I'll help you pick a song. . . ."

She went on like that for a while, suggesting songs and ways to spend the money I would earn, never once questioning why I'd consider practicing in a supply closet. At least it took her mind off James for a while, and I didn't have to listen to her describe his eyes or fantasize about the same lips I was fantasizing about. Off-limit lips.

Maybe that's why my face was so red.

"Okay. After school," she said.

I nodded, but it must not have been the most convincing nod. She held me by my shoulders and made me face her squarely. "Promise?" she said.

I nodded again. "I promise."

TWENTY-TWO

"Costume shopping this weekend, girls!" Willow squealed.

It wasn't even October yet, but that hadn't stopped her from flitting around all day handing out save-the-date cards for her Halloween party. Mrs. Goodwin had succeeded in hiring the jazz band from Lincoln Center and the "Roaring Twenties" theme was official. Wynn was Googling flapper dresses on her phone and kept holding them out for us to see. Their giddy enthusiasm was actually one of the reasons Reesa and I were friends with them. It was easy to get swept up in that kind of excitement—the anticipation of something big.

And if the Halloween bash wasn't enough to push them over the top, Willow and Wynn were still basking in the glow of their ascension to the "fairest of them all" potato club.

I went to my lunch period in the cafeteria at 11:45, though my mind was on James in the library at noon. There was some discussion as to where on earth Lazarski "came from" that had this unusual tradition. Poland? Lithuania, perhaps? Reesa babbled on about how she read somewhere that peasants would bring baskets of crops as a gift to female royalty during medieval times. The fairest of them all received the most.

"That's how sweet potatoes got their name," she said.

I gave her a warning look. If she laid it on much thicker, even the W's would realize she was bullshitting them.

"I never knew that," said Wynn, happy to accept any version of history that ended with her being singled out as pretty or sweet. She had conveniently forgotten that it was Lennie Lazarski who'd given her the stupid potato.

I glanced around the cafeteria, wondering what Lennie thought of the whole thing . . . but he wasn't there. I hadn't seen him since I'd walked away from his Jeep that morning. And whenever his bruised eye surfaced in my mind, I pushed it away. That kiss . . . that was just a peck, the kind you might give a friend to say hello or good-bye. *It was nothing.*

I glanced at the clock on the cafeteria wall. It was exactly noon. I clutched my seat to resist the magnetic pull coming from the library. I couldn't do that to Reesa, not after the way she'd saved me with the whole potato thing. But then I imagined James standing there amid the books, checking his watch. Waiting for me. Thinking I didn't like him.

Reesa nudged me under the table with her foot. "You okay?"

"Yeah. I . . . uh . . . have to use the bathroom." Scrambling to my feet, I hurried for the door. Five minutes past twelve. Heel-toe-heel-toe, I fast-walked down the hall. The library wasn't far.

If he was still there, I would simply explain that it wasn't going to work out. I turned the corner and came to a sliding halt outside the library, took a deep breath, and pulled open the door.

I didn't see him at first. He hadn't mentioned exactly where to meet, so I strolled past the computer workstations and along the shelves, glancing left and right. I finally reached the "quiet study" section. No James. There was one more place I hadn't checked, a little nook where periodicals were kept. I turned the corner and nearly bumped into him.

"I was looking for you," he whispered. "I didn't think you were coming."

I bit my lip. "Neither did I."

James pulled me farther into the nook and frowned. "You didn't like the drawing?"

"I loved the drawing. It isn't that. It's just . . ."

"What?"

"I . . . don't know." I couldn't tell him that Reesa liked him, or that I wasn't who he thought I was. I just stood there, silent. It felt like someone had taken a novel, torn out all the pages, and thrown them back together in the wrong order. I couldn't make sense of anything or anybody. It was all turned upside down. "I could really use that yellow portal right about now. Step into a different world where nobody knows who I am, nobody expects me to be something I'm not."

James tilted his head back, looked up at the ceiling, and laughed. "I know exactly how you feel," he said.

He moved away from me and motioned drawing a big rectangular shape. Then he reached through the imaginary space and held out his hand to me. "Brand-new world," he said. "Come on over."

I took his hand and pretended to step through the window. I glanced around at the periodical room. "Funny, it looks exactly like the library."

"Parallel universe," said James. "Much better than that other one."

I had landed very close to him when I came through the imaginary window, and his face was now inches from mine. We weren't touching, but I was definitely within his gravitational force field. I swallowed. "If you say so."

"I say so," he said. The joking tone I liked so much was gone and his face got serious, but I liked that, too. His gaze went from my eyes to my mouth. And at that moment, everything else disappeared. He leaned in and I closed my eyes and his lips had just barely grazed mine and I was thinking *he's kissing me right here in the library* when we heard someone approaching and quickly separated. I grabbed a magazine and plopped down at the nearest table. *Popular Science*. James snagged an old copy of *Seventeen* with Selena Gomez on the cover. The librarian who peered in at us gave him a funny look but moved along. When he realized what he was reading, his face went red.

"Smooth," he said, shaking his head.

I giggled softly. "I better go."

His shoulders slumped, but he was still smiling. "Can I drive you home today?"

"No!" I blurted, then lowered my voice. "No. My parents . . ." I left this vaguely open, hoping he'd think my parents were simply overprotective. It didn't matter if we fantasized a different world—I was still living in the real one. And I didn't want him to see me there.

"Saturday night, then?"

I nodded. "Sure." *Wait, did I just say yes to a date?*

"Where should I pick you up?"

"I . . . I'll leave you a note." I'd figure out somewhere I could get to on my bike. "In our secret place."

"Which one?" he said.

At first, his question puzzled me . . . it seemed obvious. But now we had two secret places, the supply room and here in the library. Three, actually, if you counted the cemetery. Maybe he was counting the hedge where we first met, where I hid my bicycle.

I gave a playful shrug. "That's for me to know and you to find out."

When the final bell rang that day, I headed to the band room. I didn't want to break another promise to Reesa, but I also had no idea how I was getting home. The band-room doors were decorated with a giant illustration of a snarling tiger, our school mascot. As I approached, its jaws opened and Molly burst out, nearly knocking me over. She held her clarinet in one hand, its case in the other, and had a crumpled pile of music tucked under her arm.

"Hey. Hi," I said.

Her face was red and angry. She brushed past me, dropping sheets of music as she went. I hurried after her, picking them up.

"Molly?"

She stormed off without answering, disappearing around the corner. What the . . . ? I collected her scattered papers and went to find Reesa in the band room.

She was sitting at the piano.

"What happened to Molly? She tore out of here looking supremely pissed off," I said.

"I asked her to leave," said Reesa dismissively. "I mean, why can't she practice in her dad's fancy recording studio?"

"Oh, my God. You didn't say that to her, did you?"

She shrugged, which meant she had.

"Reesa! They don't live there anymore! Remember?"

"Oh. Yeah," she said.

I groaned. "I can't believe you did that."

"Fine. I shouldn't have asked her to leave, but she was acting like she owns the place."

"This is the *band* room, Reesa. She's in the *band*. You're the one acting like you own the place."

Reesa rolled her eyes. "Since when do you care so much about Molly Palmer?"

"Since I remembered we used to be really good friends with her, and we treated her like crap," I shot back.

"Oh, give me a break." Reesa swiveled to face the piano keys, turning her back to me. "What are you now, like the voice of the little people? Standing up for the downtrodden, the po—"

"Excuse me? Are you serious?"

Reesa clunked her head down on the piano keys. "I'm sorry, Ivy. I didn't mean that. You said to make sure nobody was in here, so that's what I did."

"I didn't tell you to be a total bitch about it. You're acting like Willow."

"Ouch."

"Well, you are. And the downtrodden?" I said. "News flash! I *am* one of them now."

"Okay. Sheesh. I'm sorry. I said I was sorry."

"Don't tell me." I pointed toward the door. "Tell Molly."

"What? Right now?"

I plopped down on one of the metal band chairs to wait. "No time like the present."

Reesa huffed and trudged out, returning about ten minutes later with Molly, who was still seething. I gave her the pile of music I'd gathered up. "Here," I said. "Sorry about all that."

She took the music. "Not your fault," she said, shooting a dag-gered glance at Reesa.

"She means well," I whispered.

Molly snorted, but sat and shuffled the sheets of music into a neat pile.

"I invited her to stay, if that's okay with you," said Reesa, a slightly evil grin coming to her lips. "You really need to get used to performing in front of an audience. And there's no time like the present. Is there?"

I stared at her, my mouth open in a surprised O. Only Reesa could turn a shitty moment into an opportunity.

TWENTY-THREE

olly slouched on a metal chair near the entrance, arms folded across her chest. Reesa paced next to the piano. The doors were locked. All I had to do was sit myself down and play something, sing a few bars. Complete the lie.

I wiped the sweat from my palms onto the sides of my dress. It didn't matter if I was performing in front of two people or two thousand. My heart still raced, my chest still got tight, my breath still rasped as if someone had been chasing me. I could barely feel my fingers as they hovered over the keys.

"Just pretend we're not here," said Reesa, tiptoeing away.

I closed my eyes and imagined the twins there, just the two of them, waiting for a lullaby. I started to play, and my voice, when it came time to sing the melody, sounded like fingernails on a blackboard.

I kept going, eyes pinched tight, feeling my way across the keys. When I finished, I held my breath until Reesa broke the silence.

"That was amazing," she said.

I didn't believe her, but Molly had shifted from slouching to perching on the edge of her seat. "Really beautiful," she said.

"But you have to sing something receptiony," said Reesa.

"Receptiony? Like, what . . . the Macarena?" The only thing worse than embarrassing myself in a performance would be doing it in the process of singing cheesy wedding songs. "This is a really bad idea."

Reesa started rattling off names of soft-rock pop tunes that made my teeth ache. Molly didn't say anything, but I saw her cringe a few times.

"You want elevator music," I said.

"No!" Reesa sashayed across the room like she was walking a runway while holding a wineglass. "Think, like, classy cocktail party."

Classy cocktail parties were about as far away from my reality as I could get. I fiddled around on the keyboard. Freddie Mercury found his way into my head again, with the song I fell asleep to the other night: "Crazy Little Thing Called Love." But nobody could sing it the way he did, so I decided to go for a bluesy-baroque version. Billie Holiday meets Bach, which sounds weird, but I loved mixing styles. It was part of what made me nervous to perform in front of other people, though, because they might not get it. Kaya and Brady didn't know any better, after all. They'd grown up with my crazy songs.

"Ready?" Reesa waggled her fingers, prompting me to get started.

I nodded and closed my eyes, this time pretending to be in the cemetery with James. And out there, over the top of my piano, nothing but a sea of tombstones. Listening quietly. Not judging.

My fingers danced over the piano keys. I sang. It wasn't too terrible. When I finished, Reesa was smiling like a total goof. "How do you do that?"

"What?"

"This." She held her cell phone out for me to see the video she'd just recorded.

"What did you do? Delete that!" I grabbed the phone from her, and with my thumb hovering over the trashcan icon, I looked and I *heard* myself singing and . . . I couldn't believe it was me.

"See what I mean?" Reesa snatched her phone from my grasp before I could delete it. "You're amazing."

I turned to Molly for her opinion, but she was gone. "Where's Molly?"

She shrugged. "I guess her ride came."

I don't know why her opinion meant so much to me. But now I worried that she hadn't liked what she'd heard and skipped out so she wouldn't have to tell me.

Reesa's phone bleeped as a text came in. "Shit. Mom's outside. I have to go, too." She gathered up her stuff and headed for the door. "You rode your bike, right?"

I shook my head, pointed to the windows. "Too wet."

"Oh." Her face went blank for a minute, clearly trying to figure out a graceful way to not offer me a ride.

"Don't worry. My mom's coming," I lied.

The relief on Reesa's face was easily visible from outer space. "Oh, good. My mom's already pissed that I didn't get the bus home. She'd probably kill me if I made her drive to hell and back."

Whoa. Way to twist that knife, Rees.

"Okay, that came out wrong," she said. "Sorry."

I waved off her apology. "'Hell' is about right."

She rushed over and hugged me tight but didn't linger. "I'll call you."

"Mm-hmm." I closed the lid on the piano keys and reached for my bag. There had to be a pay phone in the school somewhere. They didn't expect everyone to have their own phone, did they? One or two of those old coin-operated thingies must still be hooked up somewhere for the few pathetic students with no other options.

Just as I was about to leave, I heard the clatter of something falling to the floor. It came from the door next to the band director's office. A door that was slightly ajar. A door I assumed to be a closet.

"Is someone there?" I asked. "Molly, is that you?"

Then the door opened and I yelped.

James walked into the band room. "Sorry. It's only me."

"Oh!" I backed away as he stepped slowly toward me.

"I know this looks weird," he said.

Yes. Very weird.

"I was in the library. I heard music coming from a closet. So I followed it." He held open the door so I could see that the closet opened into the library on the other side. Our school was apparently a maze of secret passageways. "Was that you?"

"You heard me? You were listening?" I bumped into a music stand, knocking it over.

He came closer, reaching out to help.

I held my hands up to stop him. "Don't."

"Ivy." He let his arms drop to his sides. "What's going on?"

"It's just . . . I didn't think anyone was listening. We locked the doors and I . . . I . . ." I sounded completely ridiculous and paranoid.

"I shouldn't have snuck up on you like that. I'm sorry."

"It's okay," I said. But it wasn't. If he heard me sing, then he must've heard my conversation with Reesa afterward. He knew I lived in a place even my best friend was afraid to visit. "I have to go."

"Whoa. Wait up," he said. "What's wrong?"

I forced a smile. "Nothing." *Everything.*

He held out a hand but I didn't take it.

"Let me drive you."

"No, that's okay." I kept backing toward the door.

"Look, I'm sorry I heard you singing. I'm sorry I scared you."

"No, it's not that." I shook my head. I couldn't explain why I was so upset. I hardly understood it myself. I just didn't want him there, where I lived. I didn't want him to know. He was an escape from my reality. I didn't want him to *see* my reality.

"I just . . . I have to go." I made it to the door and pushed it open.

"Talk to you tomorrow?" he called after me.

I turned back, gave a quick nod, and rushed out.

It was still raining. The entire planet was pretty much conspiring against me. I headed toward home, my umbrella keeping little more than my face dry. I made no effort to avoid the puddles. My boots were already soaked through. Anyway, it was water.

Water couldn't hurt me.

After about twenty minutes, I heard the familiar *meep-meep* of the red Jeep before I saw him approach. Lennie rolled to a stop beside me, and the passenger door swung open. He surveyed my soggy state from top to bottom but said nothing.

I silently climbed in.

He made a U-turn. "Kaya said you hadn't come home. I thought you might need a ride."

"Thanks." I couldn't figure out why he was being nice to me.

"'S okay."

We drove the few miles to our neighborhood in silence, but he didn't turn down our street. "You mind if we stop at Save-a-Cent? I gotta pick up my paycheck."

"Okay."

Lennie found a spot near the front and hopped out. The rain had let up to a light drizzle, at least for the moment. He walked toward the entrance holding his fingers to his temple, trying to hide the black eye from view. At least the swelling had gone down.

The minutes ticked by. I thought back to James, what he'd said, how crazy I must have seemed. How had things gotten so complicated in such a short time? Mom was always saying things had a way of working themselves out. But they were *not* working themselves out this time. They were working themselves into knots—really tight ones that I would never be able to untie.

Lennie finally came back out, still scratching his forehead so the palm of his hand shielded his eye. He was halfway across the lot when he stopped to talk to someone approaching the store. As he moved to the side, I gasped and dived to the floor of the Jeep.

It was James.

Please don't tell him I'm here please don't please. I waited, tucked under the dash. After another minute, I heard the slap of feet approaching on the wet asphalt. I peeked up from my hiding spot and saw Lennie staring at me through the driver's-side window. He yanked the door open and got in. I steeled myself for whatever wiseass remark he was preparing to make, but he didn't say a thing.

And his silence made me feel small.

I climbed back onto the seat as he pulled out of the shopping center. "Sorry, I didn't want him to see me."

"With me," Lennie said.

"No, it's . . . he . . ."

"Look. You either like me or you don't. You want to be friends, or you want to pretend I don't exist." Lennie stopped at the light and turned to face me with the full force of his bruised eye. "If you could decide which one it is and stick with it, that would be great. Because I really hate being jerked around."

He floored the gas when the light turned green. I fell back against the seat and was tossed to the side when he turned sharply onto our street. I braced against the dashboard as he slammed to a stop in front of my place.

"Len, I . . ."

He reached across my lap for the handle of my door and shoved it open. "Good-bye, Ivy."

I sat rigid for a moment, then slowly collected my backpack and umbrella and got out. I pushed the door closed and watched him drive in reverse the short distance from our house to his. He stayed in the Jeep for a while. I could see him sitting there, leaning on the steering wheel. Finally, his door swung open. I don't know why I kept watching, why I couldn't seem to move. He turned and looked at me looking at him.

Then he spat on the ground, like he was spitting at *me*, and walked into his house.

TWENTY-FOUR

"I'm going to invite him to Willow's party," said Reesa on the way to AP English. "I mean, everyone will be there. We don't want him to feel left out or anything. And if he wants to go, I could ask him for a ride!"

I stayed silent. It was a no-win conversation I didn't want to have.

"Or maybe I should just give him my number," she said. "Do you think that's too forward?"

"I think he'll ask you for your number if he wants it," I said.

She huffed. "Why should I wait for the boy to make the first move?"

"Then ask him for *his* number," I suggested.

"Maybe I will." Her mouth twisted side to side while she pondered her strategy. "Maybe instead of waiting for Willow's party, I could tell him I'm getting some friends together. We could all go to the movies, or that Little Invisibles concert."

"Or maybe we could all fly to Paris for the weekend." I

mimicked her breathless excitement.

"Sorry." She cringed. "I forgot."

"You go ahead," I said. "Just because I can't afford anything doesn't mean you have to take a vow of poverty."

She looped her arm around mine. "Once you get that job at the country club, everything will be back to normal."

"Yeah, normal," I mumbled. I slipped my arm out of hers as we approached Mr. Eli's room. James was standing outside. His eyes followed me through the crowded hallway.

"Now's my chance," Reesa whispered. She bopped ahead of me to talk to James. When I slipped past them, she was saying, "I'm getting some people together this weekend . . ."

They followed me into the classroom. "We might just hang out and watch movies," said Reesa. "You want to join us?"

I sat at my desk and buried my head in my backpack, as if I was having a hard time finding my ginormous Shakespeare textbook.

"I . . . uh . . . have plans Saturday," said James.

"Oh! Oh, well," Reesa chirped. "Maybe next time."

I glanced up at James, but Reesa was blocking my view. Then Mr. Eli called him up to his desk, and while they were talking, Reesa leaned halfway across the aisle between our seats. "Screw him," she whispered. "Saturday is girls' night. My house. Just you and me. 'Kay?"

I couldn't say no. After complaining that I didn't have the money to do anything, I couldn't exactly claim to have other plans. Besides, I missed her. I missed lying on her bed and staring at the glow-in-the-dark stars, talking about everything. Maybe everything would feel normal again at her house.

I smiled. "You and me."

James didn't look at me again during class, but on the way out he shoved a note into my hand. I went to the bathroom and closed myself in a stall to read it.

I'll be your secret if you'll be my girl.
Are we on for Saturday?
Tell me when and where.

I shoved the note into my pocket. At least he'd figured out that I wanted to keep him a secret. But now I had to choose between my best friend and the guy my best friend claimed to be falling in love with. My subconscious must've sensed my need for some piano therapy, because I was pushing the band room doors open before I even realized where I was headed. Molly sat in her usual corner near the drums, putting her clarinet together.

"You want me to leave?" I said.

"No way," she said. "I was hoping you'd show up. Join me?" She nodded toward the piano.

I hesitated. I'd never played with anyone before. "If you want," I said.

She picked up her stuff and came to the piano, scooting a chair next to the bench. I sat down and arched my fingers over the keys.

"Warm up a bit?" she said.

I nodded, and started playing scales. Molly jumped right in, easily transposing from her B-flat instrument to the piano's C. I tried harder and harder keys, with four and five flats or sharps, and she stuck right with me.

"You're good," I said. "How about this?" I made something up then. A few measures of what I was feeling. The crazy of James asking me to be his secret girlfriend. The guilt of it all with Reesa and the weirdness that was now our friendship.

She closed her eyes and played it back for me, adding a couple of trills.

It was like the old movies when one guy would tap-dance something really complicated, a challenge, and the other would tap it back but with extra flourish. We went back and forth for a while.

Molly was winded when we stopped. "That," she said, "was ridiculous."

I swept my fingers from the very top C on the piano to the bottom one, a final glissando. "I didn't get stage-frighty at all," I said. "Weird."

"It's because you're not worried about what I think," said Molly.

"That's not true," I said. "I care what you think."

"Yeah, but you're not *worried* about it. Because nobody else cares what I think." She grinned as if this didn't bother her in the least. "My opinion means very little at this school."

I couldn't argue with the truth of the statement. But it wasn't right. "It means a lot to me."

She twisted around to look at the clock above the door and started putting her clarinet away. "We should do this again. Maybe work on a piece for open mic night. They have one tomorrow, if you want to go." She must have noticed my body stiffen because she quickly added, "Just to listen?"

I knew of the King Theatre but had never been there. The place was supposed to be huge, with a big stage for major concerts and some smaller ones for local acts. Concerts were usually pretty expensive. "I don't know...."

"It's only five bucks." Molly tore a corner of paper out of her notebook and wrote down a phone number. "Friday at eight. Call me if you need a ride."

An idea came to me then, one that would save me from choosing between James and Reesa. I took the stairs to the second floor, and sidled up to the supply closet door. The hall was still full of students getting to their next classes. I waited a moment, made sure nobody was paying attention to me, and slipped inside. The books were still stacked on the shelf in the secret room. I opened *The Outsiders* and found a new note:

Dally: Sexy or rude?

I knew he was referring to the character Dallas Winston, a friend of Ponyboy's and the toughest of the greasers. In the movie, he was played by a young, dark-haired Matt Dillon. But in the book, he had blond hair and icy-blue eyes, just like James.

That's about where the similarities ended. Dally was dangerous. And rude. But, yeah . . .

Sexy.

I wrote the word down hoping James would know I was referring to him as much as Dally. Then I added:

Change of plans:
Meet me Friday, 8:00
King Theatre

I closed the book and laid it back on top of the stack. We were just going to listen, not perform. I could handle that, though the prospect of getting close to a stage still made me nervous. It sprang from a completely unreasonable fear that someone might pull me up there. But practicing with Molly was giving me confidence. With her at my side, and James, too, maybe I could stop caring what anybody else thought.

I laughed to myself. *Yeah, right.*

TWENTY-FIVE

"This whole supper cost less than ten dollars." My mother swept her arm over the serving dishes she'd set out on the kitchen counter. I kept my mouth shut this time.

We ate buffet style, filling our plates and then gathering around the coffee table since the island in the kitchen only seated three. The food may have been cheap, but our dishes were not. Mom had stocked our kitchen cabinets with the antique bone china my father had given her for their fifteenth wedding anniversary. Each blue-and-white flowered dish was rimmed in gold leaf. She'd sold the glassware and silver, though, so our fancy plates were slumming it with plastic cups in assorted colors and a cheap set of cutlery that used to come out only for picnics.

"Looks delicious." Dad picked up the carving knife and sliced into the roasted chicken, while mom poured the gravy into the antique gravy boat. It was the twins' favorite meal, and one of mine, too. Mom was definitely pulling out all the tricks in her bag, trying to make it feel like home.

But it only made me miss my real home that much more.

"Chicken, on sale for only five dollars. The potatoes were a dollar a bag, right, Ives?" She hadn't adjusted her calculation for the missing bag, but I didn't say anything about that. "Carrots, about three dollars. A dollar or so for the herbs, butter, salt . . ."

I held up my glass. "Milk?"

"Oh. I forgot that. Extra for beverages." She knit her brows together. "But still, not bad for a family of five."

Despite my meltdown a few days ago, my parents continued to treat our family's financial disaster like we were starring on some kind of reality show. *Survivor: Poverty Island*. Mom announced every penny she saved as if it was a golden nugget she'd panned herself. Finding chicken on sale at the supermarket? That was the equivalent of hunting down a wild turkey and plucking its feathers with her teeth.

Mom waited until we were halfway through our meal to announce her next big money-saving idea. "We'll go to the food bank on Saturday. That'll really help bring our cost per meal down."

I dropped my fork and it clattered from plate to table. "I'm sorry, what?"

"The food bank," said Mom.

"But . . . that's for . . ."

Poor people.

"It's for people who need a little help providing nutritious food for their families." Mom took a delicate bite from her fork.

"People like us. You don't have to be completely destitute to take advantage of these programs. That's why they're there. To keep people from getting to that point."

I picked up my fork and took another bite, but it didn't go down so well. I couldn't even believe we were in danger of not having enough food.

Kaya made a lake in her mashed potatoes, filled it with gravy, and floated a bit of carrot in the middle. She poked at it a few times, pushing it down and watching it bob to the surface. Then she smashed the side in so her gravy streamed all over her plate.

"Are we slum bums?" she asked.

We all froze and stared at her.

"Did someone call you that?" said Dad.

She nodded. "Sienna Goodwin. I was telling my class how we moved and the houses are real close together and we can play right on the street and walk to the Save-a-Cent. Sienna said that's the slums and that makes us slum bums. Miss Fisher put her in time-out."

I was already sitting on the floor, so it wasn't far to fall when I slumped over sideways and laid my cheek on the carpet. Sienna was Willow's little sister.

"Sit up," Mother hissed at me, then said to Kaya, "You're not a slum bum, sweetie."

"But what is it?" Kaya didn't look particularly upset by the whole thing. Only puzzled.

"It's ... well, it's ..." Mom stabbed at her potatoes, as if searching for the answer in their gravied depths. "It's a not-very-nice name for people who are living . . . well, modestly."

"What's modestly?" said Kaya.

I lifted my head from the carpet. "She means poor. And you know what a bum is."

"Someone who smells like pee?"

"Yeah," I said, dropping back to the floor. "Someone who smells like pee."

Mom scowled at me. "Bum is a not-very-nice name for a homeless person," she said. "But we are *not* homeless. We have this very nice apartment, and this is not the slums. It's an affordable housing community."

"Slum bum," said Brady. "Slum bum slum bum slum bum . . ."

Dad got right in front of Brady, to make sure he was paying attention. "No, Brady. We don't say that. It's a bad word. Kaya, do you have a good word for him today?"

We all turned to my sister, the keeper of new words. "He didn't want a word today. He only wanted to say Lennie's name."

Brady's eyes lit up. "Len-nie-Laz-ar-ski," he said perfectly. "Lennie is my friend."

I moaned into the carpet, ignoring my mother's toe-nudging. My mistake, I realized, was in assuming things couldn't get any worse than they already were. Because every time I thought that . . . they did.

* * *

Friday morning I rode my bike to school with dread hanging around my throat like a too-heavy necklace. If Sienna knew we lived in the slums, it was only a matter of time before Willow found out. I wished I didn't care what she thought, but I did. Molly was right. It wasn't that I couldn't tolerate the bad opinion of one person. It was the multiplier effect. It was the fear of walking down the hall knowing that every single person you pass is laughing at you. Or pitying you.

I slunk to my homeroom, head down. Ashamed of how weak I was. The dread turned to a hard knot in my chest as I walked toward Mr. Eli's room. Every time I saw a blond head, I thought it was Willow. She'd ask if it was true, what Sienna told her. Had we really moved to Lakeside? She'd have that something-smells-bad sneer on her face, like when Lennie tossed the potato to me, before it was "cool." And Reesa wouldn't be able to cover it up with some crazy story this time.

James was leaning against the lockers outside Mr. Eli's room when I got there. He smiled and lifted a finger to his lips, which I took to be a gesture of secret-boyfriendliness.

I smiled back. I tried to say, *Yes, I'll be your secret girlfriend* with my smile. I figured I might as well enjoy the last few hours before the Willow News Network destroyed me.

His grin widened. He mimed wiping sweat from his brow.

Reesa came up next to me. "What's that all about?"

"What?" I hadn't realized she was there. "What's what all about?"

She nodded toward James. His eyes darted quickly away from me; then he waved to someone down the hall behind me. Someone who had no idea who he was.

"Oh," said Reesa. "Never mind."

Willow came stomping over to my locker before lunch, and I thought the moment of truth had come. I even felt kind of relieved, anticipating it. But all she did was thrust an orange envelope into my hand. "Here," she said. "Mother insisted on mailing printed invitations. Yours came back. What's up with that?"

I took the envelope and looked at it. It was addressed to me at our Westside house and stamped NO FORWARDING ADDRESS.

My heart thumped in my ears. Could she hear that? "Weird," I said. "Thanks."

"Did you move?"

"No. Of course not," I said quickly. My mother had forgotten to put in the forwarding order and only realized it when we didn't get a single item of mail for a few days, not even bills.

"Aren't you going to open it?"

"Oh, right. Yeah." She hovered over me as I tore open the envelope and pulled out the invitation. It was beautiful, as expected, with an art deco illustration of a flapper on the front.

"It's going to be amazing. We're all going to that theater rental place on Saturday to pick out our flapper costumes. Meet us there at eleven o'clock. Okay?"

She didn't wait for my answer but continued down the hall to bestow her presence on a pack of admiring sophomore boys.

I sank against the locker wall.

TWENTY-SIX

When I checked the secret room at the end of the day to see if James had gotten my note, the *Outsiders* book was gone.

A nervous feeling nagged at me, like maybe someone else had snuck in there and taken it. But when I got to the parking lot, his car was gone, too, so I retrieved my bike from the hedge and headed home. It was late September and getting cooler. The wind blew through my sweatshirt like it was made of gauze. Then a car passed so close, it sprayed muddy water all over me. I was fairly certain it was a red Jeep.

Cold and shivery, I left my bike in the yard. My fingers fumbled at the lock to the front door, too shaky to line up the key. It dropped on the steps, bounced once, and fell through the wooden slats of the porch to the dirt below.

I got on hands and knees and peered down at it. The crawl space under the stairs was muddy and dark. I'd have to shimmy on my belly to squeeze through the opening. I started to whimper just as Carla opened the door. The aroma of freshly baked cookies wafted out.

"Happens to me all the time," she said. "Come on in. I have extra keys."

"I'm all wet." I stood and held my arms out.

She directed me to a rug inside the door. "I'll get you a towel. What happened?"

"Got hit by a puddle," I said, accepting the towel she handed me. "Can I use your bathroom?"

Carla pointed the way. I cleaned up and made friends with a gray cat that sat next to the sink, batting its paw at drops of water that fell from the leaky faucet. It followed me out to the living room.

"I see you've met Valentino." She handed me a warm mug. "Chamomile okay? I was just making tea."

"Yeah. Thanks." I sat and sipped, letting the warmth seep into my chest.

Valentino hopped onto my lap and dug his paws into my thighs like he was kneading dough. When my lap was sufficiently softened to his satisfaction, he lay down and rested his chin on my knee.

Carla watched the whole thing with amusement while she placed a plate of cookies on the table between us. "You are hereby officially blessed and deemed a worthy human pillow for His Royal Majesty." She bowed her head and rolled her hand in the air, in that universal royal-majesty gesture that seemed unusually popular around here. I'd seen Lennie do it, too.

I rubbed the cat under his chin with one finger, and he purred. "He's not very particular, is he?"

"*Au contraire.*" Carla gave me a long look, perhaps deciding whether or not she agreed with her cat's endorsement. "He's actually a very good judge of character. Used to pee in my ex-husband's shoes all the time."

"Really?"

Carla smiled at Valentino as he stretched on my lap and then curled back up again.

"Bad kitty," I said.

"Actually," said Carla, "I should've listened to Valentino and thrown the guy out with the shoes. It would've saved me a lot of heartache. And *money*."

"Is that how you ended up . . ." I realized before I finished the question that it might be a rude one to ask, so I stopped myself.

"Yes," Carla answered anyway. "That is how I ended up in Lakeside. But it was a choice I made, to live here. We had a house in Westside. I could've stayed there."

"Why didn't you?" I said.

She smiled. "It's complicated."

I hated when adults assumed that teenagers were incapable of understanding their complicated adult lives. Did they not remember high school at all?

"Yeah," I said, nodding. "I've spent the past three weeks pretending I still live in Westside, trying to convince my best friend that I don't like the boy she likes even though I do, and basically hiding who I really am from every single person I know. So I *get* complicated. What I don't get is why someone would choose to live *here* if they didn't have to."

Carla's eyes had widened as I was speaking. "Okaaay," she said. "It's like this. When I was married, my husband made the money and he made a lot of it, but it always felt like what we had was never really *mine*."

She paused to take a bite of cookie, wiping a bit of gooey chocolate from the corner of her mouth and licking her finger. "We got divorced and I wanted to prove that I could take care of myself. I also never wanted to find myself in a position again where money factored into decisions of the heart. I stayed with my husband a lot longer than I would've because of the money, because of the nice house and the lifestyle we had."

She put her hand to her chest. "I own this house. I paid for it with my own money. It's mine. It's not much, it could use a paint job . . ."

The look on my face apparently revealed my agreement on this point, because Carla laughed. "At least I know if a man falls in love with me, it's not for the money. Or the house. Unless he *really* likes the color brown," she said. "Maybe you can help me pick out a new color. And paint it?"

"I'd love to." I sank back into my chair with exaggerated relief, and she laughed again.

"You and Molly, perhaps. And Lennie."

I looked away from her smiling eyes. Petted the cat.

"Not Lennie?" she said. "So he's not the boy you like who your friend likes, too?"

I nearly choked on the sip of tea I'd just swallowed. "Lennie? God, no. No."

"Oh!" She seemed genuinely surprised. "I thought . . . well, he certainly seems to like *you*."

"Excuse me?"

She lifted an eyebrow. "Don't tell me you haven't noticed."

"I've noticed that he's completely infuriating," I said.

She chuckled. "Of course he is. Because you like him, too."

"Um, no . . . I really don't."

She shrugged and took a sip of her tea. "If you say so."

"He's a total pothead," I said, "and a drug dealer, and . . ."

"Where on earth did you get that idea?"

"That's what everyone at school says. . . ."

"And you believe everything you hear?" Her voice had taken on a slightly harder edge. "Last time I checked, the high school rumor mill wasn't exactly a good source of credible information."

"True," I said. "But I saw him taking money from some guy in the stairwell and giving him a little bag. And people are constantly driving up to his house and handing him money in exchange for little packages. It doesn't take a genius to figure out what's going on."

Her lips pressed into a thin line. "And you know what's inside those little packages?"

"Well, no, but . . ."

She stood and carried our tea mugs to the sink. "I've known Lennie since he was a boy, and I cannot believe he would ever do such a thing."

Or maybe she just didn't want to admit it?

"Maybe you're right," I said, not because I believed it. But she was obviously fond of Lennie and didn't take kindly to me trashing him.

"Not everything is always what it seems to be," she said, sounding just like Mr. Eli. "You should ask him about it."

There was a rumbling in the distance; the twins' school bus approaching. Mom had picked up some more hours at work this afternoon, so I was on Brady duty. I started for the door. "Thanks for the tea."

"Anytime." Carla pulled a key ring from the drawer and followed me out, unlocking the door to our apartment as I ran to meet the bus. The twins hardly stopped to say hi. They dashed right past me to Carla. I watched them circling her legs, telling her about their day. I'll admit it, I was a little jealous. Even with them, it seemed, I was on the outside looking in.

Dad insisted on coming out to meet Molly and give her car a thorough visual inspection when she pulled up out front to pick me up for open mic night. I had asked him to please not grill her about her family or her favorite subjects in school or any of the usual dad stuff, so "that tire looks like it could use a little air," was all he said.

Molly assured him we'd stop at a gas station on the way and top it off. Which we actually did. "Your dad's really nice," she said, then drove in silence the rest of the way to Belleview.

The King Theatre was on a city street that was busy by day, when all the employees from downtown businesses were buzzing around, but almost deserted at night—except for the people coming and going to hear music. We found a parking spot easily—though it took Molly a few attempts to parallel park the car.

"It's a miracle I got my license," she said, attempting to straighten out the tires without bumping into the car in front of us.

I could see the theater from a block away as we approached. It had one of those old-timey half-circle movie marquees out front, all lit up and glowing. My heart pounded at the sight of it. At the box office, we paid our five dollars (finally, something I could afford!) and they directed us to the main stage theater. When we went through the double doors, my breath caught.

It was so beautiful. And so big.

The theater had been abandoned during World War II and sat vacant for decades before someone raised the money to restore it. But rather than make it look all shiny and new, they had left the ornate paintings on the walls—what remained of them—by sealing them with some kind of clear coating. The colors were a little faded and much of the paint had chipped away over the years, but you could see how glorious it must've been in its heyday.

The stage backdrop was a patchwork of textured panels that shimmered in the colored lights. But what really caught my eye was the grand piano at the side of the stage, all shiny and black. I wanted to go up there and stroke its surface, glissando my hands up and down the keys.

Molly reached over and flicked me under the chin. "Catching flies, Emerson."

I snapped my mouth shut and smiled. "This place is amazing," I said. "I don't even care if anybody performs."

She laughed. "The sound is great, too. You'll see."

There was a bar in the back, and Molly went to get us sodas while I excused myself to the bathroom. When I came out, she was getting her arm signed in Sharpie by some kid with a four-inch-high Mohawk. He looked about fifteen years old. "He'll be famous someday," she assured me. "And I'll have a photograph of his autograph on my arm." She pulled her cell phone out of her pocket and took a picture of it.

"I thought you were going to say you'd never wash it," I said, thinking of Reesa when James had touched her hand in class.

"No," said Molly. "I'm not that pathetic."

We stood in the back for a few minutes, searching for a good place to sit. I kept glancing toward the doors, looking for James.

"Waiting for someone?" said Molly.

I hadn't told her I'd invited James, hoping it might seem more like a chance meeting than a date. "I did mention to someone that I'd be here," I said. "I hope you don't mind."

She narrowed her eyes. "It's not Reesa, is it?"

"No." I couldn't blame Molly for disliking Reesa, but I felt guilty talking behind her back, even if I wasn't really saying anything.

"We'll save a spot, then," Molly said. "For your mystery date."

We found three seats in the middle of the front section. "I like to be close enough to see their fingerings on their instruments," Molly explained.

When they lowered the houselights, a flutter of nerves rushed to my throat. I had to remind myself, *It's not you up there, it's not you.* But I couldn't help envisioning myself standing next to the piano. Unable to move.

"You okay?" Molly was looking at me funny.

"Yep!" I pushed the image to the back of my mind and forced a smile, shifting to get more comfortable in my seat.

The first act was a rock band made up of three women—drums, bass, and the lead singer on guitar. They called themselves the Llama Mammas. They sang an original song of their own called "Spinning Free." The bass player twirled around and around, got tangled up in her cord. My heart raced for her. I would've died of embarrassment, but she just laughed and unplugged herself and stepped out of it and plugged back in.

I kept looking back to the entrance so I could wave James over when he came in. But he didn't, and after an hour I began to lose hope. We sat through a bunch of solo performances, people singing with guitars or a cappella. One guy played a bagpipe.

Someone told jokes. Molly applauded and whistled for everyone. It made me wonder if she really thought I was any good or if she was just supportive of music in general.

It was past nine o'clock and still James hadn't shown. Then someone tapped me on the shoulder and said, "Ladies?"

I spun around and there was . . . Lennie.

"What are you doing here?" I snapped.

"I'm supposed to meet someone." He stared at me for a moment, then looked around. "Not sure if she's here, though. It's kind of a blind date."

Molly pointed to the empty seat next to me. "You can sit with us if you want."

I glared at her.

"Or not . . . ," she mumbled.

"That's okay." Lennie grinned crookedly. The bruise around his eye was purple and must've still hurt. "I can see you're waiting for someone special."

The next performer had taken the stage, so I turned to watch. Lennie left, went I-didn't-know-and-I-didn't-care where. The seat next to me remained empty for the rest of the night.

Molly noticed my disappointment. "Sorry about your . . . uh . . . friend."

I shrugged. "The music was great," I said, eager to change the subject. There was such a crazy variety of performers, but the organizers had presented them in a way that flowed just right. It all ended with the most amazing quartet that sang a number from *Les Misérables*. The audience was on its feet before they finished.

I felt both exhilarated and annihilated, wanting to sing like that but knowing I never could. Molly squeezed my arm as if sensing my mood. But she didn't say anything, which was exactly the right thing to say.

TWENTY-SEVEN

Mom shook me awake on Saturday morning. "Time to get up. I want to leave in a half hour. I made you some oatmeal."

I looked at the clock on my little desk. "It's only seven. I thought you said they open at nine."

"Yes," said Mom. "But the lady at the food pantry told me they start lining up at eight. To get the good stuff."

Mom had broken it all down for me the day before, how the food bank collects and sorts all the donated food, then supplies it to the pantries, which dole it out to people at risk of hunger. Mom kept calling them "the hungry."

"We're not hungry," I had said.

"No, we're not." She'd been scrubbing at a stain on the counter that was never going to come out. "Not yet."

I rolled over in bed and groaned. "Do you think we'll see anybody we know?"

"We might." Her voice had that high, tinny sound like when she'd first told me about moving here.

I swung my legs to the floor. "Might as well get this over with."

Mom had already driven Dad and the twins over to Dad's office so he could get some work done while they played with the shredder. He had let them shred some documents once and you'd have thought they'd died and gone to heaven. Now he saved up all his shredding so they could do it for him when he worked on weekends. He'd even purchased a shredder with a special safety device so they couldn't shred their fingers by accident.

Mom called up to me as I was getting dressed. "Wear something, uh . . . not too flashy."

"Dress like a poor person," I mumbled. "Got it."

My hoodie supply was running a little low, so I pulled on the humblest sweater and jeans I could find. Instead of the knee-high leather boots I usually wore with it, I donned my oldest, most beaten-up pair of Chucks. I didn't brush my hair or put makeup on.

"How's this?" I said, twirling around in the kitchen.

"I didn't say you had to look like you'd been attacked by birds," she said. "Go brush your hair."

When we were finally on our way, Mom explained that the pantry was at a church. "It's a choice pantry," she said. "That means we get to choose what kinds of foods we want. Some of them just give you a box that they've preselected."

She kept rambling on about what to expect, but I honestly didn't want to know. I just wanted to get it over with.

We drove out of our neighborhood, passing my school and

heading in the same direction James had gone the day we escaped. We passed the beheaded deer and the wine-bottle tree. My heart started to pound. "Mom? What church is this pantry at?"

Mom fumbled in her purse and pulled out a square of paper. "Northbridge," she said, passing the note to me. "Northbridge Methodist."

I groaned. That was James's church. The cemetery. "Is it okay if I stay in the car?"

"I need your help," said Mom with a look of despair. "To carry things. I don't think they have carts."

We had a pile of canvas shopping bags in the backseat of the station wagon—the Volvo. My parents had sold the Mercedes but the Volvo was already paid for, so that's the one we kept. Still, when we drove into the church parking lot, it was definitely the nicest car there.

"Oh, my," Mom said as we circled around to the food pantry entrance. There was a line of about fifty people already waiting. This was "the hungry" she'd been talking about. Not visibly starving like on TV, when they show children with distended bellies and skeletal limbs. These people seemed tough, like hunger was the least of their problems. It was the rough ones who stood out to me first. The guy with wiry muscles and a face etched with lines, smoking a cigarette. A woman who looked like she'd beat me up if I so much as blinked in her direction. They glared at us as we drove past. Did they think we were going to take their food?

"Oh, my," Mom said again.

"We don't belong here," I said. "Let's go."

Mom drove all the way around the church and pulled into a spot facing a car that looked perfectly respectable, except for the passenger window was cracked and held together with clear plastic tape. It had a handicapped tag hanging from the rearview mirror.

We stayed in the car and watched more people arrive and get in line. One family drove up in an RV, which I assumed was their home. I noticed quite a few handicapped tags, and a number of people with walkers or canes. They weren't so tough. More weary. After a few more minutes, a man came out of the church and handed plastic laminated numbers to those in line, and everyone dispersed a bit, going back to their cars or sitting on a grassy embankment.

"Let's go in now," said Mom, though she didn't actually make a move.

I wasn't ready. "Not yet," I said.

A car pulled into the spot next to ours. I turned to look at the driver. It was Chandra Mandretti. My eyes went wide, and hers narrowed. We both looked away. Oh. My. God. *Chandra Mandretti went to the food pantry.*

I sucked in my breath.

Mom gave me a quizzical look but was too busy working up the nerve to go inside to ask what I was gasping about. She turned off the ignition and studied her reflection in the rearview mirror. Even in her not-too-flashy clothes, she could've been dressed for lunch at the country club. Although I was wearing my rattiest sneakers, I had forgotten and put my leather jacket on.

We did not look needy of free food.

Mom took her earrings off and dropped them in her purse. They were the small diamond studs that Dad had given her for a birthday a few years ago. "I forgot I had these on," she said apologetically.

"I thought you said we didn't have to be destitute to come here."

"We don't. We're being silly." She reached into the backseat for the canvas bags we'd brought. "Come on."

I glanced at Chandra as I got out of the car, but she had her elbow propped in the window to hide her face. Her mother had gotten out and gone to collect a number by herself. But I couldn't do that to Mom. Not this first time.

When we got to the door, a man with a brigh-orange VOLUN-TEER tag handed us the number sixty-seven.

"We're new," said Mom, as if we were joining a social club. "I understand there's some paperwork we need to fill out?"

He took us inside to a lady volunteer who gave Mom a form with questions about our name and address and monthly income and how many people were in our family. She also offered us some literature on SNAP benefits. "That's what they call food stamps now," the lady explained.

"Food stamps?" I hissed in Mom's ear. "Seriously?"

Mom just kept this smile plastered to her face and wrote her answers in the little blocks. She added up her hours of work for the past two weeks and doubled it, calculating a monthly income, and wrote the figure down.

"What about Dad's income?" I asked.

"Nothing to report," she said.

"Family income, it says. You need to put Dad's down, too."

She tapped the pencil on the paper and leaned toward my ear. "Your father is not bringing home an income at the moment, Ivy. Everything he earns is going toward the bank debt on his business."

"What?" I glanced back down at the dollar amount Mom had written, what she brought home from her part-time job at the newspaper. "Seriously? How are we paying for Brady's therapy?" I asked.

"We'll talk about that later," she whispered.

The orange-badged volunteer reviewed our form and seemed satisfied that we were as poor as we said we were. She waited with us until a man with a microphone called out "up to number seventy!"

We shuffled into line with the other hungry. The realization that we were really and truly one of them came on much the way the sensation of hunger does, with a dull ache in the stomach. Only this one felt a bit more like a sucker punch. How did things get so bad, so fast? I wanted to bend over and lean my hands on my knees to catch my breath, but that would only make it worse. People were already staring at us.

When we got to the front of the line, Mom tried to give our number to the man, but he explained that we should hand it in at the end. There were different sections for different kinds of foods. Our volunteer lady pointed out the canned stuff, like fruit and veggies and tuna, boxes of pasta and rice, cookies, and crackers. She called them "shelf-stable products." There was a center section for fresh fruits and vegetables, and another for bread and muffins and other baked goods. "The refrigerated items are in the back," she said. "Meat, eggs, yogurt, milk, cheese."

Hanging on every shelf was a sign that indicated how many of each item you were allowed to take, based on the size of your family. Mom kept reading them aloud, as if I couldn't understand the simple system. Or maybe she didn't want the others to think we were claiming more than our share. "We're a family of five, so we take three boxes of cereal," she said. A family of two was allowed to take one.

"Two pounds of ground beef." She pulled them from the refrigerator. A smaller family could take only one.

"You don't have to announce it," I murmured in her ear.

We stopped to watch a little cooking demonstration going on, teaching people how to prepare a nutritious meal from groceries that were available. They were making a chicken Caesar salad.

Mom kept saying things like, "Oh, look, they have Cheerios!" and "It's just like the market!" But it was *not* just like the market. People didn't snake through the aisles single file like this at the market. They didn't get excited about two pounds of ground beef. And the market never ran out of groceries. By ten o'clock when we finished our shopping, the shelves were almost bare. And people were still showing up.

"Should we give them some of ours?" I asked Mom as we hauled our bags to the car.

She paused and considered, resting her bags on the pavement for a moment. "No," she said firmly, snatching them back up. "I'm sorry. I can't worry about everyone else. I have to worry about us."

We got in the car, and Mom put her earrings back on. Her hands were shaking, but I didn't say anything about that. I turned and saw Chandra still sitting in the car parked next to us. She looked at me again and nodded, before turning away.

As we drove toward the exit, I saw a car I recognized. Its front bumper was held together by duct tape. Leaning against the passenger door was Rigby Jones, one of Lennie's friends. I might've pretended I didn't see him, but he raised a fist and bumped it toward me. I smiled and bumped back.

"Who was that?" said Mom.

"Kid from school." I twisted back around to wave good-bye. That's when I noticed the orange badge. Rigby wasn't using the food pantry—he was a volunteer.

"Everything is not as it seems," I mumbled.

Once we were a few miles away from the church, Mom let out a huge sigh, as if she'd been holding her breath that whole time. "I'll make that Mexican rice and beans with chicken that your father likes," she said, "and the chicken Caesar. That's a good idea. A meat loaf, or maybe a meat sauce . . ."

She was over the challenge of getting the food. Now she had to find a way to stretch it, because at our income level we were only allowed to visit the pantry once every three weeks. I wondered what poor looked like for the people who could shop there every single week.

"You were going to tell me," I said, "how we're paying for Brady's therapy."

Mom didn't reply right away. She probably didn't want to tell me, only said she would to shut me up earlier. "I don't want you to worry about it."

"Mom." This was getting ridiculous. I was worried about it. If I'd known, I would have been looking harder for a job.

"Okay, okay." She fidgeted at the steering wheel. "Insurance pays for some of it. And all the money we made from selling the furniture, jewelry, appliances. That'll pay for the rest. For a while."

"Then what?" I asked.

Mom took a deep breath. "We'll figure something out."

I looked out the window as we headed home, newly determined to find a job.

TWENTY-EIGHT

Later that day, I headed over to the used-book shop, but the elderly woman working there laughed when I asked if she was hiring. "Barely make enough to pay myself, dear," she said.

So I went into the Save-a-Cent. The man working behind the customer service counter gave me a little clipboard with an application to fill out. When I handed it back to him, he said, "We'll let you know if there's an opening."

"You don't have anything?"

"There's a waiting list," he said. "And I'll be honest. A lot of the applicants are older and have families."

"I have a family," I said.

"Are they relying on you to put food on the table or are you just looking for some extra spending money?"

I shrugged. I didn't want to admit that I might need to help my parents buy food. "Extra money, I guess."

"We'll let you know," he said, shoving my application into the back of the folder.

I started to walk out, then turned back around. "I've seen other kids my age working here. Do they support their families?"

"Actually, yes," he said, nodding. "Some do."

"Oh," I muttered, turning and walking out. Maybe I should've considered that country club job, but it was too late. The auditions had started an hour ago.

Brady was on the front lawn when I got home, throwing his gravel into the road. Kaya was sitting on the porch with a coloring book.

"Where's Mom?" I asked.

"Upstairs talking to Daddy," said Kaya.

I looked around for Carla, but she was nowhere to be seen. "Who's watching Brady, then?"

She sat up very straight. "I am!"

"What if something happens? You're six years old."

"If Brady leaves the yard, I'm s'posed to holler as loud as I can. Like this . . ." She took a huge breath.

"No!" I stopped her. "I get it." Had Mom forgotten that Brady would have a total freak-out if Kaya yelled like that?

I went over to my brother and took his arm. "Brady, come with me. We're going inside."

He yanked his arm away and went back to his rocks. "You go," he said.

"You need to come with me," I said. "Now."

He scooped up a pile of rocks and kept throwing them, one by one.

I batted the gravel out of his hand and seized his wrist. "Enough with the rocks, Brady! You can't put them all back. You'll never put them back!"

He dropped them then, and his hands went to his ears. Pounding. He started that silent-screaming thing again.

Kaya rushed over to us. She pushed me in the stomach. *Hard.* "You ruin everything," she said. "Leave him alone."

I stumbled away from them, almost falling over the bike I'd left in the yard yesterday. Mom and Dad hadn't even asked me about it. They were too busy worrying about money to pay attention to me or even Brady.

I ran up the back stairs to get them, but when I reached the top, the door was ajar and I could heard them arguing.

"What about unemployment? Can't you get that?" my mother said.

"I'm not unemployed, Susan."

"You should've been there, Mark. Those people were poor, and not because their multimillion-dollar businesses were failing. I felt like a fraud."

Dad slammed something on the counter. "I'm doing the best I can. You want me to give it all up? Go begging for a job at Sheffley's?" That was Dad's competition, and the biggest printing company in the state. They weren't known for treating their employees particularly well.

"No," said Mom. "I just hope it turns around soon. I don't know how long I can keep this up."

"It's not that bad, Susan. We have a roof over our heads, we have food, we have clothing. The kids are in their same schools. Brady is thriving here. He's—"

"He's playing in the gravel by the side of the road! He's palling around with the neighborhood thug!"

Ah, so she didn't think so highly of Lennie after all.

"That boy is no thug. His only crime is living in a poor neighborhood," he said. "Don't be such a snob, Susan."

Mom gasped. "A snob? Now I'm a snob because I want something better for my mentally disabled child? For all my children?"

"*Our* children," Dad corrected, his voice louder. "They're *our* children and *we* made this decision together. It's not going to kill them to learn that everything in life doesn't come to them on a *goddamned* silver platter."

My hand flew to my mouth as if I was the one who'd cursed. My dad *never* swore. He *never* raised his voice at Mom, either.

Their voices got lower then, and I heard Dad saying, "I'm sorry. I'm doing the best I can." It sounded like he might cry.

I pushed the kitchen door open then. Dad was sitting on one of the kitchen stools, and Mom had her arms wrapped around him. They were sort of rocking back and forth. They looked up when I stepped inside and realized I must've heard the entire argument. Or maybe they just didn't have the energy to put on their everything's-just-fine faces anymore.

"I'll get a job," I said. "I just put an application in at Save-a-Cent."

Dad's whole body slumped even farther than it already was. "You don't have to do that, Ivy."

"If they don't have anything, I can try some other places. And there's . . ." I took a deep breath, for courage. "There's this job at the Morgans' country club. . . ."

"It's too far," said Mom. "I'm already driving your father to work and myself to work and Brady to therapy and . . ."

"Okay then, I'll find something around here that I can walk to," I said, relieved that the country club option was out. "I could give piano lessons, maybe . . ."

Dad sighed and Mom stroked his back, and we all just stood there not saying anything for a few minutes. We could hear Brady's gravel landing in the road, one tiny fistful at a time.

Kaya could take care of him just fine, apparently, and I ruined everything. I climbed the two flights to my room and sat by the attic window, looking down on my neighbors. Looking down *at* my neighbors, that is. I couldn't exactly look down on them anymore, could I?

TWENTY-NINE

Reesa called around four o'clock. "How'd it go?" she asked, all breathless.

"Oh . . ." I hesitated, deciding whether to lie and tell her I'd bombed the audition or confess that I hadn't gone.

"You bailed, didn't you?" Her voice had that steady, I-am-pissed-off-but-trying-not-to-show-it tone.

"Yeah," I said. "It was too far away, anyway." I paused, waiting for her rant, but it didn't come. She only sighed. "Are we still on for tonight?" I asked.

"Yeah," she said. "Get over here already. I have something to show you."

I yanked my hair into a ponytail and splashed water on my face, threw some clothes and my toothbrush in an overnight bag, and went down to the kitchen. Mom looked me up and down. "That's what you're wearing?" I had the same clothes on I'd worn to the food pantry.

"Since when do you care what I wear to Reesa's?"

She had put on a nicer outfit just to drive me over there, maybe expecting Reesa's mom would invite her in. But Mrs. Morgan didn't even come out to say hello.

"I'll pick you up in the morning. Ten o'clock," Mom snipped.

I couldn't believe Reesa's mom would've brushed her off on purpose, but she was right there in the kitchen when I went inside. She smiled like she was posing for someone who was taking too long to snap the photo.

Reesa dragged me upstairs. "Wait till you see what I found."

I was expecting an amazing dress, maybe a couple of great flapper costumes from her mother's closet. But she opened her laptop, clicked on a browser window, and stood back.

"There," she said. "The Wickertons of New York."

I leaned in. It was a fuzzy photo of some people standing at the bottom of a big staircase.

"It's from a few years ago, but look," she pointed to a boy. "Same hair, only shorter. It's got to be him."

I looked at the caption, which identified the boy as Robbie Wickerton. "Wrong name," I said.

"Maybe it's a nickname. Because that kid looks exactly like James. You can't tell me that's not him."

I looked closer at the boy named Robbie. There was definitely a resemblance, but I refused to agree with her.

"Please. It doesn't look anything like him," I said.

"It looks *exactly* like him," Reesa insisted. But she put the photo away and didn't bring up James or his family's obscene wealth again after that. I hadn't told her about the trip to the food pantry or my failed attempts at getting a job, but even Reesa was perceptive enough to notice that something was bothering me.

"What you need," she said, "is some Reesa therapy."

She pulled out her nail polishes and gave me a manicure while we listened to music, taking turns choosing songs. Determined to cheer me up, she pulled out the big guns: her 1980s playlist. For every "Raspberry Beret" and "Girls Just Wanna Have Fun" she blasted, I countered with an "Over the Rainbow" or "I Dreamed a Dream." It was Madonna versus *Evita*, Wham! versus Wagner, Joan Jett versus *Phantom of the Opera*.

"You are not giving Reesa therapy a chance," she said, as her latest selection, "Jessie's Girl," started to play. "The first step is admitting you have a problem."

I nodded. "I definitely have a problem. But I don't think Rick Springfield is going to fix it."

She pulled me up from the bed to dance with her. I tried, really I did, but "Jessie" started with a J, like James, and it only reminded me that he'd stood me up at open mic night. It appeared he didn't want me to be his girl, after all.

I flopped onto Reesa's bed and flipped through her huge stack of celebrity magazines. She played with my hair, twisting it into ringlets, then teasing it so it stood straight out like a giant afro. It was hard not to feel at least a tiny bit better.

After dinner (take-out sushi from our favorite sushi place), Reesa grabbed our coats and led me out back to the deck. I could see our old house from there, the window of my bedroom. It was dark. Empty.

"Here." She pulled a key from her pocket and handed it to me. "I found this."

I turned it over in my palm. "A key. To what?"

"Your house, silly."

"Um, thanks. I guess my mom can give it to the bank people, or the Realtor or whatever." I slipped it in my pocket.

"No, dummy. It's for you. To get inside. Hello?" She wiggled her fingers like she was playing a piano. "It's still there, right?"

It was. My piano hadn't been sold yet.

"I know you miss it," said Reesa. "I thought you might want to go back and play it one more time."

I stared at the key in my hand. "But . . ." I missed everything about home—my old life—so badly. How did she know it was the piano I missed the most? "What if they changed the locks?"

Reesa shrugged. "Guess we'll find out."

She took my hand and we walked the short distance from her house to mine, slinking through the shadows.

"I feel like a burglar," I said.

"It's not like we're going to steal anything," said Reesa. "We're only visiting, and it's your house, anyway."

I pulled out the key as we approached the back door. We hadn't been gone that long, but everything seemed so different. The yard was sprawling, the patio immense. The flower beds so . . . so trimmed and mulched.

The key slid into the slot and turned easily. When I pushed the door open, the alarm sounded, which I expected. It was just a little tiny beep, a reminder to disarm it. I punched in the code, the last four digits of our phone number, and pressed ENTER.

It went silent. *I was home.*

We stepped inside and pulled the door closed. It was dark in the house, and cold. I knew the heat was turned off, or set very low. But there must be electricity since the alarm was working. Reesa flipped one of the six switches by the kitchen door. The recessed lighting above us flickered on.

I breathed in the smell of home. But it wasn't quite what I remembered. Whatever combination of odors made home smell like home—the cooking, the furniture, the soap Mom used and Dad's cologne, Kaya's rescued frogs and Brady's bouquets of dandelions—it was already dissipating.

I crossed the kitchen to the back stairs that led up to my room. Reesa followed me, turning on lights as we went. Everything was so big and so painfully empty. None of our furniture remained. I knew it was being sold off, but didn't realize they'd take it all so quickly. The hardwood floors were bare. Our footsteps echoed through the house. I entered my room, stared at the spot where my four-poster bed used to stand. No more desk, no dresser, no vanity, no rocking chair. It was all gone. Only the window seat remained. I walked to it and sat in my usual spot, where I used to watch Reesa crossing our yard on the way to my house. I wondered if Reesa remembered how we used to talk on our cell phones until she made it all the way up the stairs and sat down across from me.

She plopped herself down there now and put her hand up to her ear and mouth like a phone. "Bye. Hi."

She remembered.

"Bye. Hi," I whispered.

Reesa dropped her hand to her lap. "It's weird in here. Like a ghost town."

I nodded. Nothing was the same, and now that I was here, I knew we'd never be back. I just hadn't expected everything to be so . . . gone.

"You want me to stay?" said Reesa.

"I think I'd like to be alone, if that's okay."

She nodded and scooted out into the hall. I waited until I heard the kitchen door close before making my way to the piano room, tears pricking at my eyes. Everything was so different. I couldn't believe I'd lived here less than a month ago. It felt like a lifetime. And seeing the piano there, all by itself in the moonlight in the middle of the room, reminded me of a line in the nursery rhyme song, "The cheese stands alone." I plunked out the simple melody on the keys, and sang along. "Heigh-ho, the derry-o, the cheese stands alone. . . ."

I nudged the piano seat out and sat down, played one of the lullabies I'd made up for the twins. It sounded hollow.

Just rusty, I told myself. I tried again, grasping for something deep inside that would bring the song to life. Came up empty.

It didn't feel right here. No furniture, no rugs, no family . . . nothing but cold, bare floors. Only memories remained, and they were lonely here, too. I closed the lid on the piano keys, slid my hand over its smooth wood surface. Every sound I made was magnified, eerie.

I thought I heard a noise downstairs and checked my watch. Only seven thirty, not time to go. I tiptoed to the door, listened. Footsteps crossed the kitchen and started up the steps. I clung to the wall.

"Ivy?" Reesa waltzed into the room. "Where are you?"

My shoulders relaxed. "Rees, you scared the crap out of me."

She turned to see me huddling by the door. "Your mom just called." She thrust her cell phone into my hand, a pinched look on her face. "You need to call her back."

I couldn't figure out why Reesa seemed angry. "Is everything okay?"

"You have a visitor."

"A visitor?" I ran through a mental list of people who knew where we lived and might pop by unexpectedly, and came up with . . . nobody. "Who?"

Reesa put both hands on her hips. "Apparently, James Wickerton is at your house, waiting to see you."

THIRTY

I followed Reesa out of my old house, turning lights off as we went. She didn't speak to me the whole way, just stomped a few paces ahead of me. It gave me a moment to be: A, scared that this was the end of me and Reesa; and B, mortified that James was in my apartment. When we got to her yard, I called Mom.

"It's me," I said.

She had her we've-got-company voice on. "There's a young man here to see you. His name is James. He says you have a date."

"A date?"

Reesa glared at me.

"Would you like to speak to him?" said Mom.

"No, no. I, um . . ." I glanced at Reesa with pathetic, help-me eyes.

She grabbed the phone and put it to her ear. "Hi, Mrs. Emerson. It's Reesa. Why don't you ask James if he wants to pick Ivy up here at my house."

She shoved the phone back into my hand and plopped down

on one of their deck chairs, arms crossed firmly over her chest. There was some discussion in the background on Mom's end.

"He says that's fine," said Mom. "We're giving him the address."

"Thanks, Mom. Sorry about the, uh . . . confusion."

"Just be home by eleven. Here, at the apartment," she specified. "Not Reesa's."

I pushed the button to end the call and handed the phone back to Reesa. She snatched it and walked away from me into the yard.

"Reesa," I called after her. "I was going to tell you. . . ."

She spun around. "That you're dating the guy I've been pining over for weeks? You didn't think it might be appropriate to mention that he already has a girlfriend, and that girlfriend happens to be YOU?"

"I'm sorry." I put my face in my hands.

"You *promised*," said Reesa. "I asked you if you liked him and you looked me right in the eye and you promised me you didn't. And, shit . . . that day in the hall? When he was making hand signals at you? You were totally lying to me!"

I shook my head, knowing it was true but not wanting it to be. "It just happened. I didn't think he liked me that much. I was pretty sure he'd bail the second he found out where I live."

Reesa let out a sharp burst of laughter. "You really think highly of him, don't you? Must be a real catch. I guess I should thank you for saving me from the guy."

"I was wrong, okay? I'm sorry."

She brushed past me to go inside.

"It's not like I stole him from you." I followed behind her. "He never showed any . . ." Oohhh . . . I could tell that was the wrong thing to say before I even finished saying it.

She wheeled around. "I get it, Ivy! He didn't like me. He never liked me! That hurts, but it's nothing compared to my best friend lying to my face for three weeks. I guess I know now why you insisted he wasn't my type."

"I thought you'd be mad," I said. "I was afraid you'd tell everyone about . . . about my move, and . . ."

"Fantastic! I'm delusional *and* I'm a shitty friend. Thanks a lot. I feel so much better now."

She stormed into the house, and I trailed behind her, pleading. "Reesa, I'm sorry. Please."

She grabbed my stuff from her room, threw it at my feet, and slammed the door. I picked up my bag and went into the hallway bathroom to do something about my hair. It was still teased into a ridiculous Afro. I dug through my bag for a brush and dragged it over my hair until it was straight enough to braid. When I was finished, I looked like some kind of crazed Heidi.

I changed into my extra clothes—a cute skirt and boots I'd brought in case Reesa wanted to go out. I paused outside her door, but the music was blasting and she didn't answer my knock. I whispered, "I'm sorry," then hurried downstairs and outside. James was just driving up when I reached the Morgans' gate. He looked incredibly hot and thoroughly confused.

"Hey," he said.

I hopped into his car without a word and he drove off. I had no idea where we were going but didn't really care. I was pretty sure I'd just lost my best friend. Losing James, too, would be a perfect icing on the cake of my increasingly miserable life.

"You didn't get my note, did you?" I said. "About meeting at the King last night?"

"No," he said. "I looked everywhere. Where did you leave it?"

"Right on the shelf."

He shook his head. "Didn't find it. Then I thought maybe you left it at the cemetery, so I went there this morning and searched all over the place."

I groaned. "I'm sorry."

"So you thought I stood you up?"

I nodded. "How did you find me?"

"I waited at the Save-a-Cent until your friend"—he cleared his throat—"excuse me, not-your-friend Lennie came along, so I could ask him where you live."

"You didn't," I cringed.

"Yeah, and he wouldn't tell me at first. He said if you wanted me to know where you lived, you would've told me yourself."

"Well, that's kind of true."

He took his eyes off the road long enough to throw me a thoroughly exasperated look. "Why wouldn't you want me to know where you live?"

I sank down in my seat a bit. "You've seen it, haven't you? I live in the worst neighborhood in the district."

"And . . . you think I care about that?"

"I don't know," I said meekly. "You drive such a nice car. . . ."

He pulled up to a red light and squared his shoulders to face me. "Is that why you like me? Because I drive a nice car?"

"No." I bent over and buried my face in my knees. I took a deep breath, hoping the words would come out right, and flopped back on the seat. "That day when we went to the cemetery, you said truth is never as good as what you imagine. I was afraid I wouldn't live up to . . . you know, whatever you imagined."

The light turned green and he drove on. I stared at the road in front of us until he pulled to the side and stopped the car.

"All I imagined was a girl who makes me feel special," he said. "Who likes me for who I am, not for where I live, or who my family is, or what kind of car I drive. You could live in a cardboard box for all I care."

"Well, it might come to that," I said.

"Don't care," he said.

"I can't afford to go places, like into the city. Or to concerts. I can't even rent a stupid costume for Willow's Halloween party."

"*Really* don't care about any of that."

"You say that now," I said. "But when everybody else is doing something fabulous and I can't?"

"You're all the fabulous I need."

I sighed. "Stop saying the right thing."

He laughed. "I'm not trying to."

A reluctant smile came to my lips. "Stop being nice without even trying."

"I'll, uh . . . try to, um, not try?"

We both laughed, and he took one of my braids in his fingers and tugged it until my lips were close enough to kiss. And then he did, he kissed me until it felt like he was my oxygen and I was his. Cars zoomed by in the darkness, their head beams hitting us with bursts of light—like fireworks ignited by the heat of our kisses.

When we finally pulled apart, I looked into his icy-blue-warm eyes, and said, "You need to not try more often."

He threw his head back in a silent laugh and shifted the car into gear, and we sped off into the night—my lips tingling and heart singing.

THIRTY-ONE

We ended up at my favorite burger joint, the Charcoal Hut. It had mini jukeboxes at each booth, with a selection of mostly old songs. James threatened to play "Stairway to Heaven." And he insisted on ordering for me in a British accent. I couldn't help thinking how much Reesa would've loved that, if she was on this date instead of me.

"The lady will have the cheeseburger deluxe, hold the onion. And I shall have the same. A basket of fried potatoes, as well."

The waitress rolled her eyes and scribbled it down. "Anything to drink?"

"Just water for me," I said, realizing the five dollars I had in my pocket might not even cover my cheeseburger.

James leaned toward me across the table, holding the menu up to hide our faces from the waitress's view. "My treat. Don't worry."

"See? This is exactly what I was afraid of. I don't want you paying for me all the time."

"It isn't all the time. It's one time. And *I* asked *you* out. You can pay the next time."

"That's just it. I can't pay the next time. I can't pay *any* of the times."

The waitress shifted her weight from one hip to another, tapping her pencil on her order pad.

James peered over the menu at her. "Could you give us a minute? We're still deciding."

She rolled her eyes and walked away.

James laid the menu down and crossed his arms on the table, leaning toward me again. "So we'll do things that don't cost money. We'll go to the library or the park or the cemetery or watch TV or . . ."

"We don't get cable. We can't even watch real TV at my house."

"Whatever." He gave an exasperated sigh but paired it with a mischievous smile. "I wasn't actually planning to *watch* the TV."

I felt my face go red.

"I really don't care where we go or what we do or how much it costs," he said softly. "Every single other girl I've ever dated has . . ."

He stopped abruptly and looked down, fiddling with the corner of the menu.

"Has what?" I whispered.

"Cared more about money than they have about me," he said.

I lowered my face to catch his downcast eyes. "How is that

even possible?" I said. "You're so much better than anything money could buy."

He smiled, chin still tipped downward. "Stop saying the right thing."

I laughed. "I almost *never* say the right thing. You should seriously be savoring the moment."

"I am." He looked up at me out of the top of his eyes, through the sweep of hair across his brow. "There's just one thing that would make this moment even better."

I felt the blood rush to my face, sure he was going to ask me to kiss him. Right in the middle of the Charcoal Hut. But he opened the menu instead.

"Please share a milk shake with me," he said in a pleading voice. "I've been thinking about it all day. Two straws."

"All right." I smiled.

He opened the menu again. "Chocolate okay?"

I nodded and he sat back to look for the waitress. When she finally sauntered back to our table, he struck up the British accent again. "Chocolate milk shake. Two straws, if you please."

"Anything else, Your Highness?" She was begrudgingly enjoying herself.

"That will be all, kind lady."

Our milk shake arrived and we slurped away at it quietly, laughing each time our foreheads touched.

"So," he said. "Your parents seemed nice—a little confused when I showed up—"

"Sorry about that." I took another sip of milk shake.

"You're, uh . . . new to Lakeside?"

I paused, and then everything I'd been holding in or hiding from, pretending wasn't there . . . it all started tumbling out. What happened with our house, my dad's struggling business, Brady's disability and needing the money for his therapy. Even the trip to the food pantry at the church that morning.

"I've seen people lined up there before," he said.

"It was scary. I mean, the volunteers were nice and everything but the people . . ." I didn't want to act like I was any better than they were, but some of them had genuinely frightened me—the hardness of their gaze and the way their struggles seemed to be etched into their faces. "They made me feel like a fraud, I guess—"

"Like you hadn't suffered enough to be there?" he said.

"Yeah. Exactly." I felt lighter, like I'd been wearing a heavy cloak and had finally managed to shrug it off. "Now you know all my secrets," I said playfully, "You have to tell me yours."

He shifted uncomfortably in his seat. "What makes you think I have secrets?"

I shrugged. "Everyone has secrets."

"I'm pretty boring," he said, stirring his straw in the bottom of the glass to break up a chunk of ice cream. "At least I'm not a secret from Reesa anymore. Am I?"

I shook my head. That heavy feeling I'd just shed was starting to come back. "Could we talk about something else?"

We both leaned in to sip from the shake and our foreheads

touched. "What do you want to talk about?" he said in a voice so low, it sent a tingle up my spine.

I pulled back a few inches. "Um, I . . . uh . . . how about Shakespeare?"

He smiled and sat back, too. "You want to talk about Shakespeare?"

"Okay, no. But I do have a new appreciation for *Romeo and Juliet.*"

"I totally butchered it," he said. "We should go see it onstage sometime, with real actors. . . ."

It was yet another thing I couldn't afford to do. I looked down at the plate the waitress had just slid in front of me, the juicy burger and mound of steaming French fries. I'd never realized how much money ruled our lives, every activity, every conversation. It was impossible to avoid.

"They have free performances in the park sometimes," James said quietly. "Or we can go back to the cemetery and read the lines to each other. Or . . ." He paused, a slow grin lifting the corners of his mouth. "I read the lines, you sing them."

"Uh-uh." I shook my head. "No way."

"Come on." He shook the ketchup bottle and squirted a blob onto his plate. "I want to hear you sing again."

"I can't."

"Why not?"

I dipped a fry into the ketchup and took a bite. "I'm afraid."

"Of me?"

"No. Of *me*."

It was a ridiculous thing to say, but James didn't laugh at me or joke about it. He seemed to understand or, at least, he didn't *mis*understand.

"It's hard to explain," I said.

He had stopped eating and was watching me, listening to me.

I stared into his pale-blue eyes. "There was this talent show when I was in the fifth grade, not just for the fifth grade though," I said. "It was a big deal, the whole school district was involved, kids a lot older than me performing—it was held at a huge auditorium. I wrote a song and I practiced for months. I imagined it every night before bed, how I'd get up there and play perfectly and sing perfectly and everyone would applaud and I'd take bow after bow.

"But I tripped on my way onstage, just a little bit. Probably nobody even noticed, but I started thinking how I'd already messed up. It wouldn't be perfect. Then I saw everybody staring at me and I felt nervous and I never felt that way when I practiced. It wasn't how I imagined it. And I thought, 'Now I've really ruined it.' And the longer I stood there, the worse it was. I really *had* ruined it then. I completely froze onstage. I could hardly breathe. Some kid had to lead me away."

"But you were little," said James.

"I know that, but I can't get rid of it," I said. "The stage and the audience—that's just what sets it off. The rest happens in here." I tapped the side of my head. "It's my own brain. It's *me*. My throat closes up. I can't even sing to the twins at bedtime anymore because someone might hear me through our walls."

"You sang in the band room that day, in front of Reesa, and . . . you know"—he lowered his voice—"that creepy guy in the closet."

I tried to a smile. "Yes, but I didn't know you were there. And I've known Reesa my whole life."

"But you did it."

"Barely. And I had to pretend. . . ." I hesitated, not sure I should trust him with the full magnitude of my weirdness.

He reached across the table to rub his thumb across the back of my hand. "Pretend what?"

"I had to imagine myself in your cemetery," I said. "Singing to the tombstones."

He grinned madly. "My tombstone trick worked?"

"Yeah," I mumbled. "But I don't know if I can trick myself like that again. And now my friend Molly wants me to perform something with her at open mic night."

"Ah," he said. "That's why you were there?"

I nodded.

"And the audience was scary?"

"No," I said. "They were pretty supportive, actually."

"And you still think perfection is a requirement at open mic night?"

I shrugged. It wasn't something I required of anybody else, but I expected it from myself. I don't know why.

James leaned across the table, bent low. "Okay, so here's the plan. You go to open mic night. You don't have to tell anybody. Just show up and sing to the tombstones. Write a song about imperfection, and then mess it all the hell up. Do it for yourself."

I shook my head. "I don't know. I'll think about it."

He took another slurp from the milk shake, and I leaned in, and our noses almost touched. His hair fell across his eyes and he pushed it back. "Seriously," he said. "If the last sound I ever hear is you singing, I'll die happy."

I didn't know how to respond to that. My family and Reesa had been telling me for years, and now Molly, too. Maybe I could start believing it was true. I looked away so he couldn't see that my eyes were watering.

"Too much?"

"Nope," I said. "Just right."

THIRTY-TWO

I went to sleep Saturday night nearly delirious over my date with James, but Sunday morning the joy was gone. Reesa hated me. I kept picking up the phone to call her, to apologize again, but what more could I say? I *had* lied to her. She had every right to be mad.

I took a walk around the neighborhood after breakfast and found Molly sitting on the stoop of her house, which was small but cute. The yard was neatly trimmed, and flower boxes hung below the windows. She smiled as I approached. "Hiya, neighbor."

"Hey," I said. "I think I can see your house from my bedroom." I pointed toward my attic window, which peeked out above the squat houses. Molly had picked me up on Friday night, so I hadn't been sure which house was hers until now.

She craned her neck sideways to see my window. "Ah. Cool."

"Lennie calls it 'Turd Tower.'" I crinkled my nose.

She smiled. "At least you have a view."

"Luxurious Lakeside penthouse with spectacular view," I said with exaggerated enthusiasm, like I was reading a real estate advertisement. "Extra-brown exterior hides the dirt!"

Molly swept her hand to the side to present her own house. "Charming mobile home poorly disguised to *not* look like it belongs in a trailer park!"

I laughed. "It doesn't! Not at all."

"Yeah?" she said, standing and motioning me to follow her. "Wait till you see the lavish interior."

We went in, and it was nicely decorated but there was no hiding that it was a trailer once you stepped inside. It was long and narrow. Molly's room was on one end. We walked through the living room, kitchen, and bathroom as she led me to her room, and my mouth fell open as I stood in the middle of it and looked around. Unlike the drab décor of my attic, which clearly evoked that I had no intentions of staying long, Molly's was a work of art. She had painted a collage of images and words directly onto the walls. There were poems, quotes, lines from books. It was a cocoon of self-expression, of grief and joy and everything in between.

"Wow. This is amazing." My eyes scanned the walls, reading quotes by Mark Twain and Dr. Seuss, Emily Dickinson, and Charlie Brown. I pointed to one that had no attribution:

Reality is for people who lack imagination.

"Who said that?"

"Anonymous," said Molly. "Anonymous has a lot to say."

Some of the quotes were scribbled with pencil or marker, others were applied neatly with stencils. There were colorful designs twined through and around them, like a complicated dance of snakes and vines and fireworks.

"This is my current favorite." She pointed to one scripted beautifully in purple ink.

It was by Picasso. "I'd like to live as a poor man with lots of money," I read.

"When I first saw that, I was like, huh? Who would live like this if they didn't have to? But then I thought about all the stuff that's actually kind of cool about this place."

I gave her a skeptical glance. "Seriously?"

"I can scribble on my bedroom walls and nobody pitches a hissy fit," she said.

"You can eat supper on the living room floor," I said. "You can talk to somebody at the other end of the house without getting up."

She laughed. "Nobody cares if your lawn isn't mowed just so, or what kind of car you drive, or if you have the right clothes or the right friends or . . . you know. All that crap."

Or if you shop at a food pantry, or let your disabled brother play in the road, or . . .

"Money does come in handy now and then," I said. "For, like, food and stuff."

"Yeah. There's that." She grinned.

"Speaking of which. I looked for a job yesterday," I said.

"Where?"

"A used-book store. And Save-a-Cent."

"Any luck?"

I shook my head. "Do you have one?"

"Nah. My mom wants me to focus on school, get a scholarship if I can."

I hadn't even asked what had become of my college plans. There was supposed to be a fund for that, but I didn't know if it was still there.

"I don't know what I want to be when I grow up," I said.

"Me neither. It's impossible to think that far ahead," said Molly. "I hardly know what I want to be *tomorrow*."

I lay back on her bed. "Why did we ever stop being friends?"

"I was ousted. Remember?" The slightest edge came to her voice. "Queen Willow didn't want me in her court anymore."

I kept staring at her ceiling, not sure what to say to that. I'd been a member of that court. I still *was*. I had felt horrible about what had happened at the time but I hadn't *done* anything. I hadn't questioned Willow's version of the truth. I hadn't said anything about my suspicions that Willow was the one starting all the terrible rumors about Molly.

I swallowed. "I wasn't a very good friend to you. I—"

"Don't." She held up a hand to stop me. "It's done. I don't blame you."

"But I should've stuck up for you. I just went along, like a sheep."

"It's okay," she said. "I got off the ride and you stayed on."

I watched her spinning on the chair and realized that was exactly how I felt—like I was spinning around and around on a ride that was moving too fast to get off. I'd been hanging on and trying not to fall, or at least not vomit. Keeping up appearances, being the girl they thought I was . . . it was dizzying.

"I really need to get off that ride," I said. "I can't take it anymore."

Molly smiled. "So do it."

"Just jump off?"

"Walk away. Don't look back," she said. "That's what I did."

"But, they're my friends—I . . ."

Molly stretched her arm out to tap her finger on one of the wall quotes:

A friend is someone who knows all about you and still loves you.

I leaned closer to see who said it, which was written smaller. "Elbert Hubbard," I said. "Who's that?"

"Writer, philosopher. Died, like, a hundred years ago. Smart dude."

"So I should just tell them everything." That about-to-vomit feeling started to come back.

"Or not." Molly shrugged. "Do you even care what they think? What Willow and Wynn say?"

I bit my lip, afraid to tell her that I *did* care what they thought. At least what Reesa thought. Maybe I shouldn't, but I did. I lay back on her bed while she doodled at her desk. What was the worst thing that could happen if I told everyone about the move to Lakeside, the food bank? James didn't care. Molly certainly didn't care. I was faking it for the wrong reasons, for the wrong people. It was too much work. I could see what it was doing to my parents, pretending everything was okay when it wasn't. It would've been easier if they'd told us all along.

When I got up from Molly's bed, I still felt a little dizzy, but I knew what to do. "I'm going to ride the bus tomorrow," I said.

She twirled her chair around to face me. "You want to sit with me?"

I shook my head. "No, actually. I want to try and face it on my own. Is that weird?"

"Nah," she said. "But I'll be there if you need me."

Monday morning, before I left for the bus stop, I checked myself in the full-length mirror Mom had hung on the inside of our front door. She would've considered that garish at our old house, but her standards were different now. I looked okay. My hair was still slightly damp so it was behaving itself. Skirt, tights, boots, jacket . . . all good. Since I wasn't riding my bicycle, I traded my backpack for an oversized tote bag I'd bought at Bloomingdale's a couple of years ago and used maybe once.

Molly was waiting at the bus stop, swinging her clarinet case, when I arrived.

"Hey," she said. "Nice bag."

"Thanks." I started to say where I'd gotten it but stopped myself.

Lennie drove past us in his Jeep. He was very intently not looking at me, but he did slow down and ask Molly if she wanted a ride. He looked at *her* and said only *her* name, to make it perfectly clear I was not invited. "No thanks," she hollered, and he continued on.

"I'm cultivating a reputation as a badass," she told me, "and the state pen bus is a key part of my strategy."

"Is it as awful as they say?"

"Nah," said Molly. "Most of these tough guys are just big talkers. Talk back and they usually leave you alone."

She kicked at the gravel a bit. A few pieces went into the grass. *Brady will get those later,* I thought.

Our bus, number thirteen, rumbled up and we climbed on. The so-called "cool kids" were sitting in the back, the ones who were afraid of them in the front. I found an empty seat in the middle. Molly sat across from me diagonally and slumped down, propping her knees on the back of the seat in front of her.

I tried to assume an equally relaxed pose, but it was a little more difficult to accomplish in a skirt. The bus wasn't crowded, so nobody bothered me for my seat. Then this guy got on who looked like he should've graduated three years ago. He strolled down the aisle, giving a couple of the kids in front a less-than-playful shove. I kept my eyes focused on the dark-green faux-leather seat back in front of me and waited until he passed to let out the breath I'd been holding.

Too soon.

He stepped backward and sat right next to me. "Mind if I join you?"

He angled his body toward me with one arm draped over the back of the seat. I could feel his hand grazing my shoulder. "I'm Mick," he said. "What's your name?"

Turning my head slowly, I considered a fake name. But I'd had enough of the lies. "Ivy."

"Where you from?"

"I live here in Lakeside." Time to own it.

"I didn't ask where you lived," he said. "I asked where you're from. 'Cause you sure ain't from Lakeside."

Someone in the back of the bus yelled, "She's one of those snobby Westside bitches."

"Thought so." Mick grinned, looking me up and down. "Aww, what happened? Lose your trust fund, sweetheart?"

"Get lost," I said.

"Now, don't be like that." He slid his thumb down my arm.

I jerked away from him, and he laughed but pressed even

closer. His knee jabbed into my thigh. I felt a surge of anger, like everything I'd been holding in these weeks was about to explode. In one swift movement, I scooped my hands under his leg, lifted it off the seat and shoved him away. I may or may not have let out one of those tennis-player grunts in the process.

He fell backward, his arms flailing but unable to grasp anything. The surprise on his face was matched by my own. I had toppled the guy. He landed with a loud *thwack* in the aisle, his arms and legs sticking upward.

"Hey!" He scrambled to right himself and lunged for me, but another set of hands came out of nowhere and pushed him back down.

"You heard her," said Molly. "Beat it, asshole."

"What the . . ." Mick's face reddened, whether in anger or embarrassment I couldn't tell.

Molly leaned into him before he could regain his balance. "Back off," she snarled. If she hadn't been saving my ass at the moment, I would've been more scared of her than Mick.

He ambled away, trying to salvage his tough-guy image. There was a smattering of "nice try" and "don't take that shit" remarks from the back of the bus. Molly reached her hand out and said, "C'mon," and led me to her seat.

"Thanks." I slid toward the window, strangely calm now that my anger had found an outlet.

"He did the same thing to me when I moved here. The jerk-off." She plopped down, flushed and breathing heavily.

"How long ago was that?" I said.

"Last fall."

Beginning of sophomore year. Months after Willow had ousted her from our circle, which explained why I hadn't known about it at the time.

"Did one of your parents lose their job or something?"

She didn't answer right away, and I thought perhaps I'd gotten too nosy. "Sorry, none of my business," I said quickly.

"No, it's not that." Molly looked down at her hand and began tracing the lines of her palm with a finger. "My dad died."

I closed my eyes. "God, Molly. I didn't know. I'm so sorry."

"Thanks." She sighed. "Anyway, we couldn't afford the house in Westside after that."

"We lost our house, too," I said.

"Sucks," said Molly.

I nodded. "The worst part is losing my piano. That's why I went to the band room to practice that day."

"I can't practice at home either." She drummed her fingers on the clarinet case sitting in her lap. "Mom works nights, sleeps days. It's too loud."

"Sucks," I said back to her, and we both laughed.

Having someone to talk to—and laugh with—was helping, but not enough to completely calm my anxiety about stepping off that state pen bus in front of everyone. When we pulled up to the school, I was surprised that nobody seemed to notice I even existed. Molly nudged me with her elbow. "It's really not that bad.

You think everybody's watching you, but they really only care about themselves."

I looked around as we walked into the school, at the girls smoothing their sweaters and skirts and hair from the rumpling of the bus. At the guys shoving each other in the arm, nervously glancing at the girls derumpling their sweaters and skirts and hair. At kids who laughed a bit too loud. Or rolled their eyes at the kids who were laughing too loud. Everyone was pretending to be something—cool, aloof, carefree. Something they weren't. I was so tired of pretending.

Willow and Wynn were already taking out their containers of organic vegetables and finger sandwiches when I got to our lunch table later that day. Jenna Watson was there, too. She sat with us when she was between boyfriends. But Reesa was nowhere in sight. She had sat in stony silence through AP English and had breezed past me and James when we stopped to talk after class. I kept trying to catch her in the hall, but she kept disappearing. I never got a chance to tell her what I planned to do at lunch.

I sat down at our table with the apple I'd brought from home and a carton of chocolate milk. There was no way Taco Surprise would make it down my throat today.

"Did you see that skirt Chandra Mandretti is wearing today? Sooo cute. Must be vintage," said Willow.

Wynn's eyes lit up. "She probably went into the city. There are some amazing vintage shops in Manhattan."

"Remember that Pucci dress I found last summer?" said Willow.

Wynn mewed appreciatively, but Jenna stayed quiet. Did she know Chandra was more likely shopping at the Goodwill or Salvation Army these days? She caught me watching her and looked down at her uneaten sandwich, pushing it back into its wrapper.

Reesa finally appeared and sat in her usual spot across from me, but she refused to meet my eye. Her silent treatment further weakened my already-dwindling courage, so my voice came out in barely a whisper. "I have something to tell you all."

Nobody but Reesa even noticed I said anything. She kicked me under the table, gave me a warning shake of her head. At least she cared enough to do *that*.

I cleared my throat and spoke louder. "I have something to tell you. All of you."

Wynn's head snapped in my direction. "Ohmygod, you're pregnant."

"What? No! Why would you think that?"

"She's not even dating anyone," said Willow. "Please."

"You got a car," Wynn declared.

"Did she ask you to guess? Stop guessing!" Willow scolded, turning a patronizingly patient face toward me. "What's the big news, Ivy? I hope it explains why you didn't show up Saturday to shop for our costumes for the Halloween party."

A guilty expression came to Reesa's face briefly. So she'd gone without me, without *telling* me. "So much for honesty," I muttered.

She looked down at her lunch and I turned my attention back to the other girls. "I just wanted to tell you that we moved. My family. We moved to a new place."

My announcement was met with a chorus of surprise. "I didn't know you were moving!" "Why did you move?" "But you have the best house!" "Where?"

I took a bite of my apple to buy some extra time while I formulated my next sentence. Every coherent thought seemed to evaporate from my mind. I chewed thoroughly, took a sip of chocolate milk. And a deep breath.

"My parents decided we needed to downsize, because of the shaky economy and all that." I decided not to get into the part about the foreclosure and the expense of Brady's therapy. "We're renting a place. It's out past Jackson Boulevard," I said, waving my hand in that general direction.

"Oh. My. God," said Willow. Her eyes were huge. "It's in Lakeside, isn't it? My sister came home last week rambling on about Kaya living in the slums and I did not believe her. Are you serious?"

"Yeah," I said as breezily as I could manage. "No biggie. It's not that bad. It's temporary, anyway."

"Oh, my God," said Wynn.

They didn't laugh, but the looks they gave me were far worse. It was a horror-disgust-pity combo of facial expressions that made me want to crawl out of my skin and under the table. Then Reesa opened her mouth. Maybe she thought she was coming to my rescue, or maybe she was trying to throw me under the bus.

She said, "Aren't you going to tell them about your billionaire boyfriend?"

Willow and Wynn and Jenna and everyone else within earshot swiveled their heads to hear more, and Reesa delivered. "The guy's loaded, and he doesn't care where she lives. Apparently."

I shrank at her mention of his wealth. I didn't care if he was loaded, and we didn't know that for sure.

"Who are you talking about?" said Willow. "I didn't even know you had a boyfriend."

"We just started dating," I mumbled. "His name is James Wickerton."

"Does he go here?" said Wynn. "Why haven't we met him?"

Reesa crunched a carrot stick and waved it as she spoke. "He's in our AP English class. Really cute."

They were clearly finding it hard to believe a cute, rich guy had been roaming our halls undetected. "He's homeschooling part-time," I explained. "He only takes two classes. That's probably why you haven't seen him."

"I've never heard of anybody doing that." Willow turned to Reesa. "Have you ever heard of anybody doing that?"

Reesa looked to me for an explanation, but I had none. I hadn't questioned it. And when we'd gotten in trouble for ditching, Mrs. Lanahan had been aware of his part-time status. She'd referred to it as unusual, but clearly he was attending our school. As dreamy as he was, I was pretty sure I hadn't conjured him entirely.

"He got special permission to take AP English and art history. That's all I know." I slurped my chocolate milk.

Willow wouldn't let up. "Do you have a picture of him?"

I shook my head.

"I do," said Reesa, pulling her phone from her bag. "Snapped it in class the other day when he wasn't looking."

She scrolled through her images until she found the one of James and turned it toward Willow, who leaned in to get a better look.

Her face lit up. "That guy?" she said, a wide smile spreading across her face. "I've seen that guy. And believe me, he's no billionaire."

I didn't care if James was a billionaire, but Willow's bait was too tempting not to rise to it. "How would you know?"

"I've *seen* him," she said, "doing things that . . . let's just say no billionaire would ever do."

"Like what?" I tipped my chin up. "His own grocery shopping?"

"Oh, no." She batted her eyelashes. "It's much worse than that. You really need to see for yourself. How about I pick you up at Reesa's house after school. We'll all go on a little field trip."

"Just tell me," I said.

She pinched her lips together and motioned turning a key and throwing it away over her shoulder.

"I have to be home by four," I said.

"No worries," Willow said, smiling as she nibbled her sandwich. "It won't take long."

After school, I got on my old bus to Westside Falls with Reesa. She begrudgingly let me sit next to her.

"Do you know what this is all about?" I asked.

She shrugged, still not talking to me.

As the bus pulled out and circled around to the exit, I found myself gazing longingly at the state pen bus. I should've gone home with Molly.

"Why am I doing this?" I muttered.

Reesa sighed. Said nothing.

"I didn't care if he was a billionaire, you know. I don't care."

She rolled her eyes.

"Honestly, I was hoping he wasn't, because it would only make me feel poorer than I am."

She stared straight ahead. I was clearly having a conversation with myself, so I stopped talking. We got off the bus when it pulled up to her gate, the ornate letter M flaunting her family's wealth in my face. I used to love that sculpted gate, but now it seemed over-the-top.

Reesa punched her code in the keypad by the little foot entrance at the side, and it clicked open.

"Aren't we waiting here for Willow? She's supposed to pick us up any minute." She had driven her Miata to school that day and had to switch to a bigger car.

Reesa stood at the little gate like she was about to shut it in my face. "I'm not going," she said, and then she did. She shut the gate in my face.

"But—"

"I'm not interested in Willow's little field trip, and I don't care what she thinks of James Wickerton," she said. "Maybe he's a billionaire, maybe he's not. I really do not have the slightest interest in wasting one more minute of my life on James Wickerton."

"Because he might not be filthy rich? You were obsessed with him when you thought he was."

"I was obsessed with him when I thought he might like me, but that clearly isn't the case," she snapped. "I was just curious. I mean, what's this billionaire kid from New York doing here, anyway?"

"Come along then." I really didn't want to do this without her. "Please? Don't make me go with them by myself."

She shook her head. "I'm sure they'll tell me all about it tomorrow. You have fun now." She wiggled her fingers good-bye and turned, walking up her driveway without another word.

I didn't have to wait long before Willow pulled up in her mother's Lexus, with Wynn riding shotgun, the music blaring.

I climbed in the back.

"Where's Reesa?" said Willow.

"Not coming. Can you just drive me home?"

"Oh, come on. It'll only take a few," she said. "Besides, I need a latte."

"Me too," said Wynn. "Tall, with a shot of caramel."

"Where are we going?" I asked.

"You'll see," Willow singsonged.

A few minutes later she pulled up in front of Bensen's, the gourmet market. "If you're stopping here for lattes then just take me home after. I really have to be there by . . ."

"Four o'clock. I know," said Willow. "This is our final destination, anyway. So chill."

She turned off the ignition. I followed them into the little coffee bar, where they ordered their lattes. While the barista was making them, Willow took me by the wrist and led me around the corner to the produce section. She stopped by the onions and pointed across the store where the fresh-squeezed juices were.

"There's your billionaire," she said.

His back was turned to me, but I could tell it was James. He was wearing an apron. Not bright green like Lennie's. It was light blue, same as the walls and the shopping carts at Bensen's. As I slowly walked toward him, he dipped a mop into a bucket and pushed down on a lever to squeeze it out, then slapped it to the floor. He was oblivious to the small audience behind him—Wynn had joined us with a latte in each hand. A white cord ran from his ear to his pocket. He was mopping to the beat.

I had walked slowly closer, and when he finally turned, there was surprise, even delight in his eyes, at seeing me. He pulled the earbuds out.

"Ivy. What are you doing here?"

"Wh-what are *you* doing here?" I stammered.

"Uh . . . mopping?" His gaze flicked to where Willow and Wynn stood sipping their drinks, then nervously back to me. "Someone dropped one of those half-gallon containers of OJ. Didn't even tell anyone, so it got stepped in and carts rolling it all over the place. Big mess."

He leaned on the mop pole.

"So, you, um . . . work here?" I said. "As a janitor?"

He pushed the mop away and looked at it, like it had magically appeared in his hand and he had no idea how it got there. "No." He laughed. "Not a janitor. More like an errand boy. Stacking shelves, unloading trucks, carrying groceries to cars. Occasional mopping."

"Oh," I said. It all sounded perfectly reasonable, except that he'd never mentioned it before.

"No food prep, though," he said. "I absolutely draw the line at wearing a hairnet."

He was trying to be funny, and I wanted desperately to laugh or smile but I couldn't seem to make the muscles of my face move. Not with Willow and Wynn watching and judging and . . . I tried to swallow but couldn't. It was like being onstage again and I froze. An audience of two—two miserable, horrible friends I didn't even care about—and I couldn't speak, I couldn't budge.

I dropped my gaze to the pocket of his apron. There, stitched in white, was the name JIM.

I didn't hear them walk up beside me until Willow's hand was on my shoulder. "You'll have to excuse our friend," she said to James. "She may be in a state of shock. She thought you were a multibillionaire!"

"You really had her fooled," said Wynn.

I stood paralyzed, like someone was shining a giant spotlight on me. I kept opening my mouth to say something but nothing came out.

I could only stare at the stitching on his pocket: JIM, JIM, JIM, JIM. What had Lennie called him? *Jimbo*. The janitor? No—errand boy. Stacker of shelves. Why hadn't he told me? He knew everything about me. I hadn't held anything back.

"Ivy?" James stepped toward me.

Willow pulled me away. "Maybe you should leave her alone now. You've done enough damage."

James let the mop clatter to the floor and stepped over it, coming closer as Willow continued to pull me away. "You thought I was a billionaire?" he said. "That's why you liked me?"

It felt like I'd been slapped. I shook my head. "No, that's not ..."

"After all you went through with your family—" He tore his apron off. "I thought you were different," he said.

I watched him turn and storm away from me, my vision closing in like a tunnel. Then I was in Willow's car again and she was gunning the engine, tearing out of the parking lot. She and Wynn were talking over each other. ". . . mopping . . . what a loser . . . can't believe . . . who does he think . . . poor Ivy . . ."

Then Wynn was shaking me. "Where do you live? We have no idea how to get there."

I pointed, and said "turn here" a couple of times. When I saw the Save-a-Cent coming up, I told Willow to stop. "This is good," I said.

"You live *here*?"

I didn't answer, just pushed myself out of the car and stumbled across the parking lot toward the wooded area next to our neighborhood. I couldn't find the walking path that cut through it, though. So I just pushed my way into the brush. Branches scraped my bare arms, but I didn't care. I didn't . . . Where was my jacket? I stopped and dug around in my bag, but I must've left it in Willow's car.

"Shit," I said, then laughed at myself.

Losing my stupid jacket is what I can finally speak up about? *Brilliant, Ivy. Just brilliant.* Stand there like a fucking idiot in front of James and let him think you care if he's rich and don't say a fucking word and fuck fuck fuck fuck *fuck.*

I mouthed the word, repeating it soundlessly because as pissed off at myself as I was, I still wasn't the girl who said "fuck" out loud. And that *really* made me laugh. Everything that had happened—losing my house and my piano and my best friend and my boyfriend, my parents fighting and the food bank and . . . and . . . I was still going to watch my language?

My mind darted and swirled around the frantic conversation in my head as the tree branches tore at my arms and clothes. The strap of my bag got caught and I couldn't get it unstuck so I shoved it from my shoulder and left it there. I stumbled and fell forward, my hands and knees slamming into the ground. I cried out from the pain and then I . . . I just rocked back onto my heels, then sat and cried.

Tears ran down my face, and my body convulsed with shuddery gasps. I didn't remember ever crying like this before, so out of control. I couldn't make it stop as I replayed the past few weeks—had my life really fallen apart so thoroughly in that little bit of time?

My hysterics finally turned into minisobs and hiccups, and I stood up, wiping my hands on my skirt and my nose on my sleeve. My bottom was soaked and my knees were stinging. The skin exposed through my torn tights was scraped and bleeding.

I searched the ground for my bag and finally found it hung up in a tree directly behind me. About three feet away from where I stood was the path.

I've totally lost my mind.

I stepped onto the path and started walking toward home, and that's when I heard it: the distinctive rumble of a school bus.

The twins' school bus.

Four o'clock, oh, my God, I was supposed to be home at four o'clock. I pulled my not-a-phone out of my bag to check the time. It said 4:12. Ohmygod ohmygod *ohmygod.* I ran as fast as I could, tearing down the path and bursting from the woods onto the playground. There were kids on the swings—kids who rode Brady and Kaya's bus!

I ran toward then, shouting. "Did Brady and Kaya get off the bus? Did the driver let them off?"

They stared up at me like startled little fawns stuck in a car's headlights. Nobody answered so I shouted again. "Brady and Kaya Emerson? We live over there." I pointed to Turd Tower. "Did they get off the bus?"

One of the boys shook his head nervously. "I . . . I don't think so," he said. "They can't get off without a grown-up 'cause that kid's retarded."

"He's not . . ." I started to correct the boy, to explain that we don't use that word anymore. That he's mentally disabled. That he's special and wonderful and . . . I just shook my head and ran from them, sprinting for the road, my feet pounding on the gravel until I reached the bus stop, crying and gasping and . . . *there was no bus.* I ran up Jackson Boulevard, hoping the driver might be lingering at the next bus stop, or the next. But it was gone. The bus was gone.

I limped back to the house and pounded on Carla's door, hoping maybe she'd seen the bus arrive and had the kids with her. But the windows of her apartment were dark and she didn't answer. I looked toward Lennie's house. His Jeep wasn't there.

The bus driver probably wouldn't have handed the kids over to him, anyway.

I was really crying now, not for myself but for Brady, who must be so scared. And for Kaya, who would be scared, too, and mad. She would never forgive me for this, for ruining everything once again.

I let myself in the back door as the phone rang in the kitchen. I lunged for it. "Hello?"

"You're there?" It was Mom. "I just got a call from transportation. They said nobody was there for the bus!"

"I wasn't here. . . . I was late. . . . I . . ."

"Ivy!" Mom said sharply. "The bus driver had to take them back to school. I'm leaving work now to pick them up. And you better hope this hasn't scarred your brother so badly he'll never ride the damn bus again, because I don't know what I'm going to do if that happens."

"Mom, I . . . I . . ."

"One simple thing, Ivy. That's all I asked, and you couldn't even do that?"

I stammered to answer her, but I couldn't find any words— only the shuddery hiccups that remained from my cry. Then I heard a *click* on Mom's end and a few seconds later, a dial tone.

My mother had hung up on me.

I returned the phone to its cradle and walked toward the front stairs so I could be waiting for them when they got home. Then I caught a glimpse of myself in the full-length mirror on the door. Scraped arms, torn tights, muddy skirt. I couldn't let Brady see me like this.

I watched out the window from my parents' bedroom, which was in the front of our apartment. When our car pulled up, Mom and Kaya got out, but Brady wouldn't. I heard Mom pleading with him. "Come on, buddy, it's okay. It's safe." The bus driver must've said it wasn't safe, and he thought that meant it was *never* safe here. Mom turned and looked up toward the apartment. It was one of those all-hands-on-deck moments, and my hands were inexplicably absent.

Lennie drove up then, parking his Jeep along the road in front of his house. He got out and waved and Kaya rushed over to him, and then he and Mom were talking low and . . . Lennie leaned into our car. Like *that* was going to help.

Then I couldn't believe it. Brady got out of the car. He was smiling and holding his arms out to Lennie. Lennie lifted him up, then sat him in the grass and took him by one hand and one foot and . . . gave him an airplane ride. Once around, so he wouldn't get too dizzy.

But I did. I got dizzy, watching Lennie save the day, while I sat there helpless and pathetic and wrong, wrong, *wrong* about everything. And *everyone*.

THIRTY-THREE

Mom found me asleep on top of her bed in my mud-caked skirt. She shook me awake, a look of horror on her face.

"Mom." My voice was raw. "What's wrong?" I'd forgotten for a moment what I must look like.

"What happened to you?" Then a more panicked expression came to her eyes.

"No . . . I . . ." How could I explain my breakdown? "I fell, in the woods . . . I . . ."

"Oh, sweetie." She gathered me in her arms. Everything hurt when she touched me, but I didn't want her to let go. I just wanted to cry on my mother's shoulder and let her take care of me.

And she did. "Come on, let's get you cleaned up."

She led me down to the bathroom and filled the tub, helped me peel off my clothes without taking too much skin along with them, and gently washed the dirt from my wounds. She spoke in the soothing tone I remembered from before the move, not the sharper more harried one that had replaced it lately.

"So what happened?" she asked softly.

"I just, I got home late—my ride left me by the Save-a-Cent, and I walked through the park. Only I couldn't find the path and I got tangled and fell, and . . . and then I heard the bus, and . . ." I started to cry again.

"I'm so sorry I yelled at you. I was on a deadline at work. . . . If I'd known . . ." Her own eyes filled with tears and she reached for the corner of a towel to wipe them away. "Look at us. We're a mess."

I cry-laughed, nodding. "We really are."

"Okay, finish cleaning up. I need to check on Brady and Kaya. They're still outside with Lennie." She got up. "You know, maybe we were wrong about that boy. The twins adore him."

When the bus unloaded in front of the school the next morning, I pushed against the flow of students going in to head the other way—toward the back parking lot. I stood where James always parked his car, waiting until the first-period bell rang. But he didn't show. I waited again outside Mr. Eli's room.

Reesa must've thought I was waiting for *her*, because she stopped halfway down the hall and pretended to tie her shoe. When she looked up and I was still there, she dug around in her backpack for a while. Wow. She *really* did not want to talk to me. Join the club. Reesa, James, even Lennie . . . nobody could stand being around me. I was like poison. *Poison Ivy.*

I snorted at my own joke and went into class. Reesa finally came in a second before the bell rang, so there wasn't a moment to talk to her even if I wanted to. Instead, I spent most of my morning classes drafting a letter to James, in case he showed up but refused to speak to me. At least I could shove it into his hand and hope he'd read it. I tried to explain everything—how Reesa thought he must be a member of this wealthy Wickerton family from New York that she found online. How I didn't care. How I was glad he wasn't. How I didn't want a boyfriend who could go places and do things that I couldn't do. I was just surprised that he'd never mentioned a job. I would've felt better about my own circumstances if I'd known about his.

But I never had a chance to give him the letter. There was no sign of James all day, not even in our secret room, where I'd left an especially long note after English class. I started to worry that he was gone for good, not just the day. But his books were still there. He wouldn't leave without his Shakespeare, would he?

At home after school, I searched my room for the Charcoal Hut receipt James had written his home phone number on. I took the phone to my room and pressed my shaky fingers to the buttons. It rang nine times, and I was about to hang up when someone finally answered.

"Hello?" An elderly woman's voice.

"May I speak to James, please?"

Silence.

"Ma'am?"

"May I ask who's calling?" she said.

"It's Ivy Emerson."

There was a muffled sound on the other end, like her hand was covering the phone as she spoke to someone. It had to be him. She wouldn't have asked my name if it was a wrong number. Right?

She came back on. "I'm sorry. He's not available at the moment."

"Oh. Um, could you please tell him . . ."

Click.

I stared at the dead phone. My first instinct was to call back. I pressed my finger to the redial button, but let it go and placed the receiver in its cradle.

It rang almost immediately.

I swooped the phone to my ear. "James?"

"No. It's me." *Mom.* "I'm picking the twins up from school today and taking them directly to Brady's therapy appointment, okay?"

"Oh, yeah, okay."

She rattled off some instructions for me, something about starting supper, and I heard her but I wasn't listening, because all I could think about was that James was at home. The woman who answered the phone had spoken to someone before telling me he wasn't there. That he wasn't *available*. I flipped open my laptop while Mom was still talking, and typed the phone number I'd just called into the search window. Wasn't there some kind of reverse directory where you could put in a phone number and find the name or the address?

"Ivy? Did you hear a word I just said?"

"Yeah, Mom. I'm just doing some . . ." I caught myself before another lie came out. "I'm just searching for something online, for an address," I said.

She let me go as I hit the RETURN key and the name IDA MCDANIELS popped up with a Belleview address. I typed her name into another search window and found an obituary, not for Ida but for a man named James A. Robertson

Then everything started falling into place. The cemetery. The tombstone where James and I sat on the bench. *James Aloysius Robertson*. And J.A.R. . . . from the Shakespeare book. I searched the obituary for any mention of James. It noted grandchildren but didn't name them. Just a sister, Ida McDaniels, and a daughter—

Sheila Wickerton.

I went back to the listing that showed Ida's address: 845 Clayton Street. I quickly mapped it, hoping it wasn't too far to get to on my bike. When the directions popped up, I scrolled down to see the total distance. Seven miles.

I scribbled the directions on the back of my hand, grabbed the letter I'd written to James, and ran for my bike.

THIRTY-FOUR

I pedaled faster than ever, ignoring honks of the early evening-rush-hour drivers. My legs were on fire and my hair wet with sweat when by the time I rolled onto Clayton Street. It was the kind of neighborhood I had hoped we might move to, with nice two-story houses lined up next to each other. Brick, not brownstone, with cute little porches and sidewalks and cars lining the street. I bicycled as close to the parked cars as I could get without bumping into their rearview mirrors and slowed as the house numbers got closer to 845. A sleek red sports car with New York plates turned in front of me and zipped into an empty spot . . . right behind a black BMW. I steered to the opposite side of the street and pulled onto the sidewalk beside an SUV. Unbuckling my helmet, panting, I heard a familiar voice.

"What are you doing here?" snarled James.

The tone surprised me and I turned immediately, a pit in my stomach. But he wasn't talking to me. He strode toward the girl who emerged from the red car like she was stepping off a fashion runway. She had sandy blond, wavy hair and a straight, delicate nose. I ducked farther behind the SUV so I was mostly hidden but could still see them through the windows.

"Nice to see you, too," she said. "No hug? No kiss?"

James took a few steps forward and gave her a stiff hug, followed by a quick peck on both cheeks. It made me think of Wynn, who kissed that way, too.

"What are you doing here?" he asked her again.

"Came to see how the other half lives." She gestured toward the houses along the block, as if there was something unseemly about them. "Aren't you tired of slumming it?"

"Staying with Aunt Ida is hardly slumming it."

"Fine. But working as a stock boy in a grocery store? Come on," she said. "You could've gotten a dozen other jobs that easily paid more. You're only doing it to annoy Daddy."

James shrugged. "Think what you want. I told Dad I could take care of myself, and I have. How I do it is my business."

She stepped back and leaned against her car, crossing her arms under her chest. "Fine. You've proven your point. Now it's time to come home. Hopefully, it's not too late for Daddy to pull some strings and get you into one of the Ivies. I'm sure the academy will fudge those two credits you're missing, with the proper incentive. A nice donation—"

"I don't want him to pull strings for me or buy off my school, Rebecca. That's the whole point," said James, his voice rising. "People look at us and all they see are dollar signs. Don't you ever wonder if anybody would give a fuck about you if they didn't know who your daddy was?"

She laughed. "Yeah, Robbie. Life's rough all over."

Robbie?

James turned his back on her and marched into the house. The girl—Rebecca—remained leaning against her car, inspecting her manicure. My legs were so shaky I was afraid to move—afraid I'd fall flat on my face if I did—so I stayed behind the SUV. Then James emerged from the house carrying a large duffel bag. He strode to his car, popped the trunk, and shoved it in.

"I was leaving anyway," he said, slamming the trunk closed. "Happy?"

Rebecca shrugged. "I'm just sick of all the yelling and crying and . . ."

James whirled around. "Who's crying? Mom?"

"Well, it certainly isn't Dad."

Something seemed to collapse in James, his defeat evident in the slump of his shoulders and the sag of his head. I don't know why I didn't run to him then, stop him and explain myself and—and . . . ask him what the hell was going on. But I hesitated, and before I could blink, he got behind the wheel of his car and drove away.

Rebecca got into her red car, too, and zoomed off after him. When I finally stumbled out from behind the SUV, all I could do was stare at the spot where they had stood arguing, stunned that James was gone.

A gray-haired woman emerged from the house—Aunt Ida, I

presumed. She offered me a sympathetic smile. "You're the one who called?"

"Yes."

She nodded slowly, arms folded around her middle, then turned to go back inside.

"Wait!" The note I'd written to James was clutched in my hand. I ran up to the porch and held it out to her. "Can you get this to him?"

She took the folded paper and tucked it into the pocket of her dress. "Can't make any promises," she said. "But I'll try."

It was dark by the time I got home, and Mom was furious. She followed me up to the attic, scolding me as quietly as her anger would allow so as not to upset Brady. "You were supposed to start supper. Where have you been?" she hissed.

"I screwed something up, Mom, and I was trying to fix it. It's a long story," I said, hugging a pillow to my chest.

"Well, I don't have time for a long story right now, because I have to make supper," she started down the stairs, then turned back. "You're grounded, by the way. Until further notice."

I wasn't even upset about that. It made sense, at least, when nothing else did—like whatever I'd witnessed between James and his sister. *Robbie.* Reesa was right all along. But James had left home, apparently, to fend for himself? To prove something to their father? My chest ached when I remembered the worst part, what he'd said about wanting to see if anybody would care about him if he didn't have money.

I lay down and stared at the ceiling, aching for my piano. I needed to get this horrible feeling out of my chest and put it to music.

The ukulele I'd retrieved from our old house sat dusty and unused in the corner next to my dresser. I got up, took it in my hands, and strummed, cringing at how off-key it was. I fiddled with the tuning pegs. Strummed again. Better.

But it was a ukulele, and it sounded too happy for my mood.

I closed my eyes and let my voice take over. I don't even remember what I sang, if there were words involved or just sound—moaning or humming or bellowing open vowels of agony. I didn't care if someone out there heard me. I just had to get it out.

When I stopped and looked up, Brady was standing in my doorway. His little face was twisted into a question mark as he struggled to assess the situation.

"It's okay," I said quickly. "I was just . . . I was singing."

His eyes lit up. "Sing for Brady?"

I nodded as he shuffled to the bed and sat next to me, his legs dangling off the edge. I wrapped my arms around him and held tight. After what I'd just seen, the way Rebecca talked to James, so cold and uncaring . . . I craved the warmth of a good hug.

We sat close with the ukulele on my lap. "What kind of song do you want?" I asked.

"La-la," he said, and I smiled.

"Okay," I said. "One la-la lullaby coming right up."

I strummed and plucked until a tune came tumbling out. It started a bit slow and mournful, but Brady's la-las were too exuberant to be satisfied by a sad song. I picked up the pace and let the music cheer me up.

"You know what? I think we need Kaya," I said to Brady.

Brady smiled and shouted, "Kaya!" at the top of his lungs. I did the same. "Kaya! Kaya!"

She bounded up the stairs. "What are you doing?"

"We're singing la-las," I said.

She grinned and threw herself at me, a laughing tackle-hug onto the bed. "You're back," she said.

I paused, realizing she didn't mean I was back from my bike ride. She meant I was *back*. Back to myself. Back to being part of my family. "Yeah," I said. "I'm back."

THIRTY-FIVE

The next few days at school were quiet. At lunch I started sitting with Molly and Rigby, the friend of Lennie's who had air-fist-bumped me at the food pantry. I didn't see the point in subjecting myself to more torture at the hands of Willow and Wynn, and Reesa's ongoing silent treatment was unbearable. Molly slid her tray over and made a spot for me, no questions asked.

On Saturday, Mom lifted my grounding, and I immediately went back to Clayton Street. When Ida saw me standing on her front porch, she gave a big, weary sigh and held the door open. I stepped inside and followed her to the front room. The house was beautiful, with its hardwood floors and Oriental rugs and lamps with fringed fabric shades. There was a quiet, fragile feeling to her home, like an antique shop. The only sound was the tick of a clock coming from another room.

"Have a seat," said Ida. "Can I get you something to drink?"

"No thank you," I said. "I can't stay long."

She lowered herself slowly into a flowered chair that seemed to hug itself around her as she sat. There was a table next to it, with books and reading glasses. I wondered if James had sat here, too, on this same couch when they talked.

"So, you're Ivy," she said.

"Oh, sorry . . . yes," I stammered. "Ivy Emerson."

"Well, I've always been partial to three-letter names that start with *I*." She winked and held out her hand, its knuckles swollen with arthritis. "I'm Ida McDaniels."

I closed my fingers gently around hers. "Nice to meet you."

We settled back into our respective seats and I tried to find the right question, the right thing to say.

She rescued me. "You're wondering about Robbie."

It was hard for me to think of him that way. "Was that his real name? Robert?"

"Middle name. Robertson, actually. James Robertson Wickerton, named after my brother, his grandfather."

"James Aloysius Robertson. He's buried at the Methodist cemetery, isn't he?" I said. "With his wife, Clara. They died a week apart."

Ida smiled. "Robbie took you there? He was very close to his grandfather." She pointed to the fireplace mantel, which was lined with framed photos. "There they are."

I walked over to see the picture. It was a young James, maybe five years old, in bare feet. His grandparents stood on either side, each holding one of his hands while he swung like a monkey between them. He was grinning like crazy.

"He spent a week here every summer. They let him really be a kid. Not like . . ." She let her voice trail off.

I smiled at the boy in the photo. "James didn't tell me they were his grandparents. He didn't tell me . . . a lot."

"Well," said Ida, returning to her chair. "I'll leave him to explain why he left home, what happened with his father and all, because that's his business not mine. But I took him in. This was his grandparents' house, and he's always welcome here. I called my friend Olivia Lanahan—Mrs. Lanahan to you—and got him enrolled at the school so he could finish high school. And the rest, as they say, is history."

"Why didn't he tell anybody who he was?"

"He wanted to start with a blank slate—no money, no status, none of that—and see if people would treat him differently."

"So I was an experiment?"

"Not you specifically. People in general, I suppose," she said. "But he liked you. He came home that one night and told me, 'She didn't even want me to pay for her milk shake!' The girls at his school all expected him to pay for that and a lot more."

A pang of guilt caught in my throat. I had been drawn to James before I'd known anything about him. But had Reesa's speculation about his wealth played a role as well? I couldn't deny the possibility. He had everything I'd lost, and more. If I'd thought, from the very beginning, that James worked mopping grocery store floors, would I have ever gotten into his car that first time? Or would I have treated him like I'd treated Lennie?

I sat the photo back on the mantel. "Have you heard anything from him? Did he . . . did you give him my note?"

"I mailed it to him, but I haven't spoken to him since he left. I tried calling, but that snooty butler of theirs kept telling me he was unavailable." She chuckled in a humorless way.

"Could you give me his phone number? An email address?"

"I don't use email, so I don't know if he has one of those," she said, reaching to her table for a piece of paper and pen. "But I can give you his mailing address and phone number. Can't promise you'll get through."

"Thank you," I said, the thought of James believing nobody would ever like him for himself gnawing at my stomach. "I have to try."

I sat on my bed with the phone cradled in my lap. I had dialed his number eight times now, always chickening out at the last minute and slamming it down before anyone answered. What if he hung up on me?

My hands trembled as I punched in the number Ida had given me once more, then lifted it to my ear.

On the fourth ring, a deep, male voice answered. "Hello?"

I'd expected something fancier, and it set me off to a bad start. "I . . . um, could I speak to James . . . uh . . . Robbie . . . Wickerton?"

"May I ask who's calling?"

"Ivy Emerson?" I immediately cringed at how ridiculous I

sounded, like I was guessing at my own name.

"One moment," the man said. They had hold music. Classical. Chopin's Nocturne in C-sharp for piano, to be exact. I knew it, because I'd played it. So *there*, snobby butler guy, who was taking way longer than "one moment." It was at least ten minutes before the man came back. "I'm sorry, but Mr. Wickerton is not available at this time."

He didn't offer to take a message, but I gave him my name and phone number, anyway.

THIRTY-SIX

After my failed attempt to call James, I gravel-kicked my way down to Molly's house. She held a finger to her lips when she answered the door and motioned me into her room.

"Mom's sleeping," she said, quietly closing her door. "What's wrong?"

"Life sucks." I flopped backward on her bed and gazed up at the new additions to her wall. "You can quote me on that."

She pointed to a far corner. I could barely make out where she'd written in pencil:

Life sucks.—Me.

I snorted. "See? My life even sucks at sucking. It's a rerun of somebody else's sucky life."

Molly tapped her finger to yet another quote, this one a clipping from a magazine:

Been there, done that.

Moping around at Molly's was my new favorite pastime, but it made me miss Reesa. She never let me mope. Not for long, at least. She always came up with the plan to fix whatever needed fixing. A completely insane plan, usually. But a plan.

I turned on my side and bent my arm to prop up my head. "What do you do when a guy—the guy you like—won't even acknowledge that you're alive?"

"Which guy?" said Molly. She didn't know about me and James. Hardly anybody did, since I'd kept it such a secret. It was like it had never happened.

"Any guy," I said. "Hypothetical Guy."

She twirled slowly on her desk chair. "Is Hypothetical Guy dating someone else?"

"Not that I know of," I said.

"Does he know you're trying to get his attention?"

Had James gotten my letter or my phone message? "Hypothetical Girl is uncertain."

"Ahhhh." Molly spun back around to face her desk and bent over her journal. She collected quotes there, including random things she overheard people saying during the course of her day. I had a feeling I'd just been quoted. She clicked her pen a few times. "You could throw a party."

"A party."

"You know, one of those things where people gather and

dance and drink and talk and laugh?"

"Yes, I know what a party is."

"So, you throw a party and you invite Hypothetical Guy. But it's not a date. If he comes, awesome. If he doesn't, it's a party. You're still having fun."

Considering I was presently estranged from most of my friends, throwing a party sounded like a great way to make a complete fool of myself. But heck, I was on a roll.

"Halloween," I said. "We could invite all the people who weren't invited to Willow's bash."

"We?" Molly raised her eyebrows.

"Well, yeah. It was your idea."

An hour later we had decided on a theme for the party: "Come as you are." And not as in "I'm too lame to figure out a costume" but rather, "This is who I really am." Our invitation would encourage guests to let it all hang out, reveal their hidden identities, show their true selves. I didn't know how I'd get James there, but after what happened between us, maybe this theme would hit home. I just hoped I could get through to him.

Walking back to my place from Molly's, I was nearly sideswiped by a souped-up truck that stopped in front of Lennie's place. I slowed my pace to witness the transaction. Lennie came out with a small paper bag, handed it to the guy, took his money, thank you, good-bye, the guy drove off. Carla's advice came back to me:

Ask him about it.

Lennie disappeared around the back of his house, into the shed. I hurried across the gravel road and followed him. The small wood-and-metal structure was windowless. I stood at its door, my imagination conjuring visions of pot plants and grow lights.

Before I could change my mind and retreat, Lennie burst out and nearly crashed into me. We both jumped.

"Whoa. Hey." His hands went to my shoulders, to steady me. Then he quickly dropped them to his sides. "Didn't see you there. What are you doing?"

"Yeah, I . . . uh . . . just . . ." I tried to peer into the shed but his shoulders were blocking my view. "Wanted to thank you for helping out with Brady the other day. I royally messed up, and you seem to always swoop in and save the day when it comes to Brady. So, uh, thanks."

"He's a great kid," he said. "I like him a lot."

"Yeah." I smiled nervously. "He really likes you, too."

Lennie kicked at the dirt with his boot. We hadn't spoken in a while, since open mic night, and I hadn't exactly been friendly to him then.

"You, um, want to come in?" He motioned with his thumb inside the shed.

"Oh . . . okay." I nodded.

"You've probably been wondering what I do in here, anyway . . ."

"No, I . . . well, yes." I gave a nervous laugh. "People are always driving up and buying something from you, so . . ."

"It's not drugs, if that's what you're thinking."

"No, I . . ."

Lennie smirked, reached back, and pushed open the shed door. "Welcome to my den of iniquity."

I stepped gently into the small space, which was lined with shelves, each one about six inches deep. Covering the shelves were gears and chains and mechanical-looking pieces I couldn't begin to identify. In the corner, on a plywood workbench, sat a computer—a brand-new desktop Mac. And in the middle of it all, a table with a postage meter, and some packing tape, scissors, and boxes. Everything was super neat and organized.

I strolled around the table, browsing the bits and pieces on the shelves. "What is all this?"

"Small engine parts, out-of-stock stuff mostly," he said. "I take them off junkers, put them up on my website, people order them for old cars they're fixing up, stuff like that."

"You have a website?"

He walked over to the computer and hit the space bar. The screen lit up. Across the top it read, LAZO'S ENGINE PARTS. The artwork was similar to Lennie's tattoo.

"Lazo?"

He shrugged. "Better than Lazarski. I didn't want my business to get confused with my dad's. He used to have a body shop."

I took the computer mouse in my hand and scrolled around

the site. There was a section for automotive parts, and another one for other types of engines—lawn mowers, chain saws, washer/dryers. You could order an item to be shipped or pick it up. Voilà.

Not a drug dealer, then, but a budding entrepreneur? "Did your dad teach you all this?"

"Some." He picked up a part that was lying on the desk and placed it next to a similar one on a nearby shelf.

"You said he had a body shop. . . ."

"Yep." Lennie ducked down to search for something in one of the boxes beneath the counter. "Messed up his back when a car fell on him a few years ago. So now he mostly sits around smoking weed." Lennie found the part he was looking for and stood up to face me. "Medicinal purposes."

I stepped back. "So your dad's the pot smoker?"

"Didn't see that one coming, did ya?"

I swallowed hard. "I'm sorry."

He shrugged. "Not your fault."

"I mean, I'm sorry about what I said, before. About you smelling like a bong. I thought you were a total pothead."

He snorted. "Guess you were mistaken."

It'd been happening to me a lot lately.

"Why didn't you say something?"

"I don't know," he said. "I figured you'd decided who I was, and nothing I said was going to change it."

"Not being totally freaking scary might've changed it," I said.

He laughed. "I'm not that scary."

"Seriously? That first day when we moved in? You and that guy with the scar?"

"That's my cousin Frankie. He's such a bonehead."

"Well, he's a scary bonehead. He called me a Westside bitch. He didn't even know me."

Lennie leaned back against the workbench, arms folded across his chest. "And what do your friends call me? They don't know me, either, but I'm pretty sure they don't think very highly of me."

All the words we'd ever used to describe Lennie's crew ran through my head. *Druggie. Stoner. Lowlife. Loser.* But I didn't say them out loud.

"That's because you hang out in a pack, like you're part of a gang—"

"And you don't?" he interrupted, coughing like he'd just swallowed something the wrong way. "Your friends are a *way* scarier pack than mine are. I mean, that day I brought you the potato? I was just trying to be funny, and Willow Goodwin nearly sliced me open with her *eyes*. That bitch is scary."

"Yeah, okay. I see your point. But your friends have *tattoos*, and they, I don't know . . . they *snarl*."

Lennie bent and unbent his elbow in my direction so show off his tattoo of gears and chains. "Oooh. Scaaary," he said, then gave me his best snarl. "Like this?"

"Yeah, like that." I smiled, then stepped closer and pointed to his tattoo. "Can I see it?" I had been curious, but didn't want him to think I was staring before.

"Sure," he said, pulling his sleeve up over his shoulder. His arm was more muscular than I would've thought, since he was so tall and lean, but I pretended not to notice. I focused instead on the intricate gears on his elbow and shoulder, and the chain that wound around them. I wanted to trace it with my fingers, the way it bulged across his biceps.

"Stop flexing," I said.

He laughed. "I'm not. I'm just naturally buff."

"Right." I gave his shoulder a gentle shove.

I suddenly heard Mom calling for me from the side yard, looking up toward our kitchen. I stuck my head out the shed door. "Over here, Mom."

"Oh!" She spun around, surprised to see me with Lennie. Or maybe it was the way he was pulling his sleeve back down over his tattoo. "We're home from therapy," she said. "Can you watch Brady for a bit?" She pointed to where he was gathering his stones out front.

"Sure," I said, then turned to Lennie. "I have to go throw gravel now. Thanks for giving Brady a new hobby, by the way."

He laughed. "No problem."

THIRTY-SEVEN

"Does this answering machine work?" I held up the ancient device and shook it against my ear, to see if anything rattled. Mom had resurrected it from a cardboard box in our Westside basement so we could cancel the answering service through the phone company and save money on our phone bill. "Has anyone actually received any messages?"

Mom pulled it out of my hands. "Yes, it works." She pressed the PLAY button. Molly's voice blasted our kitchen, "So, about the Halloween party. I can only fit three people in my house and you can probably fit about seven. Can we have it in your yard? Do you think Carla will mind? Call me!"

"Party?" My mom looked at me and raised her eyebrows.

I grinned sheepishly. "Oh, right." That's how my parents learned that we were hosting a Halloween party. Once Molly and I assured them our costs would be minimal—we'd make lemonade and serve chips—they agreed to it. Honestly, I think they were just happy I'd made a friend here and was no longer begging to leave.

But it had been more than a week since James had left and still no call. I'd sent him a paper invitation and countless letters. I phoned Ida to see if she'd heard anything, but her answer was always the same: "Nothing, dear. I'm sorry."

Molly had made the invitation to our party, cutting words out of magazines and taping them together like a ransom note. Then she snuck into the office at school and made photocopies on that hideous orange-yellow copy paper they use for notices they don't want parents to ignore.

"Goldenrod," Molly clarified. "It was the Halloweeniest color I could find."

"Weeniest," Rigby said, snickering.

Molly handed us each our allotment. Rigby was an honorary cohost of the party. "Don't invite any douche bags," she said to him.

I took one and wrote in the margin above the COME AS YOU ARE heading:

I don't care who you are.
I just want to see you.
— Yours, Ivy

I addressed it to James in New York and dropped it in the big blue mailbox at the entrance to our neighborhood. I mailed one invite every day, in different kinds of envelopes. I always included my email address so he could reply more quickly. But I was careful not to print a return mailing address on the outer envelope. Maybe one of them would get through.

On my way back from the mailbox one day, I saw a woman with salt-and-pepper hair come out of Lennie's front door with a blanket wrapped around her shoulders. She fast-walked toward an old Honda Civic that was parked in the grass on the other side of their house, ducked into the backseat, and shut herself in. Her head dipped to the side and she disappeared from sight. I slowed my pace to see who would follow, if Lennie or his dad would come out and drive her away.

But nobody came.

Then I noticed that the car had a flat tire and one of the taillights was out. I walked along the hedges between our houses and knocked on the door to Lennie's shed. He opened it a crack and peeked out.

"Hey." He smiled and nudged the door wider when he saw it was me. "Come on in."

I stayed outside and gestured toward the Honda. "No thanks. I just . . . There's a woman hiding in that car. Do you know her?"

He sighed and his shoulders dropped a bit. "That's my mom."

"Oh." I looked toward the Honda again. "Is she okay?"

He wiped some grease from his hands with a rag. "Probably just hiding."

"Oh," I said again.

Lennie held up a finger. "Wait here."

He strode over to the car and tapped on the back window. The woman sat up and rolled it down. I couldn't hear what they said, but she reached a hand out and stroked his cheek. He nodded and turned back to me.

"Is everything okay?"

"Sorry," he said. "Can we talk later? I—"

"Yeah, sure. No problem." I backed away toward my house, lifting my hand in a little wave. "See you later."

"Thanks." He locked up the shed and went in the back door to his house.

I found my mom in our kitchen, chopping onions. "Have you met Mrs. Lazarski?" I asked.

"Couple times," she said. "She's very quiet."

I hadn't even thought about Lennie having a mother, to be honest. I'd never seen her before. "What does she do?"

Mom shrugged. "Takes care of her husband, I guess. Why don't you ask Lennie?"

"I will," I said.

The tenderness between Lennie and his mom made me wonder about James and his mother. Rebecca had been all "Daddy this" and "Daddy that," barely mentioning their mom. But James had looked like he'd been punched in the gut when he'd heard she'd been crying.

I opened the obituary of his grandfather on my computer again and stared at his mother's name. *Sheila Wickerton.* She'd grown up here, in a family that went fishing and bowling. Had she turned her back on that long ago, immersed in her high-society life? All

I had to go on was a hunch that she had a soft spot for this place, and for James. I took out a sheet of paper and wrote *her* a letter.

I told her how James and I met, how we'd gone to the cemetery and left daisies on her parents' grave. I told her how much I liked her son, that there'd been a misunderstanding and if she could give him a message for me . . . I very much wished he would call.

When I carried the letter to the mailbox fifteen minutes later, Lennie's house was still quiet. I hoped everything was okay in there.

THIRTY-EIGHT

I knocked on Lennie's shed door after school the next day. I'd been half expecting to see an ambulance or a hearse drive up, as quiet as it had been around his house. There hadn't even been any customers.

Lennie opened the shed door and pulled out his earbuds. "Hey, come in. Sorry about yesterday—my mom and all," he said as I shut the door. He moved back to the far counter and fiddled with a pile of bolts.

"What happened?" I'd been worrying about it more than I cared to admit.

"Ah, nothing, really. My dad was having a bad day. Mom needed a little break is all."

"Oh." We stood in awkward silence for a few seconds. I noticed a little section of his shelves that had books instead of engine parts, so I went to peruse. They were mostly automotive manuals, but also some paperbacks. A thesaurus and a Spanish-English dictionary, a copy of *The Great Gatsby*. I pointed to it and said, "Summer reading?"

He nodded.

He had all the same books that used to sit on my shelf, from English class. The books that made you look like you were serious about literature. *The Bell Jar* by Sylvia Plath. *Howl* by Allen Ginsberg. There were copies of *Jane Eyre* and *The Outsiders*. I stroked its spine. Couldn't seem to get away from reminders of James.

I hadn't been to our secret room for a few weeks now. What was the point? James was gone, my secret of living in Lakeside was out. But looking at these books made me miss it a little. I shook my head and turned, nodding toward Lennie's iPod. "What were you listening to?"

He stepped closer and held the earbuds out. I put one of them in and handed the other back to him.

"So you don't totally blast me out," I said.

We had to stand really close to share the earbuds, shoulder to shoulder. He glanced sideways at me. "You might not like this."

"You'd be surprised."

He smiled and tapped PLAY. The song started out in Latin, with eerie church choir voices, and I quickly realized the lyrics were all words for Satan. "... Behemoth, Beelzebub ... Satanas, Lucifer ..."

My eyes widened. "Oh, my God. What is that?"

Lennie just bobbed his head to the beat as drums and electric guitars came in. Then he grinned. "Swedish metal band, Ghost. Cool, huh?"

"I guess . . ." I gave him a wary look. The music was cool, actually, though I didn't usually get into metal. Or Satan.

He laughed. "Don't worry. I'm not a Satan worshipper . . ."

"You just play one on TV?"

"Gotta keep up appearances." He flexed his tattooed arm and gave me the badass scowl I recognized from the old days, before we ever met. Just as quickly, he shrugged it off and turned back into the kinder, gentler Lennie I was getting to know. "They're not really Satanists. The band. It's just their shtick. The lead singer dresses like a cardinal, with skeleton makeup. They all wear hoods and capes and their concerts are like a horror show."

"You've seen them in concert?"

He nodded. "In Philly once."

"Nice." ·

We started talking about bands we'd seen live, or wanted to. He played a song from another favorite group. I recognized it immediately, because I'd been totally obsessed with them for a few months last year. I loved the way they mixed piano and symphony and choral music into a hard rock sound.

"I'm teaching Brady how to play the ukulele," I said.

Lennie scanned his music and pulled up a ukulele recording. "Jake Shimabukuro. You know him?"

I shook my head and listened for a moment. "Is that 'Bohemian Rhapsody'?"

"Yep," said Lennie. "Dude is amazing."

"I always thought of the ukulele as a wimp of an instrument, something to use in a pinch if you didn't have anything more substantial. But I love it now. And this guy really is amazing."

Lennie smiled and let me scroll through his music selection while he went back to work sorting through a box of odd parts. I played a few more Shimabukuro tunes. ("Ave Maria" on ukulele? Bach's Invention No. 4 in D minor? Crazy.) I found lots of heavy metal, too, but also stuff like the Beatles and Bob Dylan. Then I saw something that really surprised me.

"No way." I bit my lip so I wouldn't laugh.

"What?" He tried to grab the iPod from me but I held it out of his reach.

"The sound track to *Titanic*?" I said through giggles. "Céline Dion?"

Lennie groaned. "She only sings one song. The rest is instrumental. You know in the movie when the musicians are performing right up to last moment before the ship sinks? That stuff is on there, and . . ."

I held up my hand. "It's okay, Lennie. I won't tell anyone about you and Céline."

He shook his head, smiling. "I hate you."

"Trust me. You're not alone," I mumbled.

He narrowed his eyes at me for a second, then went back to his gadgets. He was photographing each of them on a white background. I offered to help, and soon we had a rhythm going where I stood behind the camera and took the pictures while he positioned one item after another.

It was nice, comfortable. I didn't think about Reesa or James. We just played music and worked in silence. After a few minutes he said, "I don't really hate you."

I looked up and smiled. "I know."

We continued to work for another hour, logging the parts I had just photographed into his online inventory. He read off model numbers and descriptions and I keyed them in.

"I should pay you something," he said.

"It's okay." I could use the money, but didn't feel right taking it from Lennie.

"Why not? You're cutting my workload in half. At least."

I shrugged. "I like doing it. It takes my mind off . . . other things."

He finished labeling a gear and slid it onto the shelf. "Like that guy James?"

I stayed quiet. I never did find out what James had said to convince Lennie to give him my address.

"He, uh . . . seemed to like you a lot," said Lennie. "Whatever happened to him?"

That achy feeling that came to my chest whenever I thought about James started to flare up again. It got worse with each day he didn't call or email. I was starting to lose hope.

But I didn't want Lennie to know how thoroughly I'd been dumped. "He's visiting his father," I said. "In New York."

"Oh." Lennie looked down at the label he was marking and put the item on a shelf.

"He should be back soon," I said. "Any day now." I'd given up lying, but was it really a lie if I sincerely hoped it to be true?

Lennie held my gaze for an awkwardly long time. "That's great," he finally said.

He read the model number of a tractor gasket, and I keyed it in. When I looked up for the next item, his face was dead serious. "Ivy," he said, "I have a confession to make."

I swallowed hard. "About what?"

His voice dropped to a whisper. "Promise you won't tell?"

"I promise," I whispered back. My heart started racing.

"I lied to you. About Céline Dion." He broke into a crooked grin. "I love that song." He put his hand to his chest in that pained-heartbreak sort of way and started belting it out. Really, really off-key.

I almost peed myself laughing.

We kept working and laughing, and every time my giggles subsided, he'd sing another little bit of a Céline Dion song he knew. It was horrible.

And wonderful.

THIRTY-NINE

An envelope.

In the mailbox.

Addressed to me.

The handwriting looked familiar. Not the cursive James had used to write the snippet of a sonnet on the drawing he made for me, but his printing—the way he'd jotted notes in the books in our secret room.

I tore it open, my hopes lifted at the prospect of a message at last. Please, please, *please* don't hate me anymore.

But it wasn't a letter. It was a flyer for another open mic night at the King Theatre. Whoever sent it had circled the part where it said, SHARE YOUR TALENT! But there was no note. Not even a scribble in the margin.

There was, however, a little starburst shape in the bottom corner announcing a cash prize to be awarded to the winner of this month's event. It didn't say how much, but there were four dollar signs and a couple of exclamation marks. So it had to be more than a few dollars. Maybe fifty or a hundred? It was *something*, though. A trip to the grocery store. New shoes for the twins.

"What's that?" Mom stood at the top of the attic stairs, holding freshly laundered sheets.

"Nothing." I shoved it into my backpack.

I had told James about open mic night, how Molly wanted me to do it with her. And he'd encouraged me. *Show up and sing to the tombstones*, he had said. *Do it for yourself.* And a cash prize? That was an even better incentive, since my job hunt wasn't going so well. I started to fantasize that maybe it was even more than a hundred dollars. Maybe two hundred. Two fifty. Five hundred? Mom wouldn't have to worry about day-to-day expenses for a week or two.

"Everything okay?" Mom dropped the sheets on my desk chair.

I smiled, my heart racing. "Sure. Everything's great."

She flicked a quick glance toward my backpack, then reached over to strip my bed. Mom had employed a maid when we lived in Westside. Now she held a job and did all the housework, too. The apartment was small, but I swear she cleaned it three times as much as our old house. Or maybe I just noticed it now. It was surprising how much I hadn't noticed before.

I took an edge of the clean sheet.

"Thanks, sweetie," she said.

When we finished (she insisted on hospital corners), I waited for her to disappear down the stairs before retrieving the flyer.

Maybe Molly had sent it. But why would she be so secretive? We'd talked about working on a song together, maybe trying our back-and-forth duel between piano and clarinet. She had no reason to send an anonymous flyer. She would've just walked down the road and shoved it into my hand.

It had to be James.

I folded and unfolded the ad, tracing my fingers over the words he'd circled: SHARE YOUR TALENT! Would he be there? Or watching somehow? If this was the way to reach him, if it would prove to him that I cared, there was only one thing to do.

It just happened to be the one thing that terrified me most.

I went to the secret room first thing Friday morning and opened my copy of *Jane Eyre*, almost expecting to find the page blank— that I'd imagined the whole thing. But the note was still there.

So serious? Love me some J.E.,
but what do you read for
laughs?

I pulled out the envelope that the flyer had come in, set it next to the note from James. There was no mistaking they were written by the same person.

I slumped into the old library chair and stared at the flyer again. I couldn't do this. I couldn't get up and sing in front of all those people.

But I had to. Not only for James, but the prize money . . . I had to do this.

The next open mic night was less than a week away. Next Thursday. A crazy assortment of songs raced through my mind, tumbling over each other. I needed to pick one that would speak to him. Or maybe . . .

I pulled out a notebook.

Ours wasn't a love song. Not yet. It was a song of finding him when I needed someone. Of making mistakes. Realizing I didn't have to fake it anymore. He'd been there for me, and I'd let him down.

I got up and peeked into the outer supply closet, to make sure nobody was there. Then I locked myself in the secret room.

It wasn't easy without my piano. I thought about the moment James and I first met by the hedges, tried putting it into words. *"Caught by surprise, leaves in my hair . . ."*

I wrote it down. More lyrics came. And along with it, a melody. I bent over my notebook and scribbled, singing along. *". . . Rusty bicycle, you didn't care . . ."*

Soon, my pencil could barely keep up. The song fell out of nowhere onto my lips. It didn't come out perfectly. Words didn't always rhyme where they should, but the message was there. *"All I knew was a mistake, my world a lie, my life a fake . . ."*

I wrote and erased and wrote some more. I tried to imagine the piano accompaniment. Moody and slow, eerie almost, then building faster and louder like thunder before a final calm. I couldn't wait to lay my hands on a piano. When I'd done as much as I could with paper and pencil, I gathered my notebook and bag and ran for the band room.

The band was in there.

I laughed at myself, how making music made me oblivious to everything around me sometimes. Like the fact that school was in session.

It was nearly eleven. I'd missed my first two classes, so I scurried to my third-period trigonometry class. Took my seat in front of Reesa. She didn't say anything but tapped my shoulder. When I twisted around, she handed me a sheet of paper.

It was an assignment from English.

"Thanks," I said.

She nodded. It wasn't much, but it was a start. We still were not officially talking. Our communication had advanced from icy glares to the occasional grunt or nod. I caught her watching me with Molly and Rigby, and she caught me watching her with Willow and Wynn.

I'm pretty sure I'd landed in the happier place. She kind of looked like a kidnap victim afraid to risk an escape from her captors.

* * *

Molly and I sat on the curb outside her house Friday after school, soaking up the last few rays of Indian summer sunshine. We were trying to make a playlist of music for the party.

"No Lucinda Williams," I said. "Too depressing."

"Yeah, but if I hear that song 'Happy' one more time, I'm going to scream. It's like the song that will never die."

"Don't forget, Rigby is making a song list, too." I glanced sideways at Molly and we both started laughing. Rigby had turned out to have eclectic taste in music.

"I love that kid," said Molly, "but what was that drum-circle thing he was playing the other day?"

"I liked it," I said, still laughing. "It felt very, I don't know . . . primitive."

"If you're into that sort of thing," said Molly. "Personally, I've never been a fan of the didgeridoo."

We played songs back and forth until Lennie's Jeep drove up to the corner. He beeped his horn and waved for us to come over.

"I'll go see what he wants," I said.

I jogged to the road and leaned on the open passenger-side window. "What's up?"

"I'm making a trip to the junkyard," he said. "Wanna come? Now's your big chance." He waggled his eyebrows like it was the most tempting invitation imaginable.

Lennie had promised, or rather dared me to go with him engine-surfing (his term) at the junkyard. Once a week or so, he scoured the new arrivals for parts. I made the mistake of saying it sounded like fun, and he went on and on about the thrill of the hunt. When I busted up laughing and told him I was kidding, he said I definitely had to go. He would prove how much fun it was.

"Sounds like a blast, Len," I said. "Really. But I promised Molly we'd get a song list ready for the party. You're coming, aren't you?"

"You mean to the party in my own backyard?" he said. "Yeah, I'll probably be there."

"I'm glad," I said.

Lennie gave me a thumbs-up and threw Molly a salute.

I skipped back to the curb in front of her house and sat down.

"Call me crazy," she said, "but I'd say Hypothetical Guy is plenty aware that you exist."

"Huh?"

"Lennie. He's Hypothetical Guy, right?"

"What? No! Why would you think that?"

"Oh." Molly looked away with a pursed-lip smile. "No reason."

"He's not," I said. "Absolutely, totally not."

FORTY

Mom woke me early on Saturday for our second food pantry run. We knew what to expect this time, but that only made us dread it more. We needed the food, though. Mom had served a meal she called "mixed steamed grill" the night before. It was basically little bowls of whatever we had leftover from the last few nights, and some mashed potatoes she whipped up with an egg and fried.

We pulled into the parking lot of the Northbridge Methodist Church. Again, we sat and watched for a while, working up the nerve to get in line for our number. I recognized some of the people we'd seen last month. But I didn't see Chandra or Rigby anywhere.

"I don't know that I'll ever get used to this." Mom let out a sigh. "Let's go."

We got in line.

As the door opened, the same man from last month started handing out numbers. We were seventy-five.

Mom said, "Any idea how long it will be?" Like we were in line for a table at a restaurant.

"Thirty, maybe forty minutes," he said.

She nodded. "Let's wait in the car." Mom started to walk away, but I turned back to the man.

"Is the church open?" I asked. I remembered there was a piano, when James and I were here last. And I hadn't had a chance to play the song I'd written yet. This was the perfect opportunity.

He nodded. "Around front. Sanctuary's straight ahead."

"I'll meet you back here," I called to Mom, and bolted around the corner before she could argue.

But I didn't go inside right away. I looped around to the side that faced the cemetery. Crossing the church parking lot, I followed the path James and I had taken to the giant oak tree. I even sprinted to the top of the hill to recapture the breathless intensity of that day, to remember how he'd made me feel. To remember *him*. We'd been apart now longer than we'd been together.

Was I hanging on to nothing? It didn't matter.

I dropped onto the bench that overlooked the cemetery. Something was lying in the grass in front of the Robertsons' tombstone. I went over to get a closer look.

Daisies. Fresh cut.

I spun around, searching for him. "James?" I called.

It was a cloudy day, and the sound of my voice seemed to disappear into the gray.

The only other soul in the cemetery was an elderly man.

He stood in front of a stone for several minutes with his hands clasped in front of him, then turned and hobbled slowly away.

I was alone.

I made my way back to the church and went in the same doors that James and I had entered to find a telephone. I peered into the sanctuary. It was empty, and so was the room to the side where I'd seen the piano that day.

"Anybody here?" I called out.

James told me the pastor kept it all open so people would feel free to come and go as they pleased. So I went in. The piano sat in the corner, past a long table filled with artificial flower centerpieces. I looked toward the doorway to make sure nobody was there, lifted the lid from the piano keys, and sat down to play.

It came out mostly as I'd imagined, with a few surprises from today's visit to the cemetery. An intricate, somewhat frenzied bit was my heart racing, searching for him. Then it calmed and ended sweetly. The happy ending I hoped for.

I sat motionless, breathless, for a few minutes.

Clap, clap, clap.

I gasped, turning to the sound of a single pair of hands, applauding from a dark corner.

"Beautiful," said a faint voice. A figure stepped into the light. It was the elderly man from the cemetery. "This is why I leave the church open."

"I'm sorry," I said. "I tried to find someone to ask . . ."

He hushed my apology. "Come again. Whenever you like.

Maybe you can perform for our congregation someday."

I bit back my usual reaction to dismiss such a suggestion as ludicrous, and smiled instead. "Someday," I said.

Running around to the food pantry entrance, I heard the man announcing "Up to eighty!" on his microphone, and saw Mom walking in.

"Mom!" I called.

She turned, looking peeved. "Where—"

"There was a piano inside," I said breathlessly.

That's all I had to say.

FORTY-ONE

The days leading up to open mic night and our Halloween party spilled together, an abstract painting of my rising panic. I hadn't told anyone I was planning to perform, since it was scary enough knowing James might be in the audience. I didn't want a hoard of friends and family showing up. But keeping it secret was only making me more nervous.

If Reesa hadn't been mad at me, I would've told her, but . . .

"Hey!" Molly snapped me out of my wishful thinking. I'm not sure how long she'd been sitting there across the lunch table. "Where *were* you just now?"

I smiled. I had to tell someone. "Open mic night. Onstage. Scared shitless."

"Seriously?" Her eyes widened. "You're going to do it?"

I looked around, made sure nobody was listening. Swallowed. "Yeah," I said. "Don't tell anybody. Can you come? I might need someone to drag me off the stage if I freeze up."

Molly grinned. "First of all, you're not going to do that.

You're going to be awesome. And second of all, I wouldn't miss it. Friday?"

"No," I said. "It's Thursday."

"I'll be there. Do you need a ride? I . . . wait." She opened her bag and pulled out the little agenda she used to keep track of homework assignments. "Shit. I can't go."

"Why not?" My voice was suddenly all whiny and pleading. I hadn't realized how badly I wanted someone to be there with me. To get me through it.

"It's my dad's birthday," she said.

Her dead father's birthday. "Oh."

"Not a good night to leave Mom home alone," she said. "We're going to my dad's favorite restaurant. There will be crying involved."

"I understand," I said.

"I'm hoping it gets easier. Last year was a bitch." She returned to her sandwich until she realized I wasn't eating. "You want me to help you rehearse? You look like you need a fix."

I smiled. "I do. But the band room is occupied by the jazz band. So annoying."

She snort-laughed. "How rude of them. You could always use the piano in the choir room."

"There's a piano in the choir room?"

She looked at me like I was an idiot. "You're kidding."

I skipped lunch that day and again Thursday so I could practice. But the song changed every time I played it. I was so

328

distracted, obsessing over how to fix it. Reesa would've noticed something was wrong. But Molly was busy with everyone who kept running over to RSVP for our party.

"What if all these people actually come?" She held up the list she was keeping in her Trig notebook.

"Maybe we should decorate or something," I said. "I think my mom has some Christmas lights we could drape around the trees."

Molly nodded toward Willow, who was racing up and down the halls like a lunatic. Our party was getting all the buzz, and it was sending Willow over the top of crazy. She kept reminding people about the amazing band her mom hired, and the caterer. Don't forget the caterer! All this time I thought people cared about that stuff. But somehow, our promise of a bag of chips and maybe some dip was going head to head with her beef tenderloin wraps and stuffed mushrooms. And we weren't losing.

It was Halloween, after all, and Lakeside was a helluva lot scarier than Willow Goodwin's well-appointed living room. Our "come as you are" theme was appealing, too. Guys were not interested in dressing like it was the Roaring Twenties. They had no idea *how* to dress for the 1920s.

Willow was putting the full-court press on everybody she knew, collecting RSVPs like votes in an election. "Can I count on you?" "I'm counting on you!"

Molly and Rigby and I watched it all like the circus it was. We just wanted our little party of outcasts to have fun.

"You haven't told me what you're wearing," said Molly. For a second I thought she was talking about open mic night, and almost described the shimmery purple dress Dad had rescued from our old house. I had snuck it out of Mom's closet, along with a pair of black heels. But what to wear for Halloween?

"I have no idea," I said.

"Come on. You're just not telling me."

I smiled, wishing that was the case.

"Fine." She crossed her arms. "I'm not telling, either."

The morning of open mic night I spotted Reesa standing in front of her locker—staring into its depths. She'd been doing a lot of that lately. Then she'd sort of "wake up" and look around and almost catch me watching her—just as I kept almost catching her watching me. Even Molly had noticed it. She said, "Talk to her. She clearly wants you to."

I wanted to tell her about open mic night. I wanted her to *be* there. But every time I thought to approach her, I'd remember how she'd slammed the gate to her driveway in my face that day. I don't think I could take it if I told her about my performance and she didn't show up. Not with her knowing how scary it was for me.

But the Halloween party wasn't a big deal. If I invited her and she didn't show, I'd live. So when I saw her standing there alone, and the party only two days away, I knew I might not get another chance. I opened my bag and pulled out my last invitation. She didn't even notice me until I was inches away.

"Here." I thrust the invitation into her hands. My heart was in my throat, waiting to see if she'd crumple it up or throw it at my feet. But she took it and scanned the text.

"Come as you are?" She did a pretty good job of pretending she hadn't heard about the party.

"Uh-huh."

"How very Kurt Cobain of you."

I shrugged. I hadn't thought of the Nirvana tune when we came up with the theme, but she wasn't the first to mention it. Lennie kept singing it when we were working in his shed. He had the perfect raspy voice for it. "Anyway. I hope you can come."

"It's the same night as Willow's party," she said.

"Yeah, well . . ." *Willow and I don't have the same friends anymore,* I almost said. I felt tears coming to my eyes so I blinked a few times, really fast.

"I'm late for class," Reesa said quickly, then turned and walked away.

"I can't imagine having a party without you," I said, but I don't think she heard me.

FORTY-TWO

I told my parents I'd be spending the evening at Molly's, not catching a cab into downtown Belleview to perform an original song in front of a crowd of strangers. The fewer people who knew I'd be there, the fewer people who'd witness my humiliation if I froze again onstage. After this, I told myself, no more secrets.

What I hadn't anticipated, however, was finding a note from my mother under the Buddha paperweight on my desk in place of the money for cab fare I'd put there.

Borrowed some cash for groceries.
IOU $40, will pay you back in the a.m. Hope you don't
mind. Thanks, sweetie!
~Mom

I threw my room upside down on the odd chance I'd forgotten about some hidden cash. Then I sat on the top step to the attic, nearly hyperventilating, and dropped my head between my knees. I would simply ask Dad for the money when he got home. If he got home in time. He'd been working late the last few days on a big job he said might turn things around for us. I could ask . . . *Who could I ask?* Molly and her mother were broke. I certainly couldn't ask Reesa or any of my old friends. There was nobody. Except . . .

I jumped up and looked out the tiny attic window at Lennie's shed. There was a sliver of light beneath the door, so I ran down our three flights of stairs and into his yard, and knocked. The door wasn't latched and pushed open slightly at my touch.

Lennie turned in his computer chair and saw me. "Come on in," he said, swiveling back to face his work.

I took a couple of steps toward him. "I, uh . . . have a favor to ask." I paused. "Remember when you offered to pay me for my help, and I wouldn't take it? Well, I need some money now and I was wondering if, maybe . . . if you could loan me forty dollars."

He spun slowly around to face me again. "For . . ."

I opened my eyes wide. "None of your business."

"Okay." He returned to his keyboard. "Then no. I'm not giving you forty dollars."

"I didn't ask you to give it to me. It would be a loan."

"Not until you tell me what it's for."

"Why do you even care?" I stomped over to where he sat. "Fine. It's for a dress. I need to buy a dress for . . . homecoming."

I cringed at the lie, the pathetic breaking of my promise to stop telling them.

He shook his head. "Uh-uh. First of all, where are you going to find a nice dress for forty bucks? Lame-ass lie, Emerson. And you wouldn't come begging at my door for dress money, anyhow."

"I'm not begging. You said you'd pay me."

"And you said you didn't want to be paid. But now you do. So what gives?"

"Nothing gives. I just . . . need . . . forty dollars!" I sucked in a shuddering breath and started to cry, which surprised me as much as Lennie. I buried my face in my hands.

"Whoa," he said. "What are you doing?"

"What does it look like I'm doing?" I grabbed for a roll of paper towels he kept on the counter and tore off a few sheets to bury my face in. Once the tap was open, I couldn't stop until it ran dry.

Lennie backed away from me at first, like he was afraid I might explode, then stepped closer and closer until his shoulder was aligned with my nose. He put his arms gently around my back and pulled me into a hug. I let my head fall against him, my body relax.

"Sheesh," he said. "I'll give you the forty bucks already."

"It's not for a dress," I said, still sniffling.

"You don't have to explain, really. I—"

"It's for cab fare into Belleview and back, to the King. That's all. I'm performing at open mic night tonight. Nobody knows."

His brows knit together. "What time do you have to be there?"

"Seven."

He smiled. "I'll take you myself."

FORTY-THREE

It was six thirty in the evening when Lennie pulled his Jeep around the corner near Molly's house, so my parents wouldn't see me leaving with him. I jumped in, tucking my bag with Mom's purple dress on the floor between us. He threw the Jeep into gear and we lurched forward.

As my eyes adjusted to the dimming evening light, I noticed he wasn't wearing his usual tan work boots but a black pair instead, with dark jeans. And he'd traded his flannel shirt and concert tee for a charcoal-gray button-up and black leather jacket.

He pushed his hair back and it fell forward, brushing his jawline. No ponytail, and the scraggly ends were gone.

"Did you cut your hair?"

He tipped his head down, as if to hide behind what remained. "Carla did it," he mumbled.

"Looks . . . nice."

He smiled. "Didn't want to embarrass you or anything."

I punched his arm lightly. "I can do that all by myself, thank you very much."

We rode in silence for a while, watching the headlights and taillights go by. It struck me suddenly that I was about to see James. Finally. But instead of being happy and excited about it, I was terrified. Why hadn't he just called, let me explain? This performance felt like some kind of weird test. Did I have to risk total humiliation to prove my sincerity?

"You'll do great." Lennie reached out to stop my knee from bouncing up and down like a jackhammer. "Don't worry."

He'd misread my jitters about James for nerves about singing, which only reminded me how nervous I was about singing.

"You're pretty confident, considering you've never heard me sing," I said.

He pinched his lips into a smirk, a decidedly guilty one.

"Have you?"

"Eight thirty lullaby. Best concert in town."

"Lennie!"

"What? I was over at Carla's one night and heard you singing. You can really sing."

I shook my head. "But I can't. Not in front of people. That's the problem. I freeze up. What if I do that tonight? I've done it before."

"That was a long time ago," he said. "You were only a kid."

Wait a minute. "How do you know? You weren't there."

Ignoring me, he reached for the radio to turn it on and dial past one fuzzy station after another until he found a song he liked. "This okay?"

"Lennie. Were you there? The district talent show?"

He turned to me and held my gaze longer than he probably should've while driving on a major highway. "You don't remember."

"Remember what?"

He turned back to watch the road. "Nothing," he said, turning the volume lower. "Hey, I haven't seen Brady for a few days. How's he doing?"

"You were, weren't you? At the talent show."

He took a deep breath and let it out slowly. "Fine. Yeah. I was there."

"Why didn't you say so?"

"What difference does it make? I was there. I saw you." He shot me a glance and a quick smile. "You don't want to think about that tonight, anyway. You want to think about getting on that stage and blowing everyone away."

"Right," I said.

But I couldn't stop thinking about it, and I guess Lennie couldn't, either, because then he said, "You were really beautiful that night, in your butterfly wings, you know."

His Jeep seemed so quiet then, like all the sounds of the road and the motor had completely disappeared. "Thank you," I whispered.

He flashed me a quick grin, then reached for the radio and

turned the music up louder. "So, how's Brady doing?"

I swallowed the lump in my throat. "He's . . . uh. . . he's having a lot of therapy after school. And, uh, learning to speak in full sentences, dress himself, stuff like that."

"Must be hard," said Lennie.

I didn't know if he meant to ask if it was hard on Brady, or me, or my parents, or Kaya, but in any case, the answer was yes. My mom always said it was okay to admit to that.

"Sometimes I wonder what things would be like if Brady were . . . if he didn't have his disability. Especially since we moved, I imagine it a lot. We wouldn't have lost our house. I'd still have my piano." I paused. This was something I never told anyone. I didn't even want to admit it to myself. "I'm sorry. I don't really mean that. I love Brady just the way he is."

Lennie didn't react right away, and I figured he was contemplating what a horrible person I was, maybe wishing he'd never agreed to take me to this show.

He reached over and squeezed my hand. "How would you want things to be different?"

I bit my lip, not wanting to say more, but the words kept forcing themselves out. "Maybe everything wouldn't be about Brady, about how everything affects Brady. We wouldn't have to be constantly watching him and worrying, and spending all our money on his therapy." I shook my head. "I'm a horrible person."

Lennie chuckled. "You know how many times I've wondered

what would've happened if my dad had been killed when that car fell on him?"

I sucked in my breath. "I don't want Brady to die."

"I'm just saying everyone thinks about how their life might've been different under different circumstances," Lennie said quietly. "It doesn't mean you're a bad person."

We drove in silence for another minute. My nerves had disappeared, for the moment at least. I felt lighter, saying that stuff about Brady. I'd been holding it in, like water against a dam. Releasing it was a relief.

Then Lennie pointed toward a sign looming ahead and said, "Here's our exit." And my nerves came rushing back.

A woman clutching a clipboard guarded the door as musicians arrived with their guitar cases and amps and drum kits. As Lennie and I approached, the woman asked the guy in front of us for his name. She scanned her clipboard and checked him off. "You'll be on first, so go ahead and set up."

I froze. We had to sign up? I thought the whole idea of an open mic night was that the mic was open. Lennie took my arm and pulled me toward the woman.

"Name?" She peered at me over a pair of purple reading glasses.

"I, uh . . ."

"It's Ivy Emerson." Lennie reached over her clipboard and pointed to a name on the list. "Right there."

I was right there?

"Looks like you're our finale tonight. We'll have you do a quick sound check before we start, though. Why don't you head up there now? Piano is stage left."

I nodded and let Lennie lead me toward the stage. James had signed me up? My already-pounding heart did a few extra leaps. Sending the flyer was one thing, but signing me up? I started looking for him, expecting to see him leaning against a wall, thumbs hooked through his belt loops. But nobody in the place was standing still. There was a frenzy of activity—people climbing ladders, adjusting lights, stringing wires, or wheeling things around.

I made my way to the grand piano, catching my reflection in the shiny black top that was propped open. Lennie watched me from backstage. His hands pushed the air in front of him as if physically urging me forward. Seeing him there, in the folds of the curtain, suddenly reminded me of a boy who'd stepped out from the curtains to help me once before.

A boy I remembered only as having dark hair, as pulling me to safety—off the stage that swirled around me. I sucked in a breath.

Lennie?

The memory rolled over me now, how he'd coaxed me to go on, to play. His hands pushing the air forward like they did now. But when I couldn't, he came to my rescue. *You don't remember?* It *was* Lennie. He was the one who'd led me off the stage that horrible time at the talent show, when I'd frozen solid. In my butterfly wings.

I made it through the sound check, barely plunking out a few bars on the piano and a single line of my song before a voice from the darkness said, "We're good, thanks."

I waited on a metal folding chair backstage as the first act prepared to go on. The other performers were peeking out to see the audience filling the theater. I didn't need to torture myself like that. The sound was enough, rumbling louder and louder, like a thunderstorm approaching. Slipping into the dressing room, I pulled the purple dress from my bag and slid it over my head. Amazing how a garment could convey something on the outside so completely opposite to what was inside. I looked smooth, slick, shimmery. I felt rough, sick, shaky. I attempted to tame my hair, dabbed some charcoal eyeliner along my lashes and gave my lips a swipe of gloss. The illusion was complete. Now, if I could only fool myself into believing it.

Lennie had disappeared after my sound check, though I glimpsed him pacing outside when someone had the loading-dock doors open. One hand held his cell phone to his ear and the other kept pushing his hair back. He didn't see me watching him, though.

Before the show began, a man walked onto the stage and tapped on the microphone. The audience hushed and he cleared his throat. "I have an exciting announcement to make, and this is the first time our performers are hearing about it as well."

Everyone backstage moved closer to the edges of the curtains, if they weren't already there, and a buzz of murmurs went through the crowd.

The man cleared his throat again. "As you know, open mic night is something we hold once a month. It is an opportunity for amateur musicians to share their talent. We don't pay the performers, and we don't sell tickets. But tonight, thanks to an anonymous donor, we'll be awarding a cash prize to one lucky performer." He paused as we all nearly burst from holding our breath. "And the amount of that prize is . . . five thousand dollars."

A roar went up backstage and in the audience. My heart, already pounding, thumped harder. *Five thousand dollars?* The man was introducing some people seated in the front row, who would be the judges. I could see them standing and waving but I didn't hear any of it. All I could hear was the scream in my brain. *Five thousand dollars!*

I bent over so my head was between my knees and tried to breathe slowly. In seconds, Lennie was kneeling next to me, his soft voice in my ears. "Don't think about that," he was saying, his hand moving in slow circles on my back. "You can do this. It's just you and your music. Nothing else. Nobody else. Okay?"

I sat up and whispered, "I can't, you know I can't. You were there, Lennie. It was you backstage. I remember now. It was you . . . all this time."

He came around so he was squatting right in front of me, his face level with mine. "I'm right here if you need me. Okay? But you're not going to need me. You're going to blow them out of their seats."

I laughed, then whimpered. *Five thousand dollars.*

Lennie grabbed my hands. "Just you and the music."

He looked into my eyes, and I don't know if it was the stage lights reflecting off my purple gown or if I simply hadn't been paying attention all this time, but Lennie's eyes . . . they were like dark gems that sparkled with a million colors when the light hit them just right.

"You'll be here, right?" I said. "You're not going anywhere?"

He steadied his sparkly eyes on mine. "I'm not going anywhere."

"Okay." I nodded. "I'm good now."

He gave my hands a final squeeze and slipped away. The show began and I lost myself in the other performances, even the bad ones. Anything was better than focusing on what I was about to do. From backstage I caught a glimpse of a sliver of the audience, and for a second, I thought I saw Reesa. Then someone called my name.

What happened next was like an out-of-body experience. I watched the woman who no longer held a clipboard shuttle me into place. A man with a microphone held his hand out to me. I saw myself walk to him, the purple dress shimmering in the lights as I returned his smile, took his hand. He led me to the piano.

"... my pleasure to introduce Ivy Emerson, who will be performing her own original composition, 'There for Me'..."

Everything was fine until my brain reunited with my body
and saw the audience out there ... rows and rows of people. Clapping at first, now waiting ... murmuring.

I sat at the piano, hands on my lap. Heart in my throat. Not
moving.

"Ladies and gentlemen, Ivy Emerson ... ," the man prompted
again.

A smattering of nervous applause, then a tiny voice called out,
"You can do it, Ivy!"

Brady?

Everyone laughed. My brother was here? My family? I
searched for them among the sea of faces, but everyone looked
the same from here. Then I remembered the cemetery, and what
James had told me about how the dead don't judge, they just listen quietly. And one by one, I transformed the entire audience
into tombstones. Patient, nonjudging, silent tombstones.

And I started to play.

The piano was clear and bright and strong beneath my fingers. When it came time to add my voice, I tried to imagine James
out there in the cemetery, and I sang.

I sang about how he was there for me, accepting me for who I
was, when everything else in my world had turned into a lie. ...
I sang about his eyes, his laugh ...

And as I sang, I wondered if it was still James I was singing about. If he was still there for me.

I continued playing beyond the lyrics, and the song took on a life of its own. My fingers melted into the keys, becoming part of the instrument. The piano became my voice. It breathed for me, it gasped and held its breath. It laughed. It *flew*, like a butterfly. It wasn't scared anymore. I was the piano, and I was doing it. I was playing for them. For the boy who *was* there for me.

I don't know how long I played. It was like a beautiful, musical trance. And when I snapped out of it, I played the last chord, and my fingers had stopped but were resting on the piano keys. Shaking. Nobody made a sound at first and I thought I'd dreamed the whole thing. But when I turned, the tombstones came alive, standing and clapping and cheering. The roar of their applause shook me. I clutched the edge of the piano to stand, to bow.

The house lights came up and I could suddenly see the audience. Brady and Kaya jumped around like a pair of pogo sticks. My parents hugged. Carla was there, too, smiling. But Lennie . . . I couldn't find him. I searched, suddenly desperate to know that he was there.

FORTY-FOUR

School the next day was beyond surreal. I kept thinking I had something on my face, the way everyone stared at me. And I wasn't just being paranoid. A group of kids would be huddled around someone's phone, then they'd all look up at me when I passed. And I kept hearing people say, "Five thousand dollars!" So, news of the cash prize had definitely circulated.

I still couldn't believe I had won. I'd given the check directly to my mother. "For food. For bills. Whatever." She'd taken it and slipped it into her purse, but promised the first thing we'd buy was an electric piano for my room. I didn't argue.

Amid the happiness of winning, there was a disappointment also. James hadn't shown. I'd looked for him everywhere, but he wasn't in the theater. I couldn't figure out why he'd gone to the trouble of sending me that flyer if he wasn't going to be there.

* * *

I walked into English class, where everyone had gathered around Mr. Eli's computer. I peeked between their heads, then quickly backed away when I saw what they were all looking at—me. Someone had videotaped my performance. It was right there on YouTube.

"Nice job, Ivy," Mr. Eli said when he spotted me.

My classmates buzzed around me, full of congratulations and—let's be honest—a bit of shock and disbelief. Their voices blended together into one long stream of praise. "I had no idea . . . so amazing . . . your voice . . . made me cry . . . that song . . . so good . . . where did you learn to play like that?" I nodded and smiled and thank you, thank you, thank you'd.

I looked toward Reesa, the one person I would've enjoyed celebrating this moment with. She sat primly in her chair, a secret smile on her lips.

I sat down next to her.

"Congratulations," she said, not looking at me.

"Thanks," I said back.

That was the extent of our conversation, which left an ache in my heart amid all its leaping and fluttering.

People I'd never met were shouting and whooping at me. I wanted to dig a very deep hole and swan-dive into it. Molly came running up to me just as I was about to take shelter in the bathroom.

"If I'd known you were going to do *that*, I would've convinced my mother to celebrate Dad's birthday at the King," she said. "He would've loved it."

"Aw, thanks," I said as a few of the basketball players came along and high-fived me. "This is so embarrassing."

"It's your fifteen minutes of fame," said Molly. "Might as well enjoy it. And you are totally playing something with me the next time. Some crazy-ass clarinet-piano mind-blowing shit."

"Definitely," I said. "Ours will be the craziest-ass clarinet-piano duet in history. Also possibly the first."

She hugged me, laughing. Over her shoulder, I saw Reesa watching us. I wanted to go to her and make peace. She'd been encouraging me to do something like this for so long. But the moment I caught her eye, she turned and walked away.

"So can we use some of that five thousand dollars to pimp out our party?" Molly asked. "Maybe hire a DJ or something?"

I shook my head. "I gave it to my parents. For stuff like food and shelter. You know."

Molly grinned, "Yeah, that's cool. Our lack of professional entertainment and catering doesn't seem to be affecting the turn-out, anyway."

She pulled out a list of guests. "The party's getting a little big," she said. "And these are only the people who told me they're coming. What if the entire school shows up?"

"They know we're not serving beer or anything, right?" I said. "And my parents will be there."

Molly shrugged. "I told 'em. Maybe they're all planning to get loaded before they come."

I cringed. "Oh, God."

"Well," she said, "Lennie's friends will be there in case anything gets out of hand."

"They're the ones I'm worried about," I mumbled.

I couldn't face the cafeteria at lunch, for the polar opposite of the reason I used to fear it. They wanted me today. They wanted to soak in my moment of celebrity, as brief and fleeting as it surely was. All this time I'd been so worried about being cast out, only to discover that being wanted was sometimes harder.

So I went to the secret room. I flipped through the books, hoping I'd missed something, a hidden note. But they were just as I'd left them. No more James. No more notes. I shoved the books into my backpack. I could mail the Shakespeare back to him, at least. He couldn't have meant to leave something so treasured behind.

When I switched off the lamp and closed the door to the secret room, it felt like I had finished the final chapter of a favorite book. I always observed a little period of mourning for the characters I wouldn't be spending time with anymore. Their stories were over. They had walked off the page and into my life, then disappeared. Like James. It wasn't fair. I hated not knowing what happened to him next.

I bumped into someone on the way to my next class and didn't even realize it was Lennie until he offered to carry my backpack.

"What have you got in here?" he said, throwing it over a shoulder.

"Books," I said.

"What kind of books?"

My heart felt like a brick. "Ancient history."

Lennie didn't ask any more questions. He walked me to my locker and set my backpack on the floor.

"Thanks," I said.

His eyes were still gemlike and shimmering—with no stage lights to reflect. No purple dress. I was having a hard time looking away. "See you later?" I said.

"I told Molly I'd take her to pick up some sodas at Save-a-Cent. With my discount," he said. "Meet us out front?"

I hesitated for just a second, distracted by his eyes and the weight of those books in my backpack and the party I was throwing the next day and how James had never responded to all those invitations and . . .

"Unless you're afraid to be seen with me," Lennie was saying.

"Sorry, I . . . what?"

He just shook his head. "You planning to float home or you want a ride?"

I smiled. "Both, I think."

He smiled back, and I forgot about everything else and just wondered, how did I not see how beautiful he was before?

FORTY-FIVE

Molly and I started decorating for the party early Saturday afternoon. We set up chairs that Molly had collected from the neighborhood. And my mother unpacked some strings of white lights she had stashed under the bed, a small fraction of what we used to decorate our old house for the holidays but enough to drape around and illuminate the backyard. Kaya spent the day cutting ghosts and bats and spiders out of construction paper and attaching them to tree branches or recruiting Lennie to hang them from higher limbs. Brady mostly ran around, so excited he could hardly say anything except "Boo!"

Things felt different between Lennie and me. Ever since open mic night when he'd held my hands backstage—my hands felt empty without his. And every time I looked up, Lennie's eyes would find mine. It seemed like he was afraid I'd disappear.

I helped Carla in her kitchen for a while and was stealing a taste of the *pan de huevo* she was making, with chocolate, vanilla, and coconut toppings, when my mother called to me from the screen door, waving a little slip of paper in her hand.

"There's a message for you on the machine," she said as I walked out of Carla's apartment. "From yesterday. I forgot to check until now. It's James."

Lennie looked over from the tub he was filling with ice and sodas he'd brought from the Save-a-Cent.

This was the moment I'd been waiting for, hoping for . . . for weeks. Checking messages every day. Ever since James left, my first and last thought of the day had been of him.

Until I saw Lennie backstage . . .

"What did he say?" I hurried up the back stairs to meet her at our kitchen door.

"He said he's coming to the party," she said, too loud, before glancing over my shoulder and realizing Lennie could hear her. "I saved the message."

The machine was blinking like crazy. I pushed the button to rewind. The first voice I heard was Lennie's: "Mrs. Emerson? This is Lennie Lazarski. I'm with Ivy, at the King Theatre and . . ."

My mom had told me the night before about Lennie calling, telling them all about my performance so they wouldn't miss it. I hit the button to skip to the next message. Lennie again. Then one from Carla. Then my dad looking for Mom. Lennie once more. And finally, the soft, low voice I'd been missing all these weeks.

I held my breath as the recording began to play. "Hi, it's James . . . uh, James Wickerton, calling for Ivy. Ivy? I, uh . . . got your invitation. I'll be there, okay? I'm sorry I haven't been in touch. I can't wait to see you."

I played it back and listened again. He hadn't mentioned open mic night, or the song, but he knew about the party so one of my letters must've gotten through. And he was coming!

That's what I wanted, right?

I listened to the message again and again, and once more before going back outside, where I found Molly icing the sodas alone.

"Where's Lennie?" I said.

She blinked at me a few times. "Went home on the third play-back of the message, I'd say, or maybe it was the fourth."

"You could hear that?"

She pointed toward our kitchen. The window above the sink, the one right next to the answering machine, was open.

"I should go talk to him," I mumbled as I started toward Lennie's shed.

Molly stopped me. "Might want to leave him alone for a while."

"But . . ."

"Seriously." Her voice was sharp. "You invite some other guy to the party we're having and you don't think he's going to be pissed?"

"I didn't . . . it's not like that, I . . ."

"Look, it's none of my business. Just stop torturing him, okay?" She started opening folding chairs, a little more vigorously than necessary.

I wasn't sure what to do with myself, now painfully aware of the absence of Lennie's eyes on me. My hands still felt empty and now my heart did, too. Carla's back screen door creaked open and she leaned out, her face tender with understanding. She must've heard it all.

"Can I do anything?" she asked.

I sighed. "Actually, could you help me with my costume?" I said. "I finally figured out what I want to be."

She nodded and let me in. I sketched my idea on paper and we found the perfect gauzy fabric in her bins of leftovers, as well as colorful bits of chiffon. We untwisted some wire hangers and bent them into shape; then Carla sewed and I glued. While it was all drying, I went upstairs and picked out a pair of black boots and black leggings and a stretchy black top with long sleeves. I pulled my hair up with one of those giant black binder clips, the one Lennie had made fun of that day (which seemed like a thousand years ago but also just yesterday).

Then I went back downstairs to Carla's and put on my butterfly wings.

"Gorgeous," she said, motioning for me to spin around so she could appraise our handiwork. "If I do say so myself."

"Thank you so much."

"Why a butterfly?" she asked. "Is that who you *really* are?"

I wasn't prepared to explain it, how the butterfly wings were my way of showing Lennie I *was* the girl he thought I was—a girl who wanted to fly, who wanted fly with *him*. "It's who I want to be," I finally said.

When it was time for the party to start, Molly and I stood out front—me in my butterfly wings and her in an all-white outfit with horizontal lines drawn across the front and back. "A story yet to be written," she explained.

I glanced at Lennie's house as guests began to arrive, but he didn't come out. There were assorted superheroes, as I predicted, and one girl came dressed in full-on princess garb, tiara and everything. The guy Molly liked had simply hung a compass around his neck and declared himself an explorer. Rigby showed up with a bunch of newspaper articles taped to his shirt, all with horrible news about car accidents, fires, earthquakes, unemployment.

"What are you?" I asked.

He flashed a mischievous grin. "Bad news. Get it?"

I groaned, then laughed.

Rigby looked past my shoulder. "What's up, man?"

I turned to see Lennie approaching. He wasn't wearing a costume, just a black T-shirt and black jeans. He folded his arms over his chest when he reached us, his tattoo flexing.

"Let me guess," said Rigby. "Batman? No, a hipster?" He stroked his chin. "Really need a goatee for that. How about . . ."

Lennie didn't answer. He barely acknowledged Rigby's presence. He was too busy staring at me in my butterfly wings, as surprised as if I'd just flown in on them and landed right in front of him.

"Yeah, uh . . . I'll just . . . get myself a drink," said Rigby, flashing me a quick glance. "You okay, Ivy?"

I nodded. "I'm good."

I stepped closer to Lennie and laid my hand on his chest. On his heart. "Who are you?" I whispered.

"Me?" He looked down at my hand. "I'm nobody. Nobody at all."

"That's not true," I said.

"Sure it is." He smirked. "You said so yourself."

"When?"

"Plenty of times," he said. "To your friends. To yourself . . ."

I opened my mouth to protest but he was right. I had said it. "That was before I knew you. I don't think that anymore."

"What *do* you think?" His dark eyes sank into mine, and I didn't look away. I'd done this for him, this costume. Now I was going to have to tell him why.

"What I think is . . ." I took a deep breath. "I think you're the only one who ever really saw me. Like *this*." I lifted my arms so my fingertips could brush the edges of my wings. "You're the only one who thought I could fly."

He took a step toward me, put a hand to my waist. "Now I'm just afraid you will."

My lips parted to tell him I wouldn't, that I wasn't going anywhere. But Brady ran up and squeezed right between us in his pirate suit. Lennie stepped back.

"What are you?" asked Brady, poking his plastic sword at Lennie's chest.

"He's not wearing a costume," I explained.

Brady looked thoroughly troubled by this news. We had told him everyone would have a costume, that it was a costume party. Not having a costume was a *problem*.

Lennie seemed to sense it, too. "Maybe you could find one for me," he said quickly to Brady. "An extra sword or something?"

My brother's face got very serious and he marched back into the house.

"You are in serious trouble now," I said.

Lennie smiled, gazed down at my costume again, and said, "I sure am."

I gave him a playful shove. More guests were arriving, and I soon got caught up with hellos and pointing people to the drinks and giving Rigby a thumbs-up on the music he was playing. When I danced my butterfly wings back over to Lennie, he was kneeling down in front of Brady by the hedge that separated our yards. There was a bundle of red-and-blue cloth in Brady's arms.

"Costume for you," he was saying to Lennie.

I bit my lip, trying not to laugh at the Superman pajamas he held up. "This is great, little dude," said Lennie. "But I don't think it'll fit me."

"Here." I stepped in and separated the red cape from the rest of it. "This is just your size."

Lennie sighed but didn't argue. He let me tie it around his neck. Then he zoomed around Brady like he was flying. My brother clapped, he was so happy. Then he dug something else out of his pocket and held it out to us. Lennie took it and his eyes went wide. He showed it to me.

It was a Wonder Woman Band-Aid.

"Oohh," I said, laughing now. "This is just what Lennie needs, Brady. Very nice."

My brother beamed and ran off, satisfied that his mission was complete. Lennie handed me the Band-Aid. "Would you like to do the honors?"

I unwrapped the package and held the sticky part of the bandage toward him. "Where do you want it?"

He tapped his chest, right over his heart. "This spot could use a little mending."

I swallowed. "Did I do that?"

He shrugged. "It's a recurring injury."

I stepped very close and pressed the bandage to his shirt, rubbing it against his chest with my thumbs to make sure it would stick. "All better now."

"If you say so," he whispered, cupping his hand over mine and pressing it to his chest. He took a few small steps backward into the shadow of the hedge, pulling me with him.

I literally had his heart in the palm of my hand, and it was pounding hard. My thumb slid up to the base of his throat and caressed the hollow spot there. I hardly knew what I was doing. It was as if my body had rebelled against my brain, and my brain wasn't putting up much of a fight.

"Len," I whispered as his lips brushed my jaw. "I . . ."

He inhaled my unspoken words with a kiss so soft and so warm, it made me want to fly. My whole body sighed into his.

When we pulled apart moments later, he smiled at first, his mouth pink from my lip gloss. Then his eyes flickered past me to the party now in full swing, and his body tensed. His hands dropped away from me.

I turned and saw James standing in front of our house, searching the crowd. He was wearing his apron from Bensen's grocery. I took a step farther into the darkness, but Lennie pushed me back. "Don't jerk the guy around," he said. "He doesn't deserve it any more than I do."

"But ..."

"Your prince awaits," he said as he slipped behind the hedge and disappeared.

FORTY-SIX

I straightened my costume and walked into the midst of the party—friends and strangers dancing and laughing all around. James didn't notice me until I was standing right in front of him.

"Hey, Ivy." He took in my costume, his eyes widening. "Wow. Those wings. You're . . . Juliet, aren't you? From my drawing."

I looked back over my own shoulder to the shape of my wings. I hadn't even thought of it when I'd sketched them for Carla, but they *were* just like the ones James had drawn. He'd snuck into my subconscious somehow, which made me wonder if a part of me still wanted to be his Juliet. "I . . . uh . . . something like that," I mumbled.

"And I almost dressed as Romeo," he said. "That would've been perfect."

What little composure I had pulled together after kissing Lennie was starting to unravel. "We should talk," I said, pointing toward the playground, away from the noise of the party.

"Lead the way, fair maiden," said James, bowing like a Shakespearean actor. He was doing everything that had charmed me before, but all I felt now was confusion and hurt bubbling up in my chest. After disappearing without a word, he thought he could just come back and things would be the same? That we could pick up where we'd left off?

James seemed to sense the tension in the air between us, because he didn't say anything more until we reached the playground. He stood next to the monkey bars while I sat on one of the swings, careful not to knock my wings off.

"I don't know where to start," he said.

"Well, your aunt kind of filled me in."

"I heard." He looked at his feet, kicking at the dirt around the ladder.

I had imagined the moment of James's return a hundred times with a hundred different scripts. And none of them started out with us shuffling awkwardly around my neighborhood, mumbling at each other.

It probably didn't help that Lennie was in my head, the tingle of his kiss still on my lips.

"You got my invitation," I started.

He smiled. "All twelve of them."

"Sorry about that. Your aunt said they might not get through."

"They didn't," he said. "Until my mom got your letter."

I had poured my heart out in that letter, told her how much I liked her son. How he'd taken me to the cemetery that day. How sorry I was . . .

"She showed it to you?"

He nodded. "And we found the other letters. Dad's assistant had been *sorting* my mail." He made air quotes around "sorting" with his fingers.

"Was he *reading* them?" I tried to remember if I'd written anything I should be embarrassed about.

"No," he said. "But my mom was pissed. And they had a big fight. Mom convinced Dad to let me come back if I want. Make my own decisions. I'm eighteen now, so . . ."

"You're coming back?" I shouldn't have been surprised by the news; it was exactly what I'd been hoping for all this time. But it still caught me off guard. I wasn't ready.

James shoved his hands in his pockets, teetering backward on his heels. "Do you want me to? Come back?"

I couldn't believe the answer to that question might be no. But open mic night had changed everything. I didn't answer, only scuffed my feet beneath the swing.

"When I heard from Reesa," he continued, "I assumed . . ."

My head snapped up. "You heard from Reesa?"

"She sent me a message through Mrs. Lanahan. To make sure I saw the video of your performance."

"Oh. So you saw it."

He lifted an eyebrow. "You didn't want me to?"

"No, I did. I wanted you to *be* there. You sent me the flyer and then—"

"What flyer?" he said.

"The flyer about open mic night? 'Share your talent'?" I motioned circling the words with a pen. "The handwriting on the envelope was just like yours, and . . . I thought . . . "

He shook his head. "It wasn't me," he said. "I mean, I knew open mic was that night, and I thought you might do it. I hoped you would. Sing to the tombstones and everything." He was pacing the grass in front of the swings now. "I really wish I could've been there."

"Why weren't you?" I asked quietly.

He shrugged. "My dad made me go to some charity thing with him. He funded this women's shelter—it's . . . Anyway, I couldn't get out of it. I'm sorry."

I sat there in numb silence for a minute. "So Reesa told you about the video?"

"She must've run home and posted it right after your performance."

I stopped the swing from swaying. Reesa took the video? My heart raced. Reesa didn't hate me. *She didn't hate me!* I stood up, my wings snagging the chains of the swing. I wanted to run to the house and call her. I wanted to tell Lennie!

"Reesa said you wrote that song for me," James was saying.

I realized in that moment that the song really wasn't his anymore. Or maybe I knew it even before I sang it. Because Lennie was the one I wanted to run to with my happy news. It was a gut reaction, nothing I could control even if I wanted to.

I walked over to James. "I did write the song for you," I said. "But . . . everything's changed."

His pale eyes searched mine and I wondered what he'd find there. I wasn't sure myself. "Changed . . . how?

"I . . . I'm just different now. These last couple of weeks have been . . . eye-opening."

"So you didn't mean what you said in your letters?" he said. "Were you messing with me?"

"No. I meant every word. I liked you so much. I still do."

He took my hands in his. "So, be with me. I'm here now. It'll be just like it was before. I'll move in with Aunt Ida again. . . ."

I shook my head. "You can't. That's not who you are." I tapped the JIM embroidered on his apron. "Not you."

"Fine, so I'll get a different job." He tore off the apron and threw it to the ground. He wore jeans and a dark shirt, the kind that looked casual and effortless but undoubtedly cost hundreds of dollars. "Would you rather I work at the Save-a-Cent with your friend Larry?"

"Lennie," I said. "His name is Lennie."

"Right." He paused and looked at me. "And he's not your friend."

"He's . . ." My face grew hot. "Actually, he's . . ."

James's eyebrows shot up. "Hold on. Lennie? He's the reason your feelings have changed?"

I lowered my gaze and nodded.

"I thought you said he was a drug dealer."

"I was wrong about that. About a lot of things."

James stepped close and looked at me with his pale-blue eyes. Then he leaned in and kissed me softly. Just once.

"Were you wrong about that?" His smile was hopeful.

I missed that smile.

"I wasn't wrong about you," I said. "I like you so much. It's just . . . this is all make-believe for you, James. It's not real."

"My feelings are real." His voice broke. "You're more real to me than any girl I've ever known."

"But you've been hiding from your real life," I said. "We both have."

He shook his head. "I didn't choose that life any more than you chose this one. So why can't I pick a different one?"

"Because it's a *lie*, James. Pretending to be poor when you're not? It feels like, I don't know, an insult to people who don't have any other choice, who are scraping to get by and would give anything to have what you have."

"But I don't want it!" He clawed his fingers through his hair. "My last girlfriend called me 'twenty-nine' behind my back. You know why?" His voice was full of anger and hurt.

I shook my head. "No."

"Because that's what number my dad is on the Forbes list of the wealthiest Americans."

"I . . . I didn't know."

"Exactly," he said. "You didn't know. You didn't care. I thought you actually liked me for *me*."

"I did," I said. "I do like you for you."

"But you like him better." He nodded toward Lennie's Jeep, parked in front of his house.

"It's not about liking him better," I said. "It's about wanting someone who understands what I'm going through, who isn't going to disappear the minute I screw up. Because, believe me—I screw up a *lot*."

James got very still. "I'm sorry, Ivy. About disappearing. I—"

"You were gone for weeks. Without a word. You listened to Willow and Wynn, but you wouldn't listen to *me*."

He shook his head. "I didn't want you to know who I was."

I sighed. It sounded all too familiar. "I just don't think it'll work," I said. "One of us would always be pretending, and I can't do that anymore."

He walked over to where he'd thrown his grocery apron and picked it up with a sigh. "I actually liked this job. Being normal . . ." He rolled the apron into a ball. "Walk me to my car?"

I nodded and reached for his hand. As we approached the house, he started swinging our hands between us, like we had that day in the cemetery. The day of Romeo. It reminded me of his Shakespeare book. "Hold on," I said. "I have something of yours inside."

I ran in to get it, taking the steps two at a time. I grabbed his *Hitchhiker's Guide*, too. He was waiting on the porch when I came down.

"Here," I said, breathless, handing the books to him. "Your Shakespeare. And your *Hitchhiker's Guide to the Galaxy*. I don't know what happened to *The Outsiders*."

James's eyes opened wide with surprise. He flipped open the cover of the Shakespeare. "I've been looking for this everywhere," he said. "Where did you find it?"

I laughed nervously. "You know where."

He spotted the note I'd written on the inside and read it aloud. "*And what do you read for fun?* Did you write that?"

All the air went out of my lungs. I lowered myself to sit on the porch steps. "You didn't leave that for me, in the little room off the supply closet? The one on the second floor near the girls' bathroom?"

"Uh . . . no." He handed the *Hitchhikers* back to me. "And that one isn't mine."

I swallowed. "What about *The Outsiders?* Dallas Winston?"

He shook his head slowly. "I've, uh . . . read it. But . . ."

"You never went into that supply room on the second floor, down from Mr. Eli's room?"

"Oh!" he said, recognition finally lighting his face. "I did go in there to find paper clips once. Mr. Eli told me there was a box of them on a shelf in there, and . . . is that where I left it?" He smacked his palm to his head. "I'm such an idiot."

"So you didn't leave *any* books for me in there? With notes in them?"

James slowly shook his head.

It all came into focus. Lennie, hanging out at the end of the hallway that day. He must've seen me go into the supply room. "That's where I left the note," I said, talking as much to myself now as I was to James. "To meet me at the King that Friday. On the shelf."

"I thought you meant the shelves in the library," said James. "The periodical shelf."

I shook my head. Had I been trading notes with Lennie all that time? Which meant the handwriting on the flyer, it was his handwriting. And the girl he was looking for at the King that night—that was *me*.

"I am sooo stupid," I said.

He gave a breathy snort. "It seems to be going around."

I stood and James took my hand again, and when we got to the car I kissed him on the cheek. He slid into the driver's seat and started the car.

When I lifted my hand to wave good-bye, he rolled down the window. "I knew you'd win it," he said.

I leaned closer. "Win what?"

"Open mic," he said. "I knew the judges would love you. Nobody sings like you do."

I stepped back and he drove off, a secret sort of smile on his face. And as I watched him go, I thought, *How did he even know there were judges?* Because there never were, normally. It wasn't meant to be a contest. It was only because of the anonymous donor. . . .

I sank down and sat on the grass. Had my prize money come

from James? I didn't want it to be so. But something told me it had to be. I knew then I'd made the right decision, because I couldn't be with someone who would always be resisting the urge to pay my way. Or to solve my problems with money. I wanted someone who was there for me—but not like that.

I wanted Lennie.

FORTY-SEVEN

Lennie was precisely where I expected him to be: in his shed, wiping the grease off some parts with a shop rag. His face was washed clean of my lipstick, and he'd changed back into his flannel shirt.

He didn't look up when I entered.

"Come to say good-bye?" he said.

I walked straight to his little collection of books and tipped the top edge of *The Outsiders* down. "Not just yet," I said, snatching the book off the shelf and flipping the cover open.

Lennie spun around in his chair. "What . . . ?"

"'Greaser or Soc,' huh?" I read from the exchange we'd written. "You wanted to know if I think Dally is sexy or rude? I should've known it was you."

He scratched his head. "I thought you did."

"No, you didn't."

The party music pulsed on the other side of his shed door, accented by occasional bursts of laughter and conversation.

"At first I did." Lennie leaned back in his chair. "I thought you were messing with me or maybe liked me but didn't want anybody to know. So I played along. Until I showed up to meet you at the King that Friday and, yeah . . ."

"I wasn't playing with you. I thought I was leaving notes for—"

He held up his hand to stop me. "James. I know."

"Why didn't you say something?" I paced angrily around his workshop. "Why did you let me keep thinking it was him?"

"Because that's who you wanted it to be."

"But if I'd known . . . if you had told me . . ."

"Ivy, I gave you a bike helmet," he said. "I picked you up off the side of the fucking road. You still acted like I was a leper."

"I was scared!" I sucked in a shuddery breath. "I didn't know you!"

He twisted and untwisted the greasy rag he was holding. "You didn't *want* to know me."

Maybe I didn't at first, but everything had changed. *I* had changed. Why couldn't he see that? "I just wish people would tell me the truth for a change."

He looked up. "Fine. The truth is you never thought I was good enough for you."

"That's not true."

"Come on, Ivy. At least admit that much."

"It's just . . . we came from two different places and . . ."

"And yours was way better than mine," he finished. "You *never* would've talked to me if you hadn't been forced into this situation. And don't give me this crap about being scared of what your friends would think. It's what *you* thought that mattered. And you thought I was the scum of the earth. Not because I was scary or had a tattoo. Because I live *here*."

I inhaled a sharp breath, wanting to deny it. But the truth of his words stung me. I stumbled to the door, my wings knocking something off the shelf. It clattered to the floor. Lennie stepped over it, reaching me in a single stride. He leaned his arm against the door so I couldn't open it.

"Don't go," he said.

I pulled at the handle. "Let me out, Lennie. Please."

"I'm sorry," he said. "I didn't mean it."

"No. You're absolutely right. I don't belong here. I don't belong *anywhere*." I could feel the tears starting and didn't want Lennie to see me cry again. I grabbed the door handle again, looking down at my hands on it. "Please."

He paused for a moment, then dropped his arm and I flew out, diving through the sea of costumed bodies bouncing to the music. Thank God Molly had the volume way too loud. Nobody had heard our fight, though a few people turned and watched the crying girl run by, butterfly wings askew.

The back stairs to our apartment were full of people coming and going to the bathroom, so I ran to the front porch. I stumbled up the steps and past a girl in a dog costume. She grabbed my arm and spun me around.

"Oh, my God. Ivy. What's the matter?" she said.

"Reesa?"

She nodded.

"Reesa!" I threw my arms around her, squeezing her so tight. "I'm so glad you're here." I held on to her, sobbing and laughing at the same time.

"Hey, it's okay," she said, patting my back as I clung to her. When we finally pulled apart, she lifted one of her fuzzy paws and wiped my face with it. "I leave you alone for a few weeks and look at you. You're a mess."

I nodded. "And you're . . . a dog?"

"Female dog." She smirked. "A bitch. That's what I am."

"No, you're not." I shook my head.

"I am. I was." Her puppy-dog eyes matched her costume perfectly. "And I'm sorry."

"It's not your fault. Everything was so messed up."

"Still," she said. "Major BFF fail."

"I should never have lied to you about James. I don't know why I did that."

"Maybe because I was acting like a complete lunatic? About a guy who barely even said hi to me?"

I smiled through my tears. "I was so afraid of losing you, and then I pretty much did everything I could to make that happen. I was such an idiot."

"Me too," she said.

"I've missed you so much." I sniffled, then started full-on crying again.

She wrapped her arms around me. "I missed you, too. Willow nearly drove me insane these last few weeks."

I stood back with a gasp. "You're missing her party! She'll never speak to you again."

Reesa shrugged. "She's going to have very few people to talk to then, because it looks like her entire guest list is *here*."

I had been so focused on James, Lennie, and now Reesa, I'd hardly noticed how massive the party had become. Our tiny yard was packed, and the overflow had spread across the street to the playground. My dad was chatting with a neighbor by the gravel road, probably wondering when the police would show up and send everyone home.

I turned back to Reesa. "And you were at open mic night. You took that video."

She nodded. "I was so proud of you. You know how hard it was not to run up on that stage and hug you?"

"How did you even know I was performing?"

"Molly told me."

"Molly?" I shook my head. My friends had been rallying around me, and I didn't even know.

I hugged Reesa again, still crying, and dragged her up toward my attic room. Mom had brought the twins in for bed and was trying to convince them to get their pajamas on. Brady started clapping when he saw Reesa. I couldn't believe he still remembered how she'd helped him learn how to clap. She clapped back and gave him a hug, and Kaya, too.

It only made me cry more.

I took her arm and led her up to my room, and she twirled around in the little bit of space in the center. "I love it. You're like Rapunzel, up here in your tower."

I pouted. "More like Cinderella."

"All you need is a prince."

My laugh came out a sob. I hugged her some more and we fell onto the bed.

"Tell me everything. Who did this to you." She motioned to my blubbering face.

"That's the thing," I said with a hiccupy sniffle. "I think I did it to myself."

"Tell me," she said.

I took a deep breath and filled her in on what had happened between James, me, and Lennie. After ten minutes of detailing everything, Reesa stared at me, her mouth gaping a bit. She shook her head. "Wow."

"And I haven't had anyone to talk to about it."

She pulled my head to her furry shoulder. "What about Molly?"

"Molly's great. But she's not you."

Reesa smiled. "Well, I'm here now," she said. "And I'm not going anywhere."

She patted my shoulder and rocked us side to side, saying "there, there" every now and then, like a mom. My shuddery sniffles quieted.

I stood up and looked out the dormer window at the light beneath the door of Lennie's shed. "I don't know what to do."

"So." She sighed. "Lazarski, huh?"

I nodded.

"And James?"

"I really like him, too. He's just . . ." I paced circles around my tiny rug. It wasn't that he'd done anything wrong. If he'd never gone away and I hadn't discovered the fascinating puzzle that was Lennie, I'd probably be trying to sneak behind the hedges with him right now.

"He's good-looking and sweet and funny and perfect in every way," said Reesa. And she was right. He *was.* "He's that guy on dating shows who everyone's rooting for and they can't figure out how the stupid bachelorette could possibly let him go."

I nodded. "But she falls for the one nobody expects her to fall for. The one *she* never expected to fall for."

"The hot, sexy bad boy."

My mouth fell open a little bit. "You think Lennie's hot and sexy?"

Reesa rolled her eyes. "Please. I may be a snob, but I'm not blind."

My mother hollered up the steps then that people were looking for me and I wasn't being a very good hostess, disappearing from my own party.

"Coming!" I hugged Reesa again and let her fix my makeup and hair, then led her to the drinks, where we found Jenna and

Rigby and Molly and her explorer dude. I think his name was Seth. One of Seth's friends, whose geek costume of thick black glasses and a button-up shirt didn't hide how cute he actually was, asked Reesa what she was supposed to be.

Reesa blanched. "I'm, uh . . ."

"The best friend ever," I said. "Loyal, faithful . . . all that."

Geek guy smiled. "I'm Reese."

Reesa and I burst out laughing.

"What?" said Reese. "What's so funny?"

"It's just . . . I'm Reesa."

Reese's laugh was more of a guffaw, which only made Reesa giggle harder. The two of them quickly forgot I existed. I wandered the party, never stopping long enough for anyone to realize I wasn't paying attention to a word they said. Molly dragged me over to dance with her and Seth and company, but didn't notice when I wiggled out of the circle and into the shadows.

I stood at the edge of our yard, watching everyone, Lennie's shed behind me. I could feel it there, though, like warm breath on my neck. When I couldn't stand it anymore, I turned toward it. Toward *him*.

FORTY-EIGHT

On my way to Lennie's shed, I cut through a dance line that was snaking around the backyard. He didn't answer the door or even say anything, but I went in, anyway. He was still twirling around slowly in his chair. I pulled my arms through the straps of my butterfly wings and laid them on the counter, then walked around the workbench to where he was sitting. He still didn't look up, so I stood between his knees and pushed his shoulders back. When his eyes finally met mine, they were red.

"I'm sorry," I said. "Can you forgive me?"

He lifted his hands to my waist and pulled me toward him, so his face pressed into my stomach. He inhaled a deep breath and let it shudder out.

I wrapped my arms around him, holding him tighter, then slid onto his lap. His arms moved slowly up my back and into my hair, lowering my face to his.

"What are you doing with a loser like me?" His voice was low, a bass note that vibrated through me.

"You're not a loser."

He let out a single snort of laughter. "Said nobody ever."

"Said me. Am I nobody?"

He smiled. "You're somebody."

I lifted Brady's red Superman cape that sat crumpled on the counter next to Lennie's chair. "You're a hero."

He grinned. "They don't call me Wonder Woman for nothing."

I laughed. "I'm sorry I looked down on you before, on this place. I don't anymore. And you aren't who I thought you were. Not at all."

He inhaled a slow breath. "What changed your mind?"

I couldn't hold his gaze, so I studied the collar of his shirt instead. "The way you are with Brady," I whispered. "And with your mom."

"Ah," he said. "Nothing to do with you and me, then...."

I shook my head, a shy smile coming to my lips. "Nope."

There was no way I could admit that his touch practically made me forget my own name—the way he was tracing my face with his eyes, the heat of his legs under mine. If he didn't kiss me soon, I was going to explode.

He stood abruptly and I nearly fell to the floor. "Hey!"

"Sorry," he said, not sounding very sorry. He turned his back to me and leaned over his computer. "I just think we're too young to be together because you think I'm nice to children and my mother. If that's all you got, then ..."

I grabbed the collar I'd been staring at a moment ago and

spun him crashing into me.

"Whoa," he said.

I stood on tiptoes, my whole body leaning into him, and kissed him hard.

"I changed my mind about you," I said angrily, my arms still locked around him, "because you do this to me, you big jerk."

"This?" He kissed me back hard, one hand tangled in my hair and the other holding me so tightly against him I could barely breathe.

"Yes," I said when we broke apart, panting and laughing. "That."

He grinned his crooked grin. "But I've never kissed you like that before."

"Let's not get hung up on technicalities, shall we?" I wasn't about to confess that I'd imagined him kissing me like that quite a few times. And the reality was way better.

He sat down and pulled me to his lap, and I sank right into him like he was custom-carved to fit. We may or may not have kissed for a really long time before we heard a faint knocking at the door.

"Who is it?" Lennie called out.

No one answered, but the knocking continued.

"Brady," I gasped. "It's Brady." I don't know how I knew. But I did. I untangled myself from Lennie and lunged for the door.

The moment I swung it open, Brady dived past me, crying, and wrapped himself around Lennie's leg. I rushed forward with soothing sounds, shushing softly in Brady's ear.

"He must've gotten lost in the dark," I said.

Lennie gently pried my brother off his leg and scooped him up. "I got ya, buddy. You're okay."

Brady clung to Lennie's neck.

My mother ran up then, in a panic. "Oh, thank God. You found him. I tucked him into bed and then he . . . he disappeared." She held her hands out to take Brady, but he only burrowed deeper into Lennie.

Mom looked to me with wide eyes.

I shrugged.

"Hey, little dude." Lennie spoke softly into Brady's ear. "You want to dance with me and Ivy?"

My brother pulled his face from Lennie's shoulder and smiled.

Lennie carried him to the yard as I pulled my butterfly wings back on, and we danced around and around with Brady hugged between us.

Reesa and Reese joined us, and Molly and her explorer dude. Soon my dad came and took Brady up to bed. Lennie slid his arms around my waist, beneath my wings. He pulled me close and the music pulsed through us, and everything else seemed to disappear. It was just me and Lennie, and as his shimmery eyes smiled into mine, I finally knew where I belonged. And it felt like home.

ACKNOWLEDGMENTS

Where to start? So many people have helped me achieve this goal of writing a novel and—even more challenging—getting it published! Perhaps the best place to begin is where the dream ultimately came true: with HarperTeen and my wonderful editor—Karen Chaplin. I wouldn't be writing this sentence if she hadn't pulled Ivy from her pile and helped me bring this story to life. Thanks to everyone at HarperCollins who played a part in making *Between the Notes* a real, live book, and to my agent, Steven Chudney, for his patience and expertise along the way.

There are many others I want to thank, and hope I don't miss anyone: To author Mary Kennedy, who was the first to say "go for it" when I shared my wish to write a novel; to Annie Norman and Patty Langley at the Delaware Division of Libraries and to Janet Hughes for asking me to work with them on the Delaware Book Festival, where I was inspired by authors like Laurie Halse Anderson and Jon Scieszka; to Stacey Burr for all the brainstorming and for not telling me how terrible those very first chapters I ever wrote truly were; to Rhe De Ville for the twist on a kernel of an idea that got this story rolling; to my fabulous writing friends and critique partners—Tamara Girardi, Joy McCullough-Carranza, and Hilary T. Smith—for suffering through early drafts (and revision after revision) and for always being there when I need you, as well as readers Sarah and Cate Kastringer; and to the fabulous YA writing community, especially the TeenLitAuthors group and Fearless Fifteeners . . . thank you all so much! I am also indebted to Renee Bowers and Aaron Fichtelberg and their twins, Theo and Oliver, for giving me a glimpse into their very special life; to Little Invisibles' singer-songwriter-pianist Gina Degnars and singer-songwriter Leah Awitan for insights on songwriting and stage fright; and to so many other friends and family members who have been cheering me on and anxiously awaiting the publication of this novel!

Finally, thanks, Mom, for the lessons in persistence, and Dad, for showing me that hard work pays off. Rich, I'm so glad you were totally on board with my decision to quit PR and start writing fiction. This novel probably won't get us that house in France you've been wanting, but I'll keep at it. Maybe someday . . .

And to Sebastian and Anna—thank you for inspiring me, believing in me, and always being eager to read my books. I hope there will be many more to come!

JOIN THE
Epic Reads
COMMUNITY

THE ULTIMATE YA DESTINATION

◄ **DISCOVER** ►
your next favorite read

◄ **FIND** ►
new authors to love

◄ **WIN** ►
free books

◄ **SHARE** ►
infographics, playlists, quizzes, and more

◄ **WATCH** ►
the latest videos

◄ **TUNE IN** ►
to Tea Time with Team Epic Reads

Find us at **www.epicreads.com**
and **@epicreads**